A Dance of
CRANES

PREVIOUS BIRDER MURDER MYSTERIES

A Siege of Bitterns
A Pitying of Doves
A Cast of Falcons
A Shimmer of Hummingbirds
A Tiding of Magpies

ABOUT THE AUTHOR

Steve Burrows has pursued his birdwatching hobby on six continents. He is a former editor of the *Hong Kong Bird Watching Society* magazine and a contributing field editor for *Asian Geographic*. Steve now lives with his wife, Resa, in Oshawa, Ontario.

A Dance of
CRANES

STEVE BURROWS

A Point Blank Book

First published in Great Britain, the United States and Australia
by Point Blank, an imprint of Oneworld Publications, 2019

First published in English by Dundurn Press Limited, Canada. This edition
published by Oneworld Publications in arrangement with Dundurn Press Limited

ISBN 978-1-78607-577-2
ISBN 978-1-78607-576-5 (ebook)

Printed and bound in Great Britain by Clays Ltd, Elcograf S.p.A.

Visit our website for a reading guide
and exclusive content on THE BIRDER MURDER SERIES
www.oneworld-publications.com

Oneworld Publications
10 Bloomsbury Street
London WC1B 3SR
England

Stay up to date with the latest books,
special offers, and exclusive content from
Oneworld with our newsletter

Sign up on our website
oneworld-publications.com

MIX
Paper from
responsible sources
FSC® C018072

For Elizabeth and Warren,
who have already started their story.

And for Graeme and Amanda,
who are about to begin theirs.

1

VI. Six. The most dangerous number of all. It meant perilous conditions. It meant violent, unpredictable forces. And for Annie Prior, it had meant death.

The man stared back up the river, transfixed for a moment by the raw energy of the water boiling down through the narrow chasm. A low roar reverberated off the rocks, filling the air with its dull thunder. He had never seen Category Six rapids before, but he knew these would qualify. Surely, no level of river danger could exceed the way this water was churning through the steep-sided gorge, crashing down in explosions of white spume onto the jagged rocks below. Even for the most experienced white-water canoeist, any attempt to navigate this stretch of rapids would be madness. For a novice, without a helmet or life jacket, it was tantamount to suicide. But for someone who is in fear for their life, any escape route must be tried, no matter how terrifying.

The man still found it hard to believe that this stretch of river was undocumented. In most places on earth, such waters would have been part of the local folklore, highlighted on the maps, most likely with a sidebar warning about their dangers. But in this vast, remote wilderness, even deadly Category Six rapids could go unrecorded. They were merely one more hazard in this unforgiving landscape that offered no quarter to those who dared to challenge it. Those like Annie Prior.

He had suspected the body would end up in this eddy. The two of them had noted it during their earlier reconnaissance of the river, when they had decided the drops and ledges of this section were far too risky, far too treacherous to be navigated. He'd headed for this spot as soon as he'd seen the canoe disappear into the rapids. Annie Prior hadn't bailed out by then, and that meant she wasn't going to. All that remained for her now was a short, dizzying descent towards death. As the raging waters thrashed the canoe to pieces on the razor-sharp rocks, she would have been rag-dolled into a state of near-unconsciousness, even before the craft flipped and submerged her in the frigid currents. After that, there would have been no hope. Annie Prior's body would be pounded against the boulders time and again by the force of the churning water, until it eventually broke free of the rapids and drifted downstream to this spot.

He saw Annie's lifeless form now, a few metres from shore, turning in a slow spiral. Set against the manic rushing of the river beyond, the movement of the water in the eddy was as benign as the swirling of cream in a coffee cup. The silence here seemed to fill the air like a pocket of empty time. But despite the peace of this place, he could not allow Annie Prior's body to remain like this.

He took off his clothes and laid them in a neat pile on the shore. As cold as the water was going to be, it would be vital that he had warm, dry clothes when he was done. In these temperatures, damp clothes wouldn't dry for a long time, and as evening approached, they'd leach out what little body heat he had. With no heavy jacket to protect him, it would leave him vulnerable to the cold night ahead.

After two steps, the shallow incline disappeared into a steep drop-off, plunging him thigh-deep into water so cold he couldn't even breathe. Numbness seized his legs, freezing out all feeling, the still air all around him seeming only to heighten the intensity of the icy chill. Carefully testing the footing, he began wading forward. He felt his chest contract as the icy water rode up his ribcage, and he opened his mouth repeatedly, as if trying to bite off chunks of the cold air to gulp down into his lungs.

Part of him had hoped he would not see her face, but as she drifted round towards him, he could not bring himself to look away. She stared back at him through cold, dead eyes, her face so bloated and battered it was almost unrecognizable. He had not seen many smiles from Annie Prior, amid the firm set of her jaw, her intense concentration, her determined expressions, but those few that had come his way had been worth waiting for; face-brightening moments of unfettered joy. *She should have let herself smile more often*, he thought.

He stretched out his arm across the glassy surface and his fingertips touched the rough Gore-Tex material of Annie's jacket. He tugged at it and the body began to drift gently in his direction. He felt in the pocket of the jacket to retrieve Annie's inReach device and clicked it off. Then he removed the battery and threw both parts of the unit into the fast-flowing waters beyond the eddy. He reached out once again and pushed Annie's head under the water, forcing the body down against its natural buoyancy until it snagged on a submerged log.

His grisly task completed, he was in the process of turning away when the body broke free and burst up beside him in the water. He recoiled from the grotesque mask of discoloured flesh with its dead, unseeing eyes, sputtering and gasping furiously as he splashed back into the frigid water. Recovering, he approached the body and tried again, pinning it beneath the log and securing it firmly. He paused for a moment, in case the

9

body broke free and once more floated to the surface. But this time, it held fast and he backed away carefully until he reached the shore.

He emerged from the water, shivering violently. He pulled on his clothes as fast as his numb hands would permit, hugging his thick, lined sweater around him tightly when he had finished. As he stepped into his boots, he stopped to fish out his own inReach device. He pried off the case and removed the battery. Pausing, he held the two parts as if testing their weight. And then he slid them both gently into the water. For a moment they seemed to hang suspended on the surface, and then they slowly sank, until through the clear water, he saw his only contact with the outside world disappear.

He stood up and took one last long look out over the eddy. From this shore, the body was completely invisible, as he knew it would also be from the air. Annie Prior's final resting place in this empty landscape was now a secret known only to him.

Out beyond the body, the foaming white waters of the river continued to race past the eddy. It may have been the Category Six rapids that had claimed Annie's life, but it was the two men who had pursued her who bore the blame. They had come looking for her, tracking her through this uncharted wilderness until her only way out was to plunge a flimsy canoe into the deadly waters of the Little Buffalo River. But with Annie Prior's death, the men would now be turning their sights on another target. They would have already found the campsite; found the two backpacks, the two coffee cups, the two metal food dishes. And the two sleeping bags; but only one unrolled. They would have surmised that couples who shared a sleeping bag also shared secrets. They would be wrong. He didn't know what Annie Prior had been involved in. But these two men who had pursued her to her death would think he did. And that meant they would be coming after him.

2

There was grace in the turn. That would have been important to the man, once. A slight lowering of the shoulder blade to lead into the spin, the chest held square, the other shoulder sweeping around to complete the move. It had been a signature movement in some of the man's best routines; the slow, elegant swirl transporting the audience seamlessly from one sequence into the next.

The only thing the turn lacked was symmetry. Both hands should have been held to the sternum, drawn up, making butterfly wings of the elbows as the performer clutched them in tightly to enhance the spin. But only the right hand was raised, pressing against the chest. The left hand trailed off awkwardly, reaching towards the floor, leading the body down into an inelegant backward pirouette. The clumsiness of the turn's conclusion would not have pleased the man at all. His legs seemed to collapse beneath him as he spun, and his body slumped to the ground, splaying out across the width of the hallway, flat on his back.

From the open doorway, the visitor looked on with astonishment. The blood had come more quickly than expected. It had gushed from the chest wound immediately, seeming to bubble up even before the knife was fully embedded. It hadn't sprayed, pooling instead in a dark red stain, first around the knife, then spreading over the man's white shirt. Now, as the body lay on the floor, it continued to flow, out across the torso and onto the harlequin-tiled floor.

From the doorway, the figure peered down at the man sprawled in the hallway. The left arm was extended, the hand still clutching the telephone receiver. The phone's grey cord coiled back up to the base mounted on the wall. It was an overlong cord, designed specifically to allow a wide range of movement in the days before untethered home phones became the norm. The visitor looked again at the clunky, old-fashioned receiver in the man's hand. It could have just as easily fallen from his grasp as he stumbled back in his final death spiral, but instead it had remained clasped in his vice-like grip. The evidence would tell investigators that the man had died instantly from the knife wound, collapsing back and falling where he now lay. It would be obvious there had been no time to hang up the receiver or press down the pegs on the wall-mounted base. A rueful smile curled the corners of the visitor's lips. You could plan things meticulously, plot them with the minutest precision, and still, there would always be these chance details for which no amount of choreography could account. Taking care to avoid the spreading pool of blood, the visitor stepped lightly over the body and moved towards the interior of the house.

It seemed like only seconds, although time was always going to be an elastic commodity when one's mind was dealing with the knowledge that a newly dead body lay in the hall-way behind you. Still, it was hardly credible that in such a short space of time, so much blood could have flowed from the body. Returning now to the tiled hallway, the visitor saw it had spread across the entire floor, covering the pitted black and white diamonds from wall to wall. There was now no way to reach the front door without stepping in blood. To take the back door would mean leaving the interior bolts unlocked, and anybody who knew the man would point out these would have been secured when he was at home. Leaving by the front door was crucial, perhaps the most important detail of the entire sequence of events. There needed to be no trace at all that anyone had entered the house after the stabbing.

Beyond the body, the front door was still slightly ajar. The front of the house was shrouded by a hedgerow, a small screen of privet behind which the visitor had waited patiently until the time was right. But perhaps a faint sliver of light from this dimly lit hallway might still be visible from the street. It might encourage casual inspection, even a neighbourly call, to remind the man that the door had been left unlocked. A knock might follow the answering silence, and a solicitous inquiry, just to check that everything was all right. With the knock, the door would swing slowly open to reveal the sight of the homeowner sprawled out in the hallway, lying in a pool of his own blood. The visitor needed to get out of here before that knock came.

There was enough room, just, between the far edge of the blood and the front door. With the right momentum it might be possible to land there. But to judge the leap, so you could clear the body and the pool of blood and still plant a firm landing on the far side, in such a narrow margin of safety? Perhaps it could be done, by someone with enough agility and athleticism. By the dead man himself, perhaps, in his youth. But certainly not by this visitor. There was only one other solution. In its way, it was every bit as challenging as the leap. It would require balance and precision; it held great risk, but time was moving, and that knock on the door could

13

come at any moment. The receiver in the dead man's hand, too, meant there were only minutes left to get out. The chance had to be taken.

Approaching the near edge of the pool of blood, the visitor leaned one gloved hand on the wall of the hallway for support, took a long, steadying breath, and stretched out a foot. The hilt of the knife moved unsteadily beneath the weight, even as it drove down deeper into the man's chest. Teetering dangerously, the visitor reached out to press the other gloved hand hard against the far wall, fighting for balance. The calf muscle was clenched in tightly and then released to launch its owner off the knife handle and into the air. As the foot landed in the narrow space between the blood and the door jamb, the sole of the shoe skidded on the polished tile. The visitor's body began to sway back into the hallway, the momentum dragging it into a fall. With a desperate lunge, leather-clad fingertips scrabbled for purchase on the inside edge of the door frame and held on tightly. Pausing for a moment to drink deep breaths into grateful lungs, the visitor eased upright again on taut arm muscles. Pulling the door open slightly, the figure squeezed out into the waiting night. There was no backward glance.

A calm demeanour was a minimum requirement for a Front Desk Associate of the Demesne at Saltmarsh. How much greater, then, the need for poise under pressure as one ascended the management ladder? To have attained the lofty rank of Evening Duty Manager, Nigel must have had a considerable supply of ice in his veins. Which was good, thought Front Desk Associate Stephanie, as she carefully replaced the phone receiver. He was going to need it.

"That was the Saltmarsh Police Department. They're on their way, but they're requesting we send a hotel representative down to Room 111 immediately. They'd like someone to stay with the guest until they arrive."

Nigel broke off his survey of the hotel lobby and turned his eyes to Stephanie. "Do we have a problem?" Nigel liked to remind his staff that they were in this together. Whatever endangered the smooth running of the five-star resort posed a shared threat to all of them.

"I really think you should go over there as soon as possible, Nigel. The police are also insisting that on no account should the telephone connection to Room 111 be interfered with in any way."

Even if Stephanie's tone hadn't piqued Nigel's interest by now, the police's instructions would have done so. "Why on earth would they care about that?"

Despite her training, Stephanie couldn't maintain her own calm demeanour any longer. "For God's sake, Nigel, get over there, now! The bloody woman is on a call with someone, and she thinks she heard him being killed."

3

"Cheese puffs."

Lindy Hey licked her fingers and tucked the package guiltily into the drawer as the man set a coffee on her desk. "Large, one cream, no sugar."

"Thanks, Jeremy."

"I've already told you, it's Jer to my friends." He pointed a forefinger at her in a gesture that was usually accompanied by a wink or a clicking of the tongue. But in this case, all he offered her was a hopeful smile. "So, we on then? For tonight?"

Lindy gave him a puzzled frown.

"The pub. Remember? Trivia night?"

She shook her head, surprised still at how it felt with her new, shorter hairstyle. She'd worn her corn-blonde hair shoulder-length for as long as she could remember, and was only a couple of days into her new look, and feel. "I don't think so, Jeremy. I'm not really up for it tonight."

Jeremy nodded, his disappointment obvious. "Oh. Only you said you'd see. Still, it is what it is. Perhaps next time. Whenever you're ready, though, no pressure. I understand it takes a bit of time to get over these things."

She offered him the same confused look as before.

"Your cold. You said you thought you might be coming down with one. Last time."

She hadn't expected him to have stored away her previous excuse like this, but if it served a purpose … "Yes, right. I think a quiet night in might be the best thing for me."

"A quiet night in at Emma's," said Jeremy, as if confirming the plans, "with her being away and all."

Lindy looked at him carefully. For somebody who'd only recently begun delivering coffees from the local café, Jeremy was remarkably up on the office tittle-tattle. Everyone at work was aware that Lindy had been staying at Emma's since her breakup with Domenic. For the most part, people had managed to avoid making reference to the fact, but discretion was not something Lindy would have called one of Jeremy's strengths. He seemed to be lingering with intent, and she was afraid he might be gearing himself up for another try at the pub date.

"Great chatting, Jeremy, but I've got a mountain of work to catch up on, so …" She gave him what she hoped was a kind smile of dismissal.

"Do you want to settle up now, then? Only, I've got to cover my 'outgoings,' haven't I?" He tweaked the word with quotation marks in the air. His *bunny fingers*, the girls in the office called them. It wasn't Lindy's favourite gesture at the best of times, and the frequency with which Jeremy managed to trot it out had done nothing to increase its appeal for her.

As Lindy fished in her bag for some change, Jeremy affected a look out of the window, and she took in this awkward person who'd suddenly become such a major feature of mornings in the office. Nobody could ever remember actually agreeing when Jeremy came in and offered to begin delivering coffees and pastries in the mornings. "Order first thing, I'll whip down and get them from the café, you settle with me on delivery."

For the most part, the staff of the magazine supported his enterprise. In truth, Lindy suspected they felt the same way she did about Jeremy: willing to tolerate his annoying habits to support an awkward young man struggling to make a living. Life wasn't going to offer many chances to someone with limited social skills and a wardrobe seemingly consisting exclusively of shabby shirts with frayed collars and cuffs that he always kept buttoned. She added a small tip and handed the money over to him. "Sorry, I don't have any more change."

"I get what I get." He lowered his voice and looked around him furtively. "I take it you haven't found those keys yet."

Lindy shook her head. In the turmoil following Domenic's departure and her temporary move, she had mislaid her keys. It wasn't catastrophic: Emma's place had a keyless lock and the car dealer had provided a spare fob when she leased her new Volkswagen Jetta. There was also a spare key to the cottage beneath one of the marram grass planters, if she ever felt like returning to the scene of the crime — the place where Domenic had killed their relationship. But her office keys had also been on her key ring, and revealing to her boss that she'd been careless enough to lose them was out of the question. Eric Chappell had been watching for signs that she'd been damaged by the breakup, that she really did need the time off he had been advocating so insistently. The loss of the office keys would provide him with all the ammunition he needed. Lindy couldn't imagine what had possessed her to confide in Jeremy in the first place, but her normally sound judgment had been a bit off lately. Chopping off her hair may have been one example; leasing the diesel version of that Jetta certainly was. She suspected enlisting Jeremy's help with the keys might be another. She was fairly sure he had read more into her whispered confidence than she'd intended; and while he would undoubtedly get the message sooner or later that it was just an innocent request for help, sooner would definitely be better.

A tall, willowy woman came over to pick up her soy latte. It eluded neither of the women that Jeremy never quite seemed to make it all the way to Claire's desk to deliver it directly, the way he did with Lindy's order. "I saw that man again this morning," she said. "The one I told you had been watching you that day."

Jeremy's interest was immediate. He bent to look through the window and scoured the street intently. "Nobody out there now. Did you say he's been here before? What day was that, then?"

Behind Jeremy's back, Lindy offered her friend a pair of extravagantly-raised eyebrows. "Don't worry about him," she said. "As I say, Jeremy, it's been lovely to chat, but …"

"I do think you should take it a bit more seriously, Lindy," said Claire earnestly. "Perhaps even mention it to the police."

Lindy gave her a soft smile. "He *is* the police, Claire. His name's Sergeant Maik."

It was an inadvertent turn in the High Street a couple of days earlier that had allowed Lindy to catch the brief glance of her watcher. He'd ducked out of sight as soon as she spun around, but she'd seen Danny's bulky form often enough to have no doubt who it was.

"If you know him, why doesn't he just come up and say hello? Why keep shadowing you like this?"

Because somebody asked him to, Claire, thought Lindy. In truth, it seemed like pretty menial fare for Danny Maik, checking up on Lindy and reporting back to his old boss, Detective Chief Inspector Domenic Jejeune. And why bother, anyway? It had been weeks now and there had been no word from Lindy's ex-boyfriend. He wasn't coming back. That much was clear. But even if he was having trouble letting go, involving his former sergeant in this silly spying game seemed a bit much. And, it seemed stranger still that a sensible, no-nonsense man like Maik would have agreed to have anything to do with it.

"Well, as long as you're sure he's no threat, Linds," said Claire uncertainly.

"No, no threat at all."

Despite Lindy's assurance, Jeremy surveyed the High Street once more. Apparently satisfied, he turned and approached Lindy's desk as Claire moved away. "Don't worry, Lindy. I'll keep an eye out. See you tomorrow."

Lindy watched him as he made his way to the door. As cloying as his attention seemed at times, at least it was an indication that somebody out there was interested in her. *Disappointment.* That was the word. The dissolution of a relationship was never easy on the circle of mutual friends, but the way that lot at the police station were carrying on, you'd have thought it was a contagious disease. Beyond this foolish, furtive surveillance by Danny, there had been no contact from anyone at all. She'd have expected, at the very least, a call from Domenic's boss, Detective Chief Superintendent Colleen Shepherd. She'd been through her own share of troubled relationships, and she knew how close Lindy and Dom had been. The suggestion of a quiet chat over an afternoon tea wouldn't have been too much to ask, surely? Lindy might have refused, probably would have, but the offer would have been nice. It would have at least shown that she was still in the thoughts of somebody down at the station.

She shrugged aside her resentment and brought herself back to the present. She stood by the window, sipping her coffee absently, watching the people moving along the street outside, oblivious to their surroundings, to the emotional earthquakes that might be ready to shake them to their foundations at any moment. The pain of the breakup with Dom had been almost paralyzing at first, but the rawness of the feelings was dulling slightly with each passing day. Perhaps it helped now, with distance, that she could understand some of the reasons for Domenic's sudden departure. He was tormented by the guilt over a boy's death that he felt he could have prevented. Compounding it, he felt he had let so many people down. His findings in the case had been mistaken, allowing them all to believe in a solution that he now knew was wrong. For a while, Lindy had tried to convince herself that there was some hope in the anaemic comments he had left with her about his return. *He wasn't sure. Maybe. Perhaps.* But one word stood out, the one that had cut so deeply: *Alone.* He had things he needed to work out *alone.* It was the word that told her Domenic could no longer find what he needed from her, or their relationship. The word that told her it was over between them.

Lindy focused again on a sunny Saltmarsh High Street, busy with midmorning activity. So many of the places flashed memories at her. The trattoria where she and Domenic had shared an occasional glass of Chablis, the travel agency where they'd stood shoulder to shoulder and considered tropical destinations they might visit, if he could ever get time off work. A sudden wave of sadness swept over her. It doesn't come when you're ready for it, she thought, when you've steeled yourself and are prepared to handle it. It lies in wait, ready to ambush you when you're distracted by other things. So, you have to be on the alert, prepared at all times. But it was so wearying, this constant vigilance. It wrung you out, until eventually you couldn't do anything but let your guard down. And then sorrow snuck in, delivering its stab of pain before melting away again like the coward it was.

She gave a deep, soul-shuddering sigh. No more. No more sadness, no more dwelling on the past, or what might have been. It was time to move on. She'd have a quiet night in tonight, and in the morning, she'd find a way to tell Danny Maik that he could end his watching brief. Perhaps she'd just go up to him and deliver the message straight to the sergeant's stoic, world-weary face. *I'm okay, Danny, really I am. Look at me, footloose and fancy-free, without a care in the world.* Well, perhaps one care. She still had to find those bloody keys.

4

Juan "Traz" Perez took a long drink of his Lone Star beer and considered his reflection in the neon-framed mirror behind the bar. Even without the disturbing hue the blue light gave his complexion, the expression that looked back at him was a long way from the easygoing one he usually wore. Three days ago, he was a Saint Lucia resident with loose plans for a trip back home to Canada. One text message later, here he was in the south of Texas, preparing to embark on a task he didn't really understand, but one that troubled him just the same.

The bar was called the Stock Pond, and it billed itself as *Amblin's Favourite Watering Hole*. There wasn't much water in evidence, but Traz believed they'd got the other part of the description pretty much spot on. He'd been hoping a casual beer or two might give him the chance to collect his thoughts, but he'd known as soon as he set foot in here that this wasn't going to be the place for quiet reflection. On the stage behind him, a morose guitar player was sharing his three-chord anguish with the half-empty room. He had just concluded a song called "I'm Gonna Put a Bar in My Car and Drive Myself to Drink," and while Traz could have pointed out there were a number of levels on which this might be inadvisable, if the singer's circuit consisted of many places like this, he could at least understand the man's sentiment.

He looked over his shoulder and listened to a few bars of the singer's newest offering before turning away again with a slight wince. The woman who had just taken the vacant bar stool beside him offered a sympathetic smile. "Country and Western oldies not your thing?"

"It's not even the end of the third verse, and already his truck has broken down, his dog has died, and his truck's broken down again." Traz shook his head. "Makes you wonder why he doesn't get a more reliable truck."

"Or a more reliable dog. His sweetheart's gonna be leaving him any time now, too," said the woman. "Hardly surprising though, with the run of luck he's on. I mean, who'd want to hang around a loser like that?" She held up her bottle by the neck and chinked Traz's glass. "Verity, by the way. Verity Brown. My friends call me Verry."

As she turned to watch the singer, Traz took the opportunity to study the woman in detail. She wore a lip ring, and her fingernails were individually painted with tiny designs, but her chopped auburn hair had a lustrous shine and her suntanned skin glowed healthily. There were no signs that sitting in Amblin's Favourite Watering Hole was a long-time habit for this woman. Perhaps her bright eyes held a touch of discontent, but just because people took their troubles to a bar didn't necessarily mean they were open to sharing them. Besides, Traz had enough problems of his own just now. He looked toward the stage, where a haze of blue smoke hung over the empty dance floor.

"They still allow smoking in here? Is that even legal anymore?"

"This is south Texas," she reminded him. "They don't take kindly down here to folks tellin' them what they can and can't do. I take it you're new in town."

Traz nodded. "Flew in today. I came to visit the Aransas Wildlife Refuge."

24

"You're a bird watcher, huh?" She didn't sound overly impressed. "Down here doing the South Texas circuit?"

Traz shook his head regretfully. "I'm driving north in the morning, so unfortunately, I won't have a chance to see any of the other sites around here."

The woman's slightly skewed expression could have indicated a number of things, a comment on his itinerary among them. For a birder to come here for a single day in Aransas and then drive out without taking in the Gulf Coast's other rich birding opportunities suggested either very bad planning or another agenda. But if Verity Brown had any further interest in the matter, she masked it with a long drink from her bottle. She waved the empty in the bartender's direction, gesturing for two more.

The final notes of the song were greeted with what could only generously be called applause, but more enthusiasm accompanied the announcement of the next tune. Traz pinched the bridge of his nose with his thumb and forefinger and closed his eyes.

"If you don't mind my saying," said the woman, "I wouldn't exactly have you figured for a place where the set list includes songs like 'I'd Rather Have a Bottle in Front of Me than a Frontal Lobotomy.'"

"What gave me away?"

"Well, for one thing, you're way too neat to be a cowboy. Don't get me wrong, some of these guys clean up pretty good when they put their minds to it, but you take things to a whole 'nother level."

Traz gave her an ironic smile. "Thanks, I think." It said something about the alienation he felt in this part of the world that he was genuinely unsure if the woman's comment on his well-groomed appearance was a compliment or not.

The bartender set two opened beers on the bar before them. Verity handed one to Traz and cast him a quizzical look. "I'm curious. How'd you manage to book a car to drive on out of here, if you only got in this morning? I tried a couple of days back and all the rental agencies were cleaned out for the week."

"This drive's not a rental. Some snowbird has been down here restoring a car over the winter, and now he's flown back and he needed somebody to take it up to Saskatchewan for him. There's an agency that arranges these things. A few of them, I guess."

The singer ended his set to more lukewarm applause and told the audience he would be taking a short break. As far as Traz was concerned, it was the best thing he'd heard through the P.A. system since he'd walked in, but as the singer trudged off stage to slump dispiritedly against the far end of the bar, he couldn't help but feel a pang of sympathy for the man. However difficult Traz's own task was going to be over the next few days, at least he knew his efforts wouldn't go unappreciated.

The audience, such as it was, broke up and people moved off in various directions to stretch their legs. Verity smiled and nodded to some of the people as they passed, exchanging pleasantries with one or two.

"You're obviously from here," said Traz.

"Not originally. I was born and raised in Lafayette, Louisiana, but I don't get back there much these days. What you call snowbirds, they call 'winter Texans' down here. I come here in autumn and do some research over the winter months, but once my subjects leave in the spring, I head up to a place called Scenic, South Dakota."

"What's the big attraction in Scenic?"

"Not much of anything anymore. It's a ghost town. Kinda sad and kinda scary at the same time. But my grandmother has a farm just on the outskirts. As a place to sit on your front porch on a summer's night, listening to the crickets and watching the sun set, it's about as good as it gets. 'Course, whether I can ever get there is a whole 'nother question."

"Can't you get a flight?"

Verity shook her head and sipped her drink again. "I need to take a bunch of lab equipment along with me. I'd rather not run the risk that some bored airport worker thinks *Fragile* is some kinda secret code for *Indestructible. Please Try.*" She smiled sadly and nodded towards the singer at the end of the bar. "You know, you listen to enough of his songs, you might come to believe all of life's problems can be solved by sitting in a bar and having one more cold beer." Verity raised her bottle and took another long drink. "Just not mine, I guess."

Traz scrolled through his phone and turned it towards her. "This is the agency that set up my drive delivery. Perhaps if you call them in the morning, they might have something for you."

"Yeah," said Verity ruefully, "'cause my luck's been running that way." But she put the number into her phone anyway. She scooted off the bar stool, heading for a door beneath a sign that read FILLIES.

While he waited for the return of the woman he was already finding strangely captivating, Traz thought once more about his task. Three thousand miles. Forty-eight hours of driving time. A week out of his life. And for what? He didn't know. He'd been sent only a series of coordinates that tracked straight north for the first half of his journey and then veered off to the northwest for the second part. He had no idea what he was going to find when he reached each of his checkpoints. The implication had been that this was all going to make sense at some point. But at the moment, it made none to him. He packed away his doubts when he saw Verity returning and offered her one of his best smiles. In her absence, at least one light had gone on for him.

27

"Your subjects leave town after the winter, you said. As in migrate. You're studying birds, aren't you? And down here, that probably means Whooping Cranes."

"Avian genetics, specializing in migratory imprinting." Verity eyed him warily. "And there's that look. The one that says an accent like this has no business in the company of such fancy-soundin' words."

"No, not at all." But Traz's guilty grin suggested the thought had at least crossed his mind. "But, working with Whooping Cranes, I mean, wow," he said, giving it a little extra by way of apology, "that must be great."

"It is," she conceded, "but now the birds have mostly moved on for the season, I'd kinda like to do the same. Instead it looks like I'm gonna be stuck here listening to this guy's tales of woe for a few more days yet."

"You know, I'm heading that way myself," said Traz casually. "Oklahoma, Kansas, Nebraska, then the Dakotas. Leaving tomorrow, bright and early. There'd be room for one more. And a few fragile packages." He raised his eyebrows, perhaps not even sure himself how serious the offer was.

"You seem nice enough and all," she said uneasily, "but driving across the country with somebody I just met in a cowboy bar isn't right up there at the top of my bucket list, if you know what I mean. Thanks all the same, but my rent is paid to the end of the month, so all waiting's gonna cost me is time. And now the birds have all but gone, I have plenty of that."

Traz nodded his understanding. "Probably wouldn't have worked out anyway. I'll be making some stops along the way. If you were looking to get to Scenic in a hurry, I wouldn't be your best bet."

The woman seemed grateful that he hadn't taken the rejection to heart. She indicated the singer, beginning to make his way slowly from the bar back towards the stage. "We should get another round in before he starts," she said. "He tends to feature some gospel songs toward the end of the night. Trust me, 'Dropkick me, Jesus, Through the Goalposts of Life' is not something you want to experience with a clear head."

A clear head was not something either of them needed to worry about by the time they stumbled from their shared taxi into the motel's neon-lit forecourt. They had packed in a couple more beers and even a brief swirl around the dance floor during the singer's last set, and as they watched the departing lights of the taxi, both would have admitted the night had turned out a good deal better than they'd been expecting.

They stood for a moment, listening to the silence that seemed to hover somewhere beyond the glare of the motel's lights. Above them, a halo of insects swarmed around the neon sign. The sultry air still held the last remnants of the day's warmth, and the soft coastal breeze played around them, riffling the fronds of the nearby palm trees with papery snaps.

"This is me, neighbour," said Verity. As she mounted the curb, she lost her footing and lurched into Traz, supporting herself with a hand on his chest.

He helped her upright and smiled. "Allow me," he said, taking her keys and unlocking the door. He peered inside the room to make sure all was well and then stood aside, holding the door open for her.

"Well, you don't find old school manners like that much anymore." Verity paused in the doorway and looked up into his face, teetering slightly as she tipped back. "You know, if it wasn't so late, and I wasn't so drunk, I do believe I could enjoy the company of a gentleman like you."

"Of all sad words of tongue or pen," quoted Traz wistfully, "the saddest are these, *It might have been*. I hope you make it to Scenic, Verity Brown. You and your fragile packages. Goodnight."

5

Domenic Jejeune stood on the shingle beach and looked west across the flat surface of Lake Ontario. The haze had robbed the Toronto skyline of its edges and now the distinctive profile of the CN Tower and the cluster of skyscrapers surrounding it seemed to hover over the water like a distant grey mountain range.

Jejeune marvelled at how many new buildings had sprung up in his absence. But if the view had changed so much since he was last here, how different, then, must it be from when the spies had gazed upon it, when this place had functioned as a training centre for covert operations during the Second World War. In those days, a man approaching this area with a pair of binoculars and a backpack might not have been met with the same polite disinterest that Jejeune had encountered today.

He left the shoreline and retraced his steps back up to the paved lane leading into Thickson's Woods. Stopping along the way to check the tops of the overhanging trees for signs of movement, he entered the tall stands of white pine, and turned right, heading for the northwest corner. From here, he would follow the track across to the marshy area in the northeast, before doubling back to cross the lane and check out the meadow on the far side. It was his long-established, unvarying route in these woods. *Patterns*, he thought. What a hold they have on us, staying in our memories even during our absences, ready to impose themselves once again the moment we return.

The interior of the woods still held much of the day's earlier coolness, as Jejeune had known it would. The spring arrivals were in by now: the warblers, the vireos, the thrushes, but the numbers seemed lower than he recalled. Individual birds were sprinkled through the trees and undergrowth like garnish. Perhaps this was what normal days had always been like here. Maybe there was no place in our memories for the mundane, only for the glories, or the disappointments. So perhaps a typical day in Thickson's Woods wasn't one where the spring migrants were dripping from the trees, as he had so fondly recalled when he was overseas.

A figure flickered in and out of view behind the stands of dark tree trunks. Jejeune picked up the approach in his peripheral vision and knew immediately who it was, in that way the familiar can sometimes form itself in the mind even before the senses have a chance to register it.

"Known whereabouts," said Roy Ducannon as he approached. He offered Jejeune a smile, but there was little warmth in it.

"You didn't have to track me down, Roy. I'd have come to you if you'd called."

Roy shrugged easily. "No trouble. Just found out why Damian never responded to the invitation to the family reunion. He never got the voicemails." Roy had a habit of jutting his chin forward slightly when he spoke. When he was first dating their sister, Suzette, Damian had secretly referred to it as Roy's gecko move, but for a long time now Domenic had found something slightly more sinister and confrontational about his brother-in-law's gesture. "Damian's somewhere out in Wood Buffalo National Park, miles out of range of the nearest cellphone tower. The comms equipment he has with him seems to be out of order. Same with his partner's."

"His partner?"

"He's in there with some researcher. Her device doesn't appear to be working either. The park staff don't think there's any cause for alarm, though. They're not overdue on any reporting schedule and they've both got back-country experience. If one had got into difficulties, the other would have had plenty of time to reach somewhere to get help by now."

Roy paused to let the information sink in. When the two men had renewed their acquaintance recently, Jejeune had been too preoccupied with other matters to pay much attention to his brother-in-law's appearance, but now he regarded him carefully. In overall terms, Roy was little changed from his youth. Always stout and barrel-chested, his frame had filled out a little as he approached middle age, and there was a touch more colour in his cheeks. There was a dash of salt and pepper in the closely-trimmed hair now, too. But Roy Ducannon still projected an imposing presence. In his capacity as an RCMP sergeant, it was a useful trait to have.

"What's that one then?" Roy pointed at a small, sparrow-sized bird flitting through the tops of the cedar trees along the side of the clearing. It had a crimson dusting on its cap and chest.

"House Finch. Male," said Jejeune, when the bird had ducked out of sight deeper into the cedars.

"Rare?"

"Common enough. Though you don't usually see them down here. At least not when I was here before. Perhaps they've expanded their range since I've been away."

Roy nodded. "Perhaps we all have."

Silence settled over the men again, heightened by the sound of the wind brushing through the tops of the tall pine trees. There had always been wariness to their exchanges. Roy had never made much effort to hide his contempt for Damian's undisciplined lifestyle, but his issues with Domenic traced back to a different source. The family attributed the men's strained relationship to Roy's annual hunting trip in the autumn, but while Jejeune had never been able to fully understand the appeal of killing as a recreational activity, both men knew there were deeper issues between them. Roy was a faithful husband and a good father, but his career was central to his identity. Only *he* had to work hard at it, pouring every ounce of energy and dedication into being a police officer. For Domenic, on the other hand, the job always seemed to come so easily. Solutions occurred to him, suspects materialized seemingly out of nowhere. And he always appeared to be so unappreciative of his gifts, so dismissive of his God-given talents. Despite the veil the two men drew over Roy's resentments for the sake of the family, whenever it was just the two of them together like this, a faint thrum of discord would always flow between them.

But that hadn't stopped Jejeune from seeking Roy's help when he needed it. And despite the prelude about Damian's whereabouts, Jejeune knew it was this that Roy had come to discuss today. Wordlessly, he handed Jejeune an envelope. Although Domenic didn't look inside, he knew what it contained: a thin gold bookmark, with three birds intricately traced into the metalwork. "Single print," said Roy with another chin jut, "spread across the filigree work. It'd be open to challenge if you were planning to use it as evidence." He waited, in case Jejeune wanted to offer confirmation, but after a moment's silence, Roy continued. "Our guys are good, though. They say it's a match to that name you gave us; Ray Hayes. They did an entire workup, DNA, fibres, chemical traces, but the fingerprint is the only thing on there."

Jejeune nodded slowly. Through the silence, the flute-like call of a Baltimore Oriole came to the men from the black cherry trees beside them. It had been a gamble, and it had not paid off. To his DCS in the U.K., Jejeune had sold his sojourn here in Canada as a temporary situation, just until Ray Hayes emerged from hiding and could be captured. Whether she had ever truly believed it, or merely willed herself to, Shepherd would know by now that Hayes was not going to resurface. Jejeune's unauthorized gambit in having the bookmark examined had been one last attempt to find some evidence that might lead them to Hayes. A single fingerprint was not enough to do that. With no new leads to follow, it seemed that the final doorway back into his old life had now been closed forever.

Roy looked around. "So, this is where Camp X was located. Supposed to be where Ian Fleming came up with the idea for James Bond. I never was much of a one for stories about evil geniuses and all that. Seems to me there's enough villains in real life to keep the likes of you and me busy, eh?"

Jejeune peered into the dark, quiet spaces of the cathedral-like groves of trees. He thought about Fleming and those long-dead British spies who had been stationed here, contemplating their temporary new home, nestled in this remnant of white pine forest on the shores of Lake Ontario. Would they have experienced the same sense of dislocation he now felt, the feeling of transience, of a life held in abeyance while the rest of the world turned without him?

"Do you think you could get me Damian's records from just before contact was lost?" he asked quietly.

"They were both using a system called inReach." Roy allowed himself a small smile at the irony. "I'm sure Damian and his new lady friend are fine, Domenic. Apparently, she's intelligent, single, and good looking. According to the park super, the two of them seemed to be getting along very well, even before they went into the park." Roy looked at Jejeune frankly. "I don't imagine they're in any great hurry for their cosy little holiday in the woods to be over."

"Still, if it's not too much trouble." Jejeune summoned a smile from somewhere and Roy responded in kind. There was too much between them for a genuine friendship, but Jejeune still respected his brother-in-law as a father and a husband, and perhaps as a surrogate son to their parents, too, during the prolonged absences of the brothers. This was a long way to come to deliver the findings from the bookmark in person, whatever Roy's motives, and Jejeune knew he should make some overture to acknowledge the fact that he had made the journey.

"Do you want to get a coffee before you head back? There's a doughnut shop a little way up the road."

Roy declined with a shake of his head. "I'm going to see if I can grab the last flight out tonight. Surprise Suzette and the kids." He reached out for Domenic's hand and shook it. "I'll send you those inReach records, but believe me, communications in the interior of Wood Buffalo are a lot sketchier than you might imagine. The authorities up there get a hundred reports like this a year. You can count the number that amount to anything on one hand."

Jejeune watched him walk up the tree-lined laneway and checked the time on his phone. There was no chance Roy could get back to the airport on Toronto Island in time to catch a flight north tonight. But part of his commitment to his job meant Roy was a fully paid-up member of the police officers' brotherhood. No summer barbeque, no poker night, no retirement party fell beneath Roy's radar. As he disappeared around the corner behind the bank of trees, it occurred to Jejeune that even though the inhabitants of Camp X may be long gone from this place, the ghosts of secret lives still lingered.

6

Detective Chief Superintendent Colleen Shepherd often singled out individuals in the morning briefings, for praise or otherwise, but she rarely summoned them to the front of the room. Today, though, everyone gathered in the Incident Room at Saltmarsh Police Station knew what was coming. Lauren Salter coloured slightly as she stood. She took a moment to smooth her crisp white blouse, but seemed to accept that further hesitation was only going to delay the inevitable; whether she welcomed the invitation or not, she, too, had been expecting it.

"With so much emphasis on the team approach to policing these days, I always feel there's a danger that individual achievements might not get the credit they deserve," said Shepherd as Salter joined her in front of the assembly. "But when a member of this department does something worthy of note, you can rest assured, it won't be allowed to pass unnoticed." She looked across at Salter, whose expression suggested she wished she'd chosen a blouse that might have done less to emphasize the pink flushing of her cheeks and neck. "I don't think it's a surprise to any of us that Constable Salter was able to pass her examinations, though I'm not sure even she would have expected to achieve such, frankly, ridiculously high scores on the written component. And I'm reliably informed she did just as well in her interviews. Her ideas about the application of new technologies in policing seem to have struck a particular chord with the panel. Which I suppose means we'll now have at least one person in the police service who knows how to use the new phone system."

Detective Sergeant Danny Maik had always felt Shepherd's attempts at humour in these situations were received far more warmly than their actual merits deserved, but today's generosity from the assembled group, he recognized, was more about the popularity of their colleague. The DCS turned to Salter once more as she made her announcement. "Congratulations, Detective Sergeant Lauren Salter."

The derisive cheers and apathetic, half-hearted applause reinforced the genuine affection among the ranks and Salter shifted slightly with embarrassment. As she stood there, with her frozen smile and her eyes flickering for an exit sign, Maik's heart went out to her. Shepherd had grasped one of her hands and placed the other on Salter's shoulder, turning her to face the room like a new midfielder being welcomed to the local football club. As stilted and awkward as the moment was, even Danny realized it was a photo op. Only he'd never yet taken a truly successful photo with his phone, and even if he did, it would likely take him the better part of a day to work out how to post it anywhere. Eventually, one of the bright young things from Traffic grabbed Salter's own phone and took a few shots that could be posted on her social media network, where they could be instantly commented on and just as quickly forgotten.

"And as it turns out, Sergeant Salter," said Shepherd, "your timing could hardly have been better. With Inspector Jejeune off on his leave and Tony Holland on secondment to the Met, there is room for a second sergeant here at Saltmarsh, at least for the time being."

Others in the crowd turned to seek out Danny Maik's face. He was renowned for his stoic expressions, but it was obvious he had already been informed of Shepherd's decision — and approved. From the front of the room, Salter flashed him a smile, equal parts gratitude and nervousness.

"With the temporary manpower shortage, you might both find you have to go it alone a bit more than usual, but make no mistake, I'll be expecting you to share out the sergeant's duties equally," Shepherd told her.

"That means Danny puts the kettle on while you fetch the biscuits," offered somebody from the cheap seats.

Salter shook her head gravely. "Sorry, no can do."

Shepherd looked slightly startled by the new sergeant's response.

"I'm off the biccies just now," explained Salter, patting her stomach. "Doing a bit of running, too."

"I do hope these are not new requirements for the position of sergeant. Jogging and no biscuits? Sergeant Maik will have his retirement papers on my desk by the end of the day."

Like the crowd, Maik was in a generous mood today, and he rewarded the effort with a smile. Of sorts. He watched Salter now as she thanked those who came up to offer their individual congratulations. He'd already taken care of that, as soon as she walked into the building.

As the assembly broke up, it crossed his mind that if it had been anyone else at the station being celebrated in this way, the event would almost certainly have been marked by a cake, courtesy of Lauren Salter. He felt disappointed in himself that he hadn't thought to arrange something. It wasn't as if he could have expected any of this useless lot to have done anything. He was still watching Salter, from his safe distance, when he heard Shepherd's voice beside him.

"I'm going to give her the lead on this domestic stabbing, Danny."

Sergeant Maik wasn't a man who normally went about avoiding people. If anything, he was aware people sometimes found his own presence a touch on the intimidating side. But he had studiously avoided getting anywhere near the orbit of his chief superintendent recently. It wasn't a situation that could continue for much longer, so there was almost a relief for Maik that she had finally caught up to him. Almost.

"I trust you'll be keeping an eye on things, though. There's something about this one that I don't like. This business of the extra force for the second stab wound, for one thing."

By making it about the case, rather than the investigator, Maik realized Shepherd had hoped to draw him out. But even if he had any misgivings about giving a new detective sergeant such a tricky case as her first lead, he would have kept his silence. He'd be ready to offer his thoughts whenever she wanted them, but he'd let her make her way alone until she asked. Only, he suspected the new sergeant wasn't going to ask, no matter how bogged down her progress became. She'd be too afraid of looking out of her depth. Nor would it do any good for Danny to reassure her they were all out of their depth, in every situation, every minute of the bloody day. So if Shepherd did want him to keep an eye on this case, it wasn't only for the developments in evidence gathering and investigative procedure and such like. It would be to watch Salter, too.

Shepherd left her shoulder-to-shoulder position and turned to face him. It was what you might do if it was important to see somebody's reaction when you spoke. "I've received a report about a request that came through from the RCMP in Toronto recently, asking for access to fingerprint records for Ray Hayes."

"Yes, ma'am." Like his expression, Maik's tone was giving nothing away.

She looked at him dubiously. "*Yes, ma'am* as in 'how interesting,' or *yes, ma'am* as in you already knew about this? There's only one reason I can think of why the RCMP might be making such a request. How about you? And where do you suppose they may have obtained a fingerprint for comparison?"

She waited.

"There was a bookmark in Lindy's car," said Maik eventually. "I believe the DCI may have taken it with him when he left."

"Are you telling me Inspector Jejeune removed evidence from a crime scene? Evidence that he's now having independently assessed in another country? Has he taken leave of his senses?"

"It wasn't a confirmed crime scene at the time he took it," said Maik, "just the scene of a motor vehicle collision."

Shepherd's complexion darkened slightly. "A word of advice, Sergeant. If this goes as far as a review board, I would strongly advise you not to voice an observation like that. They're not overly tolerant of people who insult their intelligence." Shepherd shook her head incredulously. "God almighty. What was he thinking? That bookmark could have been vital in a case against Hayes, but there's no hope we'll be able to use it as evidence after this."

"With respect, ma'am," began Maik. He stopped at her stare. The phrase was bandied about at the station far too easily for Shepherd's liking, but she could usually be at least reasonably sure Danny Maik's use of it was sincere. "Since we didn't request the print match, the results won't be reported back to us. But the one thing we can be sure of is that there was nothing on that bookmark that could bring us any closer to finding Hayes. If there was, the DCI would have already let us know."

"If you believe that in any way excuses his actions —" She stopped, accepting Maik's point. It didn't excuse them, but until anyone asked, it gave them some breathing room. "So the two of you have not been in touch?" Despite her frustration, Shepherd had lowered her voice slightly. Maik's search for Hayes had been purposely kept from the rank and file. Ray Hayes wouldn't have the resources to breach the sophisticated firewalls of the police department's secure communications systems, but he might well tap into a source of equally rich information — the unguarded gossip of officers patrolling the streets of Saltmarsh, or having a quiet pint at the Boatman's Arms.

"No, ma'am. No contact, as agreed."

Shepherd gave her sergeant a look designed to remind him that, in the past, both Maik and Jejeune had occasionally followed procedures that were not entirely *as agreed*. "I've not had a chance to check my inbox this morning. Anything in there from you that might help push this bookmark business to the back of my mind?"

"No new leads to report, ma'am. All the existing ones have been rechecked, but there's nothing come to light there, either. We're no closer to finding Hayes than we ever have been."

Shepherd nodded slowly. It was a variation of every update she'd received from him so far. He'd even stopped adding the other part, she noticed, some vague assurance that he was doing all he could; a statement so vapid it sounded like it had come directly from a police press release. Not at all what she might have expected from the sincere, straightforward officer to whom she'd entrusted the most important task of his career. She knew the probability of Hayes's arrest was diminishing with each passing day, and with it, the prospects for Domenic Jejeune's return.

"Your latest written report suggests you've stepped down your surveillance on Lindy."

Maik understood her need to check and recheck the small details. It was always that way with one's superiors when there had been no progress on the larger ones. "I didn't want to take any unnecessary chances that I'd be seen, on the off-chance Hayes is still around these parts." But Maik's tone did not suggest he felt this was a very real possibility any longer. If it ever had been. Shepherd knew he believed they were now out of options, and while she didn't want to accept it, at the moment she could find no reason to disagree.

"You feel Lindy's safe, then?"

"There's been nothing to suggest otherwise."

Shepherd nodded. So, DCI Jejeune had been proven right. He had predicted his absence would ensure Lindy's safety. He'd always felt Ray Hayes would only pose a threat to Lindy again if Jejeune himself came back to Saltmarsh. But unable to confide his reasons for leaving to Lindy, he had left her discreet surveillance in the hands of the one man he trusted most. It was a duty Sergeant Maik would execute as diligently as any he had ever taken on, and Shepherd knew that Danny would never have scaled back his watching brief unless he, too, was convinced there was no longer any threat to the DCI's girlfriend.

The two officers watched as the last of Salter's well-wishers left the room. With a final lingering glance in Maik's direction, the newly-minted sergeant followed them. Shepherd gave a sigh and looked at Danny. "As I say, Sergeant, keep me apprised. Any developments. Any at all."

In either case, she meant. But they both knew there was only one he would be reporting on. The other one was already closed in all but name. And soon, DCS Shepherd was going to have to make it official.

7

"Mints."

In truth, Jeremy's constant habit of identifying the items he saw Lindy holding was beginning to wear a bit thin. *Mints, cheese puffs,* and once recently, even *lipstick.* He was like someone learning a new language, trying the words out loud to show he had mastered them. But if this minor irritation was the price she needed to pay for having a fresh coffee delivered to her desk every morning, she continued to find it worth it. For now. She proffered the pack of mints to Jeremy and he took one eagerly.

"You're later than usual, Jeremy. Busy day?"

"Trying to drum up a bit more 'business,'" he said, punctuating the word with his air-quotation-mark fingers. "No go. Still, we have what we have."

As if his Captain Bunnyfingers routine wasn't enough, it didn't help that Jeremy was a fully paid-up member of what Lindy referred to as the *inanity squared* mob. His response to a depressingly wide range of subjects seemed to revolve around variations on the same theme, each delivered as if it was a new frontier in profundity: *it is what it is, we have what we have, we know what we know.*

It was the last one that separated Domenic Jejeune from most people, she thought. He spent his days striving to know what he didn't know; to plug the gaps in his knowledge; about timelines, circumstances, motives. But Lindy's observation belonged to her past, and she was making a concerted effort these days to ensure all thoughts of Domenic Jejeune remained firmly stored there. She steered her thoughts back to the present day, and to Jeremy, who was now standing by the window, stooping his gaunt frame slightly to peer out.

"No sign of that man, the one who was watching you. Did you warn him off? Only you said you were going to."

"Did I?" Lindy sipped her coffee. "I don't think it'll come to that." She wasn't sure exactly where Jeremy called home, but she got the impression he spent enough time on the streets around the office that Danny Maik's presence anywhere nearby would have been noted. She hadn't seen Danny either, and she had also been looking, despite her resolve not to. If neither she nor Jeremy had spotted him, it likely meant the sergeant had discontinued his surveillance of her. Perhaps the man who requested it had finally decided it was time to move on, too.

"No luck on the keys front, then?"

The question startled Lindy. She'd assumed Jeremy was still at the window, but when she looked up, he was standing at her desk, staring at her with that awkward, disquieting grin of his. "I suppose it doesn't matter much at the moment, with Emma's place being keyless entry and all." Jeremy gave Lindy what he intended to be a nonchalant shrug. "She mentioned it to me once. It must be nice for you to have the place all to yourself while she's away."

"*Spain, Linds,*" Emma had told her. "You should come. Do you good. It's just me and a couple of mates. A few days in the sun and the sangria. It'll be fun."

Spain might be fun, but Lindy knew she wouldn't be. Not yet. So she had declined, agreeing instead to stay and house-sit, luxuriating in the quiet time, collecting her thoughts and readying herself for her next steps in her new post-Domenic world. By the time Emma got back, she'd have found a place of her own to move in to. It wouldn't be the cottage, though. The cottage was *their* place, their *shared* place — with its long driveway and the deck overlooking the sea, and its key still under the marram grass planter on the back patio. Lindy wondered idly if she'd ever mentioned that to Jeremy. She couldn't remember doing so, but he seemed to have a way of wheedling information out of people, and her defences weren't exactly intact in the wake of her split with Dom, so it was possible she may have let something slip. Perhaps she'd move the spare key somewhere else the next time she was over there, she thought, just in case.

The next time she was over there. Lindy knew that visit would involve sorting Dom's things out, separating his stuff from hers and making some arbitrary decisions about those they had shared. It wasn't as if Domenic would put up a fight about anything, but she wanted to do everything fairly anyway. At least there were no pets or valuables to squabble over, she thought practically. There'd need to be contact at some point, though, when she got down to the stickier point of disposing of the cottage itself. Perhaps Danny would be willing to act as the go-between one last time. It was not something she looked forward to asking of him. It wasn't really fair to impose that sort of burden on such a kind, decent man. But he had been willing to act on Domenic's behalf to keep tabs on her. Maybe he owed her one last visit, bearing an address to ship Domenic's things to, and the contact details of a lawyer in Canada.

Lindy stood up hoping it would signal the end of Jeremy's visit. "I need to speak to Kate-Lynn, some accounting thing." She flapped her hand vaguely.

"Why don't you just call her?"

"I need the exercise. That's the trouble with mobile phones. They make for immobile people."

"Oh that's good, Linds," said Jeremy. "Really, killer stuff."

Linds? Where had that come from? Had it been there all along and she'd simply missed it till now? Or had Jeremy, *Jer to my friends*, taken it upon himself to ratchet up the familiarity an extra notch? It was time to start thinking about gentle ways to ask him to back off. She caught herself in the thought. *Gentle*? The old Lindy would have already dealt with this, probably even seen it coming long beforehand and headed it off. She'd have deftly disarmed Jeremy, kept him as a friend but left him in no uncertain terms where they stood in terms of a relationship. But the one thing she wouldn't have worried about was doing it gently. Where had she gone, that old Lindy, that clear-eyed, self-confident version of herself that she'd spent so much time honing over the years? Vanished, she thought sadly, along with her dangling blonde hair, and her belief that love really could conquer all. She returned from her thoughts to find Jeremy over by the window again, peering out.

"Coast's clear." He gave her a smile that was meant to be reassuring. *I'm on the case, Linds. I'll keep watching out for you. I'll take care of you. And more, too, if you'll let me.* Poor Jeremy. She wished it was as simple as that: a slow, easy drift into another relationship. But as welcome as Jeremy's attentions had been when she needed them, he was never going to be the one, when she did eventually start rebuilding her life. It was time he was encouraged to come to terms with that reality.

Claire materialized at Lindy's desk, even though there was no order from Jeremy for her to collect. It crossed Lindy's mind that it might be in response to some perceived need on Lindy's part. Protection from Jeremy? Surely not.

"I saw him again, Linds. Your stalker."

Jeremy snapped his head around. "Again? When?"

Claire looked at him uneasily, as if unsure Lindy would want him involved in her business like this. But Lindy was making no effort to deter Jeremy's interest.

"This morning. He was watching you as you made your way in from the car park. He was hiding, Linds, tucked away in a doorway. If I hadn't been looking straight in that direction by accident, I'd never have seen him. It's getting a bit much, Lindy. Policeman or not, it's creepy."

Lindy couldn't disagree. Whatever Maik's brief from Domenic was, this nonsense had gone far enough.

"Which doorway?" asked Jeremy. "What time was this?"

Lindy held up a hand. "It's okay, Jeremy. I'll deal with this now."

For once, Claire made eye contact with Jeremy. Because Lindy's tone had left neither of them in any doubt that she would.

8

Domenic Jejeune wheeled his rented Range Rover Evoque into the car park at Fairchild Flats and drew up to the low wooden barrier. He turned off the engine and lowered the car window, looking out over a shallow stream and listening for a moment to the bird calls coming from the stands of pale grass around him. Common Yellowthroat, Bobolink, Brown Thrasher. Even after his long sojourn in the U.K., the names came back to him now as effortlessly as memories. But he could not hear the call he had been hoping for. And the lack of other cars in the lot was further evidence that the bird he had come to see was no longer here. Only one other parking space was occupied. Jejeune saw the person he presumed to be the car's owner standing at the edge of the water. He was peering into a stand of scrubby cedar trees on the far side. Jejeune grabbed his binoculars from the front passenger seat and walked towards the man, the crunching of his shoes on the gravel over loud in the quiet morning air. The man half-turned at the sound of Jejeune's approach and offered him a wan smile.

"Come for the PABU?" He shook his head. "Nothing doing, I'm afraid."

"There was a posting on ONTbirds this morning that said it had been seen."

"Ah yes, mistaken identity. A correction was sent out shortly after. But clearly not soon enough for some. It's been my unfortunate duty to disappoint people all morning."

Jejeune drew in a sharp breath. "Exactly what else could you mistake a Painted Bunting for? A Gouldian Finch?" he asked testily. He found himself quickening to frustration more easily these days. Even if he understood the underlying reasons, it was not a side of his character he enjoyed. But impatience had no place in this tranquil setting, and he found a smile from somewhere to meet the sympathetic one the man was offering him.

"Indeed, there can be few more instantly recognizable birds than a male Painted Bunting. Sadly, reports are only as reliable as their reporters. I didn't know these particular ones." Jejeune wondered whether the man had appointed himself guardian of the site, as certain individuals sometimes did when a rare sighting occurred. If he had, Fairchild Flats could do worse than this kindly, articulate man in whom there seemed to be no sense of self-importance, merely concern for the place, for the bird, for the birders.

Jejeune looked around, taking time to consider his surroundings now that the urgency to see the bird had passed. All the same features were still here, and yet, they were not quite as he remembered them. It was as if he was looking at his memories through a faintly distorted mirror. The tall blue spruce he had parked beside he remembered as a newly planted sapling. The stands of sumac, with their crazed candelabras of burgundy blooms, had spread farther along the bank. Even the water, a silver ribbon in the flat morning light, seemed wider than he remembered. Only the sounds hadn't changed; the raw, scolding cries of the American Crows from the bare treetops, the gentle chuckling of the water as it danced over the stones of the creek bed. And in the background, that soft hum that hung in the air like dust. Jejeune had always marvelled that less than half a mile from this quiet, peaceful setting, sixteen lanes of traffic soared over the Rouge Valley carrying almost a quarter of a million cars per day between Toronto and its eastern suburbs.

"Those cedars, that's where it was." Jejeune looked up to find the man was pointing to the stand of trees that rose on the far bank, dark against the aspens higher up on the hillside. "Its pattern was to show up for about fifteen minutes in the morning and then disappear for the rest of the day. But it's not been reported," the man paused to allow himself a slight tilt of the head, "*reliably* reported, for three days now. I fear it may have moved on. Caused a lot of excitement, I must say, lots of Ontario ticks, a few lifers even." He shook his head in what might have been regret.

Jejeune understood. He shared the disquiet that accompanied the sighting of a bird so far outside its range; the knowledge that the bird's survival was likely at risk. But with food now available, and the spring temperatures, this visitor to southern Ontario had a better chance than many rare visitors he had seen here. True, it would almost certainly not find a mate this far north, but there was a reasonable chance it would recover its navigational radar well enough by fall to make the southward migration. He played his bins into the branches of the trees, but he detected no movement of any kind. He tried lower down, amongst gnarls of undergrowth and the bleached grey wood of the dead trunks before lowering his glasses in defeat.

"Ever seen one?" asked the man.

Jejeune shook his head. "I've been chasing one for a long time," he said, "this and the Scissor-Tailed Flycatcher."

"Our nemesis birds." The man offered a soft smile. "I have a friend from the old country who claims the time and energy

51

consumed by his enemies far outweighed that he invested in his friends. But surely, there have been a few Sci Flys around southern Ontario over the past few years. You've never managed to catch up with one of them?"

"I was overseas. In the U.K."

"Oh, I see. You live there now?"

"Yes. No. Sort of." Jejeune was disturbed not so much at his inability to articulate his answer, but to know what that answer really was.

"I do have a few photographs of the PABU that I suspect may offer you some consolation."

It was all Jejeune could do to suppress a look of disdain at such an offer. He had driven a long way to see a bird that would have been a lifer for him, a nemesis bird at that. If he had merely wanted to see pictures of Painted Buntings, he could have looked at his field guide. Surely, this man, who seemed to know so much about birders and birding, could appreciate that photographs would provide no consolation at all. But courtesy was as ingrained as Jejeune's other traits and he managed to find a smile of gratitude from somewhere. He peered closely at the images the man called up on his camera screen and then looked up at the cedars where the photographs had been taken.

"It's not the light," said the man. "The colours really are that washed out." He shook his head. "As I say, a lot of lifer ticks ..."

Jejeune nodded, understanding the man's earlier gesture now. Not regret, but pity.

"The trouble is, feathers don't change colour once they are grown in. It's nutrition that influences feather pigmentation. I'm not sure specifically which food sources provide the carotenoids for Painted Buntings, but if we assume this bird simply migrated too far north from South Carolina or Georgia, its diet when the feathers were growing in would have been its natural one. Given that PABUs are commonly kept in captivity, and this one's plumage is suggestive of a seed diet, I'd suggest the Ontario Bird Records Committee is going to be hard-pressed to accept this sighting." He smiled. "Though, I can assure you they'll have plenty of other photographic evidence to consider besides this."

Jejeune didn't doubt it. A spectacularly attractive bird so close to a major urban centre would have received more lens time than a Hollywood A-lister. Fortunately, he suspected the fast-flowing water in front of him at least would have been deep enough and cold enough to have kept the barrage of cameras at a safe distance from the bird.

"I expect the committee will come to me sooner or later. I've probably seen the bird more often than anyone else." The man paused thoughtfully. "Of course, I'll not offer my own thoughts. Just my observations, the details, as clearly and accurately as I can recall them."

Where were witnesses like this when I was investigating my cases? wondered Jejeune. *Back in my old life, when Lindy was a part of it,* he thought sadly.

"Well, I should be getting on, leave you to enjoy the rest of your day. There are plenty of other birds to see here. A Black-throated Blue Warbler has been moving around in those sumacs, and I heard a White-eyed Vireo somewhere nearby too. And do keep your hopes up about your PABU. This could still be your year. One of the reasons such a dubious sighting has gained so much currency is because there seems to be an irruption of sorts this spring. Painted Buntings popping up everywhere. Indeed, there has even been a report of one in the U.K. recently. A place called Norfolk, I believe."

Jejeune allowed himself an ironic smile. He bade the man goodbye and watched him leave. Alone in the parking lot, he

53

looked around. He couldn't remember the first time he had visited the Rouge Valley. It seemed he had always known this natural corridor that flowed like a green river through the concrete sprawl of the city. But he had never known it as a national park. Not some distant, remote destination, as the words conjured up in his imagination, but a national park within easy access of a third of the country's population. He looked around him now for telltale signs that the new designation had left its mark on the area. The parking lot had been graded; it was no longer a minefield of potholes so deep they seemed to hold rainwater long after everything else in the park had dried up. The wooden parking rail here was new, too. But the natural areas that surrounded him seemed unchanged. He took in the dark smudge of pines on a distant ridge and the smoky purple haze of maples running down into the valley below. Would these things change, when the authorities had finished developing new access routes and public education programmes? Would some of the wildness have to be sacrificed to the proposed new hiking paths and bike trails? He was glad he had known Rouge Valley in former times, just in case.

He followed one of the older trails, now all but overgrown, and came upon the arches that supported the massive steel beams transporting the highway over the park. His thoughts turned to all those people traversing this spot twenty metres above him. They were so close to this place, but so utterly separated from it. The commuters would pass over this valley, reassured by the presence of this green space, feeling a deep affection for it, even, but content to let the highway carry them across the ravine on its massive concrete legs without every truly experiencing the wild, natural wonderland just below them. He knew better than anyone the price you paid for separating yourself from the things you loved. Perhaps it was necessary in some cases, but you always lost a part of yourself in the process. But then, perhaps the true measure of how much you loved something was how much of yourself you were willing to sacrifice for it.

He sat beneath the arches, a pocket of silence beneath the drone of traffic, amid a strange half-world of graffiti and coyote tracks. He remembered coming to the Glen Rouge campground as a child. He had snuck off one afternoon to sit beneath these same concrete pillars. He fancied he could feel the heartbeat of the city above in the vibrations, while the slow-moving river in front of him ran like blood through its veins. He recalled his young boy's excitement at his unfettered independence, at being completely free and alone. Now he was once again facing the same prospect, but this time, the thought brought him only sadness.

When he returned to Fairchild Flats, Jejeune's rented Evoque was the only car in the parking lot. He checked his phone and found a message from Roy. He had forwarded Damian's inReach records, as Domenic had requested. He knew Roy believed this was just some distraction to relieve the boredom of Domenic's endless days of waiting and holding on. Perhaps it was. But two tracking devices had failed in the same place at the same time, and that wasn't something he was inclined to write off as a coincidence. At least, not without further investigation.

As he started the Range Rover, he stared at the stand of cedars on the far bank. Was this how he was destined to spend his time now, trapped in places he had once loved, like a man imprisoned by his memories? He wanted there to be other reasons for putting his life on hold like this, for every passing day he spent in this self-imposed exile. But there were none, only the impossible hope that Danny Maik would find Ray Hayes, and he knew the time had come to let that hope go. The rest of Jejeune's life awaited his decision to move on.

He looked over one last time at the spot where the Painted Bunting had been seen. Whether it was a wild bird or the escapee Jejeune now believed it was, he knew it would not be returning. There was a point at which you simply had to accept that your nemesis had won.

9

The old Victorian house was showing its age, but beneath the rusty tears that dribbled from the drainpipe fastenings, and the peeling paint flecks around the window frames, there was something else. Character. Lauren Salter had never been one for fanciful analogies, but there was something in the red-brick facade, in the half-round columns that framed the doorway that emanated strength and steadfastness; enduring qualities that the passage of time couldn't diminish.

Well, that was settled then, thought Salter ironically. Put in her report that Wattis Wright lived in a solid, dependable house, and that would be her character profile of the murder victim in the books. She remained a moment longer on the top step, looking up at the house. She understood the reason for her reluctance to duck under the yellow incident tape and enter the building. It was because once she crossed that threshold, there would be no turning back. This would become her case, her investigation, and she was going to have to conduct it according to one simple guiding principle. It would inform her every decision, guide her every movement. *Don't fail him.*

"'The lead? Er, yes, ma'am. Great. Thank you." Even in playback, her response sounded wishy-washy and unprofessional. But in fairness, the news had come as a bit of a shock.

"You've already been to the scene," Shepherd had said as Salter was still recovering. "So tell us, Sergeant, first impressions?"

Danny Maik had been beside them, but he'd held back. He'd known which sergeant Shepherd was asking. So, Detective Lauren Salter, newly appointed to Equally Shared Sergeant's Duties, had taken a deep breath and plunged in. "There's no sign there was anyone else present, so we should probably go with … we should go with," she'd corrected herself, "the idea of a single assailant for now."

"A random attack?" Shepherd's eyes had gone to Danny here, as if the two of them might know better. She couldn't bring herself to believe it was random, Salter had told them, but if it was targeted, it was hard to see what for. "Certainly not robbery. There are no signs the attacker entered beyond the hallway. Nothing was disturbed; nothing appears to have been taken. In fact, there was a certified cheque, made payable to the victim, in plain view. Granted, it's not easy to cash a stolen cheque, but it's not impossible, either. You'd have thought it would've been worth the killer's while to take a chance on it, especially for that amount of money."

Shepherd had nodded. "And the method, Sergeant Salter? Do you have any concerns about that?"

She did. The first stab wound to the chest would have proven fatal. There would have been a lot of blood. But it was followed by a second thrust, much, much harder, delivered sometime after the first, possibly even minutes later, when it would have been obvious the victim was already dead. But what was the killer doing between those two knife thrusts? To deliver that blow, the killer would have had to step into the hallway, but why stand there all that time, waiting, before delivering that second thrust?

Shepherd had looked at her for a long moment. "Plenty for you to be going on with, then," she'd said finally. "I'd suggest you get started."

Salter drew a deep breath, unlocked the front door, and entered.

The heat from the spring morning hadn't yet found its way into the hallway of the house, but the light had. Pale swatches of colour spilled onto the tiled floor. Salter thought at first they might be spots the post-crime clean-up crew had failed to mop up, but turning to look over her shoulder she realized it was sunlight, filtering through the small stained glass panels in the front door. She stood for a moment looking down at the place where the victim had been found, still clutching the telephone receiver, a carving knife driven into his chest up to the hilt.

A large room opened off the hallway to the right and she entered through the wide, door-less archway, hearing the soft creak of the wooden floors beneath her footsteps. A parlour, the room would no doubt have been called on the Victorian builder's plans. It was an office now, a curious jumble of old furniture and antiquated electronics. An oak rolltop desk dominated the facing wall, flanked by a fax machine and a cumbersome, freestanding photocopier, of the kind Salter had not seen since she was a teenager. On an exquisite reproduction Elizabethan writing table stood a computer set-up of only slightly more recent vintage than the photocopier. The tiny screen and keyboard shared the standard grey-beige colour of computer generations past, as did the bulky tower resting against one of the legs of the desk. No wonder the SOCO team had dubbed this place *Jurassic Park*.

She moved from the office into the room behind it, another empty space, ringing with silence. She had never felt so much an intruder in a crime scene. It was the solitude, she realized. Usually she was in attendance with a senior investigator, Danny or Inspector Jejeune. Often there were forensic techs around, fingerprint teams, even a medical examiner. Now, it was just her, DS Lauren Salter, and a house full of secrets. And her mantra: *Don't fail him.*

It was cooler in here, at the back of the house. The room drew no warmth from the sparse furnishings: a well-worn armchair, a set of heavy brocade curtains, a faded area rug that looked like it would have been worth a lot of money when its colours were vibrant and new. Along the back wall was a heavy wooden sideboard on which a turntable and receiver stood. Beside the sideboard was a shelf unit holding a neatly arranged stack of vinyl albums. Neither had the coating of dust Salter had seen on such items in other crime scenes she had visited. These were not relics from some forgotten past. They had been used recently, and regularly, she suspected.

She crossed to the chair and sat down, listening to the silence in the room, trying to collect her thoughts. What had she seen so far, what had she learned that might help her? Beside the chair was a side table. Salter silently recited SOCO's inventory: *two empty beer cans, one glass.* The brand was Danny's beer of choice. Perhaps there was a marketing campaign there somewhere, she thought idly, *Pardham's: the choice of men who prefer to stay home at night and listen to old songs.* Should have the stuff flying off the shelves. Neither the cans nor the glass were here now. They had been bagged and taken for analysis, as likely the last items the victim had touched before he went to answer the door for the final time in his life.

In a holder beneath the table there was a small address book. Salter took it out and riffled through the alphabetized pages. Most of the categories were empty, page after page of blank sheets. In fact, there were so few entries she was able to count them individually: eleven. Perhaps somewhere in the list lay answers about what had happened here. Certainly, at this stage, she had none. She took leaned back in the armchair to consider what, if anything, she knew about the case so far. The silence of the room settled in around her and she closed her eyes, enjoying the peace of it for a few moments.

The shrill ring of Salter's phone startled her awake but she'd reflexively answered it before she was fully alert.

"Sergeant Salter? Susan Bonaccord. I understand you've been trying to contact me."

"I'm sorry?"

"About that night, when I was on the phone with Wattis Wright?"

"Oh, right, yes." Salter rubbed her face awake with a hand. "Yes, thanks for getting back to me." She stood up and began to move around the room, getting her thoughts in order. *Don't fail him.* "I wanted to go over things again with you. If you're still at the hotel, I could come over." A thought struck her as she looked around the empty house. "Although, perhaps you could just talk me through it now."

"Now? What, you mean on the phone?"

"I'm at the house. The scene ... the crime scene." She sighed irritably at her own fumbling.

"Well, if you're sure ..." Bonaccord sounded dubious, and in truth, Salter could think of no good reason to do things this way. Except she was here, now, and Bonaccord's first recollection was always going to be the clearest one, the most visceral, closest to the emotions. Setting it against Salter's own observations as the woman's account led her through the scene might just help the sergeant to see things in a different light.

"We'd been talking for some time when I heard the doorbell go in the background. It was one of those old-fashioned chimes, I remember. Quite loud."

Salter entered the hallway, its pitted, harlequin-tiled floor still dappled by pools of stained-glass light. Beside her, the wall-mounted phone sat on its cradle, its long, twisted cord dangling almost to the floor. She stood facing the doorway, recalling the large round doorbell on the door jamb outside.

"He asked me to excuse him, while he spoke to the ... person at the door. And then I heard ... it was like he was gasping for breath, drowning almost. Only not quite."

Salter stared down at the tiled floor, at where Wright would have lain as the blood bubbled up, filling his lungs, creating the gurgling sound Bonaccord had heard.

"I asked if he was all right, what had happened. But of course, he didn't reply."

Salter saw Wright now, lying on the cold tiles, the phone in his hand, the life spilling out of his body in a pulsing red stream. He was listening to Bonaccord's voice, wanting to say he'd been stabbed, to tell her he was dying, but unable to move or speak. Or finally, to breathe.

Perhaps the silence on the phone meant Bonaccord was dwelling on those details, too. Salter needed her not to. They could distort other impressions she might have.

"Did you hear the other person's voice at all?"

"No."

"And Mr. Wright didn't say anything, after he excused himself to open the door? A name? Anything?"

"No. *Hello*. That was all."

"*Hello*, like he knew the person?"

"I suppose so. I never thought about it."

Salter stared at the doorway, imagining someone standing there, someone he knew. The address book provided meagre pickings, but perhaps that was no bad thing. It certainly limited the suspect pool.

"Are you still there?" Bonaccord's inquiry sounded slightly impatient. "Is there anything else, Sergeant? Only I have rather a lot to do this morning."

Salter looked at the stained tiles in the empty hallway once more, at the phone cord hanging forlornly down the wall, at the door with its pastel patches of light shining through. They were discussing a man's violent death, and still Bonaccord had her mind on other priorities.

"This cheque your company issued. The accompanying letter says something about a rights purchase."

"That's correct. We purchased the rights to some properties from Mr. Wright. He wrote all the music for the Shammalars. I'm too young to remember them, frankly, as I imagine you are, but they were a big act in the sixties."

The name may have rung a distant bell somewhere in Salter's memory, but she couldn't conjure up any pertinent facts. She'd ask her dad, Davy, when she got home. As hard as it was for her to believe, looking at him these days, he'd apparently been an avid music fan when he was young. If the Shammalars were as big as Susan Bonaccord seemed to be implying, Davy would likely have heard of them.

"This deal, was everybody happy with it? No disgruntled parties being forced into something against their better judgment?"

"Absolutely not. In fact, we were both delighted to have concluded our agreement. Mr. Wright was, quite frankly, very keen to have the money, and we needed the rights. Our clients are staging a large West-end production that should be a strong fit for the current nostalgia market. This represented a very good deal for both sides. I'd be happy to discuss this all further at some point, Sergeant, but I'm afraid I really do have to get on just now."

Salter tucked away her phone and looked around. From the hallway, she could see the chair she'd been sitting in when she'd fallen asleep. How many nights had Wattis Wright sat there, she wondered, immersing himself in the tunes from another era, reliving the memories of some earlier time. *If only it was that easy*, she thought. *If only we could revert to the inno-cence of our past lives just by spending a couple of hours listening to music.* Whether it had ever worked for Wattis Wright, she couldn't have said. All she knew was, it would take more than a few old songs to bring back her own carefree days. A lot more.

10

Shadows of birds tracked across the pink gravel of the parking lot. Their calls told Traz they were Laughing Gulls even before he looked up. Dozens of them had been roosting on the waters of San Antonio Bay when he'd left for the Stock Pond the previous night, and now they were up, riding whatever thermals they could find, their incessant squeals filling the warm morning air. He was standing in the doorway of his motel room, sipping thoughtfully on a coffee as he admired his ride for the next few days. The tangerine bodywork of the 1971 Buick Riviera glittered under the tinfoil-bright sunshine of the Texas morning, the metal flake finish twinkling like a constellation of tiny stars. Traz wasn't somebody who sought attention as a rule, but he had little doubt that the elegant lines of this boat-tailed beauty would be turning heads wherever he went.

He leaned back on the door jamb and closed his eyes for a moment. The breeze carried the salt tang off the water to him, and played pan pipe music over the hole in the lid of his Styrofoam coffee cup.

"I thought you would be long gone by now."

Traz opened his eyes to see Verity Brown poking her head out of the doorway beside him. "That was the plan, but that low-down Lone Star beer had other ideas. How about you? Sleep well?"

"Well enough. Rapid recovery is a trademark of field researchers. If not, it would mean no drinking the night before early-morning fieldwork. And that would just be no fun at all." Verity's short hair was wet and spiky. However long she'd been awake, it was enough for her to have had a shower and get dressed in tight jeans and a loose cotton pale blue blouse. She looked out over the bay, holding up a hand to her brows as she squinted at the light spangling off the water. "Nice day for it."

Traz nodded. "Can't wait. As soon as I finish my coffee, I'll be on my way."

"You're not going to eat breakfast first?"

Traz held up his coffee cup and smiled.

"Caffeine and hydrogenated creamers are no way to start a day. Your blood sugar levels will be low after the beer last night. Your body needs proper nourishment. C'mon, I'll buy you a decent breakfast before you go. It's the least I can do for an old dancing partner. We can reminisce about all the great tunes we heard last night."

"Not if you want me to keep my appetite," said Traz.

"Maybe you could just quote me some more poetry, then. I've always had a soft spot for Whittier. Give me five minutes and I'll meet you by the car."

As he watched her disappear back into her motel room, it occurred to him that Verity might not have been as drunk last night as he'd thought. It occurred to him, too, that this meant all the compliments she'd paid him couldn't just be written off as the beer talking. Though, if that was the message she'd intended to convey, he couldn't have said.

They were sitting on the outside patio of a restaurant called Pop's that was perched on a wharf overlooking the bay. The waitress brought them their orders and told them if they needed anything else, all they had to do was holler. He enjoyed the easy courtesy of the south Texans, and the strain of gentle, self-deprecating humour that lay just beneath the surface. But if he was being honest, in Verity's presence he seemed to like pretty much everything down here.

"You going to eat that?" she asked.

Traz looked down at the bacon sandwich he was holding. "It crossed my mind," he said. "I hope you're not going to tell me bacon's not good for you. I'd remind you, I am Canadian."

"There can be a lot of antibiotics in bacon if it's not responsibly sourced. But if you are intending on eating it, at least give the white bread a miss. You may as well be eating furniture upholstery for all the nutritional value that stuff has. Plus, there's that whole gluten thing, not to mention this wheat belly, wheat brain business." She held up her hands. "Hey, just the messenger here. My parents are both nutritionists. I got a lot of home-schooling in this kind of stuff."

Traz's eye was caught by a couple of birds slowly circling the bay. Though they were deeply silhouetted against the cloudless sky, he finally decided he's seen enough to identify them as Gull-billed Terns. Eventually, one settled to roost at the end of a battered wooden fishing pier that stretched at least a hundred metres out into the bay. With its missing boards and twisted support struts, the structure looked barely capable of supporting a man's weight. At the pier's entrance stood the trunks of two palm trees, each snapped off at a height of about three metres. A "No Entry" sign that had also been severed from a post somewhere lay propped against the base of one of the trees.

"I guess Hurricane Harvey hit this area pretty hard," he said.

"'Bout pounded it back into the dark ages," Verity told him. "They'll rebuild, though." She pointed along the wharf, where skeletons of new timber framed a fishing hut and tackle shop. "Stubborn breed, the south Texans."

To Traz, it seemed not so much a question of whether the town would rebuild, but whether it should. Before the storm, Amblin had taken advantage of its proximity to the winter home of Whooping Cranes, offering a range of services for visitors to the reserve. There was a petrol station, a motel, and a couple of places to eat. From what Traz had seen of this part of the world so far, that made Amblin practically a metropolis. For all the devastation brought by the hurricane, the carnage had provided new opportunities for reconstruction and development. But the town also had the option now of allowing itself to dwindle back into the sleepy farming community it had once been. Backsliding would be the easier option. The wide flat fields of dark earth surrounding the Aransas Wildlife Refuge meant farming was always a viable alternative in these parts. It would take a significant act of will to re-establish the infrastructure needed to support any kind of tourism industry here again. When it came to hurricanes and South Texas, it wasn't a case of *if* but *when*. In Traz's view, daring Mother Nature to come by and wipe out all your hard work over and over again went some way beyond stubbornness. It required a resilience he wasn't sure he would have been able to find in himself.

Verity had turned her head away from Traz. "I was wondering," she said, staring out over the water, "whether that offer of yours was still good."

Traz set down his sandwich so hard the plate banged against the table, startling a pair of Laughing Gulls from their wharf-side perches.

"I'm on your bucket list now?"

"A drunk woman who doesn't even know your real name all but invites you into her room? With you already planning an early-morning getaway? If you chose to do the right thing in those circumstances, maybe you'd be okay to travel with, after all."

A breath of soft, warm air came to them across the bay. The piercing squeals of the disturbed gulls had subsided now, and all they could hear was the water gently lapping against the shoreline. Traz picked up his sandwich again to give himself a moment to process the wider implications of Verity's statement. "Well, I suppose it's nice to be trusted."

Verity shrugged. "Trust has got nothing to do with it. In case you haven't heard, all us southern girls sleep with a gun under our pillow. But at least if you're given to gentlemanly behaviour, I wouldn't have to shoot you."

Traz smiled, but he realized it was time to take things seriously. If Verity's proposal was genuine, he'd need to remind her of his plans. They weren't up for negotiation. "I'll be making a few stops," he said. "Overnighters. Four at least, maybe five. If there's time, I'd planned on visiting a couple of bird reserves along the way, too." He realized even as he spoke that something inside him was hoping these details wouldn't put her off. The prospect of travelling with Verity Brown for the next few days had suddenly become very appealing.

"I'd be okay with that," she said easily. "I've got the whole summer off. A couple of extra days to get where I'm going makes no difference. Can you tell me where your stops are, or is this gonna be some kind of a mystery tour?"

Traz shook his head. "I know it sounds a bit crazy, but I don't really know. A friend sent me a series of coordinates and asked me to check what's at each one. I'm hoping it makes a little more sense as I go, but at the moment, I've got no idea what'll be waiting for us when we get there."

"Nothing you're saying is making this any less appealing," said Verity. "Like I said, if that offer's still on the table, I'm in.

I'd just have to pack up at the motel and grab a few things from my research station at the reserve, and I'd be ready to go. In fact, if you'd care to give me a ride over to Aransas, I could make it worth your while."

"And just how might you do that?" asked Traz, standing up. He put an upturned saucer over the remains of his half-eaten sandwich, in case the marauding gulls scavenged it before the waitress returned.

Verity stood to join him. "By showing you a secret place or two," she said, "where you can see some pretty special birds close up."

11

From a live oak at the edge of the small gravel parking lot, a Northern Mockingbird trilled out its twice repeated phrases, running through its repertoire of the calls of the local species. Traz had offered no resistance when Verity had suggested taking the Jeep after she had emerged from her porta-cabin office at the reserve's visitor centre. It wasn't a decision he regretted. If he had been forced to subject the pristine Buick to these rugged dirt tracks, he was fairly sure his nerve would have failed him long before they reached this place.

He'd asked about the porta-cabins as they'd pulled away from the visitor centre and Verity had told him the researchers used to have work areas in the main building. Until Harvey. "It was eight days after the hurricane hit before anybody could get in here to assess the damage. The rain had pounded in through the soffits and the water inside the building was a foot deep by the time folks got here. South Texas heat and standing water isn't a great combination for buildings. They were never going to get the mould out of that visitor centre, so they decided to tear it down and rebuild. The crane researchers, and everybody else, too, are out in the porta-cabins until they finish."

They climbed out of the Jeep and strolled towards the edge of the lot, where it looked over a small marsh. "There wasn't a leaf left on the trees in this reserve by the time Harvey was done with us," said Verity. "The live oaks, the blackjacks, even the hackberries. All of them totally stripped. It was kind of amazing to watch how quickly the reserve greened up again, though. Nature's ability to regenerate itself is pretty amazing, huh?"

Traz looked around at the abundance of vegetation surrounding them in every direction. His gaze stopped at a ragged line of dried grasses and other natural detritus.

"Is that a —"

"Tide line? M'mm. The storm surge drove stuff a mile and a half inland. We were really concerned about the impact on the crane habitat. Places like the sandbanks at Heron Flats were just about wiped out. But by the time the cranes got back from Wood Buffalo, there were plenty of places for them to settle in. There's your Whoopers."

She pronounced it *whuppers*, like the locals did, but the announcement was so nonchalant it had Traz looking up in the live oak for a moment. Then he saw her pointing to a stand of tall grass at the edge of the marsh, and he noticed the two birds, resplendent in their stately white plumage and distinctive black masks, carefully picking their way through the water. He raised his bins and looked at them in wonder. Whooping Cranes; once one of the most endangered creatures on earth. Only fifteen migrating adults were known to survive when a recovery plan had been put in place in 1941 to pluck the species from the brink of extinction, and rebuild the population. And that had happened here, on this small stretch of nondescript shoreline around St. Charles Bay. He shook his head as he took in the breathtaking significance of the place he now stood.

Verity watched the birds intently. "Can you imagine what would have happened if they had allowed the last few Whooping Cranes to be taken into captivity?"

"They were seriously considering doing that?"

"They sure were. They could have even ended up in Cincinnati Zoo," she said. "It was a leading destination for rare species at that time." She shuddered. "The thought of them ending up there just about turns my blood cold."

Traz looked puzzled.

"The world's last Passenger Pigeon died there. Four years later, the world's last Carolina Parakeet did, too. In the same cage."

"What? You're not serious?"

Verity nodded. "How's that for luck? To think the last Whooper might have died in there, as well. Talk about an unwanted hat-trick."

"So, you don't think taking those Whoopers into captivity would have saved them?"

Verity shook her head. "I'm convinced preserving the migration mapping in the genes was what saved the species. If they'd have been taken into captivity, their ability to trace those routes to the summer breeding grounds would have been lost forever."

"You don't think it could have been re-established, once the numbers had recovered?" Traz spread his hands. "They've successfully led captive-bred birds on migrations in Wisconsin."

She nodded. "But they've never created a viable breeding population there. Too many wild characteristics have been lost. Species restoration is not like rebuilding that old car of yours. You can put all the shiny new parts in place you like — enhanced habitat, breeding resources, predator protection — but you can't restore natural instincts. Once they've been lost from the DNA, they take many generations to redevelop. Maybe some never do. That population of Whoopers out in Louisiana, for example, just seem content to stay put."

Traz looked back at the birds and Verity let him have his observation in silence. It was only the cranes' sudden burst of activity that broke the spell. The male reared up and extended its neck, flapping its wings and kicking out its legs before him. Traz watched every movement, drinking in the experience, storing up the images. For all the ease of finding these birds, he hadn't lost sight of what an incredible privilege it was to see them in their natural habitat, and even more so, to watch them displaying their most celebrated behaviour right in front of him.

"Somebody needs to warn him that dancing can lead to all sorts of unforeseen consequences," said Verity darkly. "Males can get pretty worked up. I watched one get so excited during a dance he lost his footing and took a face plant straight into the mud." She smiled at the memory. "And they say females have trouble corralling their hormones."

They watched as the male jumped again, its legs flailing in awkward spasmodic movements, like someone having their reflexes tested with a knee hammer. "It's not the most elegant thing you'll ever see, is it?" she asked. "Still, it works for them, I guess."

"But why here?" asked Traz. "Isn't dancing a courtship ritual? I thought they'd wait until they're on their breeding grounds up north."

"These stragglers will be on the move soon enough," said Verity. "There's a strong link between the hormones that drive the courtship display and the migration instinct. Brain activity in the areas that trigger migration increases significantly when the breeding hormones kick in. If you track the synaptic functions, your monitor lights up like a Christmas tree." She paused and looked at him. "Too much information?"

"No, not at all. It's fascinating."

The birds disappeared into the bank of tall grass and Verity turned to go. The heat was building and Traz could feel the sun on his shoulders through his shirt. Another couple of hours, and this open, exposed area wasn't a place he'd want to be. He said as much to Verity as they got back in the Jeep.

"Yeah, the cabins are kinda cramped when I've got my equipment set up, but at least the air conditioning works."

"Maybe they'll surprise you with a nice new lab in the visitor centre when they rebuild," said Traz brightly.

Verity shook her head doubtfully. "I'll be surprised if I even get my work station in the main building back, never mind a lab."

Traz looked across at her. "Really? You're studying one of the most iconic birds in North America. It sounds like pretty important work to me."

"Oh, it is, but my research doesn't get taken real seriously down here. Well, pretty much anywhere, come to that. I don't know what in the world difference it makes the way I say things, but it sure does seem to matter to some people. They hear this accent, they figure I should be in a kitchen somewhere, fixin' up biscuits and gravy."

"I can't believe that's true. You only have to talk to you for a couple of minutes to realize how much you know about your subject."

"A couple of minutes is more'n I usually get. All I know is every time I say 'evidently' instead of 'apparently,' the academic world's estimation of my IQ goes down about fifty points. Just like yours did last night."

Traz tried to laugh off the accusation, but he couldn't deny it. Nevertheless, he doubted things were as bad as Verity claimed. It was possible, likely even, that she'd encountered some prejudgment because of the way she spoke, but the wounded are rarely interested in giving a balanced view of their injuries.

Verity pulled off the road onto a narrow track so overgrown with vegetation Traz would have missed it completely if he had been alone. The Jeep rattled along the track for a hundred metres or so and emerged into a small clearing. A shallow pond of still water was fringed by the same tall grasses as at their previous stop, but here, a pair of large blackjack oaks leaned in from the water's edge, bathing half of the clearing in cooling shade. Verity drew the Jeep to a halt beneath the nearest tree and put an arm on Traz's as he moved to get out. "No need."

On the far side of the pond, a small dance of cranes stood still, their elegant stances reflected in the mirror-smooth surface of the water. It was a family group, two adults and their single off-spring, a colt with rusty colouring still trailing up its neck. Raised last year and ready now to begin the single-most important flight of its life, the one that would show whether the route it had taken on its southbound journey last autumn had imprinted itself deeply enough to allow the bird to return safely to the breeding grounds of Wood Buffalo National Park in Canada.

On some unseen cue, the birds all turned and lifted into the air, their wing beats as slow and effortless as an unfolding dream. In seconds, they had disappeared from view. Traz looked at the empty pond. Not a ripple disturbed its surface. It was as if the birds had never been there at all. *Vanished from the face of the earth*, he thought. *How close we had come.* The thought stayed with him for a long moment until Verity spoke.

"You all ready to head out?"

"I am, but I'll have to check with the rest of us."

The smile that met Traz's mischievous grin seemed just a touch colder and more forced than Verity's usual efforts. There were no-go areas for all of us, he thought, and he had just touched upon one of his travelling companion's. He was sure there were going to be plenty of topics they would have fun with during the next few days. Verity Brown's speech patterns wouldn't be among them.

The shrill ring of Traz's phone saved him from the uncomfortable silence that had settled between them. "JJ," he said delightedly as soon as he recognized the voice. "I'd heard you were back on this side of the pond. Is Lindy with you? ... Oh, I'm sorry to hear that. But hey, I'm sure you guys will work everything out eventually. So what's up?" he asked, ensuring his tone didn't reveal the true sadness he felt about the news of his friend's breakup with Lindy. "I'm in Aransas," he said in answer to Domenic's question. "I was just thinking about you, as a matter of fact. Know what I'm looking at right now? A Scissor-Tailed Flycatcher." He looked at Verity and pointed up to a dead snag on one of the oaks where a bird with an extravagantly long tail was perched. Even from below, the delicate salmon pink flushing on the bird's sides was clearly visible, contrasting with the soft grey plumage of its back. Verity didn't seem too enthralled by the sight and it occurred to him that she probably saw these birds all the time down here. "I seem to remember that's one you've dipped on a few times. Did you ever see one?"

He smiled at the answer he heard. "Really, wow. Pity you're not down here, then. They're all over the place. In fact, there's another one now. And another. Are you kidding me? Another one just dropped in, right in front of me. Man. It's just raining Scissor-Tailed Flycatchers down here."

Verity hadn't seen any other birds come in, but when she looked at Traz, he gave her a big wink. "You should see the travelling companion I've picked up, too, JJ," he said. "Gorgeous body, and looks to die for." Verity raised her eyebrows in surprise and he offered her a smile. "A 455 V8 under the hood, with a Rochester Quadrajet four-barrel carb and Positive Traction differential. A Buick Riviera GS boat-tail. She's a dream. I'm also with a pretty special woman who's going to be road-tripping with me for the next few days. Her name's Verity. Want to say hi?"

He handed his phone over.

"So you've actually met him and you're still prepared to travel with him?" said Jejeune.

Verity laughed. "Yeah, he seems harmless enough. We've only just met, but we found out we were heading the same way, so everything just kinda worked out. It's cool when stuff like that happens, huh?"

There was a beat of silence. "It is," agreed Jejeune.

Traz came back on the phone. "You'd love her, JJ. She studies Whooping Cranes. Her field is brain activity."

"What's she doing with you, trying to establish a baseline?"

"Ah, comedy gold. I'm so glad you decided to carry on when Curly and Moe called it a day. From here we're heading to Oklahoma. Know what the state bird is? Why, that would be the Scissor-Tailed Flycatcher. I hear the place is just lousy with them. They're a garbage bird up there."

A dirt bird, Jejeune's British birding acquaintances would have said. He knew Traz's use of the derogatory term for over-common species was just to needle him. In truth, his friend despised the phrase as much as he did.

"Is it Verity's work that's taking you up there?"

"No, she's heading up with me to her home in Scenic, South Dakota." There was a long silence on Traz's end of the line. "Hold on," he said eventually. He held up a finger to Verity and climbed out of the Jeep, retreating to a safe distance along the dirt track before speaking again. "JJ, I'm in Aransas because Damian asked me to come here."

"Is that what his text to you last week was about?" Jejeune didn't say it was Damian's last text.

"You don't know about any of this, do you? Damian sent me a list of coordinates and asked me to check out the sites. They run in a straight line north from Aransas to North Dakota and then veer off to the northwest."

"Whooping Crane stopover points?"

"Couldn't be anything else. I was at a loose end, so I said sure."

"Did he say why he wanted you to check those sites out?"

"No, but I'd really like to know, if you're planning on asking him."

Traz knew when Domenic spoke that he had not imagined the uncomfortable pause.

"I would if I could reach him, Traz. His tracker is off. He's somewhere in Wood Buffalo Park, but there's no way of getting in touch with him."

Verity and the Jeep were still a long way down the track, but Traz lowered his voice and hunched over the phone slightly anyway. "Damian didn't want me talking to anybody about what I was doing, JJ," he said guardedly. "Anything I found out was to go straight back to him. I don't know what your brother's mixed up in, but you know Damian, it's probably nothing good." Traz gave a momentary pause of his own. "If Damian is out there in the middle of Wood Buffalo and he's gone dark, that could mean he's in a lot of trouble, JJ."

"Yes," said Domenic quietly. "That's what I was thinking, too."

12

The room seemed different. Everything in it was familiar, but DCI Jejeune had left a large gap when he returned to Canada. Salter was surprised at the impact the absence of such an unassuming personality could make. But other things had changed within the room, too. There was a new dynamic to the association between the two occupants. It filled the space between them like an awkward piece of furniture, and it wasn't something Salter intended tiptoeing around for very long.

"Sarge, we're okay, you and me?"

To Maik, the question came from nowhere. He looked at Salter for a moment before answering. "We are," he said earnestly.

"I mean, this new situation, this new *relationship* between us, I suppose you'd call it," she said with a half-hearted laugh.

"You've worked hard to get your promotion, Sergeant," said Maik. "It's well deserved."

If it wasn't exactly what Salter had been asking, she'd accept the response for now. Maik had his music on, as usual. From his laptop, the Temptations' "The Way You Do the Things You Do" provided a backdrop to the silence between them. Tony Holland had complained about Maik being mired in songs of melancholy and loss recently, but this one was lively enough.

Come to think of it, the other songs Maik had been playing since she'd returned to active duty had been noticeably upbeat, too. She began to walk towards his desk and Maik looked up. In the past, she had often come over for a chat, but this time her approach seemed just a touch more hesitant. "Would you mind if we listened to something else today?"

Maik muted his laptop and looked at her over the top of it. "Did you have anything particular in mind?"

She held up a flash drive. "The Shammalars. Wattis Wright wrote their songs. I'm not really expecting to get any clues from them, but I thought I should probably give them a listen anyway. You know, just to be thorough. Only, I wouldn't dare listen to this stuff at home. Max already thinks that I spent my teenage years eating dinosaur meat. If he thought I was listening to this kind of music, it would only confirm to him that I'm older than dirt."

"The Shammalars it is," said Maik gallantly. He inserted the drive and opened the file. The sound of swirling strings and punchy brass arrangements began to drift from the speakers. Maik gave the music the courtesy of a short listen before deciding it was time to move on to other topics. "How are your inquiries progressing?" he asked.

She shrugged. "Somebody named Albert Ross is looming large. And I mean that literally. Apparently, he's a mountain of a man. He's an acquaintance of Wright's. Of a sort anyway. I'm not sure what the connection is yet, but he's one of the very few people who made it into the victim's address book. He was heard by a neighbour in a nasty shouting match with Wright the afternoon before his death. Apparently, Ross was standing on his doorstep, literally screaming at him about something."

Maik looked interested.

"It's not as promising as it sounds," said Salter. "Ross has got a file as long as your arm for public order disturbances, breaches of the peace. He's clearly got impulse control issues, anger management, all that. There have been several spells in facilities for treatment, but …"

Maik inclined his head. "But none of the previous targets of his anger have ended up dead."

Salter nodded. "Still, I suppose it wouldn't hurt to have a chat with him. I mean, just because there's been no serious afters with anybody else, he does seem to have had run-ins with most of the inhabitants of Saltmarsh at one time or another — over the most ridiculous stuff sometimes. He even assaulted a fortune teller at the Saltmarsh Fete one year, for God's sake."

"Was the fortune teller laughing at him?"

Salter looked puzzled. "I've no idea. Why?"

"I thought it might just be a case of him wanting to strike a happy medium."

Salter laughed out loud. "You're wasted here, Danny, truly." She became suddenly serious. "But really, have you never considered taking the next step up the ladder yourself?"

"I've been out of school a long time," said Maik frankly. "The studying might be a bit of a stretch, if I'm being honest. I get the feeling I'd have to dedicate so much time to it that the promotion would end up taking priority over the work. I suppose I just could never really convince myself that it was worth that. Besides, there's plenty enough you can achieve working away in the background. Look at Herb Dixon."

"Who?"

"My point exactly."

A joke from Danny Maik was a rare enough commodity. A wink was a genuine collector's item. But the two in combination? The effect left Salter wondering who this imposter was, and what he might have done with the Danny Maik she knew. She looked over to the vacant desk of Tony Holland, another absentee who had often filled the room with his personality, albeit in a completely different way to DCI Jejeune. "I wonder what Tony and the Met are making of each other. He said he's enjoying himself, but you know Tony, that doesn't necessarily mean the work."

"You've spoken to him, then."

"He called to congratulate me. He said somebody had tipped him off that I was back." She paused to see if her suspicion was correct, and despite Maik's impassive expression, she decided it probably was. "I have to say, he was amazingly supportive. And sincere. I'd expected a bit of banter, but he was very complimentary." She paused and looked at the empty desk again. "Full of surprises, our Tony."

"Well, you were missed."

Was I, Danny? By any one individual in particular, or just by the universe in general? Why was it so difficult to talk about something that had never happened between them? Was it because the faintest glimmer of hope remained deep down inside her somewhere that the possibility was still there? She'd have given the idea short shrift if Tony Holland, or anyone else, had suggested it, but she had to at least be honest with herself.

"They know their harmonies, this lot, I'll give them that." Danny's comment brought her back to the present. His expression suggested he wasn't as impressed with the song itself. To be honest, Salter wasn't overly taken with the doo-wop sound, either. In her opinion, if the best you could come up with for lyrics was *bip bippity doop*, you were probably better off leaving the song as an instrumental in the first place. But the melody was pleasant enough. And like Danny said, the Shammalars could certainly sing. To her, the silky-smooth harmonies were every bit the equal of those Motown artists Danny liked: The Temptations he'd just been listening to, the Miracles, the Four Tops. She wouldn't say that out loud, though. Danny had obviously gone out of his way to try to find something positive to say about the Shammalars. There was no point in pushing her luck.

She moved her shoulders and rolled her head gently to the beat of the music. "Isn't it amazing how something from so long ago could suddenly gain this sort of popularity again, all because of the internet? It started as a meme, you see." Salter paused for a moment, toying with the idea of asking Maik if he needed a translation, but thought better of it. It was one thing for Maik to have a curmudgeonly contempt for today's frivolous trends; having to confess to missing them entirely as they hurtled on by was another matter altogether. "Somebody used one of the Shammalars' songs as a soundtrack to a video," she continued. "Two teenage lovers who can't find the right words, so they speak in all this *shalalala doop doop* nonsense instead. It was really quite sweet." Maik's expression suggested he wasn't entirely being won over by her description, and Salter hurried on. "Anyway, it caught on, and all of a sudden the internet's on fire with Shammalarmania. These things generally peter out pretty quickly, but with the nostalgia train everybody seems to be riding these days, this one's showing no signs of going anywhere. Susan Bonaccord's company is responsible for securing the rights for a musical, all based around songs by the Shammalars."

"So, this is what that big cheque on his desk was for, the rights to these songs?" asked Danny. Not even a note of disbelief in his voice, she noted. He really was on his best behaviour today.

"Not exactly. The publishing rights to all the songs had long since been signed away. What Susan Bonaccord was purchasing from Wright were the dance moves. He had never sold those rights to anybody, so he still retained ownership of them."

"You can't copyright dance moves, surely?" said Maik in surprise. "Cholly Atkins would have spent his life in court, the number of times his routines have been copied. He was the one who choreographed all those moves for the Motown artists in the sixties," he explained.

"Actually, you can copyright dance moves," said Salter, "if you have visual evidence that the choreography was designed as a specific performance piece to accompany a song."

"So Wright had some film of his routines?"

"He'd managed to hang on to some grainy old sixties film of the Shammalars in rehearsal, with him and his assistant working out the choreography with them."

"Was Albert Ross a fan of this stuff?" Despite his best efforts, it was clear that Danny's tolerance for eight-bar breaks consisting entirely of *shamalalalalas* was reaching its limit. He looked ready to make a case for justifiable homicide if Ross had been subjected to very much of this kind of music.

Salter gave a small smile. "Motive's the thing I'm struggling with at the moment. It wasn't a targeted robbery. If you knew Wright at all, you'd know there were no fancy portable electronics lying around. There was no flat-screen TV, his only phone was fixed to a wall, and you'd need a crane and a flatbed truck to get that bulky office equipment of his away, the photocopier and computer system and such. The only thing that seems to fit at the moment is something personal. But Wright had no family, no business associates. So again, it's hard to see why anybody would want to kill a man who just wanted to sit at home listening to his old songs."

"In a case like this, I might be inclined to look at the *who* first, and worry about the *why* after," said Maik casually.

It would have been immediately obvious to the killer that the first attack had done the job. From a knife wound that had penetrated the heart, there would have been a *lot* of blood.

But there had been that second thrust, made with extreme force, long after the first one, long after the victim would have appeared dead. It spoke to rage, and it spoke to an extremely powerful individual. A big man with impulse control issues. Shepherd may have assigned the lead investigation to Salter, but she knew that hadn't stopped Danny Maik from mulling it over in his mind.

He stopped the Shammalars mid-song and removed the drive, holding it out to her. "Heard enough? If you need a lift when you go to see this Albert Ross," he said, "let me know."

13

The Demesne at Saltmarsh had created its share of controversy during the planning and construction phases, and though the active opposition had subsided now that it was a *fait accompli*, there was still a marked difference of opinion among the locals as to its merits. To the local Chamber of Commerce, the resort's state-of-the-art facilities were a sign of Saltmarsh's willingness to embrace the future. For many of the residents, however, a thirty-thousand-square-foot complex of high-tech innovation and design had no place in a quiet country town. Not even if it was set in a refurbished eighteenth-century manor house on its own twenty-acre estate and with an enviable stretch of riverfront access.

Salter hadn't really settled on a side during the contentious early times, and she remained ambivalent now. But as she pulled up in the sweeping gravel forecourt, she had to admit the developers had done an admirable job of restoring the shell of the old building. The whitewash gleamed beneath the heavy black timbers criss-crossing the facade, and the thatched roof was in better repair than any she'd seen in the area for a very long time. She remembered passing the house on her walks along the riverbank with Max when he was a baby. Even then, long into neglect, the building had impressed her with its grandeur. A remnant of another age, it had survived the centuries virtually intact, awaiting its rescue with dignity and patience. When salvation had finally arrived, in the form of an investment group with a plan to house one of the country's most technologically-advanced hotels behind an exterior restored to all its former glory, perhaps it was, for once, the best of both worlds.

Even a brand-spanking new Detective Sergeant's warrant card wasn't enough to get Salter past reception, and she waited patiently while the clinically efficient Front Desk Associate dialed Susan Bonaccord's room. In stark contrast to the rustic exterior, there was an uncompromising utilitarianism to the ultra-chic lobby. Clean edges and sharp lines gave the space a bracing clarity and definition. All in all, thought Salter, it was a good place to begin a search for the truth.

Once admitted, she walked along a corridor so plushly carpeted it seemed to suck in the surrounding sounds, leaving only a strange, unsettling silence echoing between the unadorned walls. She knocked on the door and heard Bonaccord issue a muffled command. The door lock clicked and Salter tried the handle and entered.

Susan Bonaccord was seated at a work desk on the far side of the room beside an open computer. She flashed a brief smile of greeting at the detective. "Sergeant Salter. Would you like coffee?"

Salter could see the coffee maker near the bathroom, but Bonaccord was making no move to get up. "If it's not too much trouble. Two creams, please."

"Benson," said Bonaccord to the empty room. "Coffee, medium strength, two creams."

The coffee maker hissed into action and Salter watched as the machine produced a perfectly-brewed cup. With two creams.

"Impressive," she said, walking over to collect the cup.

"Not really. Voice-activated technology has been with us for a while, though admittedly not as much in the hospitality sector. Digital-age amenities are one of the Demesne's major draws." Bonaccord closed her notebook and swivelled in her chair to face Salter, indicating that the detective should take a seat in an armchair in the corner of the room.

Salter obliged, regarding the woman closely. Even though she had never met Susan Bonaccord, she would assume the woman might be in her element in this hotel room. Her crisply efficient demeanour, her fit-for-purpose business suit, even her neat, no-nonsense hairstyle, all suggested a person who might prefer not to have to clutter up her day engaging hotel staff in small talk.

Salter looked around, taking in the pristine layout of the upscale hotel room. Every surface was shiny and uncluttered, every crease crisp and neat. Who lived like this in the real world? With Max and his friends constantly in and out, Salter's own place generally looked like a film set from *The Jungle Book*. She couldn't remember a time when her home had ever been this tidy, or this clean. Of course, this was taking things a touch far, but a bit of neatness around her house would be nice, she thought wistfully, not least for the sheer novelty of it.

"You chose to stay in the same room," said Salter, leaning forward in the armchair to sip her coffee. "I thought you might prefer to move. I imagine it must be difficult, looking around and remembering what happened on that call you took in here."

Bonaccord nodded briskly. "Oh, yes, it is, of course. But this room is convenient for me. I have everything I need here, and the fitness centre is right next door."

Salter wondered how long she worked out each day. It would be a precise amount of time, with each exercise scheduled and its output monitored. Whatever her exercise regimen was, it would be a far cry from Salter's own shambolic daily efforts, grabbing a few minutes for a jog wherever she could. Regardless of its encouraging results, or perhaps even because of them, she felt a momentary pang of envy for Bonaccord's ability to plan her day so rigorously.

"I'm trying to press on, put it behind me," continued Bonaccord. "I think that's the best way, don't you? Besides, moving to another room would cause me further inconvenience I don't need at the moment."

Further? Was this her subtle way of sending a message about the sergeant's intrusion into her day? Nevertheless, she admired the woman's determination to avoid being held hostage by her circumstances, and focus instead on the parts of her life she could control, like her work. Salter rocked forward slightly in the chair once more, still unable to find a comfortable position. If Bonaccord had been sending a message, she would no doubt appreciate the sergeant getting down to business. "I'm trying to put together a picture of Mr. Wright's lifestyle," said Salter. "Frankly, his world seems a bit on the small side, and since you played such a big part in it recently ..."

"Did I? How sad."

"Sad?"

"Well, I mean, I had so little to do with the man, really. I typically have a number of projects on the go at any given time. It's hard to think of any one of them playing a major role in someone's life."

To sip her coffee, Salter had to hunch forward in the armchair again. It was an awkward, inelegant posture. She began to understand why Danny Maik usually conducted his interviews from a standing position. "Had you ever met Mr. Wright prior to this transaction?"

"No, and the truth is there was really no reason for us to have met in person this time. It's not unusual these days for me to conclude a business deal, even a fairly significant one, without ever having laid eyes on the other party. But Mr. Wright insisted on coming down to the offices so we could meet face to face. They're like that, aren't they, these older men who've lived alone for a long time. They pour their attention into the small details: promptness, courtesy, formality."

They weren't small details as far as Salter was concerned, but Susan Bonaccord wasn't wrong. Salter could think of at least one other man who lived alone who would have checked all those boxes.

"Still, nice, in a way, isn't it?"

"Yes, I suppose it is," said Bonaccord, as if considering the idea for the first time.

Salter gave up her see-sawing in the armchair and lifted herself to her feet, still holding the coffee cup. She felt faintly pleased with herself. She hadn't been working on her abs particularly, but she wouldn't have been able to manage a manoeuvre like that before she'd begun her exercise routine. "There were no problems with the deal, you said. No points of contention?"

Bonaccord shook her head sharply. "None whatsoever. I did get the sense that in parting with these performance rights he was letting go of something that had once meant a great deal to him, but once he had decided to do so, there was never any hesitation."

"I assume you had been talking to Mr. Wright quite a bit lately. If he had other worries, someone in prolonged negotiations with him might notice. Was there anything you were aware of?"

Bonaccord had taken a moment to check her phone and laptop screen. If there was anything of note on either, it wasn't urgent enough to distract her from the sergeant's question. "Nothing at all. He seemed concerned about how the production company intended to use the dance numbers we were acquiring. That was the purpose of our phone call, actually — to reassure him the integrity of the original Shammalars numbers would be preserved in their entirety."

Salter saw the hotel phone on the nightstand, and it reminded her of a detail in the incident report from the earlier night. It was a small one, insignificant, but it would nevertheless send a signal to the other woman that Salter, too, was thorough and professional.

"The duty manager said he noticed the phone had been moved to the far side of the bed. Was there any particular reason you'd done that?"

Bonaccord nodded easily. "Mr. Wright liked to talk," she told Salter. "And in fairness, we did have a number of items to discuss. I suspected the call might be a long one. I thought I might as well make myself comfortable on the bed."

"You were expecting his call then?" The way she seemed to be peppering Bonaccord with questions smacked to her more of an interrogation than a conversation with a witness, but she suspected that, rather than finding it unsettling, such a ruthlessly efficient approach would be standard fare for someone like this.

"He'd called previously, a couple of times, but I was busy on other calls. I told the Front Desk Associate to tell him the next time he called I would be available at eight thirty."

"That's when he called?"

"On the dot." She raised her eyebrows at the sergeant.

Old school values, thought Salter. Again, just like Danny, another man whose manners seemed to hearken back to a different era, now lost in the mists of time.

"I'm curious as to why you wouldn't use an electronic funds transfer instead of issuing him a certified cheque. Surely it would have been more secure. After all, your agreement did involve a significant amount of money."

"Did it?" Bonnacord nodded thoughtfully. "Yes, I suppose it would have been, to someone in his circumstances."

Circumstances where five-figure amounts didn't slide across balance sheets like pieces on a chess board, thought the sergeant, as they apparently did in Bonaccord's world.

"He'd specifically requested payment by cheque. I'm not sure Mr. Wright would have been comfortable with something as radical as an EFT." Bonaccord gave her approximation of a smile. It wasn't one that had seen a lot of practice.

"I suppose we should be grateful he didn't ask for it in cash," said Salter. "There's no sign the attacker went any farther into the house, but he might well have done if there'd been a pile of money on the table. Are you all right?"

A strange look had flickered across Bonaccord's features and Salter let her question hang in silence until the other woman eventually broke it with a nervous laugh. "It's silly, really. It's been bothering me that the killer might have been there, listening, while I was on the other end of that call. I just kept talking, you see, saying things, even though it was obvious by then that something terrible had happened. I just felt, you know, as if I had to. It seems a bit ridiculous in retrospect."

"No, I understand," said Salter. She had once knelt beside a stabbing victim, whispering words of comfort as she watched the life slowly ebbing from the man's body. She'd held on to his hand long after it was clear he was dead. It seemed to her that it was only when she released it that he would truly be gone.

"The thought that the killer might actually have heard my voice on the other end of the phone," said Bonaccord, "even as he was stabbing that poor man to death. It felt like there was a connection between us, between me and this person … this monster. I've been thinking about it since it happened. But now you're saying the killer would never have heard any of it? That he never entered the house at all?"

Salter hadn't said that, exactly, but Bonaccord's assumption had clearly brought the woman such relief the sergeant made no move to correct her. "The events of that evening are going to stay with you for a while yet, unfortunately, but at least that's one part of it you can stop worrying about."

Bonaccord nodded her head, but not a tightly-coiffed lock moved out of place. Salter wondered what it must be like to live in a world where not even your hair was allowed any freedom. This control went some way beyond a desire for efficiency, she realized. Susan Bonaccord was someone who needed to manage every aspect of her life, to determine every outcome. The world could be a hard place for people like that. It had its own views of how matters were going to proceed, and if they didn't match your own, there was only going to be one winner. The incident the other night was a perfect example. Bonaccord's perfectly laid plans for the next few days had been disrupted by life's sudden spin in another direction.

Her points covered, Salter wrapped up the interview and bade the woman goodbye. On her way out, she looked around the well-appointed hotel room again. As she progressed up the career ladder, perhaps she'd experience some of this world herself. There would be conferences, seminars, meetings, that would necessitate stays in hotel rooms like this one. She wondered if Bonaccord ever got tired of the life and yearned for a night in her own home. All Salter knew was, it would take some time before the appeal ever wore off for her.

As she reached the door, she considered briefly whether she would be able to open it for herself, or whether she would have to ask Benson to unlock it for her first. She stopped suddenly and turned.

"Did you like him?"

From her seat at the desk, Bonaccord shrugged. "In his dealings, Wattis Wright was just as you'd wish the other party to be: organized, efficient, and reliable. But he was simply a person who owned something we needed to purchase. Liking him didn't really come into it." She paused, as if she was looking for something else to offer. "There wouldn't have been a lot of common ground between us on a personal level, I'm afraid."

In the forecourt, Salter paused beside her car and looked along the river toward the village. Behind her, the Demesne at Saltmarsh hummed on in its effortlessly digital way. It was a dispassionate world of order and precision, of relentless efficiency and uncompromising functionality. It crossed Salter's mind that on the far side of the forest, less than a mile along the riverbank from here, a man had died in a house that seemed by comparison to be almost from the Stone Age. She could see what Bonaccord meant when she said there would not be a lot of common ground between them. Besides, this was a woman who seemed to have poured her life into her career, invested all she had in herself. There wasn't much space in a world like that for other people.

14

Domenic Jejeune lingered over coffee in the spartan breakfast room of the Borealis Motel, watching the building across the road intently. As soon as the doors to the Wood Buffalo National Park Visitor Centre were opened, he drained his cup, dropped some change onto the Formica table and stood up. The morning air was crisp and cool as he crossed the road. Despite North America's steady pirouette towards spring, the cold wasn't ready to give up its grip on the Northwest Territories just yet. He had seen large ice floes on Great Slave Lake as he had flown in to Fort Smith from Yellowknife the day before, and while the afternoon sunshine had been pleasant, he had already concluded the clothes in his hastily packed overnight bag were only going to be warm enough for evenings outside up here if he wore them in layers.

The cold air helped to freshen his senses. It had been a long flight from Toronto, gaining daylight hours all the way. The park offices had still been open when he checked in to the motel the previous afternoon, but he had chosen to wait. He needed to study the records Roy had sent him, to match them up to the information he'd received from Traz. And he wanted to test his theory, too, that bored hotel clerks everywhere shared the same penchant for gossip, if only they could find a willing ear. So, he'd checked in, ordered room service, and read. Only he had stayed awake longer than he'd intended, reading by the light from the window, deceived, like so many visitors to this land of extended daylight into believing it was far earlier than it really was.

He looked around the reception while the visitor services coordinator wandered off to find out if the park superintendent was available. Such waits were another part of his new life that he was still coming to terms with. When people were told a Detective Chief Inspector was waiting to see them, other priorities were generally put on hold. Without official rank, or even the urgency of a crime to investigate, private citizen Domenic Jejeune seemed to command no such consideration. Though the visitor centre had only been open a few minutes, there was already a sense of industry about the large open-plan office. Beige-shirted officers moved briskly about the building, and the space pulsed with quiet activity. He made his way into the diorama exhibit and stood for a moment in front of a glass case displaying a wolverine posed in an aggressive attack posture.

"Wouldn't like to meet him on a dark night, would you?" The coordinator had materialized behind Jejeune and startled him slightly. "There are reports of them taking down moose. That's like your house cat bringing down a full-sized deer. And the wolverine is only one of the predators you'd have to worry about on your dark nights in Wood Buffalo. Bears, lynx, wolves. Even the bison can pose a threat."

Jejeune offered the young woman a smile of sorts. He'd not yet explicitly stated that his visit was to express his concern about two people he believed to be lost in the park. He suspected the coordinator may have been keen to point out some of Wood Buffalo's more benign features if he had.

"Superintendent Bracker can see you now. If you follow me, I'll take you to her office." The woman led the way through a warren of desks and room dividers to a corner room at the back of the building. Large windows looked out onto a dense stand of white spruce from which Dark-Eyed Juncos made forays to a well-stocked feeder outside the window.

Carol Bracker noticed the close scrutiny with which Jejeune examined the hanging wire basket. "If you're interested, there's a Hoary Redpoll that's been visiting lately. Oh, can you believe it? How often does a bird drop in right on cue like that, just as you're speaking about it?"

"Not as often as birders would like," conceded Jejeune. He watched the redpoll as it worked intently to pry a seed from the wire feeder. In this flat northern light, the bird looked like an exquisite Fabergé confection, the delicate pink blush of its forehead and chest feathers almost like an embellishment, applied as an afterthought onto its frosted white plumage. Jejeune marvelled at the bird's fragile beauty, barely an arm's length away beyond the glass, unaware, or unconcerned, that two humans were staring at it with rapt attention.

When the redpoll departed, Jejeune turned his gaze to Ms. Bracker, thanking her for finding the time to see him and taking the seat she offered on the other side of her desk. In her forest green sweater and pants, she barely looked old enough for the role of superintendent of the largest national park on the continent. But then, Jejeune had often been subjected to the same prejudices about his own appearance. He couldn't speak to Bracker's administrative abilities, but she had the lithe, lean frame and healthy tan of someone who'd spent a good deal of time outside in these parts. A former field operative, he would have guessed, rather than an administrator promoted up through the ranks. She would know the park well — both its attractions and its dangers.

Bracker opened a laptop and took notes as Jejeune spoke. "Okay, so your brother is currently doing research work in the park," she summarized, "and you haven't been able to contact him."

Jejeune nodded impatiently. He understood the need for the formalities, but he was anxious to get on to the real reason for his visit, to request that a search be launched immediately.

"I see your brother wasn't issued a research permit himself, though. He entered under the one issued to Annie Prior."

Jejeune's eyes widened in surprise. "He was working for her?"

Bracker nodded. "Essentially, we would have seen the relationship as employer and employee, yes. Prior was issued an umbrella permit. It would allow her to bring in anyone she feels has the requisite skills to assist her with her research. Your brother wouldn't be permitted to operate independently in the park. Any work he would have undertaken would have fallen under the aegis of Prior's own research. Your expression suggests you weren't aware of any of this? Perhaps your brother may have told you otherwise?"

"No, not at all, I've not spoken to him directly about the purpose of his trip. But I did know he was with someone. And now, both of their inReach devices have stopped transmitting."

Carol Bracker took a moment to study the bird feeder outside. The redpoll had not returned, but a male Pine Grosbeak, resplendent in its spring breeding plumage, now sat proudly atop the feeder, defying all rivals to enter his domain.

"We weren't aware either of the devices was malfunctioning, since no one had been tasked with tracking them. It was only when your brother-in-law requested Damian's contact information that we discovered his device was not working."

"Not receiving?"

"Nor transmitting either. Unlike some tracking devices, the inReach is capable of both functions, but your brother's had ceased all data transmission in either direction. We tried to get a message to him via Prior's device, and that's when we discovered that hers wasn't working either."

"And that didn't raise any red flags for you?"

Bracker moved her shoulders easily. "An inReach device uses internal lithium batteries, Mr. Jejeune. If they weren't fully charged before they went into the park, if the USB port got wet and became corroded, if the charging cord was lost or broken ..." She opened her hands. "Any number of explanations suggest themselves."

Jejeune looked at the map of the park on the wall behind Bracker's desk. Forty-eight thousand square kilometres of wilderness, an area the size of Switzerland, filled with predatory carnivores, fast-flowing water, and mile after mile of empty, open space. "I think they may be in trouble, Superintendent Bracker," he said quietly. "I think we should begin a search."

Bracker eased herself back from her desk. It was clear she had a strategy for dealing with requests like this one. She was summoning her standard set of responses now, marshalling them into a reasoned, ordered denial. "They both have a great deal of experience in backwoods camping, Mr. Jejeune." She consulted a paper on her desk. "According to his form, your brother even has survival skills training."

"May I?"

She seemed to hesitate, but Jejeune left his hand extended. If Damian had omitted anything noteworthy from his Extended Stay permit application, or even deliberately lied about something, it may be important. Seeing that Jejeune would not relent, Bracker handed over the form. It was a comprehensive questionnaire, but even with a brief scan, Jejeune could see his brother had not misrepresented himself or his background in any significant way.

She leaned forward intently. "Mr. Jejeune, I'm not making light of your concerns, but I must tell you, Ms. Prior and your brother wouldn't be the first people to deliberately disable their devices out there. There is a psychological element to severing all connections with the outside world, even for a short time. There is an exhilaration, an excitement in knowing that you are now truly alone in the wilderness, surrounded only by natural things, with no hint of our hurried, human world, and no way for it to intrude upon your experience. It's the kind of feeling many people come to Wood Buffalo in search of, and to fully experience it, a number of them have taken the step of disconnecting themselves, literally, from the outside world."

Her eyes shone as she spoke, and Jejeune recognized the field officer starting to rise within her. Being shackled to a desk by administrative duties would chafe with Carol Bracker. She would probably seize any opportunity to be back out there, doing what she really loved, what she had signed up for. Would the draw of the wilderness be enough for her to accompany a visiting off-duty policeman on a trip into the park to search for his lost brother, Jejeune wondered.

"I understand that Annie Prior spoke to someone named Gaetan Robideau before she left. He advised her not to go into the park. Do you know why that might be?"

Although they were a long way back in the office, Bracker's eyes darted in the direction of the motel. Jejeune clearly wasn't the only one who knew about bored hotel receptionists.

"I've no idea, but he went into the park himself recently to perform a ritual. He's still in there now, I believe." She paused. "We strive to stay on good terms with the local First Nations people, and for the most part we maintain an excellent working relationship with them. But there are always outliers, individuals like Gaetan Robideau looking to make mischief." She tried hard, but she was unable to keep a small glimmer of distaste from creeping into her expression. "There's usually some element of personal gain in it."

"Did my brother go with her to see Robideau? Did he receive the same warning?"

"I have no idea, but as I say, Ms. Prior was the research team leader. I can't see any reason your brother would have met with Robideau."

"I think you need to put a search party together to go in there and look for them, Ms. Bracker." It wasn't a plea, it was a statement. But it wasn't dispassionate either.

Carol Bracker closed her laptop and leaned across the desk. "A missing person search in Wood Buffalo is no small undertaking, Mr. Jejeune. There needs to be cross-jurisdictional coordination between provincial and territorial RCMP. Dogs need to be brought in, divers prepped and equipped. Someone needs to organize volunteers. The cost for helicopters and plane flights alone can run into the thousands. We don't take requests such as yours lightly, but we don't respond reflexively either. Your brother and Dr. Prior are not overdue. They are not scheduled to return for another week. They have not missed a single scheduled call-in. Correct me if I'm wrong, but as I see it, all we have to suggest anything may be wrong is your instinct. I see your brother mentions on his form that he has previous experience working with Whooping Cranes."

"A long time ago, yes."

"The birds are just now beginning to establish their territories. The low-level flight of a search plane over the nesting areas could be incredibly disruptive to the process." She paused and gave a slight sigh. "My point is, would it be your brother's wish to compromise an entire breeding cycle of one of North America's most protected species, one he has actually worked with himself, because of a piece of malfunctioning equipment?"

"Two pieces."

The superintendent acknowledged the point with a nod. "Unusual, I'll admit, but on its, own, not enough, I'm afraid.

To get to these people's last known location, it would be necessary to fly directly past the breeding grounds."

Jejeune was puzzled. "Past them? Surely, the crane breeding grounds are exactly where they would be?"

Carol Bracker shrugged lightly. "I don't see why. Though she didn't specify any particular location for her studies, Annie Prior's permit wasn't for crane research, Mr. Jejeune. It was for anthropological exploration."

15

"I don't think anything restores a person's love for their country like its wild places," said Verity, leaning back against the Buick's tangerine bodywork and looking around. All around them, dry rangeland rolled away to the horizon on a series of low, undulating hills. The midday heat had brought a strange eerie stillness. A long-abandoned windmill stood motionless in a field of unmoving grass. Black Vultures rested on the bare branches of cottonwood trees, waiting for the sun to bring them a death. And over it all, the heat haze hovered, faint and intangible but colouring all it touched.

"To see all this open land, and to know your country had enough sense, and enough foresight, to protect it. How could you not feel good about that? Same in Canada, I guess. I hear you've got some pretty spectacular national parks up there."

Beside her, Traz nodded. "Provincial parks, too. Don't think any of them look quite like this, though." They had stopped to stretch their legs before continuing on their way to Salt Plains National Wildlife Reserve. Traz had driven them to Enid that morning to check out another set of coordinates, only to find they lay somewhere beyond a heavily secured wire fence. A military compound, he would have guessed, or an industrial research facility. They had tracked their way along the boundary roads of the fenced-off area, but it was secured on all sides, and the coordinates definitely lay inside, so Traz had abandoned his mission and decided the extra time they now had could be better spent elsewhere, watching birds.

Verity looked across at the sound of a spoon scraping plastic. "What's that?"

Traz held up a carton. "Yogurt. See, eating healthy. I took your advice."

"Dairy is healthy? Since when?"

"I'm aiming for a balanced diet. The bacon had antibiotics, this has probiotics. As far as I can tell, that should make me biotic-neutral at the very least."

"Mock all you want. I can't say I'd willingly choose to eat lactobacillus, not to mention the hormones stored in the saturated fats in dairy products, but whatever you put in your body is up to you."

"I take it that means you don't want some?"

She shook her head. "I prefer my travelling companions strong, dark, and hot."

Even before Verity indicated the coffee nestled against her chest, Traz's smile showed he had already recognized the comment as payback for his references to the Riviera's looks. She seemed willing to meet him on so many levels. He felt as connected and comfortable with this woman as he had with anyone in a long time. Which was why it troubled him so much that something was bothering her. He saw it in her unguarded moments, when she was staring out at the passing countryside as they drove, or while she was waiting for him to return to the car. She was able to let it go quickly enough when they began chatting, so whatever it was, he supposed it couldn't have been anything too serious.

A car slowed down almost to a stop to look at the Buick, but drove on before Traz could acknowledge the interest with a wave. He watched it go. Along the side of the road, a row of telephone poles disappeared into the distance like a procession of penitents, arms outstretched as they marched away. He looked again at the land around him, at the orange sand that burst through the seams of the hills like stuffing, and at the horizon, so far away it looked like it was a day's walk in any direction.

"This gig you're on," said Verity, "checking out these spots for your friend. It's a lot of trouble to go to. I just wondered why you'd take it on."

Traz shrugged. "Because he asked me to, I guess. We've known each other a long time. He knew I'd help if I could."

"He's lucky to have a friend like you."

"Yeah, his brother, too. I make sure I tell them so all the time, just in case they forget." He paused for a moment. "How about you? Any special ... friends?"

Verity shook her head, the highlights in her hair catching the sun. "I'm one of those people whose best friend is her work."

"What is it you're studying, exactly?"

She gave a sigh and sipped at her coffee. "I'm trying to track how changes in DNA over time affect the migration impulse. Why are the Aransas cranes driven to migrate, when others, like the Louisiana population, are content just to stay put? I get that birds may lose their migration route imprints over time, but have these just lost the drive to migrate altogether? I think the allele variations that trigger migration are being irretrievably lost in birds in captivity. If I'm right, it calls into question the whole idea of captive breeding programmes to supplement wild populations."

"Then I'd say the cranes are lucky to have you."

She shrugged. "I guess it's just too bad nobody else feels that way." She cocked her head to one side and looked at him frankly. "It's okay to want a little bit of respect, isn't it? I mean, to want the value of your work to be acknowledged, to be appreciated as the one doing it? There's nothing wrong with that, is there?"

It was the first sign of insecurity he'd seen in her, and it was all the more surprising coming from someone he had thought of as so self-assured. Perhaps it was this that gnawed at her in her quiet moments.

She reached to take his empty yogourt container and looked at him. "I take it you're biotically balanced enough to continue?"

She climbed back in the Buick without waiting for an answer.

Verity stood beside Traz, waiting for him to finish his survey of the glittering salt plain. In front of them lay the flat expanse of bleached gypsum deposits that gave the reserve its name. In the autumn, upwards of sixty thousand American White Pelicans would populate the shallow pools of water that interspersed the wide salt flats, but today Traz wasn't looking for pelicans. A report on the board at the park offices said a pair of Whooping Cranes had been seen earlier that day; there was mention of other species Traz wanted to have a look at, too.

Behind them, dark scars stretched across the land all the way back up to an area of pine forest. Tussocks of shiny black vegetation dotted the ground like wads of chewed-up liquorice, charred and blackened and still holding the acrid scent of smoke. A controlled burn, Verity told Traz. She knew about burns like this; they did them at Aransas from time to time. This one was done recently; a couple of days ago, at most.

The fire had reached the point where they now stood, but it had been in its final throes here, finding little vegetation on the white sand plains to fuel its onward march. Pockets of scorched sand plums stood beside thriving clumps of wild millet and smartweed in a tapestry of black and beige. The wind picked up slightly and moved a stand of charred cattails at the edge of the water. Verity pointed to them. "Sometimes in Aransas, the cattails way out in the water catch fire," she said. "I go out late at night to watch them burn out. They look like candles, reflected in the dark water. It's one of the prettiest sights I've ever seen."

She'd been hesitant to come through the woods at first, telling Traz tales of cottonwood trees that had smouldered away for days after a burn. "I've seen logs two weeks later with their ends still going. It wouldn't take much to set them off again." But she knew getting out to the plains was important to him, and although there was still a layer of unburned vegetation in among the trees, she could see no indication of live fire, so they had cautiously entered the trail. Evidence of nature's astonishing resilience was all around them. A spring of Blue-winged Teal drifted unhurriedly around a dark slough fringed with fire-licked tree stumps. Farther on, a plague of Boat-tailed Grackles gathered to pick at the insects in an area of blackened stubble. Eventually, Traz and Verity had emerged from the forest out onto this point of land, on the edge of the wide white sea of the salt plains.

"No cranes," said Traz, finishing his scan. "Snowy Plovers, though. I'll take those. They're the tiny white blobs scurrying around out there." He turned and handed Verity his bins, and she took a quick look before handing them back.

"I could have used these when I was doing my classes in college."

"For your fieldwork?"

"So I could see my professor at the front of the lecture hall."

Traz smiled. "Yeah, I heard at some colleges there can be as many as five hundred students in a single lecture."

Verity nodded. "It's why I decided to do most of my courses

online. I figured if my professor and I weren't going to be in the same zip code anyway, I may as well study from home."

"Do you think that has anything to do with why your work isn't as ... well-regarded by your peers?"

She shook her head. "It wouldn't have mattered where I studied. Or how much. Undergrad, couple of post-grads, I got more degrees 'n a thermometer. But when I speak, all they hear is my accent."

"In fairness, there does have to be some consistency in academic language. You start allowing people from all around the world to use their own colloquialisms, and nobody's going to know what anybody else is talking about."

"Oh, I can write in Academic-ese when I need to. I just prefer not to talk in it, that's all."

He began to understand her frustration. There was no reason why this engaging, knowledgeable person should have to compromise anything to be taken seriously. He was sure he would have been outraged if he was confronted with the same dismissive attitudes. He raised the bins again for another scan of the salt plains, but the plovers had gone. Not a single flicker of movement disturbed the shimmering stillness now. When he lowered his glasses to look back at Verity, he found a stillness there, too.

"We shouldn't be here, Traz. The wind's picking up again. I don't like this."

"We're fine. They wouldn't have opened the path back up to the public if it wasn't safe. But if it's making you uneasy, we can go."

They turned to leave and were already on the path through the pines when Traz realized everything had stopped. The birdsong had disappeared, the branches had ceased moving, even the air seemed to be still. And then there was a faint breath of wind, and a ribbon of scarlet began racing through the undergrowth. "Fire!" Verity shouted. "Run!"

The flames raced through low vegetation, tracking them through the trees on both sides of the path as they ran. They were both fast, and that was good. There would have been no time to wait for anyone. As the fire pursued them, they could see flames ahead of them, too, tearing through the trees towards the trail, consuming the low brush and dead tinder in a crackling trail of glowing orange.

They sprinted over the hard-packed earth of the trail, the fire closing in on them now on both sides, threatening to overtake them and cut off their exit. Ahead of them more flames flared up, setting the undergrowth aglow as they raced beside it. Still they sprinted on, urging more from their bodies until their lungs burned with the effort.

Finally, through the smoke, Traz could see the clearing at the end of the trail; beyond it the gravel parking area and safety. But first they had to reach it. If the fire got to the end of the forest, it would leap the narrow trail and they would be trapped. Beside him, Verity had reached the same conclusion and she surged ahead, digging down for one last burst of energy.

Traz's feet hit the gravel surface, and suddenly there was light. They kept running and didn't stop until they reached the far side of the parking lot. They turned, doubled over with their hands on their thighs, drawing deep breaths gratefully into their lungs. On the far side of the lot, the fire burned on, spitting and clawing against the gravel barrier like a caged animal. It was still burning when they had recovered their breath enough to begin making their way to the park offices.

"This your car?"

Traz was momentarily startled. He'd had the exquisitely-sculpted trunk of the Buick up, searching for a fresh shirt in his kit bag, and hadn't seen the ranger approach.

"Some guy came asking after you. Said he'd noticed it up around Enid earlier today."

"The owner lives in Canada," said Traz, pulling on a shirt and closing the trunk. "He spent the last couple of winters restoring the car down in Texas. I'm just driving it up there for him."

The ranger indicated the park offices with a tilt of his head. "Your girlfriend's just been telling us about that flare-up you were almost caught in. I'm truly sorry to hear about that. We had that path blocked off with a warning sign this morning. I guess folks don't always think through the consequences when they remove things like that." He paused to see if Traz was buying the apology. "We have someone heading up there right now to rope off the area properly. The fire'll burn itself out soon. It rained here yesterday, and the flames won't run for long on moist ground. They just take the top dead biomass, which is why the fire was moving so fast. It must've been pretty hairy."

Traz shrugged. "It's all good now." Behind the ranger, he saw Verity approaching them from the offices. "You said this guy was asking to talk to the car's owner. Any idea what he wanted?"

"Didn't say. Maybe he took a shine to it. It's a fine-looking automobile. He sure spent a long time looking at it."

Traz shook his head dubiously. "I doubt the owner would be willing to sell, given the amount of time and money he must've put into the restoration, but if this guy left a number, I could pass it on."

The ranger shook his head. "I asked, but he said since you weren't around, he'd let it go." Verity had joined them now, and the ranger turned to her. "Again, I'm sorry about the fire. But at least nobody got hurt. Might not've been such a happy ending if you'd have been caught out on those salt plains. No place to escape it there. You folks have yourself a nice day."

Traz watched the ranger leave. He turned to Verity. "In the future," he said, "if anybody isn't interested in listening when Verity Brown has something to say, how about you just refer them to me."

16

The light from the pale Norfolk sky filtered through the Perspex roof of the greenhouse, suffusing everything with a soft, milky glow. It was like being inside a light bulb, thought Salter, the world outside now a curious place of opaque shapes and undefined shadows. All around the quiet, airy space, potted plants were arranged on steel tables in rows so neat they looked like designs printed on a silver tablecloth. Standing in the doorway, Lauren Salter found the pattern of the endlessly receding pots almost hypnotic. It was easy to forget she was looking at living objects. Colour, height, size — if there was variation between the individual plants in any given row, she couldn't see it. In the centre of them all, the massive form of Albert Ross looked like a rocky outcrop in a sea of green.

Although he had his back to her, Ross seemed to sense her presence. "You can get to the ones at the back by going along the walls," he called out. "For anything in the middle of a table, you'll have to ask me."

He turned slowly and watched Salter's approach with undisguised interest. What was he seeing, she wondered — the confidence, the sense of authority that she was trying to project? Or her inner anxiety? She gave her approach a bit extra to make sure she didn't falter as she got closer and took in the man's true size. Albert Ross was a colossus; six foot seven according to his file. He had a large head and enormous tree-trunk arms. The way he held himself straight, with no hunching forward, as so many tall people did, suggested he had come to terms with his immense size a long time ago. She introduced herself and Ross inclined his great head slightly.

"About Wattis, is it? I thought you'd be by."

"Any particular reason you'd think that?"

"Murders. They're usually done by somebody the victim knows, right?"

"In the vast majority of cases, yes."

Ross nodded, like a man confirming something troubling. "Wattis didn't have many friends. Not sure you'd count me as one, come to that. But I knew him, right enough."

"For a number of years, I understand. I'm told you had an argument with him recently."

"I have lots of arguments." Ross picked up a potted plant and turned it slowly in his massive hands, peering in closely at the leaves before returning it to the same spot on the table. "Arguing with people is mostly what I do, when I'm not in here."

"Can you tell me what your argument with Mr. Wright was about?"

"He'd made me a promise. Then I heard he was going back on his word, so I went round to see him." Ross's eyes fixed on some distant place and he began to pound a massive fist rhythmically on the steel tabletop, making the potted plants dance to the beat of the words. "Usual story." *Thud.* "Sorry, Albert. A change in plans." *Thud.* "Not possible at this time." *Thud.* His breathing seemed to quicken and he picked up the pace. "Not possible." *Thud.* "Not possible." *Thud.* "NOT POSSIBLE." He hammered his fist down with such force that pots at the far end of the table juddered violently.

Salter was startled by both the speed and the power of the action, but she managed to avoid flinching, and her voice was nice and level when she spoke again. "You've had trouble controlling your temper in the past. It's got you into some difficulties."

"It goes a bit beyond that," said Ross ironically. His eyes had swum back to the present, and his breathing had returned to normal, but there was a faint sheen of sweat on his face. "I have Intermittent Explosive Disorder. At least, that's what the experts call it."

"I see," said Salter in a tone that suggested she didn't really see at all.

"Clinically diagnosed debilitating rage. Not a pretty sight when it kicks off. Or so I've been told."

"Are you receiving professional help?"

"I see a psychologist twice a week. She's big on CBT — cognitive behavioural therapy. Spot the initial triggers, remember the anger doesn't need to rule you, understand you can learn to control it, develop a self-care plan." He gave a short laugh. "Sounds straightforward enough when she says it."

Salter was struck by Ross's ability to speak in such an informed and dispassionate way about his condition. She'd seen the same thing in other people who suffered from serious illnesses. At times, it was almost as if they were describing someone else's diagnosis, some third party with whom they had little personal connection. But then, perhaps that was who they were describing, after all. Ross had picked up a small African violet, and he rotated the pot slowly in his hands. A number of its outer leaves were turning brown and he removed them with a delicacy that bordered on tenderness. "I have a sponsor, too."

"A sponsor?"

"Like in AA. Somebody I can talk to about things. Only drinking is a slow danger. You've got time to call somebody when you feel your problem starting to come on. These rages I get happen so fast, there's no time for all that. All you can do is chat to somebody when it's over."

"So, you're never in contact with your sponsor when you're having one of your episodes?"

"It wouldn't be a good idea. I can't tell the difference between friends and enemies when I'm in the middle of one of my 'sessions.' I only call after I come back."

"Come back?"

"From the dark side, Sergeant," said Ross, leaning in to add a touch of mock-menace. "I have blackouts. Sometimes seconds, sometimes more. The first I know about what I've been up to is when I wake up. There's usually a few reminders laying around — broken stuff, torn up papers, furniture knocked over." Ross's impassive expression gave her the sense once again that he almost felt he was describing someone else.

"Is it possible you could have forgotten even if you'd been in an altercation with someone?"

He looked at her directly. His eyes swam for a moment with troubling thoughts. "Are they saying I'm the one who killed Wattis?"

Salter recognized she was on the verge of something important. A swell of eagerness built within her, but she knew she had to approach the next few moments carefully. A man as unstable as Ross was likely to bolt back into his emotional cave if she pressed too hard, too fast. "You didn't hurt him when you went to see him at his house that afternoon. We know that much. You just shouted at him, repeating the same thing over and over again."

"Repeating?" He shook his head. "It can get bad when I do that. It winds me up, see, the repeating, gets me going. That's one thing my sponsor keeps telling me. *Stay away from the repetition, Albert, don't let it drag you in.* Easier said than done, though. What did I say?"

"You said Wattis Wright was a dead man. You said the same thing at least a dozen times."

"I said that?" Ross fell silent.

He looked so devastated by the news that, despite herself, Salter's heart went out to him a little. "It's about now that people normally tell the police it wasn't meant to be taken literally."

But Salter's attempt at comfort found no resting place with Ross. He was staring blankly down the uniform rows of plants, trying to come to terms with something that Salter could not understand. She looked around the greenhouse. The diffused light filled the space. For the first time, she noticed the faint scents, too, hovering at the edge of her senses like a promise of spring. He picked up another African violet, identical to the earlier one, at least as far as Salter could see. He began the same process of gently removing the dead leaves from around its edges.

"It's very peaceful in here, isn't it? I imagine you must like working in a place like this."

"Lot of wasted space, though." He shook his head. "You've got a big gap around the walls." He nodded, agreeing with himself. "Wide central aisle, too, and still you can't get to the plants in the middle. Circular tables would fix that, and narrower aisles. They should come off a central display area. Easier traffic flow, that way." He tapped his temple with an enormous forefinger. "I've got the ideas, see. No problem, the ideas. But nobody will listen to me, will they?" He raised his voice. "No, nobody here will listen to me. Just ignore me, don't they. Oh, it's Albert, we can ignore his ideas," he shouted to the empty space again. "Just ignore me, and my ideas!" He had gripped the edge of the steel table and she saw his knuckles getting whiter. She could sense the struggle within him as he battled to suppress the welling anger, to drive it back down inside him. It must be so wearying, she thought, to be permanently hovering on the edge of the abyss like this, constantly fighting to retain his grip on the world.

He looked down at his hands as if seeing them for the first time. "They tell you to do that, hold on to something physical, when you feel it coming on. Chair, table, whatever's at hand. It obviously works." The ironic smile was that of a different person, one Salter could go back to questioning. Perhaps.

"Are you capable of moving during these episodes you have?" she asked carefully. "I mean travelling from one place to another?"

"Must be. Sometimes I'm lying in my own bed when I come back, with no idea how I got there. I get tired, you see, after. Exhausted. Sometimes I sleep the whole next day."

"Do you think it's possible you could have had a blackout episode the day of your argument with Mr. Wright? Or perhaps later that night? Do you remember going to his house later on, a few hours after the first time?"

Ross shook his head, but he didn't speak. Salter couldn't tell if it was shame at what he remembered or frustration at what he didn't. But perhaps it was something else altogether; perhaps it was just the evasiveness of a guilty man. His eyes began to float slowly into focus once again, as if he was drifting back toward her once more.

"I can't help you, Sergeant. In fact, I don't think I can tell you anything else at all about that day."

"I'm sure your sessions with your psychologist are covered under doctor-patient confidentiality, but do you think I could talk to this sponsor of yours?"

"She won't talk to you. She's not allowed to."

"Even with your permission?"

"Permission denied," he said. Ross looked to the door at the far end of the greenhouse. "You can show yourself out."

At the doorway, Salter took a final glance back into the greenhouse. The way the pale light bathed the neat rows of plants, the way the gentle silence settled over this space, it would be easy to lose yourself in a place like this. It might even be possible to convince yourself that bad things in the outside world had never really happened. If you tried hard enough.

17

Danny Maik's briefing had lived up to its title, and Colleen Shepherd looked out her office window in frustration.

"And you're sure there's nothing we've missed?" The royal pronoun wasn't lost on Maik. Finding Hayes was his job, but the DCS's stake in the outcome made her an equal partner, at the very least. Maik let his silence stand as his answer and Shepherd thought for a long moment. Finally, she turned from the window and looked at him. "Could Hayes have gone back overseas, I wonder? Border Services have no record of him leaving, but perhaps he could have slipped out. He had that relative in Australia; an uncle, wasn't it? Is there a possibility he could be hiding out with him?"

"The uncle's dead."

Not *passed*, thought Shepherd. The ending of a life might well be a passing, but for Danny Maik, who had seen so many lives end, it would always remain a death. In Sergeant Maik's reports, people *died*; they were *killed*. It was as if he wanted to remind himself, and everybody else, of the stark truth of what had happened, to make sure the reality wasn't diminished by softer, kinder words. Maik said what he meant. Which is why when he told his DCS there were no leads, he meant no new ones, and no old ones that were still alive, either.

"You're still keeping an eye on the cottage, I take it, in his ... *their* absence?"

He was, he told her, now and then. The motion detector lights Jejeune had installed were still in working order. They'd keep any vandals away for the time being. It wouldn't last forever, though. Lindy would need to move back in soon. Either that or she'd need to put the place on the market. Maik didn't add the third option, the *as-you-were* one involving Domenic and Lindy moving back in there together. That one didn't seem to be on the table anymore.

Shepherd's sigh suggested she had mentally filed the subject as "pending." She turned now to a new one. "Sergeant Salter tells me she interviewed a suspect in her case. One Albert Ross. Does he sound like a viable suspect to you?"

Maik shrugged. "From what I understand, he has a history of violent outbursts, and he was heard earlier in the day issuing verbal threats to the victim." His expression suggested if you were looking for viable suspects, you could do worse.

"Verbal threats of a sort, though, Sergeant," said Shepherd. "It was the same phrase repeated over and over again. And even then, it was hardly what you'd call a string of invective, was it? You'd hear worse than that in the police canteen when somebody has left the milk out of the fridge."

"What did she make of him?" asked Maik.

"I think she rather came down on his side, though I'm not at all sure what her thoughts are just yet. I'm still waiting for an official report." Shepherd looked at Maik over her glasses, as though Salter's failure to submit the necessary document might have something to do with nefarious coaching on his part. She turned from him and contemplated the world outside her window again. Whatever it was that she found out there, it seemed to have a soothing effect. Her tone when she returned to Maik was gentler and more measured. "You don't worry that her tendency to get too close might be a problem, do you? She's always connected to them as individuals, the victims and the suspects." Shepherd held up a hand. "I'm not saying that's a bad thing, but I'd hate it to compromise her objectivity. She seems fixated on the idea that Wright died on the cold floor of an otherwise empty house, friendless and alone. She asked the ME if he would have suffered, how long he would have lain there on his own. His loneliness seems to be playing on her mind a great deal."

"We can't know whether he was lonely," pointed out Maik reasonably.

"The man's address book had eleven entries, Sergeant. Most of them were professionals — doctors, lawyers, accountants. I think we can fairly surmise his life wasn't a round of cocktail parties and gala openings, at least not anymore. It was just him and his record player these days."

"Speaking of his record player," said Maik, "I don't remember seeing anything on the SOCO reports about a record being on the turntable. Are we sure he was listening to music at the time?"

"There was no TV in the room," said Shepherd, "no book by the chair, no crossword puzzles. And the computer was in a different room from his beer glass. It's what you do, isn't it, if you like playing records on those turntable things. You pour yourself a drink and settle in to listen to all your old favourites?"

"I was thinking if there was nothing playing when he answered the door, perhaps it was because he was expecting his visitor."

Shepherd inclined her head to acknowledge the idea.

"Conversely, if Susan Bonaccord could remember hearing any music in the background during that call ..."

... and there was nothing on the turntable when SOCO arrived, it would be a significant lead. Shepherd nodded slowly.

This was Danny giving Detective Sergeant Lauren Salter a few new directions in which to take her inquiries. Only he wasn't doing it directly. Shepherd was going to be the conduit. She understood. Direction from a superior officer was to be expected by a new sergeant. Somebody of the same rank showing her just exactly how much she still had to learn wouldn't do anything at all for Salter's fragile confidence. From her seat, Shepherd looked up at Maik, towering above her in his standing position. "The money wouldn't sit well with him, would it?"

No, thought Maik, *it wouldn't.* The certified cheque couriered to a house the day before the homeowner was murdered? DCI Domenic Jejeune wouldn't even have made passing acquaintance with the idea that this was a coincidence. Its mere presence in the house suggested some sort of connection with the death. Jejeune might not have worked out what that was yet, but he wouldn't have been ready to look beyond the money as a motive until a lot more questions about it had been answered.

Shepherd drew in a deep breath. Jejeune always brought such a reassuring sense that things had been considered, evidence noted, possibilities weighed. He may not always have been able to prevent cases spiralling off in unforeseen directions, and he often got his own reasoning wrong, but you got the sense that any investigation in which Domenic Jejeune was involved was unlikely to get blindsided because something obvious had been ignored. Like the presence of a certified cheque at the crime scene, for example. Shepherd missed the comfort that it brought, knowing that Jejeune was on your side. Without the DCI's oversight on this case, she felt vulnerable in a way she couldn't quite explain. Not that she would have needed to. She suspected Danny and the rest of the team at Saltmarsh felt exactly the same way.

"Sergeant Salter was looking for you this morning, by the way. She wanted a bit of background on all that old technology." She shook her head in wonder. "Record players, free-standing photocopiers, VHS machines. Remember when we used to think all those lumbering great old things were indispensable?"

"Some of us still have our uses," said Maik.

Shepherd gave him a crooked grin as payment for his deadpan delivery. "Those old photocopiers were all retired due to security concerns, though, as I recall. No danger of that with you, is there, Sergeant? You haven't said anything to Salter about the Hayes investigation yet, I take it. It may be wise to loop her in on it. Especially now, given her new rank."

Maik shifted uneasily. As much as he respected Lauren Salter, he had shied away from revealing any details of his task to her. Lindy Hey had once remarked Danny liked to keep his emotions under house arrest. How much more so, then, his secrets? He had no doubts about Salter from a professional point of view, but *need-to-know* was the watchword here. That meant Danny and his two immediate superiors. So, if it was all the same to the DCS, he'd carry on solo on this one, with only his misgivings for company.

"There wouldn't be much point in telling her anything at this time," he said. "It's not like there's a lot to report."

"Point taken," said Shepherd quietly. Another thoughtful silence seized her, and as before, she staring unblinkingly at the scene outside. Maik could see the fields, the wide open swatches of brown earth, tilled in preparation for planting. A new season, he thought; a new phase. Salter left her gaze on the fields for so long, Maik wondered if she'd already made some gesture of dismissal that he'd failed to pick up on. But she stirred finally and turned, reluctantly it seemed, from the window. "Tell me honestly, Danny. In your opinion, is Lindy safe?"

"Hayes has had plenty of time to act if he was going to. There's been no hint of any threat to her. I'd have to go along with the DCI's assessment that as long as he stays away from her, Hayes no longer has any reason to be interested in Lindy."

Shepherd nodded and sighed deeply. There was a moment of stillness as she considered her next comment, seeming to drag it up from somewhere inside her. "Then it's time to wrap this up. We'll give it forty-eight hours, and if there have been no new developments, I'll end your active search for Ray Hayes. We all need to move on."

Given the complete lack of leads, Maik couldn't see what purpose a forty-eight-hour extension could serve from an operational point of view. But sometimes there were considerations that went beyond the operational ones. DCS Shepherd had long since worked out what Maik and his DCI had known from the beginning. Maik was never going to find Hayes. He was too resourceful, too intelligent, to allow himself to be arrested. The extra forty-eight hours was for Colleen Shepherd to come to terms with the knowledge that the day she terminated the sergeant's search was the day Domenic Jejeune's ongoing, twice-extended leave of absence in Canada became a permanent arrangement.

18

Domenic Jejeune strolled slowly along the narrow streets of Fort Smith. He could feel the sun on his shoulders, but the air carried a hint of coolness, and many of the gardens he passed were still struggling to display their spring flowers. In some ways, the tidy fenced-off plots in front of the single-storey houses reminded him of Saltmarsh. The vegetation was different, of course, with the preponderance of conifers and subarctic shrubs here, but there was the same orderliness to carefully-tended gardens; the same evidence of pride.

There were other ways in which the town resembled the English village half a world away; like how the residents flapped a hand or nodded at each other with familiarity. Domenic got the impression that here, as in Saltmarsh, the sense of belonging would be strong. Victories would be shared; tragedies, too. A family member lost in the wilderness just beyond the town's tidy grid pattern of streets would be a public concern, and the community would rally round to offer their assistance and support.

He headed north and walked along the top of the ridge, looking down at the Slave River as it curved around the town's northern perimeter. Was this wide, glittering band of light a barrier, hemming the town in, or a protective blockade against the untamed lands that existed beyond the far bank? He supposed it depended on your point of view. He mounted a rise and stopped at an open information pagoda that told him the white water he could see from his vantage point was the Rapids of the Drowned.

A man approached and stood at Jejeune's shoulder. For a moment, neither of them spoke as they watched the water coiling into rope-like wraiths of white foam as it threaded its way between the rocks.

"The Dene could have told those trappers running these rapids is a bad idea," said the man. "Seems nobody thought to ask them."

Jejeune turned to look at the speaker. His lean, tanned face was patterned with deep lines, but there was no hint of grey in the long black hair that hung loosely over his shoulders. He was wearing faded blue jeans and a black shirt with a white eagle embroidered between the shoulder blades. The man's black hat, like the jeans, showed signs of wear. It was a wide-brimmed style known as a Plateau. Even with no elaborate band, if it was the one hundred percent beaver felt it looked to be, it would have been an expensive item when it was new. Jejeune suspected he might already know the man's name, but he waited for him to introduce himself.

"Gaetan Robideau." The man didn't offer a hand. "Guessed you'd probably come looking for me sooner or later." He moved his head. "Thought I'd save you the trouble."

"I heard that you'd gone into the park," said Jejeune, "to observe some kind of ritual."

"Drinking birch sap. A traditional purification ceremony. One-man show," said Robideau flatly. "Done now."

"How were the conditions? I mean, would it be easy enough for a person ... people to survive in the park at this time of year?"

Robideau gave a small shrug. "Water's still cold, ground's still hard. Be a while yet before the last of the snow disappears. But life is coming to the land. The temperature won't get much above ten degrees this time of the year, cooler at night. But if you had the right equipment, I suppose a person ... people would be okay. Still hard to find food, though, unless you took enough in with you. You'd need to know where to find edible plants this early in the year."

"The kind of wisdom that would be passed down by the tribal elders," said Jejeune, nodding earnestly.

"Or you could Google it. This person you have in mind, it's that woman?"

"Annie Prior. Yes. I'm told you met with her before she went into the park."

"And now she's gone missing." Robideau shook his head slowly. "Those park people don't like me much. They'd be happy to tie me into this woman's troubles in some way."

"You think she is in trouble, then?"

Robideau spent some moments looking out at the rapids, following the tumbling of the white waters intently. Despite the bright whiteness reflecting back at them, he wasn't squinting. "A few weeks, there will be pelicans down there. You fly or swim, that river's a good place for you. You sit in a boat and float along, maybe not so much. I told her she must pay the water, to ask for its protection and safe passage — nothing elaborate, a small offering of tobacco, just before she entered it. But she said she had her own faith. She would get all the protection she needed from her own god." He fixed the detective with his look. "You start telling the spirits you don't need their help, bad things are going to happen to you."

"Can you tell me why Ms. Prior came to see you?" Jejeune was surprised to find how uncomfortable he felt asking these kinds of questions without the safety net of his police identity.

"She wanted to know if the Dene created middens. I told her the Dene moved with the seasons. We never stayed in any one place long, and anything the spirits gave us, we returned to its rightful place. You took an animal from the land, like a deer, you put its bones back in the earth; a creature from the river, like a beaver, you put those bones back in the water. There was no one place we'd stockpile them."

Jejeune was quiet for a long time, but Robideau seemed content just to stand there, letting the wind wash over him as it crested the ridge. Whether or not he had more business with Jejeune, he appeared willing to wait for him to process the information he had just given him.

"Was she interested in where the Whooping Cranes were nesting?" asked Jejeune eventually.

"She didn't ask me about them."

To Jejeune, it seemed that Gaetan Robideau was being careful to make sure his responses were true. But that didn't necessarily mean they were complete. There was more that he and this woman had shared, Jejeune was sure of it. But if a man as taciturn as Robideau had decided to keep secrets, it was unlikely, to say the least, that the detective would be able to extract them.

"There was a man with her when she went into the park," said Jejeune.

"He missing too? Two people have got a better chance out there than one, providing at least one of them has some knowledge of how to live off the land."

"He does," said Jejeune. "He's got survival skills, and he's spent quite a bit of time in the area. He knows the park and the ways of the people. The traditional landowners, I mean ... the First Peoples, the Indigenous Peoples," stumbled Jejeune.

"Can't help you with that one," said Robideau evenly. "Last I heard, I believe I was some kind of Indigenous First Person.

Singular, presumably." He shrugged disinterestedly. "I'm Dene. That's all I need to know."

Jejeune coloured with embarrassment. Would he have been better-versed in these cultural nuances if he had spent his recent years in Canada? Or would he still have felt as disoriented as he did up here, as alien in this tiny, tidy outpost teetering on the edge of the great northern wilderness?

"I saw her once before," said Robideau flatly. "Long time now, when she lived here."

"Annie Prior was a native … a local?"

Robideau shook his head. "No. But she stayed here for a while. She came to the band one time to ask if the elders would re-enact some of the old rituals while she filmed them. Wanted them for a degree she was doing at that university in the south, Black Hills State. Elders didn't think the spirits would like them acting out sacred rituals for the camera, so they refused. Didn't stop her asking a couple more times, though. She was persistent, I'll give her that."

Jejeune was silent for a moment. "You said the park staff don't like you. Why?"

Robideau looked Jejeune in the eye. "I cause trouble. The water management programmes in the park are being mishandled. Too much interference has disrupted the natural channels and drainage systems. These days, the water levels in the lakes rise too high too fast after a storm. That one that hit us recently will have backfilled the rivers way up into the interior of the park. We get another one anytime soon, the land's going to drown."

"So, you're asking them to address this?"

"No, I'm asking a lawyer to make them."

"You're suing the park?" Jejeune looked at Robideau in surprise. Suddenly the claim that the man caused trouble seemed to make a lot more sense.

He nodded. "Them, and Parks Canada, and the federal government they represent. At least I would be, if I could get my lawyers the proof they need."

"What proof is that?"

"They say they're going to need empirical evidence, like a dying ecosystem leaves a track in the sand or a snag of fur on a bramble." Robideau shook his head sadly. "The land is giving us all the empirical evidence we need, every day. Fish are drowning, plants are dying of thirst. People keep telling me the effects of climate change will be with us soon. They're already here. Every time I go down to visit my brothers, the Mikisew Cree down in Fort Chip, the poplars are filled with caterpillars. That never used to be the case. Fewer mosquitoes, too, now that the land is drying out."

Jejeune, who had already been chewed upon by more than his share of insects since he arrived, reflected that some impacts of climate change were going to concern people more than others.

"What are you hoping to get the authorities to do, if you eventually succeed in bringing a lawsuit?"

"Nothing."

Jejeune gave a puzzled look.

"They say they are working to restore the natural balance. As if this is something that is in their power to do. Humans cannot restore nature. Only the Great Mother Earth can do this. Forget management, forget remediation, forget restoration. The best thing humans can do is stop causing the damage. Do nothing. Cause no harm, and let the park take care of healing itself."

Robideau fell silent, and Jejeune got the sense it was a long speech for him, and now he had made his point, he had nothing more to say.

"When Prior came to see you, did you happen to notice if she was left-handed?"

An updraft from the escarpment tugged at the brim of Robideau's hat like a polite inquiry, tousling his hair. His eyes showed no surprise at the question, only a kind of understanding. "You thinking of going after these people?"

"Would you have any advice for me, if I was?"

"Get yourself a comfortable pair of slippers and a housecoat."

"To go into the park?"

"To wear in your hotel room while you wait for them to return. College degrees like that woman has are one thing, but you need a different kind of knowledge out there. Anybody planning to go into Wood Buffalo had better ask themselves if they have it. You believe you are a wise man, and I think maybe you are. But yours is not the kind of wisdom that will keep you alive in that park. You won't be able to out-think the challenges the land offers. You start convincing yourself you're in control out there, and the spirits will pretty soon show you otherwise."

"The man who went into the park with the woman is my brother."

This time, Robideau's expression did change. He seemed to recognize now that nothing would prevent Jejeune from going after them. "You plan to go in there, you need to think about making your own offering to the waters."

"I don't have any tobacco," said Domenic simply.

"Then you'd better hope any rivers you come across are non-smokers." Robideau turned away and looked out over the river once again. It was clear he felt he had no more to offer this man. Jejeune murmured a word of thanks to Robideau's back and began to descend the steep slope leading from the overlook. As he reached street level, he heard Robideau's voice calling him. "Hey, mister people person." Jejeune turned to see the man still at the top of the rise, his lean frame silhouetted against the bright sky. "That woman, Prior. She was right-handed."

19

The wide canvas of the American Midwest lay along the sides of the highway as the Buick and the countryside rolled past each other; images and impressions that told the story of America's development through the ages. There were pristine valleys that still looked as they would have a century ago, small towns that had long since seen their glory days, new communities that seemed to be prosperous and thriving. A journey like this was as much about driving through times as it was places, Traz realized.

He turned north onto an arrow-straight county road cutting through the heart of the Kansas farm fields. The flat land stretched to the horizon in all directions; green fields of winter wheat, sorghum, and soybean. Western Meadowlarks trilled at them from the fenceposts, and from a lonely telephone pole, a Prairie Falcon tracked their progress carefully. Verity was sitting beside him quietly, contemplating the passing scenery. Her bare feet were resting on the dashboard. Traz might not have been so tolerant if it was his own lovingly restored car, but his remit was to get the Buick to Saskatchewan unblemished, not to ensure there were no traces of human DNA on it. Besides, Verity's presence wasn't making much else of an impact on the car. She'd even chosen to leave her boxes of delicate lab equipment behind in the porta-cabins at Aransas.

Traz's early-morning coordinate search had been successful, and he had stopped the car on a rise overlooking a wide slough. It was within sight of a large complex of buildings, but far enough away that a group of migrating Whooping Cranes might consider it a safe resting place on their journey north. From his vantage point, he'd scanned the area carefully with his bins, but he could detect no movement, no unusual features, other than the vast spread of structures, grey and indistinct, in the haze beyond the slough. From somewhere high above, he heard the distant drone of an airplane engine. It was the only sound that had intruded on his survey of the still, shimmering landscape.

He slowed up now as a truck trundled out from a field onto the road ahead of them. It was laden with cotton, a relatively new crop here, a strain developed to withstand the harsh winters of the plains. It was a sign that change was inevitable even in the timeless tradition of farming.

With the car's momentum already checked anyway, the snap decision was an easy one. "Lunch," he announced suddenly, turning into a roadside opening and slowing the Buick to a stop in front of a silver Airstream trailer.

From the outside, Denzley's Roadside Dinah had the appearance of a genuine mid-century roadside diner, but as soon as they entered, Traz realized this was a faithful reproduction rather than a true original. The black-and-white-checked floor bore no scuff marks, the Formica-topped counter was unblemished by cigarette burns or elbow wear. Instead, the entire interior had been refurbished in a pristine tribute to a vanished past. From the gleaming porthole windows to the shiny silver jukeboxes along the walls, Denzley's pride and passion glittered back at them from every surface.

They sat at the counter on chrome-stemmed swivel stools with red plastic upholstery. Traz rubbed his hands together. "Okay, I promise I'll be full of remorse later, but I have to tell you, I'm going full on in here. The whole way. Heart attack on a plate coming right up."

A waitress in a period uniform bearing a badge with the name Dinah approached. She placed a menu on the counter between them and Verity picked it up to peruse it. Unbidden, the waitress poured them both a cup of coffee.

"This place is great," said Traz, looking around with genuine appreciation.

"Why, thank you, honey. Denzley and me always dreamed about opening our own restaurant, so when this old trailer went up for sale a few months ago, it just seemed like the perfect vehicle for us. That there's a pun," Dinah informed him.

"I take it you're the *Dinah* in the name," said Traz, indicating her name badge.

She leaned forward confidentially. "My name is actually Lacey, but it doesn't really go with the ambience we were aiming for in here." She gave him a wink. "Denzley's really Denzley, though. He's out back, cookin' up a storm as we speak."

Verity laid down the menu. "I'm just going to freshen up," she said. "I won't be long, though. I'm looking forward to seeing what you order off there."

Traz looked at her as she left, but once he'd read the menu's preamble, he understood her strange parting glance. *Welcome to Denzley's Roadside Dinah. Our vision is to provide our patrons with a healthy dining experience in a setting from a bygone age. We proudly serve a wide range of organic, non-GMO, gluten-free fare for your dining pleasure.*

Traz felt his appetite waning even as he read, and closed the menu solemnly. He pointed at a chalkboard on the wall. "What's the soup du jour?"

"Hold on, honey," said Dinah. "I'll go find out."

Verity returned from the bathroom with a crooked grin on her face. "Your choice," she reminded him. "Can I get the keys to the car? I have some ground flaxseed in my case that might go with a couple of the things on that menu if I sprinkle it on."

He handed over the keys and watched her leave, still smiling to herself. Dinah had returned by the time he swivelled back around on the stool.

"Soup du jour is 'soup of the day,'" she said. "Denzley thinks it might be French."

She paused just long enough to let the look of astonishment spread across Traz's face before offering him another lavish wink. "It's a *terrine de grenade puree.*"

In defeat, Traz ordered pasture-raised, grass-fed chicken on Ezekiel low-sodium sprouted-whole-grain bread. As Dinah/Lacey left, a stirring of interest among the other diners had him turning around on his swivel stool. Through one of the diner's curtain-framed portholes he could see a military Jeep that had just pulled up, and from which two Military Police Officers had emerged. They were standing splay-legged at two points of a triangle. Verity was the third. He rose to go out and join her but she had manoeuvred herself into a position where she could stare casually through the window of the diner as she spoke to the men. Her eyes were fixed on the spot she knew Traz was sitting. The head shake would have been imperceptible unless you were looking for it. He sat back down on his stool, and like the other diners, watched the unfolding events outside with rapt attention.

Verity had come around to this side of the car, and leaned in to retrieve something, but whether it was for the MPs or just her ground flaxseed, he couldn't tell. From his angle, he could lip-read some of the officer's questions, but Verity had her back to the window now, so he could only supply her answers for himself.

"Are you the driver of this car, ma'am?"

"No, that would be that drop-dead gorgeous guy in the diner."

But neither of the green-helmeted heads turned in his direction, so she hadn't told them that.

"What company is that?"

She took out her phone and began scrolling, before turning the phone towards the officer. He reached to take it, but she held firm, and he leaned forward to read the information. He asked another question but Traz could only make out one word: *Canada.* He saw Verity nod her head. With a slowly growing astonishment, he realized she was telling these men she was the person contracted to drive the car. The number she had shown them was the one he had given her in the Stock Pond the night they had first met, the one for the vehicle delivery agency.

Discreetly, so as not to alert the other patrons, he checked his pockets. He had his phone and wallet with him. His sunglasses lay on the counter, and beside them the binoculars he always took with him whenever he left the car. He'd not worn a jacket that day, so the only thing of his that remained on display in the car was a black computer bag on the back seat, an item Verity could pass off as her own if she was intending to convince these men she was travelling alone. Unless they decided to search the trunk.

Here was a question about ID now, and Verity fished in her purse for a wallet. As she handed it over, Traz knew she would be accompanying it with that beguiling smile of hers, the one you'd need a heart of stone to resist. But stone hearts must have been standard issue with this military unit because neither of the soldiers responded. Instead, they seemed to be getting just a little more insistent, leaning in slightly as they questioned her, reinforcing their authority a touch more intimidatingly.

Traz was about to go out and end all this, to protect her from whatever it was she thought she was doing, when the officer handed the ID back and both soldiers took up a more at-ease stance. With a few more curt words Traz didn't catch, the men climbed back into the Jeep and drove off.

Verity re-entered the diner to a bank of furtive stares and a few more direct ones. She smiled easily at Traz, but in her eyes was a message. *Not here.*

"Mistaken identity," she said, just loud enough for any other interested ears, as well. "They thought I was their commanding officer."

When it became clear they weren't going to get any more details from this chirpy, auburn-haired girl with a lip ring, the diners returned gradually to the business of dispatching their meals. But not Traz. His appetite for his pasture-raised, grass-fed chicken had long since disappeared. On Ezekiel low sodium sprouted whole grain bread or anything else.

20

Danny stood in line in the coffee shop, behind three young girls who seemed to find the process of ordering hot drinks doubled-over hysterical. He watched them giggling and flapping hands at each other and felt like he was about a hundred and forty years old. The process of deciding over, two of them retreated to a nearby table while their friend awaited the order. The second she was alone, the girl took out her phone and began looking at it.

"They should get a delivery service in here," said a familiar voice behind Danny as he placed his order, "save us having to trek all the way down here for a cup of green tea when we're busy."

The owner smiled at Salter's comment. "Good idea, detective," he said. "We'll give it some thought. The walk is obviously doing you good, though. You're looking very trim these days, if you don't mind my saying so. Anything else?"

Salter, who'd felt her resolve beginning to crumble as she stood before the case of fresh cream cakes on display, suddenly had new reserves of willpower to call upon. "Just the tea, thanks," she said with a smile.

Maik had long ago given up attributing things to coincidence, but that wasn't quite the same thing as giving up belief in its existence. Things did still happen randomly, and perhaps Salter's appearance behind him in this queue was just such a case. But at the new sergeant's conversation opener, the idea left him, as it always seemed to do.

"I've been giving this case some thought," she said. "Who am I kidding? It's been with me day and night. I'm so distracted, I even sent Max off to school today without a lunch."

Ahead of them, the girl still had her head bowed over her phone. Maik watched her for a moment. "I understand you wanted to chat to me about it earlier," he said, his eyes still on the girl. "Something about Wright's old equipment."

"Oh, that. Yes. I was wondering about that old sound system he had, the record player and the rest. I was going to ask you how loud that amplifier would go. I couldn't get it to work when I was over there, but I was wondering if Wright could have been playing his music loudly enough to upset the neighbours."

"Did the SOCO report say there was a record on the turntable, then?" asked Maik casually.

"No, but Wright was on a scheduled telephone call at the time he was killed. He may have been intending to wait until the call was complete before putting on any music. But that's not to say there couldn't have been something on earlier in the day. If he played it all the time, loud enough to drive the neighbours barmy ..." She trailed off. "We haven't got any noise complaints on file, but I was just, you know, wondering."

Salter looked at him uneasily. He could tell she was unsure whether she was over-thinking things, or under-thinking them, or perhaps not even thinking them through at all. But admitting you didn't have the answers, and being willing to consider all angles in order to find them, were both important approaches in any investigation. She hadn't come in with any preconceived notions that might have caused her to ignore evidence that didn't fit, or rushed into developing theories for the unknown or the unknowable. At this point, Sergeant Salter was open to all possibilities. And in an ongoing investigation, that was about the most important approach of all.

At the counter, the girl's order arrived, and she suddenly found herself with fewer hands than hot drinks. She reached inside her blouse and tucked away her phone so she could carry the cups over to her friends at their table. Salter shook her head sadly. "I hate to see that. The young girls at the gym do it all the time, too, stick their phones into their bra while they're exercising. I can only imagine the health hazards they must be exposing themselves to."

Maik shuffled ahead to the counter, but it was clear his interest in hearing about Salter's progress in the case wasn't over. "You met with Albert Ross."

Salter nodded her confirmation. Danny hadn't asked for the details. She knew he'd leave it to her to tell him what she wanted to. But for once, that suited her. She lowered her voice a notch. The lineup at a bakery shop in Saltmarsh High Street wasn't really the place to be discussing the details of a case, but Danny Maik was proving difficult to track down these days. Whatever he was working on, and nobody seemed prepared to say exactly what that was, it was apparently demanding all of his time. So, she'd take whatever opportunities came her way to bend his ear. "Ross has a condition called IED — Intermittent Explosive Disorder. I've been reading up on it. If he has worse-case symptoms, and I think he has, he'd certainly be capable of enough rage to kill someone." She paused to look around her, but there was nobody else in the queue behind them. "He claims he can't remember what happened after his argument with Wright, where he went, what he did."

Danny's eyes met Salter's. He *claims* he can't remember, Maik's expression seemed to say. *Have you already made up your mind about Albert Ross, Sergeant Salter?*

"IED sufferers have anger blackouts sometimes, don't they?" he asked, reaching to take the cups as the café owner brought them over. He left enough change for both orders, and a little extra, on the countertop and handed Salter her tea, waving away her offer to pay.

"Some do, yes," she said. She nodded as the point became clear. "And if it's true that he blacked out, then he can't even be sure himself whether he did it or not. So, you think I'd be well within my rights to give Albert Ross some serious consideration?"

Maik's answer, if he intended to give one, was interrupted by a burst of giggling from the nearby table. The officers looked over to see the three girls all craned in, staring at the tiny screen between them. "Lindy's not answering her phone," said Maik suddenly. He looked almost as startled as Salter that the statement had burst from him like this, but he realized he couldn't simply leave things at that. "Someone in HR left her a message, asking if she had a forwarding address for the DCI. Some form or other they had to send him. They followed up today when they didn't get an answer." Maik could have told the HR clerk Lindy wouldn't have an address for Domenic Jejeune, but that was hardly the point. He'd never known Lindy to be out of touch by phone for very long. For one thing, the nature of her job as a journalist more or less demanded she was contactable at a moment's notice.

"She's probably out on assignment somewhere. Why don't you ask her boss?"

"Eric doesn't seem to be around at the moment, but nobody else at the office has heard anything about any assignment. In fact, nobody remembers seeing her at all yesterday."

She should have realized Danny would already have checked the obvious lead. "Perhaps she's just gone off somewhere for a couple of days. Down the Smoke, maybe, having a bit of R and R. God knows, she deserves it."

"Without her phone?"

Salter met Maik's dubious expression head on. "Not everybody spends as much time glued to their phone as you seem to think, Danny. A lot of people like to take a break from it now and then. Used to be, if you wanted to avoid calls, all you had to do was not be home when your landline rang. Now, there's no escape unless you deliberately turn your mobile off."

"Not many do that, from what I've seen. You think Lindy could do without hers for this long?"

"It's not a life support system, Danny. People leave their phones at home all the time. On purpose."

There was a metallic buzz and a second of agonized hesitation as Salter thought about ignoring it. "Sorry," she said, "that's Max's ring. I have to take this." She fished in her pocket for the phone and held it to her ear. "Hello, Sweetheart, I'm sorry about your lunch. Can you get something at school, just for today?" She listened for a moment and nodded. "Yes. Yes, I do remember our talk, but I'm sure nobody here heard me calling you that." She rolled her eyes heavenward and listened again as Maik looked on with an impassive expression. "No, Max, I would never call you that if your friends were around. Look, Sweet ... Max, I'm a bit busy, so was there something special you wanted to talk to me about?"

Maik watched the standard pauses and nodding of a one-sided conversation. "Well, did Jensen's mom say it was okay? And she's willing to pick you up and drop you off in the morning?" Salter gave a brave laugh. "Of course it's all right with me. I want you to go and have a good time at Jensen's. Just remember your manners. I'll see you tomorrow." She ended the call and looked at Maik. "That's another quiet night in for me, then," she said. She didn't look ecstatic about the idea. "Sorry, what were we talking about?" she asked with heavy irony.

"You know, for the life of me, I can't remember," said Maik with such an uncharacteristic lightness it caused Salter to leave her glance on him a moment.

"Don't worry about Lindy, Danny. She's an independent woman. She doesn't have to check in with us before she leaves town. She'll call back when she wants to. We all need some quiet time now and again. I take it you've checked the love nest … the cottage," she said to Maik's questioning gaze.

"She's not been to the cottage," said Maik firmly. Salter looked at him carefully, trying to decide if she should be reading anything into his tone. But it was just Danny being Danny, certain of his facts and ready to state them. "I drove past there this morning. You saw that place when they both lived there. Can you imagine her letting it stay the way it looks now if she'd been back?"

Salter accepted Maik's reasoning. *Tidy*: that would have been the word for the garden when DCI Jejeune and his girlfriend were living there. The lawn was always neatly trimmed and framed by carefully tended flowerbeds. The front porch was garlanded with annuals in neat terracotta pots. But the last time Salter had driven past, the cottage had the forlorn look of a place where love had died. Branches from the trees along the driveway lay scattered over the lawn, the flowerbeds were overgrown and tangled, the unwatered plants on the porch dead in their terracotta pots. Salter didn't know Lindy that well, but she suspected she would be heartbroken by the state of the garden if she had returned, and to Maik's point, would have been unable to resist the urge to do something about it.

The girls at the table were still fiddling with their phones. "If he'd had one of those, Wattis Wright could have got rid of just about everything else in his office," she said. "His sound system, his photocopier, probably even that antiquated computer."

"Some people resist change even when newer technology is available to them. I remember the push back in the military when they decided to get rid of those big photocopiers. They replaced them with electronic systems and people went haywire for a bit."

"You can hardly blame them for the decision, though. I'm sure the new system was far more secure than trusting some dopey squaddie not to leave a set of invasion plans on the glass after he'd finished copying them. Apparently, security concerns were why the hospitals got rid of them, too."

"Except people could always leave a hospital if they were uncomfortable with the new system." Maik gave her an ironic smile. "The army generally doesn't give you that option."

"It wasn't just those copiers that were huge, though. Remember the first mobile phones? They weighed about half a tonne." Salter followed Maik's stare back over to the girls. "I'd like to see these girls storing those the same way as they do now. Talk about a health risk. They'd be so top-heavy, they'd be going face first into the concrete every time they took a step."

As he watched the three girls gathered over their shared phone screens in rapture, Maik couldn't shake the feeling that something was wrong. Lindy was closer to these girls' age than to his. She would not have wanted to be away from the world her phone connected her to for long. And as one of the most conscientious people he knew, she would have checked her messages before now.

Maik drained his tea and stood up, offering Salter a forced smile. "I should be going," he said. "Plenty to be getting on with."

Salter nodded. "Listen, for all I said, I'd be happy to help you track down Lindy if you needed me to. Was there any special reason you were checking on her?"

Like his earlier lightness, hesitation was not something Salter would have generally associated with Danny Maik. For a moment, it seemed like he might say something, but in the end he merely thanked Salter for her offer, anyway, and turned to go, not even looking at the table of three girls giggling into their phones as he passed.

21

The woman in the garden was standing perfectly still, straight-backed and shoulders squared. Lauren Salter had received no response to her knock at the front door, but the sound of a woman's voice had led her to the small sunlit garden at the back of the house. She stood at the fence now, watching. The woman was standing barefoot on the grass, with her eyes closed, drawing in even, measured breaths. She spoke some words aloud and slowly extended her right leg in front of her at an angle. Drawing her arms up from her sides, she held them across her chest. Salter watched, engrossed, as the woman gently swirled her hands into the air, redistributing her balance to compensate. When she had finished the routine, she drew her body back to its starting position, exhaled and opened her eyes. She showed surprise at seeing Salter watching her, but as with her activity, her poise remained perfect.

"Jennie Wynn? I'm Sergeant Salter from the Saltmarsh Constabulary." The title still sounded strange to her. "I was hoping you could spare a few minutes for a chat. It's about Wattis Wright's death."

"Please come in." Salter entered and crossed the soft turf to stand in front of the woman. She was a head shorter than Salter and slightly-built. Although she was about a generation older, it was clear that she was in very good physical condition. Her muscles beneath the blue leotard were toned and well-developed and she'd already displayed a control over them that Salter herself would have been proud of.

"Can I ask what you were saying, just before you started that series of moves?" asked Salter.

"*Needle at Sea Bottom*. It is the name of the final movement of my Tai Chi exercises. Announcing the moves as I go helps to remind me where I am in the sequence. If I'm in the last phase of *Part the Wild Horse's Mane*, I know I should be going directly into *The White Crane Spreads Its Wings*. As *Grasp the Bird's Tail* ends, *Hand Parts the Clouds* awaits me. Announcing the names also seems to add harmony to the progression." She smiled at Salter. "And things are so much better when there is harmony to them, don't you find, Sergeant? So much more balanced."

To a working mother whose own days consisted mostly of trying to make it to the end of them, harmonious balance wasn't high on Salter's list of priorities. But she returned the woman's smile anyway. "I understand you were Wattis Wright's assistant back when he had all that success with the Shammalars," she said.

"Wattis used to refer to me as his partner. I came on board shortly after the second big hit. It was about then that the record company realized the Shammalars had gone some way beyond being merely a novelty act and were becoming stars in their own right. As the band's manager, as well as the principal songwriter, the record company wanted Wattis to provide them with the full package the Shammalars were going to need to take them to the next level — outfits, dance routines, light shows."

"They were a novelty act?"

"Originally. They were intended to be a parody of the American doo-wop groups from a couple of decades earlier," Wynn told her. "It was a time in the music industry when people were willing to try anything and everything. There were quite a lot of acts back then that would never have seen the light of day in earlier times. Or later ones, come to that."

The woman reached down to pick up a bottle of water. Even in this simple action, her movements revealed a precision and control beyond many people half her age.

"Did Wattis Wright make a lot of money from the Shammalars? Only ..."

The woman nodded in understanding. "... there wasn't much evidence of it in his lifestyle? Long gone, I'm afraid. There were halcyon days when the hits were being rolled out, but his song-writing royalties dwindled away to nothing as the decades passed. His manager's percentage, too." Wynn set the bottle down again. It was warming up in the garden, and Salter wouldn't have minded a drink herself, but there were no other liquids to be seen.

"These dance routines the producers of this new musical were paying him for, were they really that good?"

Jennie Wynn allowed herself a small smile. "Modesty forbids, but yes, they were."

"You were involved in creating them?" Salter's surprise was evident in her tone.

"If you'd call translating Wattis's sketchy ideas into viable dance routines, working out the choreography, and coaching the band on how to perform the moves being 'involved,' then yes, I was. Essentially, those dance routines were mine. As are, I might add, the literally dozens of derivations of them I've seen other artists use over the years. Of course, it's much harder to prove someone copied individual dance moves, as opposed to an entire routine, but there's no doubt in my mind that they were drawn from my original choreography."

"But Wattis Wright never offered to include your name when he applied for copyright for the routines?"

Wynn shook her head lightly. "It really didn't seem to matter at the time. It was only after it became clear the producers of this new show were willing to buy them that I realized Wattis stood to profit from what was rightfully mine."

"Did you confront him about it?" Good word, thought Salter. *Confront* carried the right connotation. It occurred to her how carefully DCI Jejeune had always seemed to word his questions. She recognized that it was one more aspect of the investigative process she was going to have to pay particular attention to.

Jennie Wynn paused before answering the question. "I admit we exchanged a few words about it. I felt I was entitled to a share of the income, even if I didn't hold any copyright. Wattis disagreed, of course. He believed since he'd come up with the original ideas, the routines belonged to him. He pointed out, too, that I had no proof to back up my claims. The video footage only proves that the routines were designed exclusively for the Shammalars, not whose work had gone into developing them." She tilted her elegant neck for a moment. "Wattis was always careful with money, even when I first met him, but he always had a core of decency about him. I wouldn't have expected this behaviour from him. Of course, he'd seen a lot of lean years, and now that all seemed about to end. Does the prospect of money change a person's true character, I wonder, or merely reveal it?"

"He was unwilling to acknowledge what seems to be your perfectly reasonable claim to a share of the rights, but he didn't seem to have any great affection for material possessions." Salter paused for a moment. "I wonder why the money was so important to him. Could his unwillingness to share be because he needed it for something in particular?"

Wynn nodded knowingly. "Like Albert's investment, you mean?"

She didn't, but if Salter could just disguise her astonishment for a moment, she realized this might lead somewhere very important. She channelled her inner Jejeune and gave Wynn her best impassive face. "You know about that?"

Wynn nodded. "Indeed, I'm the one who introduced them. A couple of years ago."

Having entered Wynn's garden with no clear destination in mind, Salter now had so many directions to follow, she didn't know where to start. The woman indicated the house. "You look warm. We can continue our conversation inside, if you like. That is, assuming you have more questions, Sergeant."

She did.

The kitchen was meticulously neat, as Salter suspected it might be. But most importantly, it was cool, and there was a refrigerator with juice in it. She accepted Wynn's offer gratefully.

A dog that looked like the sort of prize you might win at a coconut shy at the Saltmarsh Fete trotted up, and Wynn gathered it up in her arms and ruffled its ears.

"Forgive me," said Salter, "but your relationship with Mr. Wright, it was purely … professional?"

"It was," said Wynn, unoffended. "Back then, as now, I tended to prefer the company of friends like Fitz here — less trouble than people, and a good deal more reliable. Isn't that right, Fitz," she said, nuzzling the dog. "You've not asked me for an alibi, Sergeant. For the night Wattis died. Do I need one? Just in case, I was picking up Fitz here from the vet in Norwich. A neighbour saw me just as I was pulling into the driveway with him. We said hello, didn't we, darling?" she said, nuzzling the dog again.

"That's that sorted, then," said Salter. "Can I ask how you know Albert Ross?"

For the first time in the interview, Wynn seemed to hesitate. She leaned back on the kitchen counter as if to consider her answer. "I'm Albert's sponsor," she said evenly. "I'm sorry, I thought that's why you were here. I assumed Albert would be a suspect, given his condition and the argument he'd had with Wattis earlier that day."

Salter's mind was reeling with questions; about how this woman knew of the argument, about whether Albert Ross might have talked to her about it. Or other things. But if being on interviews with Domenic Jejeune had taught Salter anything, it was that sometimes, silence asks the best questions of all.

The dog squirmed in Wynn's arms and she set him gently on the ground. "Go off and find your brother. I have two," she explained as the dog scurried away. "Fitz and Startz. They're identical siblings."

"So, was it you who brokered the arrangement between Wright and Albert?" asked Salter.

"No, not at all. Wattis mentioned the possibility that he might be coming into some money. I realize now he was talking about the royalties from the Shammalars musical, but at the time, I had no idea that was what he was referring to. He simply said if he did, he might be looking for a worthwhile investment, and I told him about Albert's plans for his own plant nursery. Wattis seemed genuinely interested. As you've seen, worldly possessions weren't really his thing. Oh, he'd loaded up on all the newest gadgets back in the day when the royalties were flowing in, but that was more because he could, rather than because he really wanted any of them."

"Did he already know Albert personally?"

"No, but he'd suffered a similarly difficult upbringing — little support, no encouragement, a person who'd never really had any faith shown in him. That, plus the fact that Albert was battling a debilitating illness, seemed to go to Wattis's heart.

As I say, he always had that side to him in the old days, the decent, compassionate one. Based on my own recent dealings with him, I have to say I'm surprised it was still there, but deep down somewhere, apparently it was."

A dog trotted briefly into the kitchen to drink from a steel bowl. Whether it was the one Salter had seen earlier, or its twin brother, she couldn't have said. She hesitated over her next step. Pursue the story first? Or the suspect? She knew Jejeune would have wanted the big picture, why Wright had changed his mind about the investment, how it all played in to motive. But Salter was keen to hone in on the suspect. She sensed there was something important in Wynn's connection to both men, and she held an irrational fear that it might all disappear unless she seized it now.

"When you say you're Albert Ross's sponsor, does that mean he's supposed to discuss his IED episodes with you in detail?"

"If he can. Mostly my role is to remind him he can control the anger and to suggest some other coping mechanisms, to counsel him how he might manage future situations. But yes, we do try to look at the triggers, the events leading up to the episode that brought it on."

"It might be in his best interest if you could tell me about any discussions you've had recently."

It was clear from Jennie Wynn's expression that she didn't agree. "The relationship between sponsee and sponsor is built on absolute trust. I'm afraid I couldn't reveal details about our conversations without Albert's permission."

Salter nodded in understanding. But if she couldn't get facts, Jennie Wynn's opinion might be almost as valuable. "I realize it's a difficult question, Ms. Wynn, but do you believe that if Albert was in the middle of one of his IED episodes, he would be capable of killing someone?"

Wynn drew in a deep breath, gathering her thoughts before answering. "Yes," she said finally, with the same certainty she had answered the other questions. She looked at Salter sadly. "He normally calls me the day after one of his episodes to discuss what he can remember before he blacked out. As I say, what brought it on, the triggers. He hasn't called me yet about the day of Wattis's death."

Salter understood the reason for Wynn's sadness. There was one very good explanation why Albert Ross had not called her this time to discuss what had brought on his episode. He was afraid of what else he might have to tell her.

22

Domenic Jejeune drew up his paddle and laid it across the oarlocks. He leaned to one side of the canoe and trailed his fingers in the water, creating a silver trail on the dark surface. The water was cold, and as clear as any he could ever remember. Above him, clouds the colour of pale sand trailed across a blue sky like flecks from an artist's brush.

Jejeune allowed the canoe to drift slowly as he rested, taking in the surrounding wilderness. The stillness around him was complete, and he let it wash over him. It seemed as if all of nature had drawn in its breath for the moment, to join him in listening to the silence. A brown shape drifted in to investigate his outstretched fingers, flashing away back into the depths as he twitched them. The fish was the first living creature he had encountered since he began paddling. Although the forest on both sides of the banks must have been teeming with life, all he saw was a dense unbroken screen of pine trees, and vast swathes of open land on the hillsides beyond them. This was a raw, wild beauty, nature on a massive scale, and he struggled to come to terms with it all. The park seemed impenetrable, the spaces overwhelming. He was an alien in the midst of it, drifting along on the river, separate from this place and yet surrounded by it. Perhaps it was this sense of disconnection that he found so unnerving; the knowledge that even now, so early into his journey, his own world was out of range and unreachable. We had come to rely on our connections so much, he thought, those wireless umbilical cords that bound us to the rest of humanity, and we felt such a dislocation when they were severed.

He looked at the tattered jacket on the seat beside him. Like the water, the air was cooler than he had expected, despite the sunshine, though it wasn't cold enough to require the additional layer of another coat. But that wasn't why he had brought it.

"That ugly tiger-striped one? Why do you want me to send you that beat up old thing?"

Though the sky outside his hotel window was still light when he had dialled Roy's number, he knew that three time zones to the east, darkness would have already fallen. Roy had answered on the second ring anyway. Jejeune had expected his brother-in-law's question about the jacket, but not his follow-up comment. "If you need a jacket, why don't you buy yourself a new one? They must have an outfitter up there in Fort Smith. If you're short of a few bucks, have 'em call me. I can give them my credit card number."

He wondered why he couldn't find more affection for someone who was always so ready to step up to help him. Roy had tried for a surprised tone when Jejeune told him his plans, but he knew the man had suspected his intentions from the moment he had flown up there.

"You plan on going into the park yourself? It's better to leave these things to the experts, Domenic. Besides, I'm sure your brother and this woman are both okay."

"The park authorities won't initiate a search until they are overdue. According to the plan filed with the park offices, that's not for another six days. Even then, their first response will be to treat them as lost."

"What makes you think they aren't?"

"I think Damian turned his tracker off deliberately. It went off four minutes after Prior's stopped working. If they had gotten into difficulties together, the devices would have ceased transmitting at the same time."

Roy's silence had shown he now realized this was why Jejeune had felt compelled to head up there. "Why would Damian turn off his tracker?" asked Roy eventually.

"Annie Prior applied for a permit for anthropological exploration, but there is still ice around the edges of the sloughs where the Whooping Cranes are coming in." There had been a pause, and Jejeune realized Roy was trying to work out the birding reference, rather than the obvious one. "The ground up here is still much too hard to do any excavations. Whatever Prior was intending to do in the park, it wasn't digging for artifacts."

Roy had been quiet for a moment. "Domenic, if she was mixed up in something illegal, you need to let the authorities handle this. Let me make some calls."

"I know Damian, and I think I can predict what he might do in these circumstances. They're both right-handed, so a search party will think they veered off the trails to the right and they'll concentrate their efforts in that direction. But Damian will know this, and if he doesn't want to be found, he'll be heading the opposite way. Whatever they're involved in, I stand a better chance of finding them than anybody else."

Even Domenic couldn't be sure whether he was making such tenuous claims to convince his brother-in-law or himself. But Roy had realized now that there would be no arguing him out of his course of action. He had agreed to FedEx out the jacket and wait before informing the authorities, but he'd ended their call with clear instructions. "You file a three-day plan with the park. That's a day in to the location where the transmitter was switched off, a day to search for them, and a day out. If you're not back by noon on the fourth day, I'll make sure they send in a search team. I'll tell them where to start, so if you need to look farther afield than the original site, leave a clear signal in which direction you went. And don't wander too far, Domenic. Out there, you need to make sure you know where you are at all times."

Drifting down the Little Buffalo River, thought Jejeune, as his mind returned to the present. He began paddling again, his steady industrious strokes seeming strangely at odds with the torpor of the early evening. A curious Raven swooped in over the canoe, its plumage almost purple in the waning sunlight. Set against the wide landscape, even the bird's great size seemed diminished. The Raven followed the river's course, flying low over the water ahead of him on slow, leisurely wing beats. If one's mind tended in such directions, it would have been easy to imagine it was Gaetan Robideau, in the form of a Spirit Guide, come to lead Jejeune towards his goal.

His destination was twenty kilometres farther down the river — a fifty-metre-square grid identified as the area from which Damian's inReach device had last transmitted a signal. Despite Roy's looming deadline, Jejeune knew he wouldn't be able to reach his goal today. He'd made a late start and soon the daylight would begin to fade as the sun dipped lower behind the trees. It would be necessary to find a place to camp before the darkness came. He eased the canoe in towards the bank, careful to avoid the sweepers, the graveyard of tree skeletons that lay just beneath the waterline at the river's edge. He tethered the craft to an overhanging snag and scrambled up the bank to assess the area as an overnight camping spot. He found a large outcrop of granite with a deep fissure running down the centre, as if some life-force trapped within the rock had clawed its way out. The opening would provide good shelter, and he set about gathering materials to build a fire at its entrance: added protection against the dangers that a night in this isolated spot might bring.

The fire brought him comfort that went beyond the warmth it offered. There was a satisfaction in having mastered this, the most basic of survival skills, and in a strange way it seemed to reassure him that he could exist out here until he achieved what he had come to do. Now, with his evening tasks complete, and his preparations made, Jejeune had nothing to do but to sit and marvel at the solitude. He looked around him in the fading light, taking in the quiet forest that fringed the clearing, and the stillness of the water below. There was no sound; no bird calls, no whisper of wind through the treetops. Not even the leaves stirred. Just a singing silence that made his ears ring with its emptiness. From his spot at the top of the riverbank, he watched the last of the daylight fade. The sky began a slow glide towards darkness, taking him through shades of blue he had never seen anywhere else, deepening in their intensity as the world around him surrendered its features to the coming night. Tomorrow he would head deeper into this wilderness. He wondered how much farther he would be from the world he knew, how much more removed from his previous life.

He awoke with a start, surrounded by silence. He had fallen asleep as soon as he lay down, exhausted by his exertions throughout the day. The fire had died down to glowing embers, yet it was still casting a strange, ghostly reflection in the night sky. But no, this was something more than reflected firelight. This light was draped across the heavens, moving in waves like billowing sheets. He watched, mesmerized, as flames of shimmering green leapt up, licking the night sky, morphing into deep neon and drifting out again to white, swirling, rippling, dancing on the winds that rode the wide plains of the northern skies. His mind struggled to come up with the scientific explanations he knew lay beneath the phenomenon, but the science didn't matter at this moment. This was a gift for the heart, the soul.

The northern lights, *the aurora borealis*: from somewhere deep within him sadness rose and settled in his heart. Lindy would have loved this. She would have held his hand and turned to him, her eyes brimming with tears, overwhelmed by the sheer beauty of it all. A wide swath of light cascaded down, unfurling like a curtain of pale green silk. It curtsied and bowed, and then it disappeared, carried away by some invisible force, as strange and mysterious as the one that had brought it. He watched until the show faded, searching the sky for answers it could not provide. Finally, he rolled over and closed his eyes, inviting the sleep that he knew would not visit him again this night.

23

"Cheyenne Bottoms must be about as far from any coastline as you can get in the continental United States, and yet it says here this place sees over half a million shorebirds during migration season. I suppose the reason I've never heard of it before is that I'm not a birder."

Traz gazed around, taking in the building's elegant architecture. Behind them, a bank of large windows followed a gentle curve around the edge of a small marsh. "I'm betting there's a lot of birders who've never heard of this place, either," said Traz. He was willing to indulge Verity's interest in this vast freshwater wetland in the middle of Kansas's agricultural landscape, and even credit it as being genuine. But he was aware, too, that while they were standing at the displays in the visitor centre, surrounded by people who were also marvelling over this natural phenomenon, she wouldn't need to answer any questions about what had happened at the diner. She'd crawled into the back seat of the Buick as soon as they left Denzley's Roadside Dinah, claiming tiredness and mumbling a promise about filling him in later. She'd feigned sleep, or otherwise, until he had pulled up in the visitor centre parking lot.

He joined Verity at a display of Whooping Cranes in a glass case. "You see them up close like this," said Traz, shaking his head, "and you realize just what stunning birds they are."

"Good job, too," said Verity. "It's charisma that attracts the cash. If they looked like the Attwater's Prairie Chicken, no doubt all that conservation funding would have gone to other causes."

She moved off and picked up a box holding what looked to be shell casings. Traz nestled in beside her. "Verry," he said in a hushed tone, "we need to talk about what happened back there."

She looked up at the wall map. "Let's take this drive," she said, tracing the route with her finger. She tapped the space at the end of the track significantly. "I think that'd make a dandy place for a talk."

They trundled along the narrow dirt road in silence. On each side ran a narrow, water-filled ditch flanked by a stand of reeds. Traz pointed out a duck skulking in the shelter of the vegetation. "Cinnamon Teal," he said. But before Verity could properly take in the bird's handsome rusty plumage and bright red eye, Traz gunned the engine and began speeding over the uneven surface. "Something interesting down here."

"Man, you birders have good eyes."

"There's a group of people gathered around a scope and they're all pointing excitedly. For us birders, that's sometimes a hint," he said with an ironic grin. They pulled up at the edge of a large body of water glinting in the midday sunshine. A group of birders were gathered around two spotting scopes, murmuring between themselves animatedly. Even Verity could tell there was something different here. This wasn't just the suppressed excitement that accompanied a normal bird sighting. There was real tension in the air. On the far side of the water she saw two Whooping Cranes, an adult and a juvenile.

They were standing just above the waterline, the light on their plumage like a faint sheen of dust. But Traz was not playing his bins on the birds. Instead, he was concentrating on a dense stand of narrow-leaf cattails that fringed the water.

"See it, to the left?" asked one of the women, looking through the nearest scope. She spoke in hushed tones although the birds were nowhere near close enough to be disturbed by human voices.

Traz had already seen it, but he murmured his thanks anyway. His eyes stayed at his bins.

"What, what is it?" asked Verity. "What are you looking at?"

Traz handed her his binoculars and pointed to a stand of pale grass just beyond the reeds. "A bobcat. It's stalking the birds."

Through the veil of grass, Verity saw a tawny shape. The bobcat's stare was focused on the young bird nearest the stand of reeds. The colt was still preening itself, utterly unaware of the danger that was approaching in such a deliberate, menacing fashion.

"We should call to see if there is a ranger nearby," she said. "Somebody needs to stop this."

"It's kind of hard not to get emotional, isn't it?" said the woman at the scope. "But it's just nature taking its course."

"It's not about being emotional," said Verity. "There's some pretty good rational arguments to be made for saving that bird. Based on the costs of all the programmes involved in restoring the wild Whooping Crane population, each bird represents an investment of thousands of dollars. That's a lot of money to spend on something to have it end up as bobcat food."

"People can't have it both ways, though," said the woman. "Even though they're a protected species, these cranes are wild. And that means they're subject to natural predation."

"But other prey species come from populations that already have viable genetic diversity. The world's entire population of migratory Whooping Cranes derives from fifteen individuals. With such a narrow gene base, the loss of any one individual is potentially far more damaging to the prospects for survival of the species." She looked at Traz. "We have to do something to save that bird."

One or two of the group had momentarily turned from watching the bobcat to focus on the discussion. Traz suspected they were as conflicted over the spectacle unfolding before them as the two women were, but no one offered a comment in support of either position.

"Well, I'm sure there's lots of differing points of view on these things," said the woman uncertainly.

"Not so much," said Verity, letting her frustration rise. "The importance of genetic diversity to species survival is pretty much agreed upon, as far as I know. I'm telling you, to allow the loss of such a valuable set of allele modifications when we could still do something about it would be a big mistake."

The woman seemed to stiffen at Verity's tone, but a momentary stirring among the other birders defused the standoff. The adult bird had wandered closer to the stand of reeds, but the watchers knew it was in no danger. The kick of a fully-grown crane was formidable, and it was something the bobcat would be keen to avoid. It was the smaller bird that the cat was concentrating on. It had crept slightly closer and now it was staring intently at the colt, frozen in position. The group watched in silence, but the bobcat showed no signs of moving.

"I'm sure the professional researchers all know a lot more about this than you or I," resumed the woman pleasantly, still watching through her scope.

"I'm pretty sure they'd all say this species needs as much genetic diversity as it can get," said Verity. "Each new generation represents one more round of genetic variance. To lose those advances, even for one breeding cycle, could be critical.

There might be vital epigenetic changes being carried by those alleles. We can still stop this. Does anyone have the number for the visitor centre?"

"It's moving."

The announcement snatched the group's attention away from Verity's request. They watched as the bobcat made its stealthy, deliberate progress towards its prey. It seemed impossible the predator could approach so closely without being detected. But with each hesitant, hovering half-step it set softly down among the grasses, it closed the distance to the unsuspecting colt. A few more footfalls and it would be in range to spring, to embed its needle-like claws into the young crane's neck and draw it in for a fatal bite from the powerful jaws.

"I can't bear this," said Verity desperately. "I can't believe I just have to stand by and watch this happen."

"I think it might be too late for any intervention now," said Traz, his eyes firmly pressed against his bins. "That bobcat's going to strike at any moment."

The young crane had its head turned away from the danger, cropping at its wing feathers. There was a shimmer in the grass as the bobcat drew itself into a launch position. The action unfurled like a slow-motion explosion. As the bobcat burst from its cover, the adult reared back, wings flailing and calling loudly. The startled colt looked up in alarm, the action taking its neck fractionally out of reach of the bobcat's outstretched paw. A claw made contact, but the cat couldn't embed it into the bird's flesh, instead spinning sideways and falling to the ground. It recovered and sprang again, but by now the adult had moved in, kicking wildly at the cat and allowing the colt to lift off into the air. The cat leapt once more, a valiant, spring-loaded effort that launched it high above the ground. But by now, both birds were airborne, twisting to distance themselves from the cat's final lunges.

Within seconds, the cranes had disappeared from view over the marshes and the bobcat had melted back into the cover of the grass. Stillness returned to the scene, only the ripples on the water whispering of the drama that had just unfolded on its shores.

There was a collective expulsion of pent-up breath and even a smattering of relieved applause. Traz watched as the contented group packed their equipment and moved off, the woman with whom Verity had exchanged views studiously avoiding eye contact now.

"And to think, there are people who say birdwatching isn't exciting," he said to Verity as the others left. "I can't believe that woman didn't pick up that you were an expert in this stuff, especially after you laid out your points so clearly."

Verity shrugged. "She wouldn't have paid no mind to me, no matter what I said, not delivered in this country twang," she said, over-extending the last word derisively. "Maybe if I'd fed my lines to you, to say in that cute Canadian accent of yours."

"Like a ventriloquist and her dummy, you mean?"

"Thought never crossed my mind."

The casual way Verity had brushed off the woman's dismissive attitude was in stark contrast to the passion with which she'd defended her position. There were a lot of layers to Verity Brown, thought Traz. It was time to start peeling away at least one of them. "Now we talk about the diner," he said.

She nodded and pointed to an observation point on the northern rim of the reserve. "Up there."

From their vantage point on the North Rim observation platform, the entire great basin of Cheyenne Bottoms spread out before them. The catchment area was a mosaic of grasslands and waterways, shimmering in the distance like a mirage.

"You think about what habitat restoration must cost in a place like this, and you weigh that against the thousands of dollars spent to preserve a single species." Traz inclined his head. "It does make you wonder."

"Priority-threat management versus eco-pragmatism. That's the battle for the soul of the conservation movement, right there." Verity shook her head doubtfully. "The greater good argument might work for human society, but I'm not sure it applies with endangered species. There's a continuum of DNA variations down through the ages, vitally important information we can tap into. That would all be lost if we had let a species like the Whooping Crane go extinct."

"Surely, in the case of Whooping Cranes, most of that information has already been irretrievably lost because the gene pool dipped so low."

Verity hesitated, as if Traz's objections had knocked her argument off track. "Seems to me, then, it's even more vital that we don't lose any more." She tilted her head slightly, as if to listen to the silence out over the reserve. "Pretty quiet here now, huh? Guess it wasn't always that way. During the war, B29 bombers used to fly practice runs over these lands. They'd drop bags of flour with detonators in them and fire off shells."

Traz turned to look at her. "I thought you'd never heard of this place."

"You should have paid more attention to the displays at the visitor centre. Those 50mm casings I was looking at were recovered from the reserve." She nodded. "There were five air bases in central Kansas back in those days." She paused and turned to look at Traz earnestly. "This area has always taken its military responsibilities seriously. Those coordinates we checked out this morning, Traz, up around Salina. They're near the old Schilling Air Force Base. There is still a lot of military equipment up that way."

He nodded. "I know. I saw the signs when we were getting close."

"Those MPs at the diner were a little twitchy about what we were doing up there."

"What business is it of theirs?" he asked sharply. "We weren't on their land. They don't have any right to question the actions of people just driving around the area."

"Yeah," said Verity, shaking her head dubiously, "the U.S. military isn't all that crazy about people telling them what their rights are, especially when it comes to protecting their facilities."

"I wasn't interested in their facilities. I was looking for Whooping Crane stopover sites."

"The thing is," she said cautiously, "that compound we drove all the way around in Oklahoma, that was a military facility, too. Vance Air Force Base." She looked at the tangerine Buick behind them, the metal flake paintwork glittering in the bright sunlight. "This is a pretty noticeable car, Traz, and it's been spotted near three military facilities in the past four days. That first place we stopped, in Texas, that was near Fort Hood."

"It's just where the coordinates took me," said Traz defensively. "It's understandable, though. A lot of those military bases cover huge areas of open land. They're well protected, and for security's sake they aren't going to be densely vegetated and overgrown. Cranes like that low, scrubby habitat, and if you throw in a couple of shallow ponds, you've got pretty much perfect habitat for a stopover."

Verity shrugged. "All I'm saying is, the car is on the military's radar now. If any more of those coordinates are going to take us close to other military establishments, I'd give them a miss."

Traz looked out over the stands of honey-coloured grass in the vast basin, swaying like fields of wheat. Above them, two

Northern Harriers danced across the sky in courtship. "Why didn't you want me to talk to them at the diner?"

"I thought it was best if they believed it was an American who was driving around these places. You're travelling on a Canadian passport. Our countries are supposed to be on friendly terms. I mean, I'm sure they spy on each other all the time, but they have to at least pretend they don't."

"I'm not a spy," protested Traz. "This is crazy. I wasn't doing anything wrong." He turned away in frustration. Damian's directive not to tell the authorities anything meant he couldn't even tell them he was innocent. But that didn't mean he was guilty. Of anything.

To the west, the sun was beginning to set, casting a pink blush over the sky above the wide-open farmland of central Kansas. Clouds were piled high on the horizon like layers of grey cotton. Perhaps they would bring rain. Traz wouldn't be here to find out. They had to head north. And whether the next set of coordinates led him to a military base or not, he intended to check them out.

24

Danny Maik recognized the woman as soon as he entered the magazine's offices. He had met Kate-Lynn long ago at the cottage, when they had both been part of a gathering to celebrate some long-forgotten success of Lindy's. They hadn't spoken since, but Saltmarsh was a small enough community that Danny had seen her a couple of times around town. The woman's expression suggested she remembered meeting Danny, too, though not where. In fairness, she probably wasn't searching her memory banks for one of Lindy's social functions. Danny hardly looked like someone you'd place in her circle of friends.

She shook her head at Maik's question. "No, Sergeant, I haven't seen Lindy for a couple of days." There was an assured efficiency about the way Kate-Lynn answered the question. The training of someone who made her living asking them, thought Maik. Based on what he knew of the office structure here, there was no official office manager, but this woman would have been the logical choice and had clearly taken on the *de facto* role anyway. "It's not that unusual around here, you understand. We have people zipping in and out all the time. Nobody really keeps track of anybody else's comings and goings."

There were three ways an interview usually went from here: people either squirmed uncomfortably and looked around for an exit, they stood blankly waiting for a follow-up question, or, when Maik was lucky, they reacted as Kate-Lynn did now. "Let me find you somebody who might be better placed to help you."

She returned a few moments later with another woman in tow. "This is Claire. She seems to have been the last one in the office to speak to Lindy. That was the day before yesterday, you were saying, Claire, about nine in the morning."

Maik lifted his eyebrows in admiration. If Kate-Lynn had been able to determine all this in the short amount of time she had been away, there was a career awaiting her in the Saltmarsh detective squad.

"Linds was talking to Jeremy," said Claire. There was hesitancy in her delivery. It might just have been nervousness, but it might have been something else. Whatever it was, Claire's timidity was heightened by the contrast to Kate-Lynn's easy confidence. Whether she was simply being helpful, or had also picked up the other woman's reticence, it was Kate-Lynn who supplied the details.

"Jeremy is the guy who delivers our coffee orders every morning," she explained. "He's a bit, well, awkward, socially. Has difficulty with personal space, appropriate comments, privacy. Nothing sinister, just a bit ..."

"Creepy." Claire looked around the office. "We all think so. But he's harmless enough. Fancies himself as quite the Romeo, but he's never tried it on with anybody here."

Maik followed Claire's gaze around the office. Most of the female staff carried the same air of self-assurance as Lindy and Kate-Lynn. Any man looking to make a nuisance of himself would undoubtedly have been given short-shrift by these strong, confident women. But the fact remained that they were young, attractive, and as far as Maik could remember, for the most part, unattached. That a young man, especially one as socially inept as Jeremy reportedly was, had not at least tested the waters raised some questions. Like whether, perhaps, he may have had a particular target in mind. "Did this Jeremy pay more attention to ... anyone in particular?" He wouldn't lead the women, though they would clearly understand where he was heading.

Kate-Lynn nodded. "He did always seem quite drawn to Lindy. You know, heading to her desk first, lingering a touch longer. But Lindy's always been a bit of a one for strays and waifs. It's that kind heart of hers. So, we never thought much of it."

Except a kind heart can get you in trouble in a lot of ways, thought Maik. "Is Lindy interested?"

Both women shook their heads. "Only in Jeremy's fantasy world," said Claire. "He keeps telling me he thinks they're on for a date at the pub. Honestly, I don't think Lindy would go within a mile of him."

Maik had heard enough. "Do you happen to know Jeremy's last name, or where he lives?"

Kate-Lynn shook her head. "No idea, really. I mean, he just started showing up one day with our orders, calling himself the coffee delivery service."

A service the owner of the coffee shop had failed to acknowledge when Salter had mentioned the idea the other day, Maik now recalled. "This Jeremy, has he been in today? Or yesterday?"

"I couldn't say. I don't order anything, so he never stops by my desk." Kate-Lynn looked at Claire, who shook her head. "Not today. I don't know about yesterday." The hesitancy was still there. She seemed about to say something more, but she drew it back inside at the last moment. Another time, Maik might have tried to soft-pedal his interest, made some joke about the dangers of depriving people of their daily croissant. But unease was starting to rise within him, and he wanted answers quickly. "Is that unusual, for him not to show up?"

"I think he does come every day, doesn't he, Claire?" Again, Kate-Lynn glanced across at the woman standing at her shoulder.

"There was someone watching Lindy," Claire said, releasing the news finally like an expelled breath. "I told her I had seen him."

Beside her, Kate-Lynn's eyes had widened in horror. Maik recognized the earlier hesitancy now for what it had been; regret that she hadn't informed someone sooner, hadn't acted in some way. Maik's charged, urgent questions about Jeremy had shaken this other secret loose. It was obvious now that Claire didn't think Lindy's was a casual absence. She believed it was tied to this watching man. And Maik thought she might be right.

"It wasn't this Jeremy?" confirmed Maik urgently. "Another man?"

Claire nodded. "I told her she should call the police, but she said she knew who was watching her. It was a friend of her ex. A policeman named Danny Maik."

Kate-Lynn's look morphed into astonishment. "Claire, this *is* Sergeant Maik."

"No," Claire backed away, shaking her head. Her eyes were fixed on Maik's. "No, no it's not."

"Claire, I can assure you it is. I've met Mr. Maik before."

"No, no, this isn't him, Kate-Lynn. Lindy told me she'd seen the other man following her, the one I saw watching. She said it was Danny Maik. But the person I saw wasn't this man." She'd started to back away farther, even raising her hands slightly as if to protect herself, afraid what this imposter might do next.

"Claire, for God's sake ..." Kate-Lynn moved forward, as if to grasp the other woman's shoulders, but Maik eased himself in to block her approach.

"This man Lindy thought was Danny Maik," he said calmly. "Could you describe him to me, please?" There was something about his tone that calmed Claire. He wasn't doubting her, trying to prove her wrong. He was simply clarifying something. And she could help.

"He was small, and he was wearing a hoodie, but the hood was down. He had a shaved head. He didn't look like a policeman at all. I thought he must work undercover."

A slow paralysis seemed to seep outward from Maik's core. He knew already, but he needed to ask the question anyway. It was his penance, for his carelessness, for letting his guard down. "Did this man have any other identifying features, Claire? Anything you noticed about him that was unique? Unusual?"

Claire nodded. "He had a lot of tattoos. On his neck. They stretched all the way round."

Maik turned to Kate-Lynn. His calm voice gave no hint of the sense of alarm rising within him. "If you could show me to Lindy's desk, I'd appreciate it."

Heads throughout the office turned to watch the procession as the two women led Maik through the maze of desks to the one by the window. He scanned the surface quickly and then slid the drawer open. Amid the paperclips and mints and a half-eaten bag of cheese puffs was an item that made Danny Maik's blood turn to ice. With a red light blinking to indicate all those missed messages, Lindy's muted phone was resting on a charging cradle. Maik reached in and removed it. As he gently slid the desk drawer shut, he looked around. This desk was the one Lindy had vacated seconds before an explosive set by Ray Hayes had blown out the wall beside her. Danny had fought through the burning rubble to save her then, but Lindy had refused to be intimidated into giving up this spot when she returned to the office. Though she likely wouldn't have even recognized it herself, Maik knew that somewhere deep inside, she would have trusted that if there ever was another threat to her, Danny would be there again to save her. But this time, she'd been wrong.

25

The low sun seemed to light the stand of birches from within, flickering through the trunks like a strobe light as Jejeune rowed past. Early-morning mist hung over the river, as if clouds had fallen from the sky and come to rest on the surface of the water. On the banks, the vegetation was still veiled in beiges and browns, waiting for gathering daylight to draw their green hues out onto this sepia-tinted stage.

Jejeune's canoe sent a chevron of silver ripples scurrying across the mirror-calm surface as it carved its path through the dark water. It seemed impossible that a few days ago he had travelled through the gentle landscape of Rouge National Urban Park and felt so removed from the urban population nearby. Now he was alone in genuine wilderness, and he was beginning to realize what it meant to experience the true isolation of the north. But he was beginning to feel more at ease in this place, too. Yesterday, he had struggled to cope with the sheer, overwhelming scale of everything, but today the disquieting vastness of the park had diminished, and in its place a sense of contentment began to settle within him. Almost as soon as he had begun his day's journey, he had detected movement — a banditry of Boreal Chickadees lisping their half-hearted calls as they flitted among the low branches of a spindly Jack pine. Other sightings had come to him since: Snow Buntings, White-winged Crossbills, and once, a Spruce Grouse. They were familiar enough species, but they felt important to him anyway, as if the park was slowly coming into focus, the details that had eluded him yesterday now gradually distilling into place.

His canoe rounded a long sweeping bend in the river and he saw two birds standing in a clearing in the vegetation on the far bank, their reflections slowly undulating on the surface of the water. They stood perfectly still, tall and stately, black masks clear against their white plumage. The pale sun backlit the mist rising from the river, so that the Whooping Cranes seemed to hover behind a veil of light. He stopped rowing and drifted slowly past the birds on the current. He made no attempt to reach for his binoculars. He knew that even if the birds weren't flushed, the very act of moving would shatter the pristine moment. The cranes remained in the same position, silent and serene, until the slow drift of the river carried the canoe out of view. But though the sighting had passed, the memory, Jejeune knew, would stay with him for a lifetime.

An opaque late afternoon sun sat behind a film of cloud, bathing the river in its diffused light. The soft limestone of the karst landscape began to disappear as the terrain became dotted with sloughs and bogs, and the gradual shift of topography told Jejeune he was approaching Whooping Crane breeding habitat. He was tired. He had been paddling all day, stopping only once for lunch and to stretch his legs before pressing on again. He realized now he could have used at least one more day to reach Damian's site and find his brother; he should be deep into this area by now, not simply on its fringes. But he had agreed on three days only with Roy, and he knew his brother-in-law would dispatch the authorities if he failed to report by the deadline. He needed to reach Damian first, to find out his real story, before any rescuers arrived. He thought about pushing on to reach his goal before nightfall, but night in this park, as he already knew, was overwhelming in its intensity. Trying to establish a camp in the all-encompassing darkness would be dangerous and foolhardy. It may be necessary to push his limits later on in this trip, but for this night, at least, safety was the better course.

Jejeune tied up his canoe and scrambled up a high bank that rose above the boggy terrain. He emerged onto the top of the rocky outcrop and realized he was on an esker, a ridge of sediment laid down by the retreating glaciers. A dense stand of mature trees and bushes had become established on the top, and the vegetation snaked away along the spine of the feature, a strange elevated forest hovering five metres above the surrounding land. From deep in the trees he heard a bird call. He didn't recognize it, and yet somehow it felt right that he shouldn't, here in this strange, otherworldly landscape. He pulled on his tiger-stripe jacket and stood at the edge of the esker, surveying the terrain before him. Wide creeks threaded their way through the muskeg ponds and the spruce bogs, where the returning cranes would soon establish their nests. From up here, high above the surrounding land, he could trace the swollen waterways back to their sources, narrow streams that ran like silver tears across the low foothills. The messages from Damian's inReach device placed his camp somewhere out there in that wilderness. Domenic couldn't reconcile the features of this landscape to those he had studied so carefully on the map before he came out here, but it was often that way between the abstract and the reality, he thought ruefully. The coordinates had fixed the location of Damian's last transmission on the banks of the Little Buffalo River, and in this place where any human activity at all would stand out, Damian and Annie Prior had been out here long enough to leave traces of their presence. Jejeune was confident he would recognize the spot when he came upon it tomorrow.

As he took a final, lingering look over the raw, savage beauty of this place, something stirred faintly in the back of his mind. But it wouldn't settle, and the challenges he faced in establishing his camp for the night soon drove it from his mind completely.

The night sky curved over Jejeune like a diamond-encrusted dome. The stars seemed closer than any he had ever seen, glittering brilliantly and filling the vast, impenetrable darkness all around him. The Milky Way draped across the sky like a wide, rippling veil of lace you could almost reach up and touch.

He gathered the tiger-stripe jacket in around him more tightly as he huddled by the fire. The afternoon had seen the temperature drop, and with the darkness had come colder winds. The night wouldn't test the limits of his −10°C sleeping bag, but it would be cold enough that he'd need to ensure he had enough fuel nearby to build up the fire several times during the night.

Beyond the space he had carved out of the darkness lay a place that had retreated into nocturnal stillness. The quietness still surprised him. He had expected the sound of creaking branches, of wind in the treetops, animal calls, wolf howls even. But no sounds carried to him on the night air, only the occasional crackle from the fire and the over-magnified noise of his own shuffling around the clearing he had chosen for his campsite.

So, when the sound came to him so clearly on the cold night air, he started, turning his head quickly. He strained his ears into the silence to listen for further sounds, the low scuffle of foraging, or a repeated pattern of footfalls. But he heard nothing. Only that one single snap of a branch that had told him there was something out there, some creature to which this forest, this night, was home. He peered across the fire at the wall of darkness on the far side. From it, Jejeune detected a shimmer of movement. The orange flames of the fire would be visible for some distance, even through the dense stands of trees up here on this ridge. The animal would have been aware of his presence from a long way off, and would have had plenty of opportunities to melt farther into the forest and pass by undetected. If it was approaching now, it was because it associated fire with humans. And it was not afraid.

Jejeune picked up his torch and shone it into the trees. He saw no movement now among the shadows. He lowered the light, slightly relieved that the beam had not picked up the sinister twin reflections of animal irises. But in a way he couldn't have explained, he could sense the creature was still out there. He stood up and began to move around the fire, playing his torch into the base of the trees once more. If the animal was readying itself for a foray into the clearing, Jejeune hoped his movements might unsettle it. It would show the predator he was alert, ready, and it might be enough to discourage an approach. He bent and drew out a branch from the fire, its end glowing in the darkness. He moved closer to the edge of the clearing, armed with his dual light sources. But the sound he heard now stilled him with fear. It was behind him, to his right, from a place where a single move out into the clearing would cut him off from the fire, leaving him stranded between his attacker and the dark bank of the trees behind him.

He turned slowly to see the shape silhouetted against the fire.

"Relax. Not even a bear's gag reflex could cope with a coat that ugly," said Damian.

Damian had asked for food as soon as the extended hug of greeting was over. "Actual food sounds very good right about now. I've been living on fruit and chocolate for the past week."

"Let's see," said Domenic as he dug in his pack, "chocolate-covered raisins, chocolate-dipped strawberries, oh, hey, I've got a Terry's chocolate orange here. That do you?" He flashed a grin at his brother and flipped him a package of Ramen noodles. Damian filled a steel mug with water and set it on the fire to heat up.

Domenic examined his brother closely as he worked. His unkempt hair and beard framed a lean face that sported a number of mosquito bites. He had several deep scratches on his forearms, but otherwise his backcountry skills had helped him to avoid the normal dangers of an extended stay in the wilderness. He wasn't sunburned, or dehydrated, and he hadn't picked up any injuries. Ones that were visible anyway.

Domenic watched his brother eat the bowl of noodles, controlling his pace, not bolting the food down. When he had finished, Domenic fished in his pack once again and brought out two cans of beer. "A new craft beer from Toronto. I brought them to toast when I found you," he said, tossing one to his brother.

Damian sipped the beer and pulled a face, holding the can away from him. "You know, with all the giardia in the water around here, I wondered if my survival might come down to drinking my own urine. I think I'll keep that as my Plan A, and save this stuff in case things get truly desperate."

"Your gratitude is underwhelming." Domenic's eyes went to the dark bank of trees beyond the clearing, from which

Damian had emerged. When he turned back, his brother was looking at him.

"Just me, Domino."

"You want to talk about it?"

Damian tried to put some nonchalance into his shrug, but it didn't really come off. "Accident. Okay if I fill you in tomorrow?"

The same accident that left my brother without a jacket or backpack? wondered Domenic. But he knew he would get more information if Damian volunteered it later than if he tried to prise it from him now.

"Is that when you lost your inReach device?"

Damian looked up sharply. "Are you carrying one?"

"Just my phone."

"Useless out here," said Damian. But he didn't sound disappointed. He looked across the fire at his brother, his eyes glistening in the flames that licked light from the darkness surrounding them. He nodded towards the tiger-stripe jacket. "You have some kind of psychic powers? How did you know I'd need a coat?"

Domenic shook his head. "I didn't. I just asked Roy to send this one up to me so I could bring it into the park."

"What for? You already have a jacket. We don't really go in for evening wear up here." Domenic smiled and shrugged off the coat. Damian stared at it again. And understood. That jacket, of all jackets, being worn by somebody standing out on the edge of an esker. Even if a person in the surrounding landscape was too far off to make out who was wearing it, the coat itself would be instantly recognizable. And so would the message it sent: *Help is here.*

Damian crushed the beer can and put it back into the pack. As he stooped, the firelight painted his skin a ruddy orange. "You have a spare sweater?" he asked. "I'm going to get some sleep. It's been a long few days."

"Take the sleeping bag," said Domenic.

Damian shook his head. "I'll layer up. With one more sweater and this lovely coat you brought, I'll be way warmer than I have been for the past few nights. I'll be fine." He looked at his brother seriously. "Tomorrow we'll talk, okay?"

Domenic watched as his brother bedded down beside the fire. It had been a long few days for him, too, but he could wait one more for some answers. He had found Damian, out here in Wood Buffalo National Park, and he was safe. Not much else mattered tonight.

26

Lauren Salter liked walking through the streets of Saltmarsh after dark. The sound of traffic was all but absent, and apart from the reassuring lights from behind the curtained windows, there was little evidence of human presence. There was a sense that the town was at rest, safely tucked away behind its doors. But as the daughter of a fisherman, it was to the water that Lauren always seemed inexorably drawn. During the turbulent times when her marriage was falling apart, it was here along the quiet waterfront of Saltmarsh harbour that she'd found her sanctuary. The faint scent of salt in the air, the gentle lapping of the water against the seawall: these were the dressings for her wounded spirits. And now, when it seemed that she was facing another breakup, as her infant child gradually slipped away into boyhood, it was to the soothing waters inside the harbour walls that she once again found herself turning for comfort.

The waterfront was as quiet as it always was at this time of night. The moon parted a veil of clouds just enough to quilt the dark surface of the water with points of light, but around her, the quayside was in darkness. She sat on the seawall, mesmerized by the slow rise and fall of the water in front of her.

The sound of a footfall startled her even before the voice came. "I've been looking for you."

She rose and turned to see Albert Ross filling her field of vision. The phrase carried many connotations and Salter searched the great, hulking figure for context, but found none. Ross was standing so close to her that she would have taken a step back if she had not been pinned against the water's edge.

"Why is that, Mr. Ross?" she asked uneasily.

"You think I hurt Wattis. And that's a problem, see. A big problem."

She wasn't sure what Ross's agenda was, but there were a number of places they could have talked about Wattis Wright. There was no need to follow somebody to a dark, quiet waterfront. Not unless you wanted to make sure what you said went no further.

"I don't know what happened to Mr. Wright. Do you think you did it, Mr. Ross?" She eased into a casual sidestep and continued manoeuvring herself around until she had the reassuring mass of an old stone-built warehouse behind her instead of the dangerous uncertainty of open water. Ross turned his body as he tracked her progress. He made no move to stop her, but his breathing was becoming more rapid and his eyes darted warily. She had intended to continue circling until she had an open pathway to the street, but a large metal skip blocked her way. It was jammed against the wall of the warehouse, and to go around it, she would need to step out towards Ross. With him so close, it could easily be interpreted as a confrontational gesture. Salter eased back into a shallow doorway set into the warehouse wall. She felt behind her, keeping her eyes on Ross. But the door was locked.

"It shouldn't still be inside me." The man shook his head angrily. "It should be gone. It should be gone. GONE!"

Behind Ross, the waters of the harbour glistened like black oil. The man's building anger was starting to emanate from him like a scent. But as much as she wanted to end this, to de-escalate things to a safe level, perhaps here in the quiet darkness of the deserted harbour, she could unlock the secrets trapped inside him. If only she could find the right key. "Is it regret, Albert? Is that what's inside you? Are you feeling remorse for what you did that night, for going to Wattis Wright's house and hurting him?"

Ross was shaking his head now, a constant action in response to Salter's string of questions. "No more questions. My turn to talk now. My turn. My questions. Not yours. MINE!"

But despite her rising unease, Salter couldn't let it go. "Do you have something to tell me, Albert? Your sponsor would want you to. You know she would. Why don't we call her, and you can ask her?" Salter took out her phone and began to scroll for the number.

"No calls." Ross snatched at the phone from Salter's grasp with a lightning-quick grab and threw it violently to the ground. She heard it shatter, but she didn't watch the pieces skitter across the cobblestones. Her eyes stayed on Albert Ross, on the angry, heaving bulk of his body, on the flushed, wild-eyed face, now so close to hers she could feel the heat coming from it. Salter wondered if someone would hear her if she called out. Or would her shouts of alarm be a trigger for him? Perhaps he'd feel he needed to do something to stop them.

"This is probably not the best place to chat anyway," she said with a light laugh that did nothing to hide her nervousness. "Let's do this later, shall we?" She made a move to brush past him.

"NO. NOW. We do it NOW!" He grabbed her arm and spun her around, jamming her against the rough bricks of the warehouse wall. "You don't ignore me. You don't walk away. You stay and LISTEN." He stepped forward and closed the gap between them until she could see the pores in his skin, smell the sweat. "You don't go anywhere. You stay here and listen to me." He jabbed a giant finger into her chest, and she stutter stepped back into the doorway to retain her balance.

"Assaulting a police officer is a serious criminal offence, Mr. Ross," said Salter firmly. "You're going to go home now and try to calm down. And when you've got your anger under control, we'll hold a formal interview. But we are not, I repeat not, going to discuss anything more about this case tonight. Do you understand me?"

But Albert Ross was slipping away; she could see it in his eyes. Only this great, heaving shell would remain, filled with an animal-like rage, coursing through it with such force it was already making his hands tremble. Salter swallowed hard, tasting the metallic tang of fear in her mouth. He was losing control. Soon he would be at a place where she couldn't bring him back. She looked around, but there was no steel table filled with potted plants, no chair; nothing to tether him to this world, this place of rational thought. All that stood between Albert Ross and the abyss of his rage was her, newly promoted Sergeant Lauren Salter.

"We're going to end this now, Albert," she said. Her voice sounded calm, confident. Would Ross hear the hollow echo of fear inside the words? "We're both going to go home, and in the morning you can come into the station and tell me whatever it is you want me to hear. I'm going to leave now."

"NO. You listen to me. To ME." He slapped his chest with his open hand so hard he reeled back slightly. He clenched his jaw in frustration. "You want to pin this on me, fit me up for it?" he hissed through gritted teeth. "Well, I've got something to say about that. Let me ask you —"

"No, Albert, I don't want to fit anybody up. I just need to know if you remember anything about that night."

"No!" he shouted. He struck the skip with a violent punch, so hard it shuddered. A rat that had been hiding beneath it gave a shriek of alarm and ran out. "NO!" he shouted again, louder now, lashing out with a kick that dented the metal. "NO!" he bellowed, stomping down on the metal chain that secured the skip to the wall. "NO. NO. NO!"

Salter moved towards him. "Mr. Ross ... Albert, you need to calm down. Stop now."

"NO. NO. NO," he roared again, kicking at the chain.

"I won't tell you again, Mr. Ross. Step back."

The fist was like a hammer blow to her breastbone, sending her reeling back into the doorway. He bunched the front of her jacket and slammed her hard against the wooden doors behind her, knocking the breath from her. "You stay here and you listen. You stay here and you listen. You stay here and you LISTEN." His eyes rolled around in his head like marbles, wild, unseeing, filled with rage.

She pushed back against him and he started back, startled, as if she had just swum into focus in front of him. He lunged towards her again, grasping her jacket even tighter, clenching his other fist tightly at his side. "You won't listen," he shouted. "I try to talk and you won't listen." He shoved her back hard against the door again, raising his fist to eye level and drawing it back. She crouched back against the door, feeling her shoulder blades against the wood as she raised her arms instinctively. Words were her only defence now. Salter reached down inside herself and found a calm tone from somewhere.

"Stop, Albert. You're in control." She looked into the angry burning eyes, trying to find some connection in there, some flicker of the person Albert Ross could be. But only blankness stared back at her. "You get to say what happens here. That's a good thought, isn't it? Those feelings don't control you. You're stronger than them. You're the one who gets to decide that everybody goes home safe and sound tonight. Nobody else, Albert. Just you."

The pressure of his grip had not lessened, but she felt the judder as he drew in a breath. And another. And another. He lowered his fist, letting his arm dangle limply by his side, and slowly released her clothing from his other hand. He stood before her with his head bowed, his eyes focused unseeingly on the cobblestones at his feet.

"That's good," said Salter. Her tone was the one she used with Max, when a dispute between them had run its course. No recriminations, it said, no lingering aftermath. Just understanding, and rebuilding. She was trembling, but in the darkness of the doorway, she knew Ross couldn't see it. She needed him not to have any reminders of what had just happened, of what he might be capable of. He just needed to hear the normalcy of her voice now, the calm, measured tone of someone who was concerned for him.

"You must be tired."

He nodded. "Tired, yeah."

"Your house is only about five minutes from here. Why don't you go home and have a lie-down. You could get into your bed, Albert. You could rest. Does that sound like something you'd want to do?"

"Rest, yeah." He took in a deep breath and sighed it out with a low, mournful sound. "It's the words," he said softly. His voice had a quavering edge to it now, as if he might burst into tears at any moment. "When I start like that. They're a sign it's coming." He shook his head gently, as if he was trying to dislodge something. His huge face was still bathed in sweat, his hair plastered to his forehead. But his breathing had returned to normal now, and Salter risked a tentative question.

"The words you said to Wattis? Did they make you do something?"

"A portal." He nodded at the description. "That's what Jennie says. They're a portal for my anger to come through." He shook his head again. "Can't have that. Can't let it out." He didn't move for a long moment. He stood there hovering over her, still pinning her inside the narrow doorway with his bulk, but not threatening anymore. He stared down at the cobblestones again.

"But if I did it, why is it still here?" The words were so quiet, she wasn't sure he was talking to her. She wasn't even sure he was aware of her presence any longer. But when he looked up into her eyes finally, she could see that he knew she was listening to him. "Why haven't they gone? The feelings? If I had killed Wattis, shouldn't they be gone now? Shouldn't the anger be over? It should be gone. So why is it still with me?"

Salter couldn't answer his question, but she knew any more talk of the anger trapped inside him could cause it to build again. "You need to sleep, Albert," she said softly. "Go home now. We'll talk later. We'll talk all you want. You can talk and I'll listen. But now you need sleep."

He nodded mechanically. "Sleep, yeah. Sleep."

Salter listened as the heavy footfalls receded into the night, but she waited a few moments before she emerged from the doorway. With silence settling over the harbour again, the rat had returned and now it began scurrying along the base of the warehouse wall towards her. But Lauren Salter didn't fear the creatures of the night. She had seen the rage inside a man called Albert Ross, and that held a terror all its own.

27

Damian was standing at the edge of the clearing, looking up into the trees, when Domenic awoke.

"Coffee's on," said Damian, nodding towards the campfire. From the treetops, the short, rasping birdcall Domenic had been unable to identify the previous day came down to him.

"What is that?"

"Western Tanager, but he's deep in. You didn't do your homework?" A review of the park's species, Damian meant, of the songs and field marks of unfamiliar birds Domenic would be likely to encounter in the park. A pre-trip review was standard procedure for birders visiting a new area; at least it was for those who had the luxury of prior planning.

"I thought I might meet a good birder up here," said Domenic sardonically. "Know any?" He paused for a moment. "It's tomorrow," he said.

Damian nodded slowly. He came back to the fire and sat beside his brother, cradling his coffee mug between his hands. "The person I came in here with is dead," he said, staring down into the mug. "Drowned. Her name was Annie Prior."

"An accident, you said."

Damian moved his head. "She took on some Cat Six rapids with no equipment and no whitewater skills."

"You didn't try to stop her?"

"I was too far away." He turned to face his brother. "There was nothing I could have done to save her, Domino."

Domenic could see his brother believed it was true. So why was there this guilt behind Damian's eyes, a haunted look that went beyond regret, beyond sorrow, even? If Damian had come to terms with the truth, what was it that he was blaming himself for? Domenic waited, but his brother had retreated into his thoughts. He seemed in danger of becoming lost in them.

"What were you two doing out here?"

Damian shrugged. "She hired me to trap some cranes. She'd already filed her study plan, and received clearance from the authorities, but her crew had bailed on her at the last moment. She said she'd asked around and heard I had some experience in that area. Couple of weeks, three at the most. Premium rates." Damian turned to his brother. "She was desperate, Domino."

Domenic shook his head. Money and a damsel in distress; Prior couldn't have homed in on Damian's trigger points any more accurately if she were his psychiatrist.

"I thought she was talking about catching chicks. You know, drop from the 'copter, run 'em down, football tackle, measurements, samples, tags, and release. Under eleven minutes or you abandon the whole operation. But those flightless colts won't be around until July. Turns out she wanted me to trap adult cranes, just arriving at the nesting grounds."

"Isn't trapping a fully-grown crane a big ask?"

Damian nodded emphatically. "Especially up here. In the winter down south you can habituate them to a bait trap and spring lure them, but up here, they have all the food they need, plus you hardly have any solid ground to work with. It's all these swampy muskeg bogs, especially around the nesting areas."

"But you told her you could do it?" Domenic paused. "In fact, you told her you were the only one who could do it. You convinced her that it must have been fate that had drawn you together like this."

Damian gave a rueful smile. "I earned my money, Domino. It was hard work: dirty, cold, dangerous. Those birds kick hard and have sharp beaks. You get a hood on them as fast as you can, but they still land a shot occasionally." He pointed to one of the long scratches on his arm. "But we got the three birds she wanted."

Domenic stood up and walked to the edge of the esker, looking out over the flat, still landscape in the distance. Beneath a mottled grey canopy of clouds, large outcrops of dark spruce and grassy tussocks dotted the land. In between them, algae had turned the water in the boggy pools into swirling rainbows of colour.

"Finding three specific birds out there," he said, "that's some impressive tracking."

"They'd been fitted with VHF collars."

Domenic turned in surprise. "Not GPS or satellite tags?"

"Those are fine for telling you where the birds have been, or what their route is, but if you want to actually locate a particular individual, you need to go old school, boots on the ground. I felt like I was channelling my inner David Attenborough, wandering around the landscape, sweeping the antennae back and forth. You'd think a five-foot-tall white bird would be easy enough to see, but they can be amazingly hard to locate when they don't want to be found. I'm telling you, without those VHF collars, we'd never have been able to find them." Damian stood up abruptly. "We should get going. There's a storm brewing and we've got a long way to go. May as well get a few klicks under our belt while the weather holds."

It was Damian's way of saying he had revealed enough for now. There would be more to the story, far more. But Domenic knew it would be a slow process to get to it all. Between the brothers, it always was. He moved off to wash out the coffee cups and when he returned, Damian was surveying the land in the distance. "Portaging across there is going to be no picnic," he said. "There's no eskers or moraines running that way, meaning we'll have to slog our way through the mud. The locals call that stuff loon shit. It's like glue; it'll suck the boots right off your feet if you're not careful."

"Why would you want to portage?" asked Domenic, puzzled.

"Those aren't established waterways out there, it's a floodplain. Most of that water is barely shin-deep. There are rocky outcrops and tree snags all over the place just below the surface. Run a canoe through there, and they'd tear the bottom out in no time flat." Damian shook his head decisively. "Trust me, the only way to get this canoe safely back to the Little Buffalo River is to carry it."

Domenic looked shocked. "We're *on* the Little Buffalo River."

"Erm, no," said Damian, digging deep to draw up every last ounce of condescension from the words. "This is a tributary of some other river, almost certainly uncharted. What made you think you were on the Little Buff?"

"I hitched into the park with a guy. We put the canoe in the back of his truck and he said he'd drop me off at the Little Buffalo boat launch. He said he knew where it was."

"Was he a park employee?"

"A writer. He was up here researching locations for a mystery novel."

Damian shook his head incredulously. "Number one rule for backcountry travel, Domino, try to avoid taking advice from anybody who earns his living by making stuff up. You put in at the wrong spot. The Little Buffalo is about five kilometres east of here." He became serious. "You were lucky. This is not Ontario cottage country, where your neighbour is a couple of hundred metres away and all of a sudden you're Davy Crockett. There are ten countries in Europe that are smaller than this park. This wilderness is the real thing. It's majestic and magnificent and it will pour its beauty right into your soul. But it can also kill you if you don't respect it."

Domenic looked at his brother blankly as the information sunk in. He had planned it all meticulously, mapped out his route, worked out the timings and the distances. But encountering Damian had come down to sheer luck and nothing else. If his brother had travelled in the other direction, or not come far enough this way, or at this time, they might never have crossed paths. All Domenic's planning, all his preparations, had counted for nothing. Only fate decided what happened out here. The thought stunned him to silence.

The clouds had taken on a dull sheen, like unburnished steel. Damian looked at the sky dubiously and then out over the film of dark water lying over the plain, glistening against the pockmarked landscape. "There's a lot more water than when I came across. It's been raining up in the hills and the runoff is beginning to gather down there." He paused and turned to his brother. "I'm curious. How did you know to look for me on the Little Buff anyway?"

"Roy told me."

"Roy Ducannon? Our brother-in-law? I wouldn't have thought he'd be the obvious choice for you to go to for help. You two changing your minds about each other after all this time?"

"We've been working together on something else. He said your comms had gone down and your last inReach message was from the banks of the Little Buffalo River."

Damian pointed to a low bank of cloud hanging close to the horizon like a grey mountain range. "Storm clouds are starting to gather," he said. "We should get going."

The subject of Damian's inReach device, and the information it might reveal, was apparently one more subject to be left behind in a hurry. But Domenic already knew the secrets it held. They were in the form of coordinates sent to their mutual friend Traz. What he didn't know was their significance. And Damian was clearly anxious to keep it that way.

28

The figure was silhouetted against the window on the far side of the room, but the man was not looking out. He was staring in Lindy's direction. But not at her. His face was expressionless, his eyes still, as if he were alone in the room. Perhaps he was. Perhaps this woman he had abducted and brought here and tied to a chair was as irrelevant to him as his unfocused gaze seemed to suggest.

The fear was still with her, as it had been from the moment she was seized. But the raw, naked terror of her abduction had given way to something calmer. At first, in the stifling confines of the Volkswagen's boot, she had truly believed that she was going to die. But the fact that he'd brought her here, to this place, meant something. She recognized that, and the thought brought her some small measure of reassurance. He could have killed her in the car park, if he'd wanted to. He had overpowered her so quickly, she would have been able to offer little resistance. So, yes, even though there was still fear, even though she recognized she was still in danger, and was uncertain of what might be awaiting her, there were tiny shards of light in her darkness. And this room, in this place, was one of them.

Lindy wasn't sure whether to speak. She ran the risk of letting him hear the fear in her voice, confirming it for him, even though he must already suspect it. Should she remain quiet, in the hope that he might take her silence as strength, a sign of resistance she knew she would have no hope of ever summoning in reality? Detachment or engagement? Her life might depend on getting the answer right.

Lindy played her tongue over her lips. They felt rough and cracked. "I wonder if I could have a glass of water. Please."

The man showed no signs of having heard her. He remained motionless, as if his stare was simply to assess whether the rope binding the woman's arms to the back of the chair was fit for purpose.

"I'm not sure what this is about," she began again, her voice finding lightness from somewhere, "but I give you my word I'm not planning to try anything. I'm just really thirsty. For some reason, my lips feel sore."

"They reacted to the adhesive on the tape I put over your mouth. It'll clear up now the source of the irritant has been removed."

The man's straightforward response left Lindy struggling to come up with a reply. But his composure was no act. There had been no signs of nervousness at all since they'd arrived — no pacing, no checking the curtains, no shallow breathing — just a steady, meticulous preparation of the room for a long stay with a captive.

"You were put in the car boot with minimum force," he said in the same flat tone as before. "And taken out. There might be a couple of bruises on your arm. Nothing more than that."

Lindy twisted slightly but the rope held fast. "No. I think I'm fine. Really. But that water —"

"They'll want to speak to you, to have proof I haven't already killed you. You'll be asked about your health. First question, guaranteed." The man turned his dead-eyed stare on to her. "So now you can give them a detailed answer, can't you?"

His voice carried the indifference of somebody who was utterly in control of his situation. And knew it.

"It's only fair to tell you there's been a police officer watching out for me," said Lindy, reaching for a tone that suggested she was being helpful, rather than threatening. "He'll know by now that something's happened to me."

"We're going to call him in a few moments to confirm it. And do remember to tell him who's holding you." He gave a cold smile. It was the first sign of any emotion Lindy had seen from the man, even if it was far from positive.

"Who's holding me? I don't even know who you are."

The man considered her comment, staring at her face carefully. "You really don't, do you?" He tilted his head slightly. "It was his best chance of making it work, I suppose."

"Making what work? What are you talking about? Who?"

"Yeah, that's just like him, come to think of it. Considers himself quite the mastermind, doesn't he?"

Lindy rallied a little, all thoughts of the water forgotten for the moment. "If this is about Domenic, you should know it's over between us. He left me. Went back to Canada. We're not together anymore." She tried a brave smile, a tiny gesture looking for sympathy, some connection with the human being inside this creature that seemed to have nothing but an echoing emptiness within him.

"So, it's all over between you, is it?" The noise the man made might have been a laugh. "Is that a fact?"

He took out a phone and stared down at the screen. "Did you know," he said without looking up, "when tactical teams make a rescue attempt, it's the experienced ones they send in first? Understandable, I suppose. You'd want a bit of know-how at the sharp end of things. Trouble is, if that door there had been wired," Hayes nodded towards the front of the building, "to an explosive device, say, as the first ones through in response to some panicky cry for help, they'd be the ones to cop it." He began dialling a number, still maintaining his casual, conversational tone. "The thing is, these longer-serving types, they're the ones more likely to have families. Hard to imagine what that would be like, knowing you were the one who'd caused them to come here, the one directly responsible for their families having to live the rest of their lives without their husbands, their fathers." He shook his head ruefully and held the phone to his ear. "Sleep would be very hard to come by with that on your conscience, I would think. You'd see the faces of all those little fatherless kids, all those tearful wives, every time you closed your eyes. Terrible thing, sleep deprivation. I've seen its effects firsthand. Oh, here we go. It's ringing. Feel free to tell him anything you like."

Maik had been sitting at his desk, cradling Lindy's phone in his hand. He'd switched it to vibrate mode, but there was no danger he was going to miss a call. The phone would be staying with him until it rang. He answered it before the second pulse. "Lindy?" But his tentative tone suggested he already knew it wouldn't be.

"Sergeant Danny Maik. I suspected you'd have the sense not to hand that phone in. You'll know who this is."

Although he had never heard the voice before, Maik knew. "Do you have Lindy? Is she all right?"

"Pardon my manners. I should have told you this call is on speaker," said Hayes flatly. "I'm going to let this article have a word now." He held up the phone to Lindy's mouth.

"Hi, Danny. So this is a bit of a mess, huh?" Maik could tell she wanted it to sound playful, but her voice let her down, quavering almost as soon as she began to speak.

"It's a very good sign that Mr. Hayes is letting you talk to me like this," said Maik. *Give me something, anything that might help me find you.*

"I'm not hurt. I'm being treated well." Lindy looked across at Hayes to see if her positive comments were earning her any points with her captor. He was looking down, fiddling with another phone with his free hand, but that didn't mean he wasn't paying attention. "In fact, I'd be prepared to say there's really been no crime here at all. We could still put it all down as a misunderstanding. I'd go along with that. Honestly, I would."

Maik didn't even try to encourage the idea. "Is there enough air in the room where you're being held? Enough light?"

"He's asking if there's a window," said Hayes, still looking down at his phone. "He wants to know whether you can see anything that might be a clue as to where you're being held."

"All I can see are a few birds," said Lindy. "No idea what they are. You know me, could be sparrows, could be the national bird of Hong Kong for all I know. I'm sure Domenic would recognize them, though."

Hayes tutted and took the phone away from Lindy's mouth, sighing loudly. "Is it any wonder the intelligentsia in this country despair at our journalists? We don't ask much; pay attention to the spelling, try to get the dates right. But still, you might expect better from one who's supposed to be among the brightest and the best. As I'm sure even the sergeant here could tell you, Hong Kong is not now and never has been a sovereign state. As such, it wouldn't ever have had a 'national' anything." The shrill ringing of Maik's desk phone startled him. "You'll want to answer that," Hayes told him.

Maik picked up the receiver as Lindy's phone went dead. Hayes's voice sounded tinny through the landline, more distant and disembodied than the call from the mobile. "As of twelve thirty-two today, Lindy Hey is alive," said Hayes formally. "Detective Sergeant Danny Maik will receive a call on a separate line, and I will give him details of my demands. Meeting these demands represents the only hope that Lindy Hey will remain alive. If any other police officer besides Sergeant Maik becomes involved, she will die. If that happens, I will send a recording of this call to media outlets, and post it on the internet, so everybody will understand that her death was a direct result of the failure by senior members of the Police Service to follow a simple set of instructions."

Lindy's phone rang again as the landline went dead. "Okay," said Hayes abruptly, "when the car was wired to kill this one, there was evidence left at the scene placing me there."

"Was there?"

"A word to the wise, Sergeant, those who choose to engage me in a battle of wits usually find themselves overmatched."

Maik could think of one person who hadn't, but he let it go. It was the second reference to Hayes's own intelligence. It was something that seemed to be important to him, and that made it worth keeping in mind. "The bookmark," said Danny.

There was a pulse of silence. It might have signalled satisfaction on Hayes's part. "The bookmark," he said finally. "The one with the birds on it. Domenic Jejeune is going to return that bookmark to me personally."

Maik's heart completed a couple of beats before he spoke. "I'm sure you already know the inspector is out of the country."

"Ah, yes, the breakup. You've seen them together, Sergeant, the way he looks at her, the way he is when he's with her. Did anybody really think that I'd believe it was all over between them? Frankly, the whole thing is a bit insulting." Hayes allowed himself a second's pause. "Now, I doubt you'll have told him anything just yet. You'll have wanted to see if you could sort this out by yourself." He gave a short, cruel laugh.

"So, how's that going, Sergeant Maik?" Hayes didn't wait for an answer. Perhaps he already knew enough about Danny not to expect one. "I realize it will take him some time to get back, but I would advise him to start making his plans as soon as possible. Every moment the inspector delays, the danger to the merchandise here increases."

Maik's shame burned within him. He gripped Lindy's phone so tightly his knuckles turned white. "Lindy Hey, that's her name, not *the merchandise*, not *the article*, and if anything happens to her, Hayes, I'm going to be your judge and jury. You seem to know a bit about me, so I'm sure you already know how far I'd be willing to go to settle a score."

"Not the time for threats, Sergeant, especially empty ones. You'll want to get going. You've got some arrangements to make. I'll call this number in forty-eight hours, and when I do, I'll be expecting to be able to conduct my business with Chief Inspector Domenic Jejeune directly. If I can't, then you'll all need to come to terms with the consequences."

Maik looked down at the phone in his hand for a long moment after the line went dead. The bookmark was three thousand miles away, and the person who had it wasn't returning anybody's calls. Forty-eight hours; it was a popular deadline lately. And now, there was additional significance to it. Because unless he could find Ray Hayes by himself, Danny believed that was how long Lindy had left to live.

29

There was a constant whip crack of willow saplings as they passed, and as the lead trailblazer of their portage, Damian bore the brunt of the punishment. Domenic considered himself to be in reasonably good shape, but it became clear early in their journey that Damian's time in the park had attuned his body far better to the rigours of crossing this terrain. It went without saying that Domenic wouldn't ask for a break, but he offered no argument when Damian finally got lashed by one willow sapling too many and called a halt, as much for mental respite as physical.

Domenic lowered the canoe from his shoulders and sank gratefully to the ground, bone weary and exhausted. "How far is it back to the park boundary once we get to the Little Buffalo?"

Damian looked up from tending a willow-inflicted wound and shrugged. "Forty kilometres maybe. Downriver. With the two of us paddling, going full-on, we should be out in two days."

"I can't help feeling if we're going to be working this hard anyway, it might be worth heading straight north over land until we could pick up the Great Slave River. If you know the approximate coordinates of where we are now, I might be able to work out which is the shorter route."

"Without any paper? How are you going to keep track of all those trig calculations?"

"After I get each answer, maybe you could just remember the numbers in your head," suggested Domenic.

"Like that guy in *Rain Man*, you mean?" Damian shook his head dubiously. "That'd never work, obviously."

"Why not?"

"Well, if I'm that guy, that would make you the Tom Cruise character." He looked at Domenic frankly. "As your brother, it's my job to tell you the hard truths, and bro, you ain't no Tom Cruise."

Domenic gave his brother a weary grin. "I still don't understand why we couldn't just backtrack on the river I came in on. At least we'd have been going in the right direction."

"Yeah, well, if you move back into the frying pan from the fire, you're going in the right direction. There could be a couple of branches to that river, or five, or ten that you didn't even notice on your way down. Wandering off course is not a good idea up here. You get lost in this place, you stay lost. Better we stick to a route at least one of us is familiar with."

Domenic was still coming to terms with how far off course he'd veered, and how easy it had been to become totally, irretrievably lost in this landscape. If his brother hadn't shown up, who knew where he might have ended up? Damian's words were still with him. This was a place of stark, sweeping beauty. It could overwhelm you until you felt your heart might almost explode with the sheer scale of it all. But it was a dangerous place to be if you weren't prepared to respect its threats. And sometimes even if you were. He moved off to the edge of a small stream nearby to fill his water bottle.

"I wouldn't," said Damian. "Giardia's bad out here where the water is shallow. You don't want to spend the rest of this trip fighting beaver fever. The water quality is going to be better on the Little Buff."

"That's not the main reason you want to go back there, though, is it?"

Damian shook his head sadly. "We need to bring her out with us, Domino. I owe it to her."

Domenic reached into his pack and withdrew the lone remaining beer. He popped the top and took a drink before handing it over. He could tell from his brother's look that Damian realized he had brought it for Annie Prior, for when he found them both, alive and safe. But he drank from the can gratefully anyway.

The shadows of two large birds drifted over the men and they looked up, tracking the Whooping Cranes as their slow wing beats seemed to carry them effortlessly over the waterlogged landscape. "Forget portaging," said Damian, "that's the way to travel over this stuff."

"New arrivals?" asked Domenic.

"That'd be my guess."

The two men watched the cranes until they disappeared over the still, silent terrain. "Four thousand kilometres," said Domenic. "That's some journey. The endurance they must have, the energy resources they need to consume. You can hardly imagine the condition they must be in when they arrive here."

Damian nodded slowly. "I thought that's what she would be looking at, when we trapped those cranes Annie wanted. But we didn't check for body fat or feather wear. No blood samples, either, or measurements."

Domenic shot his brother a puzzled look. "What data was she looking for then?"

Damian fished in his boot and withdrew a plastic bag. Inside, a tiny blue memory chip shone like a jewel. "Mostly the kind that's on this."

"The birds were wearing cameras?"

Damian nodded. "Altitude-triggered." He held up the bag in his fingers and stared at the chip. "I still had this one with me when she died. I didn't even have the chance to turn it over to her. No idea what's on it though."

Domenic looked around the undulating boreal marshland surrounding them. "I wonder, did Annie Prior ever show any interest in the landforms as you were passing through?"

Damian lowered the bag and looked at his brother in astonishment. "All the time. Sometimes, it seemed that she was almost as interested in that stuff as she was in the cranes we were tracking. What makes you ask?"

"I think she was looking for evidence of Dene settlement. The trouble is, the Dene are transient, aren't they? So there would be no middens, no evidence of permanently established campsites."

Damian smiled indulgently. "Unfortunately, whoever gave you your crash course in Dene culture didn't give you the whole picture. The Dene *were* a transient people. They would have left no record of any permanent settlements, but every summer the various bands would meet up near a lake somewhere. They'd come from miles around to feast and trade. The locations of these meeting places aren't well known outside the Dene community, but if they used the same sites every year, I'm sure there would still be bones and artifacts there. But what does any of this have to do with Annie?"

"Annie Prior wasn't a biologist. She was a cultural anthropologist."

"What? No, that's crazy." Damian was half standing in surprise. "I know she was interested in the Whooping Crane's place in the First Nations culture. We talked about it all the time. The university she worked at is near the Black Hills. There's plenty of good crane habitat out that way, and a lot of it is on Indigenous land. But we were here to get tracking data from the birds. I know. I recovered it for her."

"Annie Prior entered the park on an anthropological study permit, Damian. She hadn't filed a plan to do any wildlife research at all."

Damian was shaking his head now. "I don't believe you. I don't believe any of this."

But Domenic had been decoding his brother's reactions for a long time. And he could tell that despite Damian's denials, he did.

"Did you ever hear her mention a man named Gaetan Robideau? When I talked to him, he said he had just returned from conducting a ritual in the park. Something about drinking birch sap. It means he would have been in here at the time she died."

"He your dubious Dene source? Drinking birch sap is part of a purification ceremony. It serves as a form of atonement, too, I think."

"Robideau told me it would be the water that took Annie Prior, Damian," said Domenic. "He said it was because she refused to pay."

Damian smiled softly. "He's talking about the Dene practice of honouring the river. The first time they go onto the water each spring, they ask the water for its protection: *Stay calm for me, take care of me when I am upon you.*"

"He said it as if he knew it was going to happen to her. Or maybe already had."

His brother shook his head. "It wasn't foreknowledge. It's just the kind of certainty that comes when your connection with the land is as fundamental as it is with the Dene. I'm not sure you can read anything else into it. It wasn't Gaetan Robideau who caused Annie's death, Domino. And it wasn't to do with any studies of the Dene, either."

He indicated a roiling band of deep grey clouds on the horizon. "Those thunderheads are still building. This storm's going to be a bad one. This whole area will become a lake in a matter of hours. We need to find some deeper water that we can follow up into a back channel somewhere to ride it out."

Domenic rose and lifted the canoe. Once again, his brother had successfully evaded further discussions about Annie Prior's death. But there was something about his final comment that struck a chord with Domenic this time. The emphatic way Damian was able to declare who wasn't involved in her death suggested he almost certainly knew who was.

30

Under normal circumstances, Danny Maik wasn't a person to dwell on his mistakes. He felt the time and effort you'd use mulling over what was already done could be better spent putting things right. But these weren't normal circumstances, and this was no normal mistake. This one had put Lindy Hey's life at risk. So, no matter how hard he tried to get past his missteps, his *incompetence*, the guilt continued to wash over him in great, gushing waves.

He had failed in his duty. He'd taken things for granted, made assumptions, simply because he couldn't be bothered to do his job properly. Had he really become that lazy under DCI Jejeune? Had leaving his boss to do all the heavy lifting while he merely followed along, mopping up the details, turned him into the same kind of indolent, go-through-the-motions copper he'd come to despise over the years? The thought rose like bile in his throat. The truth was, he should have raised his objections from the beginning, pointed out the flaws in his DCI's reasoning, and shown him the dangers that he seemed to be ignoring. Instead, he had meekly gone along with everything, because it was easier to convince himself that his DCI knew what he was doing than to voice his own misgivings about the plan they had put together.

But for now, he needed to put all those feelings aside. Despite the self-loathing churning away inside him, he was just a detective making a few casual inquiries today: no anxiety, no sense of desperation or panic. Patience was going to be the key. But then, at Cley Marshes Wildlife Reserve, it always was.

Quentin Senior was texting as Maik approached, the birdwatcher's great white-maned head bowed over his phone. He looked up when he heard the sergeant's heavy footfall on the gravel path. "One moment, if you'll forgive me." Senior returned to his screen until he had finished his message and then looked up again, a broad, yellow-toothed smile showing through the wiry forest of his beard. "You've chosen quite the day to visit us here at Cley, Sergeant." He indicated his scope with an extended arm and windmilled his other one to usher Maik towards it. "Come, feast your eyes upon that beauty."

Maik approached the scope reluctantly. "Now, Mr. Senior," he said, bending forward to peer through the eyepiece, "you know I'm not much of a … blimey, what on earth is that?"

"Adult male Painted Bunting, Sergeant, in full breeding plumage. A first for the U.K., we believe."

"Looks more like a painted-by-numbers bunting. I don't ever remember seeing a more colourful bird. Are you sure it hasn't just escaped from an aviary somewhere?"

"The question will be asked," acknowledged Senior with a grave nod, "but I'm all but certain this chap's a wild 'un. Got the survival skills, you see — the vigilance, the foraging." Senior touched Maik's shoulder lightly as the sergeant made to straighten up. "Please, don't hurry. I've been watching the little fellow for the past ten minutes. Take the time to enjoy one of nature's true glories. Know what they call a collection of buntings, Sergeant? A mural. A mural of buntings. Isn't that delightful?"

Maik desperately wanted to get on with the reason for his visit, but he knew if he treated the sighting dismissively, it would diminish Senior's joy in it, so he continued to view the bird a moment longer.

"The Inspector will be deeply disappointed to have missed this one, I can assure you," Senior said when Maik eventually straightened up. "Still, perhaps it will stay around until he returns. Do we have any idea when that might be?"

We don't, said Maik's flat expression.

Senior nodded in understanding. "Then perhaps he might get to see one over there. Painted Buntings are popping up in some unusual locations this spring. Another reason I believe this is more likely to be a wild one." Senior smiled. "Though admittedly, north Norfolk is somewhat outside the normal pattern of vagrancy for this species."

Senior had bent for another admiring glance at the prized rarity, and Maik knew he needed to seize the opportunity to step into the silence. He would have liked to have let the man's enthusiasm run its course, but given the chance, Senior would obsess about this bird until dark. "I wonder, Mr. Senior, would you have a few moments for a chat?"

"Certainly, but we'll need to hurry it up a bit. The unwashed hordes will be descending upon us at any moment. I've just texted them that our friend here is in full view. They'd been searching for him over on the far side, but I just had a feeling he might be over this way this morning."

Intuition: it was part of what set aside some people from others in their field. Maik had his moments, his DCI more. He wished something would come to him now, but nothing would, other than the idea that Lindy's message was more than it seemed. "I wondered if you'd ever heard of a bird referred to as Hong Kong's national bird," said Maik. "I took a quick look at a list of national birds online, but I didn't see anything for Hong Kong. I thought you'd be the obvious person to ask around here."

Senior looked puzzled by the sergeant's comment. Maik, who'd seen enough reactions to tell the difference, wondered what it might be about it that troubled Senior. But he couldn't elaborate. He knew the older man had a particular fondness for Jejeune's partner, and if he sensed that Lindy was in any danger at all, he would try to overcompensate in his eagerness to be of assistance. But Senior's over-stretching, however well meant, wouldn't help in this case. Only the facts could do that.

The birder stroked his luxurious white beard pensively, all thoughts of the Painted Bunting momentarily forgotten. "Hong Kong? The bulbuls are all common enough over there: Crested, Chinese, Red-vented, but I hardly think they'd warrant that status. The Black-faced Spoonbill would be the obvious candidate, but it's a migrant, not a resident, which one would assume would rule it out of contention." He shook his head dubiously. "I know the Pied Kingfisher is the symbol of the Worldwide Fund for Nature in Hong Kong. I suppose that might be your best candidate for a national bird, though I've never heard anybody actually refer to it as such."

He stared at Maik frankly, awaiting an explanation for the question. But Maik was as good at missing non-verbal cues as anybody else when he needed to. "Is there any chance one could have been seen anywhere in the area recently?"

Senior allowed himself a small chuckle. "A Pied Kingfisher? Not the slightest, Sergeant. A sighting like that would have lit up the local rare-bird lines like a fireworks display."

"How about farther afield?"

Again, Senior smiled, though still in kindness rather than contempt. "News of a Pied Kingfisher anywhere in the U.K. would raise the kind of ruckus the likes of which the birding community would have rarely seen. Not only would it be the bird of a lifetime for many, it's a spectacular little creature in its own right. Charismatic, colourful, a delightful hovering display before it plunges; it's the type of rarity even the general public would take the trouble to come and see. Can I ask, Sergeant, is someone reporting that they've seen one?"

"Not in so many words. Someone mentioned the National Bird of Hong Kong, that's all. I just thought I'd ask."

Senior gave Maik the same dubious look as before. "An amateur someone or a professional someone?"

"Amateur, but one who'd been around someone who knew his stuff, I would say." The two men didn't have many mutual acquaintances that fit the description; in fact, just the one. Maik wondered if part of him had wanted to tell Senior all along, desperate to coax out that bit of extra effort that he'd just been convincing himself could be so dangerous.

"I haven't seen Miss Hey since the inspector went away. I miss our discussions. She always defends her positions with such passion. She's doing well, I trust?"

Controlled expressions were Maik's stock-in-trade, but he was forced to work hard at this one. "So, she couldn't have seen a Pied Kingfisher?"

Senior shook his head. "But then, non-birders have a tendency to be a touch, well, imaginative, in recalling the details of birds they've seen. Once had a chap give a note-perfect description of a Blue-winged Pitta he'd just seen flying over Blakeney Freshes."

Maik understood the inference, if not the reference. "Eyewitness accounts," he said, shaking his head ruefully.

"Exactly," said Senior. "He'd gone on the web, found the image, and then convinced himself that was exactly what he'd just seen." Senior held up one of his mottled, calloused hands. "I'm not for a minute suggesting there was any malice in it. Nor, indeed, in Miss Hey's claim. But she didn't see any Pied

Kingfisher around these parts, Sergeant. Or anywhere else. Though if that was what she believed she had seen, it's hard to imagine what she might have mistaken it for. There aren't all that many black-and-white birds of that size. Greater Spotted Woodpecker perhaps?"

Senior was welcome to mull over the problem as long as he wanted, but Danny wasn't going to wait around while he did so. His lack of success here meant that he needed to look elsewhere for something that was going to lead him to Lindy. He thanked the man and bade him goodbye.

"Please pass on my best wishes the next time you run into Ms. Hey," said Senior. "I do hope we'll be seeing her around these parts again soon."

"Let's hope so," said Maik. But he couldn't quite bring himself to match Senior's smile.

He was halfway along the gravel path when he heard the older man calling out to him. He turned to see Senior looking in his direction, eyes shielded against the high sun. "You might ask Eric Chappell, Sergeant," he called over the distance. "He spent several years in Hong Kong. He wasn't a birder when he was there, of course, but even he might have noticed something ubiquitous enough to be considered the national bird."

Chappell! Of course. He should have been Maik's first stop. It was why Senior had looked so puzzled when he'd first asked. Why wouldn't Maik have started with a man who'd lived in Hong Kong? He gave his head an angry shake, grateful Senior had gone back to his study of the Painted Bunting and could not see the gesture. Detective Sergeant Danny Maik was going to have to be at his best to get the answers he needed. Stumbling around in this fog of remorse wasn't going to do anybody any good, least of all Lindy. It was time to put his guilt aside and get on with the job of finding her.

31

The shock of Hayes's revelation made Lindy physically sick. She felt the sourness rising in her chest and bent forward, arms still tied to the chair behind her. But the dry retching produced nothing, only a watering of the eyes that Lindy was determined to fight back, lest the man should take them as a sign of some kind of victory. Why had Domenic done this to her, sacrificed their relationship — worse, *pretended* to sacrifice it, in order to save her, without ever once letting her have any say in the matter? The stupid, selfish, arrogant bastard.

"Nice touch," said Hayes in a self-congratulatory tone, "the objectification. It'll add a bit of urgency to proceedings. If I've already dehumanized you, it'll be easier to kill you when the time comes. That's the way he'll read it." Hayes shook his head. "Conventional thinker, our Sergeant. Easy to manipulate the emotions of somebody like that. And from there, it's just a short step to controlling them completely."

Lindy lost the battle with her own emotions and her welling eyes overflowed, sending silent tears down her cheeks. They tracked to the corners of her mouth where she could taste their salt with the tip of her tongue. She tried to shake them away angrily.

Hayes considered her carefully, as if her sorrow was some curiosity at a funfair. "I suppose it's the lack of trust that hurts the most." His tone suggested he was not particularly interested in receiving an answer. "Doesn't say much for a relationship, does it, especially when this business concerns you as much as him. That's the way he is though, DCI Jejeune. Always has to be the one making the decisions. Always has to be the bright est person in the room. I don't suppose it's ever occurred to him that there could be somebody out there who was cleverer than he was. And now here we are. I imagine it's going to be quite the shock to his system when he finds out, don't you?"

Through her tears, Lindy regarded Hayes carefully. Who was he, this man who seemed to have no emotions of his own, yet understood everybody else's so well? It was exactly what was hurting, the knowledge that Domenic didn't trust her enough to confide in her, to let her in on his decision, his plan, any of it. "Why are you doing this?" she asked, drawing a deep breath to stem the flow of her tears. "What do you want?"

"Well, the bookmark for a start, obviously," said Hayes flatly. "It's the only piece of physical evidence that could tie me to an attempted murder." He looked at her. "Yours," he said. "Without it, the police can't make their case against me. So, you know, given that, I thought it might be handy to have it back."

"The birds on it, are they cranes?"

Hayes nodded. "It looked like the sort of thing that would mean a lot to him. I guessed it would hurt him all the more, that way, when he realized I had taken it. I used to like that bookmark a lot. I even managed to get it into the prison with me. Somebody stole it from me in there." He shook his head. "Shocking, eh? Getting so you can't trust anybody, these days. Know the piece, do you?"

"I bought it for him. I wanted him to go to a dance, but he said only if it was a dance of cranes. I had a jeweller friend of mine make it for him." She looked sad at the memory, and perhaps at something else. "He never told me it was missing."

"Seems to me your relationship was riddled with deception. Perhaps that's something you'll want to take up with him when he shows up."

Deception, thought Lindy, *or just protection, another misguided attempt to safeguard her feelings?* Either way, the man seemed to share Lindy's certainty that Domenic would come. Even if their breakup had been genuine, Domenic would have returned to save her. She knew it as surely as she had ever known anything. But if this man wanted the bookmark *for a start,* what came next? She thought she knew. "Whatever Domenic arrested you for," she said, "he must have been sure of your guilt. Not simply convinced by the evidence; that's never enough for him. He has to know, to be certain."

"Prison is no place for a man of intelligence," said Hayes as if he hadn't heard her. "At first, I tried to fit in." He pointed to the string of colourful tattoos on his neck. "Pathetic, I know, but things don't go well in there for those who like to show they're too good for general pop." He shook his head ruefully. "Try as I might, though, I never really could settle into it. It just wasn't for me."

Lindy might have pointed out that a man of intelligence would have stayed away from activities that would put you in prison in the first place, but her close association with Domenic's cases had shown her often enough that intelligence and criminal behaviour were not mutually exclusive. Far from it, in fact, as this man sitting across from her perhaps proved.

"So, why risk going back, just to get revenge on a man who was only doing his job?"

Hayes shook his head again, and for the first time Lindy saw some glimmer of genuine emotion in his eyes. "Oh, I'm not going back." He took a moment to fasten his detachment back in place, but Lindy had seen a glimpse of what lay behind the curtain now, and she knew that Hayes recognized that, too.

"All right, enough chit-chat. I'm going to stretch my legs. When I get back, we'll set a few rules. If you decide you want to follow them, we should be able to pass the time pleasantly enough. If not," he shrugged, "then I'll keep you strapped to that chair with a gag in your mouth, and you'll stay that way until Jejeune shows up."

Lindy stared at the closed door for a long time after Hayes left. He had spoken so matter-of-factly about killing her. It was as if he had managed to disconnect himself entirely from any trace of human feeling. How could you survive in that condition, she wondered, how could you even function if you didn't have a single thread of humanity to tether you to this world? But she had no doubt this man was capable of doing anything that suited him, and she knew he would do it without a heartbeat of remorse. She knew, too, that Hayes had meant it when he said he wasn't going back to prison. But if Domenic was coming here, Hayes's arrest was one of only two possible ways things could end. It was the other one that was scaring her now.

As promised, Hayes had imposed the rules as soon as he returned from his walk. Lindy would be allowed to move freely around the living room, but she couldn't go within three metres of the doors, or Hayes himself. She could go into the kitchen where food items and the electric kettle sat on a countertop, but she was not allowed to open any of the drawers or cupboards. Fridge, yes, stove, no. If he needed to leave the room for anything, she would be required to secure her ankle to a radiator with a lock and chain until he returned, when she would be released, providing she hadn't tried anything in his absence. The rules were a masterpiece of manipulation, she recognized. Though they didn't represent freedom in any real sense of the word, they allowed Lindy enough liberty that she would find herself weighing the risks of losing it, even as she hated herself for doing so.

Under the rules, Lindy would also have been free to watch television. But she found herself unable to draw her eyes away from Hayes, watching him from her chair or as she moved restlessly around the room. He seemed unperturbed by the scrutiny. "We can talk, if you like," he said without looking up from the book he was reading. "I can't promise the intellectual cut and thrust of those chats you'll have with the women in your office, discussing the intimate details of your reproductive systems and such over a latte," he said sarcastically. "But we might still be able to cover some interesting ground. Like that article you wrote last year, for example, the one about repeat offenders in the prison system."

"You read that?"

"Without moving my lips," said Hayes. "I read most things you write. *Nearly half of prison inmates will re-offend within a year,*" he quoted. "*In some individual prisons, the number is seventy-five percent. It's clear that a regimen of communal meals and visits by the prison chaplain is not an entirely successful formula for resetting an offender's DNA back to some earlier, more law-abiding time.*" He nodded. "Well-researched, competently written. Left nobody in any doubt as to what you thought of the prisons' efforts to reinstall some semblance of usefulness in all those lost causes."

"That isn't what I said," protested Lindy. "I don't think they're lost causes."

"*If the purpose of prison truly is rehabilitation, it's hard to make a case that the best way to achieve it is by surrounding prisoners twenty-four hours a day with people so devoid of morality and conscience that they'd kill a cellmate for a packet of cigarettes,*" Hayes quoted again. "No false modesty, please. You should be proud of yourself, holding up a mirror to society like that, allowing it to see the flaws in its reasoning, the abject failure of its stated goals, the utter futility of the entire penal system, in fact."

"That wasn't the purpose of the piece," said Lindy defensively.

"Attracted a lot of attention in the prisons, that article did," said Hayes in his same flat, disinterested tone. "In fact, I'd go so far as to say it was where all your troubles started. That's the problem with making sweeping generalizations about a world you know nothing about, you see. You're going to attract attention to yourself, and not all of it good. Not to worry, though," he said over-brightly. "The time for settling accounts will be here very soon."

Lindy was in the kitchen making tea when she looked out to see Hayes had fallen asleep. His head was lolling to one side, his book resting on his chest. She set down the tea quietly and stood still for a long moment, staring at the front door. She was closer to it than Hayes, and she knew it was secured only by a simple deadbolt from this side. Ten steps, probably half as many seconds. She could run, but could Hayes? Was he one of those wiry, whippet-like creatures that had a turn of speed? He could overpower her if he caught her, she knew that. She remembered the raw power of his grip when he had dragged her from the boot of her car. Her desperation, her fear, would be no match for somebody who was prepared to use as much force as necessary to subdue her. And then what? He was from a prison culture that didn't entertain appeals for a second chance. Would he just follow through on his threat, remaining deaf to her reassurances and her pleas, as dispassionate and disinterested as always as he cinched the ropes tight around her and jammed the gag in her mouth? Or would he end it there, on the driveway, decide he had no more use for her, now that Domenic had already been lured back to him with the bookmark? Five seconds. Ten steps. When she looked back at Hayes, his eyes were open. He was staring at her. And now, they both knew that as long as she was here, she wouldn't be entertaining any more thoughts about escaping. Whatever was going to happen when Domenic arrived, Lindy would be here to witness it.

32

Even with the canoe above his head, Domenic had been able to detect the gradual greying of the skies. The temperature had dropped noticeably in the last hour, and the wind was beginning to pick up. Mercury-coloured clouds had begun a slow, ominous roll towards them, dappling the flat landscape beneath with dark swatches of shadow.

"Break," announced Damian as they approached the edge of a watery slough. "A short one though. We have to press on before that storm hits."

Domenic slumped down beside the canoe and looked around him at the low, empty terrain in which they found themselves. What were they doing here? he wondered. They were aliens in this place, humans like himself and Damian and Annie Prior. What part did they play in the ecosystems of this park? This wasn't their home. It belonged to the animals, the plants, the elements. And perhaps, too, to people like Gaetan Robideau and the rest of the Dene, who understood this land, who were a part of it. His brother seemed to read his thoughts.

"Why did you come here, Domenic?"

"To the park, you mean, or to Canada?"

"Okay, let's start with that one."

Domenic shifted uneasily. "A man called Ray Hayes has been targeting Lindy. He was a former arrest of mine, and he was convicted on the basis of evidence I uncovered. He got out on a technicality and now he's looking for payback. I thought if I could remove myself from the scene for a while, he might back off, and we'd have a chance to re-arrest him."

"And?"

"It hasn't happened."

"This is what Roy's helping you with?"

"I asked him to have some forensic tests run on a bookmark. It was left in Lindy's car the last time Hayes made an attempt on her life."

"You think it belongs to this guy Hayes?"

Domenic shook his head. "It belongs to me. Hayes stole it off my desk when I brought him in for questioning once."

"Did the tests turn up anything useful?"

"One print. Hayes." Domenic shrugged. "But it wouldn't be enough for a conviction, even if we could find him."

Damian nodded slowly. "It must have been a hard decision for you and Lindy, to agree to being separated like this," he said sincerely. "Even if you were prepared to put up with it, neither one of you could have known how long this thing might stretch on. That kind of uncertainty can test a relationship. Still, I suppose there was no other way you could have handled this."

"There wasn't."

"I'm sure she gets it, though, Domino. I'm sure Lindy understands that it had to be this way. So what's the next step, now that you can't find Hayes? What happens when you go back? It doesn't sound like you two can just pick up where you left off, in the hope that this maniac eventually loses interest?"

Domenic shook his head. "Hayes won't lose interest. He'll want to see it through."

"But you have another plan, right?" said Damian uncertainly. "One that will see you and Lindy safely into the happily ever after? I mean, my brother Domenic Jejeune always has a plan."

"There is no other plan," said Domenic. The emptiness in his voice caused Damian to stare at him for a long moment, as Domenic's thoughts took him off to a place where his brother could not trespass.

Damian regretted having reminded his brother about the girlfriend he had not seen for so long. He should not have brought the topic up. It was time to introduce a different one.

"I've been thinking about what you said about Annie."

The sudden announcement seemed to snap Domenic back to the present.

"If what you're saying is true, it explains why she was in such a hurry to get to those birds. If she wasn't working under a wildlife permit, she'd need to get that tracking equipment off them before the park staff began their early-season breeding surveys." He paused and gave a small, rueful smile to himself. "I knew something was wrong. It's so hard to trap adult cranes. It would have been the perfect opportunity to gather all that other data; blood samples, measurements, fat stores. That she wasn't interested in any of it just didn't sit right. It didn't make any sense." He looked up at Domenic. "I sent Traz an inReach message, Domino; the coordinates of the cranes' stopover points. I asked him to check them out. I guess I just wanted to know what was so special about these particular birds."

He stood up abruptly. "Come on. Those clouds will be on top of us before long. We don't want to be out in the middle of nowhere when they eventually decide to let loose."

The storm struck like a judgement from the gods. It swept across the low land unchecked, driven by north winds that carried all the Arctic fury of the high latitudes in their wake. Blasts of chilling air brought ice pellets that raked across the flat terrain like machine-gun fire, stinging the men with their force. Sleet swept through in ragged, swirling sheets, turning the air grey and blocking out the light. All around them, the icy rain pelted the surface of the water, hammering down as they paddled frantically in search of cover. As the waters had begun to rise, the two men had tried to outrun the storm, driving the canoe across the fast-flowing waters. Now exposed, out in the centre of a lake of floodwater, the fierce winds brought the storm lashing in on them from all sides, pummelling them, rocking their craft until water slopped over the gunwales with each tilt. At the front of the canoe, Damian swivelled towards his brother. The rain was streaming unchecked down his face, plastering his hair to his forehead. His tiger-stripe jacket was open, billowing in the wind, saturated inside and out. "We have to get off this water," he bellowed over the sounds of the storm. "That lightning is headed this way."

As if to emphasize his point, a jagged fork lit up the horizon and a deep-throated growl of thunder echoed across the basin. "This wind is going to push us around like crazy if we don't find shelter," he shouted, his words all but snatched away by the winds and the rain. He pointed to a low fringe of vegetation far out into the water, barely visible through the curtain of rain. "Head for that," he yelled. He took a deep breath before turning back into the teeth of the wind. But even as they dug in with their oars, hauling the heaviness of the water back with frantic strokes, the wind swirled once more, crashing waves against the bow, driving them back.

The sudden juddering stop almost pitched Damian into the water. Domenic saw his mouth move and knew he had shouted out a curse, but over the winds he couldn't hear his brother's voice anymore. Not until Damian turned to him directly. "Sweeper. It's torn right through the hull. Keep paddling. I'll try to bail." But Damian's hand scooping seemed to have no effect, and the water level in the bottom of the canoe continued to rise steadily as the grey fluid poured in through the ragged hole in the bow. Damian shook his head. "It's hopeless," he shouted. "She's going down. We have to get out."

Their twin leaps over the side breached the canoe's last resistance against the inflowing water, and the craft pitched along its axis and rolled over. It had sunk from view before the two men had even surfaced from their plunges.

The coldness of the water seized their chests, penetrating even the chill of the freezing rain pounding down around them. Domenic looked around, but saw nothing but frothing grey waters. He felt Damian's hand grab his shoulder, spinning him around. "There! Those reeds!" Damian pointed, his head sinking under the water with the exertion. He was gasping when he surfaced again. "Go!"

They swam towards the bed of flattened vegetation and dragged themselves up onto it. The mound was waterlogged, barely strong enough to hold their weight. But it was wide enough for each of them to find a place to drag themselves onto and lie, exhausted while the rain continued to pound against their faces and bodies. When they had caught their breath, they rolled into sitting positions, drew up their knees and pulled the hoods of their jackets over their heads. Hunkered down, they sat in silence as the storm raged around them. And they waited.

33

The coffee shop in the Demesne at Saltmarsh was about as jarring a contrast to the building's rustic stone exterior as it was possible to be. Chrome and glass reflected back at Lauren Salter wherever she looked, the polished surfaces dazzling in the bright light that flooded in through the room's large picture windows. She patted the back of her hair and smoothed her skirt, but accepted it was probably too late to give the small details the kind of attention such unforgiving scrutiny would demand. If Susan Bonaccord spent much time in places like this, Salter could begin to understand the woman's fastidiousness with regard to her personal appearance. There was nowhere to hide any flaws in a house of mirrors like this.

Bonaccord was seated at a small table near one of the windows. Although she was bent over her phone, she seemed to sense Salter's arrival and looked up. Perhaps she'd caught a reflected image of the sergeant somewhere, thought Salter ruefully. She raised a hand in greeting and went over to join her.

"Isn't it strange how you need to select the right method of contact these days," asked Bonaccord as Salter sat down. "With some people, it's email, others it's voicemail. With this particular client, if I use anything but a text message, chances are

I'll never hear back from her." Bonaccord set the phone down beside her place setting, where it would be in her direct eye line the moment it sprang to life. Even in the short time she had known this woman, Salter would have expected nothing less.

"Interesting place," she said, looking around, "though I'm not quite sure what it has to do with the outside. If they were intending on changing the interior so much, I can't really see the point of preserving the outside the way they did." She indicated the room. "I mean, you'd hardly say they'd retained the character of the old place with this decor, would you?"

"It would have been a marketing decision to retain the exterior look. Based on the older demographic of this area, I would guess." Bonaccord sighed. "I do despair sometimes at the amount of time and effort we put into trying to preserve the past. I mean, I fully understand that the nostalgia movement is inevitably going to gather steam as our population ages, but surely we'd be better off concentrating our efforts on improving the way things are, rather than harkening back to the way they once were."

So even the Shammalars' work, all those songs and dances that brought so many people so much joy over the years, was just another business deal to Susan Bonaccord, thought Salter. She felt unaccountably sad for a person to whom even nostalgia was nothing more than an entry on a balance sheet.

"Are you still doing okay?" asked the sergeant.

Bonaccord looked puzzled.

"That phone call. The things you had to listen to."

"Oh, yes. Well, of course it was a terrible experience." Bonaccord fell silent, as if she recognized the hollowness of her response. She seemed like someone searching around inside herself for memories of what emotions had felt like, when she still allowed herself to experience them. But perhaps she was taking solace, too, in the rarity of truly terrible things in this world, in the knowledge that she would likely never have to encounter such horrors again. Salter knew she herself would forever be denied that consolation. These things, the cruel, the terrible, the unthinkable, were part of the world she had chosen to inhabit. She didn't get the chance to slough them off and go on with her life. They were her life.

"I was hoping we could talk some more about Wattis Wright," she said, "specifically about his attitude toward the money. I've had our legal team look at the deal. They seem to think it's a very good one from your company's perspective. They speculate that if the Shammalars' musical was even a modest success, Mr. Wright's royalty earnings would have probably doubled the flat fee you paid for the rights."

"I can assure you I did go over the numbers with Mr. Wright, even though I was under no legal obligation to do so. He wanted the cash because he wasn't prepared to put up with the world of rolling reserves, staggered reporting cycles and the like. He really didn't seem overly concerned that his decision could potentially cost him a lot of money."

"Did you get the sense he was in a hurry to get his hands on the cash?" The autopsy report had revealed no signs of serious illness, but that wasn't the only reason someone might decide to take the money and run.

Bonaccord shook her head. "I just took it as part and parcel of the man's antiquated attitude toward things; a bird in the hand and all that."

Antiquated or not, it was an attitude Salter could appreciate. Especially if there was the possibility of a counterclaim to the rights you were selling. From the top of the window, a translucent white blind began to silently descend, stopping at a point about a quarter of the way down the pane.

"Photosensitive glass," said Bonaccord. "It lowers the blind to prevent it from getting too bright." Salter looked through the window. Three young boys were walking along the tow-path, and she regarded them carefully. They were probably just into their teenage years, perhaps not even quite there yet. All wore scruffy pants and loose, billowing T-shirts. Each sported a different, but equally eccentric hairstyle.

"What *do* they look like?" asked Bonaccord, following Salter's gaze and shaking her head.

They look like kids who a heartbeat ago considered their mum their best friend in the whole world, and just about the coolest person on earth, thought Salter sadly. Now they'd prob-ably die of shame if she went up to give them a hug.

"You don't have children yourself, I believe."

Bonaccord shook her head. "My career always came first in the early days. By the time I might have been ready, any potential *y* chromosome donors had long since moved on." She looked down into her coffee and took a small breath. "So, I put all my efforts into creating a better me instead. Not that I regret it for a minute," she said brightly. "I'm very happy with the way things turned out, thank you very much. I mean, kids just tend to consume your whole life, don't they?"

Yes, thought Salter. *They do. If you're lucky.*

"And you?"

"One boy," said Salter, "nearly nine. Of course, all kids are teenagers by the time they're ten now, aren't they?" But for all the heartbreaks and disappointments that her nine-going-on-nineteen boy was going to be bringing her, Salter would never have any regrets about Max consuming her whole life.

"I'm curious as to why Wattis Wright simply didn't come over to speak to you in person. His place is not very far from here. It was a nice night. He strikes me as the kind of man who might've enjoyed an evening stroll along the riverbank."

"He hadn't been asked," said Bonaccord simply. "Appearing at a woman's hotel room, at night, uninvited? Hardly the sort of decorum one would associate with a man of his era, is it?"

It was a fair point, and Salter acknowledged as much with a slight tilt of her head. "Did he ever mention a man named Albert Ross to you?"

"I don't believe so. There was a business associate of some kind that began to make a fuss, but that was a woman. Jennie, I think — Jennie Wynn." Bonaccord shrugged slightly. "It happens. The scent of money wafts through the air and suddenly people dream up all manner of imaginative claims to it. I asked her to speak directly to Wright. I kept waiting to hear more, but then he contacted me to say he'd sorted it out. He could demonstrate sole ownership of the rights to the dance routines and so he was free to sign them over to us. Certainly, his was the legally registered name on the copyright notices." A thought suddenly seemed to occur to her. "The contract we have has been thoroughly vetted by our legal department, Lauren," she said amicably. "It's a perfectly valid transfer of rights ownership. Having purchased them lawfully and in good faith from the rightful owner, I'm informed that our entitlement to them is legally incontestable."

"I'm sure it is," said Salter, but she'd never yet met a lawyer who'd issue such a blanket assurance about moral rights. She wasn't convinced Jennie Wynn's claim on the routines was quite so spurious. And from what she could tell from her conversation with the woman, Jennie Wynn didn't feel it was, either.

Bonaccord didn't seem able to let the matter go. Perhaps Salter's assurance hadn't been vigorous enough. "I still have a signed copy of the agreement in my briefcase, as a matter of fact." She gave a short smile. "It just arrived in the mail. Wattis Wright must have popped a copy in the post to me after he signed it. I receive so few pieces of paper these days, I almost feel I should hold on to this as a souvenir. Perhaps a museum might be interested in it one day."

Is that all that Wattis Wright has become now, too? wondered Salter. A museum curiosity; this man who had died in such terrible circumstances while this woman had listened to his last breaths on the other end of a telephone, an event she now seemed able to dismiss like a bad memory. She looked at Bonaccord carefully as the woman checked her phone again. *I could have done this*, she thought, *after my divorce.* It would have been so easy then, when her world was falling apart all around her, to seize onto those things she could control: her personal appearance, her career. She might have forged herself into Susan Bonaccord in the furnace of her bitterness and her anger, if it hadn't been for Max, dragging her back into a human landscape of love and connection and caring.

She said goodbye and stood up. At the doorway of the café, she turned to wave, but Bonaccord had already taken out her laptop, immersing herself once more in the meticulous, ordered world she managed so tightly. But even when you had control over every aspect of your life, it wasn't to say you always got your decisions right. Not many people would have chosen loneliness as their preferred state. Fewer still would have pretended they enjoyed it.

34

The defining moments of our lives come upon us so suddenly, thought Maik as DCS Colleen Shepherd entered the Incident Room. No warning, no time to plan, all you were left with to confront such moments were your instincts. But the consequences of your decisions could last a lifetime; in this case, the loss of a career, a reputation, of most things that Maik held on to, that defined him. All this weighed against a young woman's life, decided in the time it took a human heart to skip a single beat.

Maik should have told Shepherd about Lindy. He should have reported the phone call; even reported his suspicions prior to it, when she disappeared. The DCS shared Maik's concern for Jejeune's girlfriend and was every bit as invested in her safety. She shared, too, Maik's desire to see Hayes arrested, clearing the way for the DCI's return to Saltmarsh. But the thing she didn't share was Danny's guilt. Inviting Shepherd and the team into his own personal quest for redemption would have made a lot of sense. They could cover a lot more ground than one man acting alone. But people made mistakes. Maik was living proof of that. He trusted his colleagues' professionalism and their discretion, but it may only take one small slip to trigger Hayes into taking the action he'd threatened. It was a chance Danny Maik wasn't prepared to take.

He leaned forward and turned the volume down on his computer, reducing the silken harmonies of the Four Tops to a whisper. "I was wondering if Mr. Chappell might be in town, ma'am," he said as casually as he had ever said anything. But he stepped his tone up immediately. Like Danny himself, Colleen Shepherd had a finely-honed detector for deceit, and excessive nonchalance was often a key. "I ran across Quentin Senior and he mentioned asking him about a bird."

Shepherd looked like she might be about to ask exactly where on earth Danny and the single most dedicated birder in Saltmarsh might have crossed paths, but she chose instead to let her eyes play across the mass of loose papers and open files on Danny's desk. If something had taken him out to one of Senior's birding haunts, it wasn't free time.

"Eric's in Scotland at the moment. He's over the moon because he happened to be already on Fair Isle in the Shetlands when a Song Sparrow was found there. It's a rarity from the inspector's part of the world, apparently. Eric tells me at least five chartered planes have already flown in to see it. Can you believe it, renting a plane to go all the way up to Scotland to see a sparrow?" She shook her head in a show of the bewilderment she knew Maik shared at the eccentricities of the birders in their lives. "I came in to see if you had managed to catch up with Lindy. I understand you were asking around recently to see if anyone had heard from her."

Maik paused.

Defining moments.

"I spoke to her yesterday," he said.

"I'm glad to hear it," said Shepherd with evident relief. "She's not come to any harm, then?"

"She said not."

Shepherd knew from experience that Maik could take terseness to a whole new level when something set him off. Generally, though, Danny Maik remained, well, Danny Maik — hardly verbose but not offhand either. "Is something the matter, Sergeant?"

Yes, very much so.

"I think it's time for the truth, don't you?" she said. "About Ray Hayes."

Maik froze. He had been prepared to sacrifice his career, and even his own cherished personal integrity, too, if it meant keeping his secrets about Lindy. But he hadn't expected the reckoning to come so swiftly. Though he knew no apology could undo the damage, he felt compelled to offer at least an explanation. But before he could speak, to set in motion the slow downward spiral towards the destruction of everything he had come to represent, Shepherd continued.

"I understand how upset you are at the decision to terminate the search for Hayes. I'm devastated, too, truth be told, by the thought that DCI Jejeune will no longer be here with us. But we must move on, Sergeant, all of us. So, I'll ask you once more, formally, and then we'll draw a line under the matter. Do you, at this time, Sergeant Maik, have any idea of Ray Hayes's whereabouts?"

The defining moments of our lives.

"No, ma'am. I do not."

"Very well. Then your assignment is over. Submit your final report to me and we'll close the file. You can join Sergeant Salter's investigation. But only a supporting role for now, Danny." Shepherd gave him a cautioning look. "I'd like to give her a chance to get things right, even if she does seem to be spinning her wheels a bit at the moment. As I understand it, this Albert Ross seems to be our most likely suspect. Are you aware of any reason she hasn't yet had him in here for a chat?"

"I don't think she wants it to be him," said Maik simply.

"Too easy, you mean? She doesn't want it to appear like she's just latching on to the first suspect that comes along?" Shepherd nodded. It was an understandable concern for a new sergeant in her first case, if not an entirely professional one. "Talk to her about it, Danny. Tell her sometimes it is as straight-forward as it seems to be, and the guilty party does just fall into our laps like this. Not as often as we'd like, it must be said, but it happens. Easy or not, if Ross is our man, I want him in custody as soon as possible." She consulted her watch. "I should be off. Eric will be calling me later. He'll want to regale me with a blow-by-blow account of his sparrow sighting once again, no doubt. I'll ask him to get in touch with Quentin Senior."

"I don't think there's any urgency, ma'am," said Maik smoothly. Deceit wrapped you in its embrace so quickly, he thought. It just kept on drawing you in until it slowly suffo-cated you. His resolve faltered, and he teetered on the brink of opening up to Shepherd. He knew if she had been looking directly at him with that steely, unblinking gaze of hers, he would have done. But she was focused on his laptop instead. The direction of a single gaze. The defining moments of our lives existed in such small details sometimes.

"Your song is over," said Shepherd. "It's not like you to have nothing else cued up. I suppose Senior wanted to speak to Eric to congratulate him on seeing this sparrow of his. There's no doubt he will have already heard about it. That rare bird net-work puts our own national alert systems to shame."

Maik shook his head. "I think it might have been about a national bird for Hong Kong."

Shepherd smiled and nodded slowly to herself. "Ah, yes. The crane."

Maik's astonishment was so profound, he couldn't speak, but Shepherd interpreted his expression merely as interest.

"Eric's little joke," she explained. "He was in Hong Kong during the boom years, when it seemed like every tiny patch of land had a building project on it. He told me he could look out of his office window and see nothing but construction cranes in every direction. He said if he was ever asked to nominate a national bird for Hong Kong, it would be the crane."

"The crane," said Maik. It was all he could manage at the moment. He cued up a song to give him a moment to bring his breathing back under control. "I can't imagine they'd be all that common in this country," he said, letting the computer task absorb all of his attention. "The actual birds, I mean, not the building equipment."

"I've never seen one," said Shepherd. "But I know Eric has. I believe they're a migratory species." She exchanged a glance with Maik to acknowledge how much birding information the two of them had absorbed simply by being within earshot when their birding associates were chatting. The opening strains of "Baby I Need Your Loving" rose from Maik's computer. "This is the same song you've just played, Sergeant. Are you sure there's nothing the matter?"

Maik ignored the question. "Would Eric have mentioned this joke of his at the office, I wonder?"

"Oh, I should imagine so. Like most men, Eric is particularly proud of his own witticisms. He seems to consider it his duty to share them with as many people as possible, usually several times."

Maik's mind was racing. If cranes were migratory, it meant Lindy could have seen one just about anywhere in Britain as it flew over. But perhaps Quentin Senior could narrow Maik's search down to some of the most likely spots. It was a big ask, but it was a glimmer of opportunity, and Danny had to pursue it.

"Keep me informed." Shepherd's comment snapped Maik back to the present. "About any new developments in Sergeant Salter's case. Not behind her back, of course, but she seems to have inherited a disturbing trend of providing as few details as possible about what she's up to." Shepherd smiled. "I can't imagine where she would have picked that up from. Oh, and remember to submit that final report, so wc can close out the Hayes investigation."

Maik shut his laptop the second Shepherd had disappeared from view. He stood up and grabbed his jacket from the back of his chair. That report was going to have to wait. Right now, Maik had to search for a crane with an intensity he knew no birder would ever match.

35

It seemed impossible that rest could have come in such conditions. Flashes of lightning had scarred the darkness around the brothers, and the crash of thunderclaps echoed off the flat landscape. Squalls of sleet billowed around the men in wind-driven sheets, tearing at their clothing and driving into their faces. Icy pellets beat down on them, an incessant tattoo that drummed against their coats and boiled the surface of the water around them into a churning lather. The winds spun like dervishes, tearing into their flimsy reed island, thrashing the stalks into a frenzied dance as they passed through with a low, mournful thrum.

As the winds began to die down, the sleet turned to rain that fell in a steady downpour that drenched them to their skins. The men gathered their jackets tightly around them and buried their heads deep inside their hoods, shrinking ever inward as they attempted to escape the worst of the onslaught. Finally, overwhelmed by fatigue, they had slept.

When they awoke, the storm had moved on, but the clear skies that they might have expected, that they might have deserved, even, were denied them. Instead, a shell of low grey cloud hung over the basin, robbing the landscape of its light and colour. The dank smell of wet vegetation hung in the air, mingling with the acidic tang of tannins in the tea-coloured water that lapped dangerously at the fringes of the reed island. The brothers had retreated farther in towards the centre of the mound as the storm had raged on. The reeds were piled higher here, but they were still saturated into a soggy, tangled mass. Domenic struggled to his feet, to try to give his body some relief from the dampness beneath him. He tested the spongy vegetation gingerly. It held.

"So, what happens now?"

"Now, we wait," said Damian. "You said Roy told you to file a three-day plan with the park office. This is day four. You don't report in by tonight, they're going to send someone out to look for you first thing in the morning. All we have to do is sit tight and wait for them to come and get you. Presumably, they'll let me tag along."

"What if they can't find us? This is a big area. Do you think we could go out on foot?"

"Not unless you can walk on water." Damian jutted his chin towards a spot far out across the water where a jumble of dead spruce trees lurched drunkenly into the water. "What is that, half a kilometre, maybe more? Slogging through that mud would be almost impossible in these conditions. We'd be wading through water for at least thirty minutes even to reach that stand of trees. We'll be wet, cold, and exposed the whole way. A wind kicks up in these temperatures, with us in these damp clothes, that's a fast train to hypothermia. And what would it achieve anyway? At best we'd be on another mound like this one, maybe even smaller, maybe less able to support our weight." He shook his head. "Trust me; we're better off staying here. These reeds don't provide much shelter, but this mound is better than anything I can see out there."

He stared out over the grey water to the line of dead trees, the skeleton fingers of their branches dragging across its surface. "You know," he said eventually, "you never did tell me what it was that made you come out here after me." He spread his arms to indicate his sodden clothing and the wider, watery desolation of their surroundings. "Not that I'm necessarily agreeing that I needed any help, you understand."

Domenic shrugged. "The timing between the two devices failing," he said simply. "It felt contrived, like maybe your inReach had been deliberately disabled." It sounded like such a small thing now, as he said it aloud, such an incidental, trivial detail. But how could he articulate all that his instincts had told him, his overwhelming conviction that Damian was in trouble? Perhaps he didn't really know himself what it was that had convinced him something was wrong. He just knew that he had trusted it.

Damian was still looking out at the vast, waterlogged landscape. When he spoke, he did so without drawing his eyes away from it. "Two of them," he said. "U.S. military. But they knew this terrain, knew how to move in it, stay out of sight. They were on our camp before I even saw them."

Domenic nodded silently. "You think they used those VHF signals to track you to your camp?"

"Those branches of the military are called *intelligence* for a reason, Domino. With those signals showing them the way, it wouldn't have been hard." He indicated their surroundings again. "Even out here."

Domenic knew from experience that now wasn't the time to interrupt his brother with objections. First you let Damian lay out his ideas; tell you what he had been holding on to. There would be time enough later to revisit the details.

"Did these two men kill Annie Prior?"

Damian shook his head. "But when she saw them approaching the camp, she ran. They chased her until she jumped into the canoe. They gave her no choice. She had nowhere else to go." Damian lowered his eyes and stared at the matted down reeds beneath his feet.

"Did they see you?"

Damian shook his head again. "No, but the campsite would have told them there was a second person around. That's why I went in-country as opposed to back out of the park. I didn't know what might be waiting for me if I came out. It's why I disabled my inReach, too. These guys have state-of-the-art technology. I'm sure reverse tracking one of those devices would be nothing to them."

Domenic saw his brother's remorse, so powerful that it gripped him even now, when their predicament should have demanded all his attention. "If she was panicked enough at the men's approach, it meant she knew why they were coming for her. Even if you'd been able to reach her in time, you wouldn't have been able to save her. If she was that afraid, she would have still got into the canoe. She would have still died, Damian. Your responsibility was to trap birds for her, not save her from the trouble she'd gotten herself into."

"I know," he said sadly.

Then what was it, wondered Domenic, this other regret that haunted his brother? Whatever it was, even here, damp and cold and stranded on an island of reeds in the middle of a floodplain, it would not release Damian from its grip.

Domenic looked out over the water, squinting into the distance. "If the park superintendent refused to sanction a search, do you think the RCMP would have the authority to insist?"

Damian looked puzzled by his brother's question, and by the suddenness with which it had occurred. "Roy personally, you mean? Maybe. But why would the authorities refuse?"

"The park superintendent did before, even though I told her I thought you were in trouble."

Damian shook his head. "You're nobody out here, Domenic. The people they trust are those who can look at the sky and tell you when it's going to snow and how much there will be and how long it will last. Those are the ones whose instincts they'd be willing to listen to. You're just some tourist with a bad feeling. Carol Bracker would have taken your request seriously, but she would have made a decision based on the information she had. Annie and I had the provisions, equipment, and the skills to last out here at least ten more days. We hadn't set up a check-in schedule with anyone. The park authorities had no reason to be concerned. But now you're missing, too, she'll make sure they come for us. Guaranteed. All we have to do is be patient."

"I was wondering," said Domenic, turning to his brother, "what makes you think the U.S. military would be interested in what Prior was doing?"

"The main migration route of the Whooping Cranes on their way north from Aransas takes them over a number of major U.S. military installations. I think the birds Annie was tracking might have attracted the interest of someone at one of these bases along the way."

"But there must be literally millions of birds flying over these military sites, and more than a few of them will be carrying tracking devices. Why would these birds attract any particular interest?"

"These cranes were wearing VHF transmitters. It's unusual enough these days that it would likely have raised flags. At the very least, the people monitoring the comms equipment at the base would have wanted to know who the frequency was licensed to."

Domenic seemed to hesitate for a moment. "I'm not sure the people who came after Annie Prior were with the U.S. military, Damian."

"What makes you say that?"

Domenic tilted his head slightly. "A couple of things. Securing the escape routes is standard operating procedure even for the Saltmarsh police force when we go after a suspect. I can't imagine highly trained military personnel would be careless enough to give her a chance to run away and get in a canoe."

"But who else is going to be interested enough in Annie's activities to come out here and track her down? That guy Robideau? You think he'd kill Annie just to protect the secrets of a few Dene sites?"

"No," said Domenic. "I don't think that."

But he was almost certain that Gaetan Robideau had come into this park to find Annie Prior. And failed to do so. Robideau was one of those people whom his brother had described, someone who knew this land, its ways, its weather, its secrets. And if a local Dene who'd spent his life in this wilderness wasn't able to find a missing person out here, what chance did anyone else have?

36

Traz stood by the car, stretching the long drive out of his joints. The restaurant they had parked beside looked like it was barely clinging to life, though the whitewash letters on the window assured them the establishment's omelettes were world famous. But it was the absence of any viable alternatives in this dog-eared corner of the town that was going to be the clinching argument in favour of them going inside.

By this point in their trip, the euphoria of being on the road had dwindled for Traz, and now the monotony of driving for hours at a time was beginning to take hold. Where he had once revelled in the tiny details of each place they passed through, now he saw only the sameness in them. The small Midwestern towns along this corridor they were following had long been strangers to prosperity. The perpetual cycle of boom and bust had finally bottomed out in these parts. All along the road north, they had seen places that had dwindled into dust waiting for an upswing in fortunes that never came. Those towns that had survived had done so at the cost of their individuality, dragged towards the homogenous conformity of big box stores and discount malls by their need to exist.

He pointed up to a distant speck in the sky as Verity emerged from the Buick. "Bald Eagle," he said, raising his bins.

"Our national symbol," said Verity, holding her hand to her brow and squinting as she looked up. "The perfect argument, if ever there was one, for putting conservation funding into trying to save an individual species. Can you imagine if the eco-pragmatism argument had resulted in this country losing the Bald Eagle? What would the bird have been a symbol of then? Sometimes you just have to save species for its own sake, never mind the bigger picture."

Traz watched the bird for a long time, tracking its slow glide across the sky.

"I like the way you look at birds," Verity told him. "You must've seen plenty of Bald Eagles, but you treat this sighting like it's still something special to you."

"There's always a chance you'll see something new, even if you've watched the species a hundred times. I understand the twitching side of birding, but I can't say it's ever really appealed to me."

"We get a lot of that kind at Aransas when the rarities are in. Birdwatchers? *Bird seers* is what I call 'em. Hop out of the car, a quick glimpse with the bins, and off again. I always thought of birdwatching as more what you were doing just now — taking the time to enjoy them."

"You never wanted to do more birding yourself?"

"I know some about Whooping Cranes, I guess. And I can identify one or two of the other local species down there. That's enough for me."

The eagle drifted out of sight, and as Traz lowered his bins, Verity leaned in to give him a hug. Their relationship had moved to a new level the previous evening. The aging receptionist at their motel had determined to turn every check-in into a comedy skit, with himself in a leading role. Despite their travel fatigue, Traz and Verity had gone along with it good-naturedly as things meandered towards the room details.

"Fifty bucks less than two separate rooms, I could let you have the Honeymoon Suite," the receptionist had told them with a lascivious grin. "Got no champagne, but I could throw in a nice free ice bucket."

There had been a sense of inevitability in their shared glance. The timing felt right, and they held hands as they left the lobby with the single set of key-cards. "Just so you know," Verity had told him as they stood on the threshold of the Honeymoon Suite's battered doorway, "there won't be any guns under my pillow tonight."

As the restaurant owner brought them coffee and menus, Traz looked out at the Buick. Set against the faded facades of the abandoned stores along the empty, brick-surfaced road, the glittering tangerine car looked like an alien spacecraft. They gave the owner their orders and watched him trudge off dispiritedly to the kitchen to begin the second act of his one-man show.

"Sorry about this," said Traz. "We could keep going if you like, maybe find somewhere better."

Verity leaned across the table and took his hand. "It's fine, okay. A world-famous omelette is just what I feel like. Just so long as it's made with free-range eggs."

"I certainly hope not," said Traz with mock horror. "You know chickens will fight to the death when they're allowed to run free. Behind every free-range egg there's a trail of spilled chicken blood."

He felt a pang of guilt at the alarm she showed at his news, but he suspected there would be no lasting damage. She would continue to order free-range eggs whenever she had the chance. It's what we do, he thought, with the things we like. We manage to find a way to accept their failings. When it suits us, forgiving is easy.

While they waited for their food, Traz called a map up on his phone. "It looks like the next set of coordinates are about fifty miles due north of here. After that, it's Scenic. And some decisions, I guess."

As the owner set the plates on the table, his eyes drifted towards the Buick outside, as if it represented an escape route from this place that he would forever be denied. Presentation wasn't the man's forte, but the taste of the omelettes almost made them worthy of their global billing. Traz was two bites in when the ringing of his phone echoed jarringly through the empty room. He reached for it with annoyance and thought about shutting it off until he noticed the number was international. He had been expecting a call from the car's owner to check on the progress of his precious toy. Traz would have been calling hourly if it had been his car being driven up this route by a stranger, so he felt he owed the man at least an update.

"Is this Juan Eduardo Perez?" asked the caller formally.

"Not usually," said Traz. "But I suppose a little extra decorum might be called for when I'm travelling with such a stunning travel companion as this one."

He winked at Verity, as he had done before, but the comment didn't receive the light-hearted response from the caller that he'd anticipated. Instead, there was a beat of silence. "This is Sergeant Roy Ducannon. I'm with the RCMP up here in Canada. I'm Domenic and Damian Jejeune's brother-in-law."

"Is everything all right? Has something happened?" Traz sat up straighter and clenched the phone more tightly to his ear. Alerted by his body language, Verity leaned in to listen.

"Domenic has missed a deadline to check in to the Wood Buffalo National Park offices. He had gone into the park looking for Damian, who we now believe is also missing. Damian's last recorded contact was with you. I wondered if he had told you what his plans were."

"They're out in Wood Buffalo? Both of them? Have they started a search yet?" Traz was standing now, the puzzled owner staring at him in surprise. Opposite him, Verity was also rising.

"One has already been organized. It will be going out first thing in the morning."

Traz looked out at the Buick, gleaming under the sun. "Tomorrow? They still have daylight up there now. Why aren't they going out today?"

"They'll be out as soon as possible." Roy's calm tone suggested he understood that the frustration in Traz's raised voice wasn't intended for the messenger. "Did Damian say anything that might shed some light on where he was heading?"

"No," said Traz, flapping a hand at his helplessness. "His text was to ask me to check out the coordinates of some Whooping Crane stopovers along their migration routes. Oh man, if they're lost out there at this time of year, they could be in big trouble."

"These stopover sites, are they in the park itself?"

"No, in the U.S. I'm in Southern Nebraska." Traz saw the owner still staring at him and he waved the man over, fishing in his pocket for cash. Verity put her hand on his arm and reached into her purse instead.

"Domenic was aware you'd spoken to Damian," said Roy. "Did he also contact you?" The tone had taken on the nature of a police inquiry. Which was what it was, realized Traz: a missing persons inquiry. He thought he and Roy may have crossed paths once or twice over the years, at social functions at the Jejeune household, perhaps even a family barbeque one time. But whether Roy remembered him or not, the man's tone suggested informality was not going to be getting in the way of his questions. Traz was okay with that. He wanted a professional police officer on this, not some headless-chicken relative tearing around in a panic.

"He wanted to know why Damian had been in touch," Traz said, "so I told him. I think he was already worried about him."

"Worried about anything in particular?"

Traz thought about Verity Brown's encounter with the soldiers. Could it be that there was some military connection to the coordinates Damian had sent him after all? He knew if he mentioned it to Roy, it would lead to more questions, detritus that might slow up the process of searching for the two men. And that was all that was important now.

"He just said he felt something bad might have happened."

"Okay, thank you, Mr. Perez. I'll be getting updates on the search, so I'll keep you informed. In the meantime, if you hear anything from either one of them, anything at all, let me know immediately. I can be reached at this number day or night."

The owner had waved away Verity's offer to pay for their unfinished food. Even from his vantage point on the far side of the room, it had been clear the couple wouldn't be staying once the phone call had ended.

"I have to go up there," Traz told her as they moved towards the door.

"Traz, the people who do those searches are experts. They'll find them."

But Traz was shaking his head. "Damian is an experienced backcountry camper, and Domenic is one of the brightest guys I've ever known. Neither one would take any unnecessary risks. For both of them to have run into trouble up there, either separately or together, means it's not going to be something as simple as wandering off track. There's something going on, and that means a conventional search operation might not find them."

"But what are you going to do?"

Traz held the door to the Buick open for her. "Whatever I can. I won't know till I get there, but I can't let those guys stay out there, even if it means going in after them myself."

He got in the car and stared through the windshield for a moment, seeming to realize something. "I'm going to have to leave this car at the airport. You'll be okay getting to Scenic from there? I'm really sorry. I'd let you take the car, but the owner is going to be mad enough as it is, having to come all the way down here to get it. If he found out I'd given it to an uninsured driver, he'd probably file criminal charges."

"I'll come with you."

"What? Why would you do that? You don't know these people."

"I know you, and I know they're important to you. If you need to be up there to try to help them out, then that's where I need to be, too."

Traz didn't argue. In fact, any words were hard to find. For so long, he'd always been the one offering the help, providing the support. But if the situation in Wood Buffalo was anywhere near as bad as it could be, Traz suspected by the time they finally found the Jejeune brothers, he wasn't going to be in a position to provide much assistance to anybody else. In fact, he was probably going to need all the support he could get himself.

37

Quentin Senior was silhouetted against the white sky hanging over the marsh; a shadowy sentinel looking out over a sea of tawny grass. As he approached along the gravel path leading to the berm, it struck Maik how many times on his visits he had found Senior alone like this. The man seemed content with his solitude, here among the quiet cells of water that faithfully reflected the skies, and the high, swaying vegetation that whispered the moods of the winds. Until very recently, Danny Maik had drawn the same comfort from his own company. But not today.

He watched Senior slowly sweep his scope across the cells. A survey, recognized Maik, rather than the focused intensity of a sighting. He understood so much of the world of birding now; its nuances, its language. Perhaps his education was coming to an end. If so, it had been an interesting experience, if not always a completely fathomable one. Once, he had considered if birding could even be something he might take up when he retired. It offered a world of tranquility and the chance to be out in the open air. But it was these aspects of the pastime that appealed to him, he came to realize, rather than the birds themselves. And there were other ways to experience the quiet pleasures of the countryside, ones that didn't involve peering through a lens trained on motionless landscapes for extended periods of time. Maik might have had his fill of silent, solitary vigils by then.

Senior straightened at the sound of the sergeant's measured, military stride on the path behind him. "Bad news if you've come for another look at the Painted Bunting, I'm afraid. It flew off shortly after you left and hasn't been seen again since. There's always the chance that it may resurface somewhere nearby, but of course it's by no means guaranteed." Senior gave Maik one of his splendid yellow-toothed smiles. "I do find the wonderful uncertainty of birding one of the most appealing aspects of the pastime. Although whether I'd be quite so sanguine about things if I'd so far failed to locate the bird, I'm not so sure. We seem so much more disposed to accept the vagaries of life once our own needs have been met, don't you find?"

Maik did, but he wasn't here to discuss philosophy. "I was wondering if you'd heard about any sightings of cranes lately, Mr. Senior?"

"Common Cranes? *Grus grus?* One or two. May one ask why? Much as I'd love to take all this new interest as a sign that you're considering joining the birding fraternity, I suspect an ulterior motive." He offered Maik another smile, but he left this one to linger slightly longer. "Not tied to your earlier inquires about the national bird of Hong Kong, by any chance? Did you ever discover what it was, by the way?"

"Eric Chappell is still out of town at the moment," said Maik, more easily than he felt. He tried a smile of his own, but for two men treating each other so congenially, a considerable amount of uneasy silence found a place between them. "I was wondering if there might be such a thing as an organization that might have a record of where cranes have been seen in the U.K. recently."

To someone outside the world of birding, Maik's hope may have seemed a vague one, but in his experience, every tiny sub-branch of birding seemed to have its own society. DCI Jejeune appeared to get newsletters from most of them.

"I'm sure the fine folks at the Great Crane Project could provide you with a list of recent sightings," said Senior, his desire to assist the sergeant winning the battle over his curiosity. "There is still a great deal of interest in the birds in this country." He descended the berm, uncomfortable at towering over the sergeant and having him squint up into the light. "The return of the Common Crane to our shores is a truly remarkable story. The birds are thought to have gone extinct as a breeding species in the U.K. around the time of Shakespeare. Wintering cranes would have occasionally turned up in the intervening period, of course, but these would have been anomalies, birds driven off their usual migration routes by storms. Nineteen seventy-nine; that was the breakthrough. Three cranes spent the winter in the Norfolk Broads. Whatever possessed them to do so, we'll never know." He smiled at Maik. "You and I have both spent enough winters here to know how inhospitable the Broads can be in the grip of winter. But remain, they did. At first, their presence here was one of the local birding community's most closely held secrets." Senior held a hand to his chest, mock-dramatically. "For my sins, I confess I was among those arguing for such suppression. It would've been a story of national importance, you see, cranes being such a charismatic species and all. We'd have had the media descending on us from all over, and the constant glare of attention, however well-meant, was the last thing a skittish group of new arrivals needed." His great snowy mane caught the breeze as he nodded in satisfaction. "I'm delighted to say our initial caution was rewarded, as a population was eventually established, and then another, over at Lakenheath Fen, and yet another up on Humberside."

Maik's heart sank, but he tried not to show his disappointment. "So, they're all over the place, then? There's any number of spots one could have been seen recently?"

"Oh, they're hardly ubiquitous, Sergeant. A crane sighting is still a thing to cherish, even in these parts." Senior nodded shortly. "But yes, we are gradually witnessing what is surely the most wonderful of all of nature's party tricks; the natural reestablishment of a species. None of that artificial reintroduction jiggery-pokery that's going on all over the place. Whatever survival instincts these birds bring with them, they'll have come by them honestly."

The comment surprised Maik. "I'd have thought you'd be the last one to disapprove of efforts to reintroduce a species, Mr. Senior. From the little I've heard about it, I understand the practice has been vital to the survival of some birds."

"Oh, I do appreciate the commitment, and the tremendously hard work such projects demand. I understand, too, the argument that we should be the ones to restore these species, since human activities have contributed so much to their decline in the first place. But I just feel nature should be the final arbiter of such matters."

But Maik understood, more than Senior knew, the human compulsion to try to repair the damage you had caused. "If I could just get that contact information for the Great Crane Project, Mr. Senior, I can be on my way. If there's anyone there who'd be particularly up on the sightings along the migration routes, I'd appreciate a name."

"There'll be a record of sightings, of course, but I'd doubt there'd be anything on migrations. There's no need."

"No need?"

"None at all, Sergeant. I'm sorry; perhaps I should have mentioned it. British Common Cranes are unique in that they are resident. Unlike all other cranes on the continent, ours do not migrate. There are a number of spots where roosts can be observed year-round."

Maik couldn't hide his welling optimism. "A map, Mr. Senior, do you have a map?" he asked earnestly. "One that shows where these resident sites might be?"

Senior withdrew a battered ordnance survey map of the north Norfolk coast from the satchel over his shoulder and jabbed at it with a leathery finger.

"This population is one of the largest," said Senior, his curiosity stilled for the moment by the urgency of Maik's request, "then this one, though we suspect it may be inactive now. And this one. Those would be the closest to our present location."

Maik tapped the map with his own forefinger. *This one.* It was intuition that guided Senior so unerringly to his Painted Bunting earlier, when everyone else had gone in a different direction. Intuition was what made some people so good at what they did. And this was what Maik was good at. This site had all the hallmarks of a hiding place Ray Hayes would choose. It was clever. It was appropriate. And it was about as unexpected as you could get. He bade Senior a hasty goodbye and began a half-sprint back to his car. Senior might feel that reparations were best left to nature, but Danny Maik wasn't going to let that stop him trying to make up for his own past sins.

38

In the milky half-light of the early morning, Domenic could almost have taken his surroundings for a field of ice — if it wasn't for the thin wraiths of mist that whispered up from the surface of the water, curtaining the motionless landscape like ghosts. It was like a scene from an earlier time, he thought, an infinite, undisturbed natural world, patiently waiting for the coming of a new cycle of life, for the arrival of a new species called humans.

Beside him, Damian stirred. "Your turn for the coffee run, I believe," he said, sitting up. "I'll take a cheese croissant, too."

Domenic forced a smile but he didn't turn from looking out over the mirror-calm water. Nothing broke the surface between them and the low smudge of the treeline that hovered in the far distance. "I think the water is still rising, Damian," he said. "There were a couple of snags out there yesterday, out past where those Common Goldeneyes are now. And a small mound of reeds, too. They're not visible anymore."

His brother looked at the uneasy grey lake around them. It stretched out across the plain as far as he could see. "That storm dumped a lot of water in the hills in the interior," he said. "Once all that reaches this flood plain, too, it's going to raise the level even higher. That search party better get here soon, or we're going to be sitting in water by the time they find us."

In the distance, the spindly reflections of the dead trees lay on the silvery surface of the water like cracks in a mirror. A raft of ducks poked around near the submerged roots. Buffleheads, perhaps? They were too far off for Domenic to tell. Above them, a pair of Whooping Cranes tracked across the white sky, necks outstretched, calling loudly.

"Looking for a home," said Damian. "This area should be perfect habitat for them, but they won't nest here if the water levels stay this high. They need it to be much lower, knee height at best."

"Don't Whooping Cranes prefer to reuse the same nest each year?"

Domenic nodded. "If they can. They always have to repair some damage that the nests have suffered over the previous winter, but I'd say they'd have their work cut out for them this year. Even if these waters do recede in time for the breeding season, they'll almost certainly choose to relocate. If they nested here last year, they won't want to move far from this area, though."

Domenic watched the birds as they continued across the landscape, gliding effortlessly on their black-tipped wings. The thought that had eluded him up on the esker that day finally distilled for him in the quiet peace of this place, like an image forming in a dream.

"I think I know what she was involved in. And why she needed to keep it from you."

Damian drew his eyes away from the birds. "Annie? You think she was mixed up in something illegal?" He shook his head uncertainly. "I don't know, Domino. Okay, she was determined, and she didn't like to be told *no*. She was uber-focused and maybe a touch obsessive, but I can't believe she would knowingly get caught up in anything really bad. She was basically a good person. A really good person."

Domenic said nothing. Damian would already know that even good people got caught up in bad things sometimes.

"Perhaps I don't need to hear it. It doesn't matter anymore, so you can spare me the details. Maybe it's more important now just to safeguard her memory. Let me do that, okay, Domino? Let me protect her, just like you want to protect Lindy."

"It's over between us." The words came suddenly. Surrounded by this desolate landscape, there no longer seemed to be anywhere for Domenic to hide from the truth.

Damian looked hard at his brother. "Now? After everything you've done for her, everything you laid on the line? To break up with you after all that doesn't sound like the Lindy I know." In the continuing silence from his brother, Damian shook his head slowly as the realization gradually took hold. "Oh, no, no, Domino. Don't tell me you didn't tell her about this guy Hayes?"

"It wasn't that simple. It's a long story."

Damian made a point of looking out at the waters surrounding their tiny, isolated perch. "You have something more pressing you need to attend to?"

Domenic sighed. "I had to keep her in the dark. It was the only way I could protect her."

"No, it wasn't. You could have told her, let her in on everything that was happening."

Domenic shook his head. "You know what she's like. She would never have let herself be cowed by Hayes, no matter how afraid she was."

"That's not up to you, Domino. However she wanted to deal with it, it should have been her choice. You took that away from her because you thought you knew better. You can't go on making decisions for people because you think it's in their best interests. You have to let people make their own mistakes."

"This one could have cost Lindy her life."

Damian looked around their reed island once more. "But look what yours has cost you."

The brothers had been silent for a long time after Domenic's revelation, each staring out from the island, lost in their own thoughts. It was Domenic who spoke first.

"At least Traz is safe. You don't want to hear about Annie's part and that's okay. But I know you've been worried that you put Traz in danger by sending him those coordinates. That's what's been gnawing at you, isn't it?"

Damian stirred. "I didn't like the thought of him out there all on his own, poking around those U.S. air bases. I liked even less the idea that I was the one that might have put him in harm's way. I've screwed up enough things. I didn't want that on my conscience, too. But if you're right, and let's face it, it has been known, if those men were not U.S. military, then, yeah, at least Traz is safe."

"He's not on his own, either. I spoke to him before I came out here. He's picked up a travel partner. A woman named Verity. He met her in Aransas."

"Aransas? He was only planning to be there one night." Damian nodded approvingly. "Clearly, he hasn't lost his touch. Not surprising, though," he said with mock pride, "I taught that boy all he knows about women."

"Then maybe we do need to be concerned about him, after all. He's obviously in a lot more trouble than he realizes."

At first, Domenic thought the noise between them was the thrumming of the wind through the reeds, the constant white noise soundtrack of their time out here. But the pitch was different this time, and when he looked up, he saw the dark speck in the sky, and a glint of light as it banked. The plane was low, flying beneath the cloud cover, the one-note drone of its engine rolling across the empty landscape towards the men.

"Cessna 210," said Damian. "It's the search plane." They stood and raised their arms above their heads, waving like cheerleaders, shouting and moving around as much as they dared on their water-laden stage.

But the Cessna banked away to continue its search farther along the river, moving inexorably away from them as if drawn by a magnet. The plane was heading for the spot where Damian's inReach had stopped working, thought Domenic, where he had told Roy he would be heading, kilometres away from where they were now.

They stopped waving and sank to the ground, their boots sodden with the water that had oozed up into the footprints they had pressed into the vegetation with their exertions. They continued to watch until the dark speck receded into the leaden skies and the sound was swallowed by the distance.

"They'll do another pass tomorrow," Damian said confidently. "We need something that will catch their eye. Do you have anything light; a white T-shirt maybe?" But the brothers had nothing between them, just the browns and greys and drab olives of outdoorsmen who wanted to blend into their landscape, not stand out from it. Even Damian's tiger-stripe jacket was perfect camouflage for the reeds that surrounded them. The clothes they were wearing would be difficult to pick out from two hundred feet in the air, let alone two thousand. If they did come again, Domenic knew, it would be to follow eskers and moraines, solid dry tracks you'd expect humans to use as they moved through the park, as generations of Dene had done before them. The search plane would trace a fifty-kilometre stretch of the river, scanning the landscape a kilometre and a half either side. One hundred and fifty square kilometres of a park three hundred times that size. The pilot would not check the middle of sodden, waterlogged swamps, areas where humans had no place, where there was no shelter for them, no sustenance. Even if the search plane returned, no one was going to look for them here.

39

Jennie Wynn led the way into her living room and resumed what Salter assumed must have been the position she had left to answer the door. On a side table beside a sofa, a half-empty cup of tea sat beside a set of reading glasses and a book. On the sofa itself, one dainty person's breadth away from the arm, a small dog patiently awaited its owner's return.

Salter made a show of looking around the tidy living room. Silk pillows embroidered with Chinois motifs lay on the sofa and chairs. On the walls were Japanese prints in soft pastel shades, and the pale tablecloth that lay on the rosewood dining table bore a stencilled print of a tranquil Asian pagoda scene. It was as if the entire space had been set up with the single aim of infusing the home with peace and serenity. Salter couldn't shake the impression that something was missing, however, but she couldn't put her finger on what it was.

The woman coiled herself back into position comfortably, Salter once again marvelling at Wynn's flexibility. "Further inquiries, Sergeant? How intriguing." She picked up her tea and sipped it. Salter had already declined the offer of a cup for herself. She had business to get to. She'd spent a long time on this case without making much progress. Now it seemed she had a chance of making some, and even the delay of a tea-making session seemed too long to put things off.

"I've been reading about these anger blackouts," said Salter conversationally. "There's a lot of experts out there who feel the phenomenon doesn't really exist. Some might say it's the majority opinion."

Wynn nodded. "I'm aware of this. But if you're thinking they might just be a convenient way for Albert to forgive himself for his sins," she shook her head, "you're quite mistaken. Albert's blackouts are genuine. I'm convinced of it."

"And he still hasn't contacted you?"

Wynn smiled her answer as another dog trotted into the room. "Ah, Startz, there you are. I was wondering whether you might join us. Bit of a loner, this one," she told the sergeant in a confiding tone. "His brother loves company, but Startz here tends to keep to himself most of the time." Wynn tousled the dog's ears with a dangling hand as he moved past the sofa. Even in the smallest gestures there was an elegance to her movements.

To Salter, the dog that had entered the room was completely indistinguishable from the one on the sofa. This one curled up on a rug, a safe distance from a pair of fragile-looking vases that flanked the fireplace. Like his sibling, Startz clearly knew the house rules. The sergeant looked in wonder at the collection of glass ornaments and bone china figurines around the room. With Max and his mates tearing around the place, none of this stuff would have lasted more than five minutes in her own home, she thought ruefully. The Salter household was no place for fragile objects. Or the faint of heart.

"I'd imagine being a sponsor in an anger management programme has a number of similarities to someone who's there to support an alcoholic," she said carefully.

"There are significant differences between the two illnesses," said the woman. "Alcoholism is always present in the consciousness of the alcoholic, as I understand it, but incidents are slower to come on. It allows the sufferer time to contact someone for help, for support. Anger, on the other hand, may lie dormant for some time, so much so that the victim may even forget it's there, or believe that they've got it under control. But rage can be sparked so quickly, there is no time for any intervention, even if the person had the presence of mind to seek it. All we can really do is discuss the incident afterward — the triggers, what might have been done to prevent escalation, coping strategies for future episodes. Empathize, really."

"*Empathize*. That's the important word, though, isn't it?" Salter said, leaning forward slightly. "Not *sympathize*. Any of us could do that."

Wynn eyed her silently, and the sergeant could see that she knew, now, what these further inquiries would entail.

"But you can only really empathize if you've also been through the same thing. Like a recovering alcoholic as an AA sponsor, or in this case, another IED sufferer."

On the couch, Wynn's lithe body seemed to take on a rigidity that jarred gratingly with the woman's normal graceful movements. "It's been a long time since I was a victim of that kind of anger, Sergeant Salter," she said, her voice taut with control. "I truly believe I can help Albert best by showing him it is possible to overcome this illness. Intermittent Explosive Disorder does not need to be the debilitating condition it is for so many of its sufferers. It can be suppressed."

"But not cured, Ms. Wynn, correct? Isn't it true that it's always somewhere inside you? That it could be triggered years later, for example, by some perceived injustice, some personal betrayal? By being cheated out of something that was rightfully yours?"

The dog beside Wynn stirred uneasily. Perhaps it had seen before this kind of stillness that had now overtaken the woman. Perhaps vigilance was necessary. "I could never have done anything like that to Wattis."

"As a matter of fact, you could. You knew Wattis Wright's schedule — when he would be home, when his guard would be down. You were one of the few people to whom he would have opened his front door without a moment's hesitation. And you had quite a record for violence when you were younger. With weapons."

"My youth, as you say. Yes, it was troubled. But that's all in the past now. Long gone." But the dog beside Wynn was not buying the woman's tight smile. It slinked away to the far end of the sofa and cowered against the armrest. Animals detected wavelengths that eluded humans, Salter knew, but that didn't mean their senses weren't to be trusted.

"The theft of your work wasn't in the past, though, was it? That was now. You've spent years watching dance moves you developed being used by other people without receiving any compensation for them. Your dance routines, ones that you'd worked so hard on, in the background, unnoticed and unappreciated. And then, when you finally get a chance to get some of the rewards you're entitled to, the recognition, the money, you're denied by a person you thought you could trust."

Salter saw that the hand that had so gently caressed the dog's ears was clenched now into a tightly balled fist. "Wattis Wright told Susan Bonaccord that he'd resolved the ownership issues to the dance rights, but he hadn't sorted out anything with you, had he, Ms. Wynn? He'd simply ignored your claims, brushed them away, and now here he was rushing off to cash in on all your hard work, your artistry, your creations."

Salter had deliberately upped the tempo. She wanted the questions to be rapid-fire, unsettling, provocative. A slow, steady approach might have allowed Jennie Wynn to keep her emotions in check. If the woman's anger was still simmering below the surface, Salter needed to bring it out. Different questioning techniques for different suspects. *Thank you, once again, DCI Jejeune.*

"He said we would discuss it," said Wynn, her voice now cold with suppressed anger, "and then I hear he has concluded the deal." A sharp intake of breath disappeared into the icy stillness of the woman's body.

"I wonder, Ms. Wynn, what would you have done, if you'd been allowed to collect on your share of those royalties?"

She nodded slowly, the movement as carefully controlled as her breathing and her words. "Yes, Sergeant, you're quite right," she said. "I would have invested in Albert's project myself. It meant so much to him. Not just the funding; but the fact that someone would have been willing to show such faith in him. To have that taken away, crushed by that man's greed, it was so callous, so unfair. *Unfair.*" The voice was low with menace, the word delivered through clenched teeth and accompanied by a violent pounding of the fist into the cushion. The dog beside her flinched and the one on the rug issued a low growl.

Wynn closed her eyes and drew in a series of deep, measured breaths. When the breathing became less pronounced, she opened her eyes again. Jennie Wynn was back, her anger stored away in the place from where it had escaped. "I did have motive, Sergeant. But the person I am now is free from the kind of anger it would take to kill someone." She leaned back casually in a way that suggested she had recovered her natural grace. "I'd remind you that I have an alibi for that time. A uniformed officer has already been next door to confirm that my neighbour saw me returning from Norwich with Fitz here. So, if that's all, I believe your further inquiries are over."

She gave a tight smile and reached out to stroke the dog on the sofa. It allowed the contact, but made no move to approach her. Trust, once lost, needs to be earned all over again.

With nowhere else to take her inquiries, Salter stood up to leave. She looked around the room one more time, taking in the soft elegance of the room's furnishings. *Music*, she thought. To complete the picture, this oasis of tranquility needed background music, something soft and soothing — wind chimes, perhaps, or dripping water. Instead, only silence filled the room, punctuated by the distant metronomic ticking of a clock from somewhere else in the house. Now that Salter had become aware of it, the music seemed a strange omission. But maybe Jennie Wynn simply preferred the sound of her own inner harmonies.

40

Salter approached the house from the rear. Despite his reserved manner, Danny's quiet courtesy and modest lifestyle would make him a popular neighbour. Eyes would be on the lookout for someone poking around the home left vacant when he went off to work each day, and Salter didn't feel like explaining her presence here to anyone until she knew what was going on. The only time Danny ever failed to show up for work was when he was recuperating from injuries he had picked up on the job. Except for that one time, when his heart began making demands his battle-scarred body proved unable to meet. It was the tremor of this memory, and the knowledge that Maik lived alone, that was causing Salter some slight concern now as she approached.

She retrieved the spare key from the top of the lintel and entered into the kitchen. She called out to make sure no one was home, or at least in any condition to answer, and looked around. One washed tea mug sat upturned in the drainer on the countertop, one clean spoon beside it. In the recycling bin, one beer can sat like an abandoned pet. She went through to the living room and then checked upstairs — both bedrooms, the bathroom. There was no sign of Danny.

But it wasn't going to be enough simply to establish that Danny wasn't here. DCS Shepherd would expect a higher threshold of curiosity than that from her new sergeant. Salter would need some clues as to just where Danny Maik might be. She returned to the living room, where more signs of one man's singular existence were in evidence. A solitary leather armchair sat near the fireplace, with a small table beside it. The other items in the room were arranged for the maximum convenience of a single inhabitant: frequently used ones within easy reach, others relegated to the backs of sideboards and shelves. Despite her concern for Danny, and her misgivings about being here, there was something about the quiet stillness of the room that she found comforting. The character of the man lingered in these surroundings: his calmness, his reassuring composure.

She walked around the room, trailing her hand over its surfaces: the flat-screen TV that managed to give the impression somehow that it was rarely used; the music system that suggested the opposite. She let her fingertip riffle across the neatly stacked album covers on the stand in the corner. All the familiar names were here: the Temptations, the Four Tops, the Miracles, groups whose dance moves Danny insisted had been passed down through the lineage to the Shammalars. The solo artists, too, she recognized: Marvin Gaye, Stevie Wonder, Jimmy Ruffin — people she'd become so familiar with over the years, she could even distinguish between their voices.

"Where are you, Danny?" she asked the empty room. "And what are you working on in the background that's such a big secret? Whatever it is, if you could possibly tear yourself away from it for a few minutes, it'd certainly be appreciated. I keep telling myself not to fail Wattis Wright but, to be honest, whether Ross killed him or Jennie Wynn did, I can't for the life of me see how I'm going to get either of them for it. So, if you've got any ideas, you know ... gratefully accepted."

She remembered sitting in this room one night, discussing another case in which there had also been precious little progress. "Some we don't solve, Constable," Maik had told her simply. He never talked about winning or losing. Closing a murder case wasn't a game. Someone went to prison, others mourned a loved one. There were no winners or losers in that scenario, just the guilty and the victims, and those they left behind.

Wattis Wright was a victim, but he had left no one behind. She knew she had made a mistake in caring too much, in relating with the man and the type of life he had led. But she knew why. She looked around this sparse living room. How could she not make the connection? Yet she knew she'd made other mistakes, too, like revealing crime scene details to Bonaccord, or advising Ross to explain away his words as hyperbole. It didn't matter that these mistakes were inconsequential, that Ross freely admitted he was prone to such outbursts, and Bonaccord had an iron-clad alibi for the time of the murder. They were stupid procedural errors of the kind that DCI Domenic Jejeune would never have made. Nor Danny Maik.

Perhaps her doubts had always been there; faint whispers drowned out by all that was going on around her. Perhaps it was just the hanging silence of Danny's living room that was amplifying them now, allowing them to grow into full-blown fears. But for the first time, Lauren Salter really began to question whether she was capable of delivering the justice that Wattis Wright deserved.

"I'm not sure I know where to go from here, Danny," she told the empty room.

"DCI Jejeune would look into the evidence," the absent Danny Maik told her from somewhere in the ether. She knew what he meant, this phantom Danny who'd come to guide her. Jejeune never simply accepted the information the evidence gave him. He was always asking it for more, trying to draw things from it that others might not even be aware that it held. Salter was just not sure she was blessed with the same talents.

"Few of us are, Sergeant," said the Danny voice, ad libbing now. "But there are other ways of coming up with answers, beyond thinking it to a solution. What do your instincts tell you?"

That Albert Ross did it. She knew Jejeune would already have arrested him by now. Ross would have made some mistake, some slip-up that the DCI would have honed in on. Perhaps he'd already made it, that one misstep, and she'd failed to pick up on it. *Look at the evidence again. Look in it, not just at it. Look for that missing piece.* She couldn't tell if it was the Danny voice this time, or her own. But it was what she would do.

Convinced by now that she would find no answers to Danny's location here, she rose from the armchair and checked her watch. A thought occurred to her and she crossed again to the rack of albums. No Herb Dixon. She took out her phone, and entered the name into Google, reading with growing astonishment as she stood in this empty room about the world of the Motown session singers. The Andantes, the Originals, Louvain Demps; names she had never heard of, but who had probably appeared on more hit records between them than any other artists in the history of recorded music. All while remaining unknown, unheralded, unacknowledged.

Perhaps she and Danny weren't so different from these people, after all; Maik toiling away anonymously behind the DCI, she performing her own supporting role for Max. She wondered what would happen when the DCI and her son no longer needed the support of some shadowy background figure any longer. Danny seemed content enough here in his cocoon, with his music for company. But for all the exhilaration of her promotion, she knew her career alone would never be enough once Max had weaned himself from her care. She was never going to be Susan Bonaccord, immersing herself in her work, convincing herself that she wanted things that way. Lauren Salter needed somebody in her life. But all her somebodys were abandoning her in one way or another. The disturbing thought stayed with her long after she closed the door on Danny's empty house.

41

Domenic flapped his arms around, batting himself on the shoulders. "My hands and my feet are getting numb, Damian. I can't get warm, no matter what I do. I can't shake off the cold. It's like it's just sitting inside me."

"You have to fight it, Domino. Keep forcing it away. Don't let it get hold of you. The sun will be up soon. It's going to be a better day today. The sun is going to come out and warm us up."

But the gathering morning light held little warmth, and by the time the last remnants of the night had faded away, there was still no evidence of Damian's promised sun in the white sky. Instead, on the horizon, a low bank of brooding clouds, laden with the promise of more cold weather, marshalled their forces.

The men spent most of their time kneeling now, or sitting on their haunches. The weight of a standing human being seemed to place too much pressure on the integrity of the mound, and they found their feet sinking quickly through the sodden reeds. Spreading their weight out at least allowed them to avoid the worst of the moisture that percolated up through the vegetation. It was no longer possible to deny the insidious rising of the water. Areas of this reed bed that had been dry when they had first hauled themselves onto it were now wallowing in a film of tawny fluid. The trampled-down sections around the edges, where the men had gone to scoop up handfuls of water, were completely submerged.

The siren song of the wind had died down for once, leaving behind a ghostly silence that hung above their tiny island like a threat. Damian turned to his brother. "If you want to tell me, it's okay."

Domenic gave his brother a puzzled look.

"Annie." Damian shrugged his shoulders "Maybe I do need to know why we're here, after all," he said, "whatever she was involved in. You said you don't think the men were U.S. military, but those birds were carrying cameras, Domenic. And you can't tell me the military wouldn't have been interested in finding out who was sending VHF tracking devices over their installations."

"Maybe so. I think they even dispatched a couple of local contractors to check Annie out, but I don't think it was because they were worried about any secret installations the cranes flew over. There are spy satellites that can read the text on your cellphone. What kind of military secrets are overflying birds going to be able to photograph that can't already be seen by technology like that?"

"But what else can this have been about?"

Domenic was slow to answer, as if he was taking the time to consider his response. "I think she made a deal with Gaetan Robideau," he said finally. "She was going to provide him with photographs. Those photographs on the chip. Robideau was looking for evidence of the changes caused by the water management policies in the park, but there was no way the park superintendent would issue a permit for a low-level flight now that the cranes were starting to return to their breeding grounds. But the cranes themselves, as they drop down to their nesting areas, they would be at the perfect height to get both the wider picture of the park's water systems and the individual details of the landscape. I believe Annie Prior offered to get Robideau the photographic evidence he needed for his lawsuit."

"But not for free, right? Not if I know Annie. In return, she wanted Robideau to show her where those ceremonial Dene sites are." Damian nodded thoughtfully.

"It would have been the chance at an insight into Dene culture that no one else had ever been granted," said Domenic simply.

Damian looked at his brother, and shook his head sadly. "I hate to say it, but I could see her making a deal like that. You know how these anthropologists are; the prospect of exclusive access to a pristine site, that's a pretty tempting proposition, especially for somebody as driven and ambitious as she was. So these contractors, you don't think they wanted to harm Annie? All she needed to do was show them what the cameras had been photographing, and they'd have left her alone?"

"I doubt they would have wanted to take it any further once they knew her interest was only in landforms up here."

Damian sat in silence for a long time, staring out over the water. "So why the hell did she run?" he asked bitterly.

"Because Whooping Cranes are an endangered species. Unauthorized trapping of them is a federal crime. You were an unwitting accomplice, but as the one who came up with the plan, she may even have been looking at jail time. At the very least, she was facing the loss of her academic reputation, not to mention her faculty position at that university."

Damian shook his head slowly, taking in his brother's ideas, accepting them fully. When he spoke again, his voice was heavy with sadness. "So, this was never about the VHF signals," he said, "or the military bases? Or any of that?"

He sank into a long contemplative silence. Domenic knew he was thinking if he had been there to intervene, to explain this to the men, perhaps he could have saved Annie's life. Domenic could have told his brother it wasn't true, but what was the point? Didn't we all need our deceptions, our indulgent vanities that we could have made a difference, have altered the course of the cosmos, if only ...

The faint drone of the Cessna 210's engine drifted to them once again across the wide, empty wilderness. It was following the same route as previously, southward along the Little Buffalo River. By now, the raft of reeds was too waterlogged to support either of them if they stood, so they simply sat and watched in silence, tracking the aircraft's progress against the high sky; a tiny black insect inching across an infinite blanket of snow.

Damian turned to his brother as the plane banked away from them. "They'll come back. Now they've checked the river systems, they'll widen their search area. They'll find us, Domino. Roy won't let them stop looking. You know that."

Domenic wasn't buying it. But perhaps it wasn't him that Damian was trying to convince any more. His older brother looked at Domenic earnestly. "We've been lucky, huh, the people we've been able to count on over the years: Roy, that Danny Maik guy you work with. Even Traz. When I sent him those coordinates, there was no hesitation. I needed them checked, he took it on. No questions asked. A couple of days to plan, and he was on his way."

"You know Traz," said Domenic simply. "Always up for a challenge."

Damian smiled dubiously. "You say that like it's a good thing. Remember that time I took that girl to Point Pelee for the weekend, and somebody had burned Leonard Cohen tracks over the top of all my AC/DC discs?"

Memories were a good place to be just now, and Domenic was happy to join his brother in them. "Ancient history," he said. "Traz thought if he left a couple of AC/DC tracks on at the beginning of your mixes, by the time the Cohen songs started, you'd already be too far into your trip to come back."

Damian smiled. "A criminal mastermind, that guy. But he would have needed an inside man, wouldn't he, Domenic?" he said, scrutinizing his brother with a playful stare. "There had to be somebody to get the original discs out of my car and the overdubbed CDs back in again afterward without me noticing. He could never have pulled that part off all by himself, could he?" He released Domenic from his stare and gazed back into his memories once more. "As it happened, Rachael turned out to be a big Leonard Cohen fan. She thought I'd brought those CDs along especially for her. Still, though, all the way down to Pelee and back, that's a lot of miles of gravelly voiced angst, Domino." He shook his head ruefully. "*A lot.*"

"I always thought listening to Leonard Cohen was a lot like birding," said Domenic. "It's only okay to admit you do it once somebody else already has."

Damian managed to find a genuine laugh from somewhere. "Good old Len, eh? I remember Lindy used to sing 'Hallelujah' all the time when I was over there. Remember?"

He began singing a verse, softly at first, almost to himself, and then bolder, raising his voice bravely as he moved into the chorus. The distant, sweet memory of Lindy singing it as she padded barefoot through the kitchen swirled into Domenic's heart, and he joined his brother's efforts. The still landscape seemed to consume their voices, swallowing them up, threatening to overwhelm the brothers' harmonies as they lifted them against its emptiness. They were nothing out here, the wilderness told them; they were as insignificant as pollen seeds floating on this vast, still lake of water. But they sang on, in defiance of nature's indifference, in spite of it, until at last their will failed them and their efforts faded into silence. The faint thrum of the Cessna came to them now that quiet had returned. But when they looked up to the sky, the plane was no longer visible.

42

Traz and Verity had plotted their strategy at a tiny table in the back of the general store next to the Borealis Motel. Like many places in the north, the store was a multi-function operation, with a small engine-repair shop at the front, a couple of aisles of grocery supplies, and a tiny café crammed into the back of the space.

"The hotel clerk heard that Domenic was seen talking to a man named Gaetan Robideau before he went into the park. Apparently, Robideau knows a lot about the park and the conditions. Maybe Domenic told him where he planned to go." Traz took a drink of his coffee and pulled a face.

"Rule one for a good cup of coffee," said Verity. "Don't order it from a place that has a gas pump in the forecourt. I'm sure the park staff would have talked to Robideau when they were drawing up the search plans."

Traz shook his head. "Word is, he and the park superintendent, Bracker, don't see eye to eye."

"Still, nobody up here would ever knowingly avoid providing information that might help find somebody who was lost in the park. In this part of the world everybody would know what that could mean ... sorry." She fell silent.

"No, you're right," said Traz, "Domenic was asking around about somebody named Annie Prior, too. That's who Damian went into the park with. I'm guessing Bracker will have all the details on the trip plan she filed. I think you should go and talk to Robideau while I have a word with her."

They lifted their cups to prevent spillage as a woman squeezed past the table to reach the cooler behind them. She grabbed a jug of milk and smiled an apology as she edged past them again on her way out.

"I should talk to the park superintendent," said Verity. "If it comes down to techno-speak about crane habitat and such, I might be better equipped to handle it." She stopped herself and looked at him. "If that's where they were headed, I mean."

Traz looked puzzled. "Where else would they go? The coordinates Damian sent me prove he was working on some kind of crane migration study. He wasn't involved in any research of his own, so presumably it must have been Prior's project." He drained his coffee and screwed up his face again. He looked at his watch. "The park offices are open now. If you go to see where things are with the search operation, I'll try to find Robideau."

"You want a coffee to go?" asked Verity.

Traz shook his head. "Better not. They may need it if somebody comes in for an oil change."

Verity sat patiently in Carol Bracker's office, waiting for the park superintendent to conclude a telephone call. A museum of Bohemian Waxwings sat in the tops of the cedars behind the feeder outside the window, but if Verity saw the birds, she gave no sign. Her mind was on the look that had crossed Bracker's face as soon as she had heard Verity's accent. Would somebody speaking Ivy League English have been made to wait this long while Bracker worked out a minor scheduling problem? The question didn't even merit an answer. She fixed on a smile as the superintendent cradled the phone.

"Sorry about that. The business of running the park has to go on, even during disruptions."

It wasn't the term Verity would have used to describe three people lost in some of the most inhospitable terrains on the continent, but perhaps Carol Bracker had more practice using fancy words.

"You were saying, before the telephone call interrupted you, that you're still verifying the details in the questionnaires they filed. Those people are in trouble out there, Ms. Bracker. Seems to me that making sure the paperwork is in order might not be the priority right now."

"I was saying," said Bracker, letting the temperature of her voice drop a degree or two, as the criticized often do, "that we intend to use the information in the questionnaire to draw up our ground search plan. The proposed route filed by Dr. Prior doesn't seem to align with the form filled out by Domenic Jejeune when he went in to find them." She gave Verity a cold smile. "There are a number of factors in establishing a viable search grid that members of the general public no doubt fail to appreciate."

Verity had been handling patronizing attitudes all her life. Finding a sweet smile for one more was no big ask, given that three people's lives were at stake. "Pardon my curiosity, but just who all are you verifying those details with? I happen to know nobody from here has called the one man who spoke to both brothers before they went into the park. His name's Traz Perez. He's here in town, in case anybody cared to check with him about what he knows."

"The details have been verified by Officer Ducannon of the RCMP. He's the Jejeunes' brother-in-law. It was Officer Ducannon who first contacted us. It was at his suggestion that we put a plane up for a cursory search yesterday. We've been coordinating things with him from the beginning."

Bracker gave Verity a superior smile. "You don't seem to be up to speed on this, Ms. Brown. Perhaps you should contact Officer Ducannon yourself and coordinate your own inquiries with him."

"Domenic Jejeune reported that he believed his brother was in trouble days ago. Some folks might think you should be well past establishing your search grid by now. Forgive me for saying so, but sending in one plane to make a couple of passes over a tiny section of a park this size doesn't seem like a whole lot of searching so far."

Bracker stiffened at the blunt reproach. Auburn-haired country girls with lip rings didn't come into her office telling her how to do her job. She maintained the professional courtesy her position required, but the iciness in her tone now was unmistakable. "We authorized one flyover of Domenic Jejeune's proposed route, but his expressed intent was to meet up with his brother and Dr. Prior. It's entirely possible he found them and has decided to stay with them until they return. They are not scheduled to be back in Fort Smith until this evening. If the party of three fails to return by tonight, we'll go out at first light tomorrow. So, if there's nothing else, I'll get back to drawing up that search grid."

"Gaetan Robideau?" Traz poked his head around the open door of the small trailer and saw a tall, lean man with long black hair standing over a tiny sink.

The man turned at the sound of his name and held up two fish on a string. "Look at this. Two boys from the reserve got into a scrape and the elders assigned them a task. *Go out and catch two fish, and take them to Gaetan Robideau for when he breaks his fast.*" The man looked at the fish again. "The boys said they caught these for me out on the lake, but the gills on these fish are grey. Healthy fish have pink ones. These fish drowned, got caught up in a back channel somewhere when the water from that big storm overflowed." He shook his head sadly. "Nature still tells its truths to those who know how to recognize them, but the young have no knowledge of the traditional wisdom anymore." He set the fish in the sink and turned to Traz again, ushering him outside where he joined him beside the trailer.

"You want to talk about the outdoors, better we are outdoors. You're here about those missing people in the park. Carol Bracker send you here, too?"

"The men in the park are my friends, Mr. Robideau. I know at least one of them came to see you."

Robideau nodded. "The younger brother. Not the older one. You like to walk?" he asked. "Let's walk."

They walked through the grid of narrow streets in silence. Traz looked across at Robideau. He recognized the man was coming to terms with something, reconciling himself to it. He was unsure whether he should press for details now or simply wait for them to come. Although Robideau was staring straight ahead, he seemed to sense the conflict within Traz.

"This woman, she your friend, too?"

"Just the men," said Traz. "I've never met Annie Prior."

"Lot of good qualities. Determination, perseverance. Dene qualities."

"She isn't Dene, though?"

Robideau shook his head. "But she spent some time up here. She has always been interested in us. Our culture." He mounted a small steep rise and Traz followed. They emerged onto a high ridge overlooking a wide expanse of river, glistening even in the dull, overcast light. "She wanted to dig at the old Dene feasting sites in the park."

Robideau's comment had Traz spinning to look at him. "Annie Prior did? I thought she was in the park to do research on Whooping Cranes. I was sent some coordinates. They were stopover sites for migratory cranes, I'm sure of it."

"She never asked me about cranes, only those sites. Not sure what she was hoping to find in them, though. The deposits would go back a long way, possibly centuries, but there wouldn't be much in there. Maybe a few cooking pots, some bones."

"Human?"

Robideau shook his head. "The Dene wouldn't bury their dead that way. Animal bones, from the feasting — beaver, deer, geese, ducks."

"No Whooping Cranes, I trust," said Traz. But his half-smile stilled at Robideau's nod.

"Them, too. Till they got rare. Don't worry; the Dene stopped eating Whooping Cranes long before the government told them they had to."

"Do you think Annie Prior could have gone to look for these sites herself?"

Robideau shook his head. "She knows she would never find them on her own."

"So she'd need you to take her to them." Traz paused for a moment. "But why would you ever agree to do that, I wonder."

Robideau was looking out over the rapids, and beyond, to where the river snaked away, winding its way back into the wilderness. Traz stared at his profile for a long time. The features never changed, the nerves never twitched. No squint, no scowl. Just the staring.

"A trade," he said, without turning. "Been something of a tradition up here over the years. Your history books may even have mentioned it." The light from the lopsided grin illuminated Robideau's craggy features for a second before dying out as quickly as it had risen. "Annie Prior came to see me. She said she had heard I needed evidence of the changing water patterns in the park and she could get it for me. Photographs, from some cameras fitted to cranes. She would hand them over in return for access to the sites. She said she knew it would be difficult to get the council's permission, but maybe if I went to them to petition on her behalf, they'd agree. I told her if she got the evidence, we'd see what could be worked out."

When he turned back to Traz, regret swam in his eyes, but with it, too, a kind of defiance.

"The band council would never have accepted Prior's deal. But they should have. Trading our history for our future, isn't that what all existence is? This is what nature teaches us, to let the older generations pass in order to secure a future for the coming ones. That water supply is our children's heritage."

The men stood in silence on the ridge, the sound of the wind in their ears. Traz looked back along the river, as Robideau had done, up into the wilderness. Out there, the steady measured cadence of nature's heartbeat continued as it always had, as it always would.

"Do you have any idea where those people might be, Mr. Robideau?"

"I looked for them. To recover the cameras, they would need to trap those cranes, and the only place you can get close enough to do that is at their nesting sites." He shook his head. "Used to be there were only a couple of places you could find nesting Whooping Cranes; Lobstick, Sass River. Now with the changing water systems, there are many new areas for the birds. I went to one or two, but there was no sign of them."

Traz leaned forward, trying to drive down his despair with the urgency of his question. "Can you give me any clues at all as to where the other places might be?"

Robideau shrugged sadly. "No one can know what's in a wild bird's heart. They go where things are good for them." He looked out over the rapids again. "I met your friend here," he said. "Water was lower then. Not so angry. I think maybe your friend felt he could control his situation out there. But the wild places are outside everyone's control. My guess is, he'll know that by now." He pointed to a thin band of powder blue sky beneath a bank of cloud on the horizon. "North wind heading this way. You better hope the search team finds your friends fast. Wherever they are, they're in for a cold night."

Traz and Verity sat at the same table at the rear of the general store. She stared in horror at the submarine sandwich he had just withdrawn from a microwave oven that looked like it might double as the store's engine degreaser. He tore off half the sub and pushed it towards her. She looked at the label on the piping hot saran wrap and pointed to the expiry date. "I should have brought a candle," she said. "It'll be celebrating its first birthday soon."

She reached around to open the cooler, handing a jug of orange juice to a boy to save him from having to inch past them. When she turned back to Traz, his face was a mask of sadness. "Robideau says a cold front is coming. It's not good. They've been out there a long time, Verry. What did Carol Bracker say about the search plans?"

Verity reached across the table and took his free hand. "Traz, they're not even going to start a proper ground search until tomorrow."

Traz looked devastated. "There's got to be something I can do."

"You need to be here, in case the search party needs to contact you. They might need more details about your friends. Their brother-in-law has been helping them out up to now, but maybe the boys told you something he's not aware of. Did you know he's an RCMP officer?"

"Roy?" Traz nodded. "Domenic's a cop, too. A detective, back in the U.K. It kind of runs in their family."

Verity looked startled. "Domenic's a police detective? Is that why he went into the park, to check on a crime?"

"What? No." Traz set down his sandwich and looked at her. "He went into that park to look for his brother. And Annie Prior. Why would you think he'd be looking at criminal activity? He'd have no jurisdiction here to investigate anything. Is everything okay?" He kept his eyes on her face for a moment. He wondered if she had learned anything from her meeting that would cause this heightened state of concern that now seemed to have gripped her.

"Traz, you might need to start preparing yourself for bad news. That park superintendent believes she's smart and all, but I don't think she can find your friends. At least, not in time."

He looked around at the haphazard grocery shelves and the cramped confines of this machine shop-cum-café. It was a terrible, soulless place to hear somebody pronounce a death sentence on people you cared about.

"I have one idea," said Verity. "I need to get to my computer back in the room to access the tracking data from Aransas. I'm not sure if it'll tell me anything, but right now, I believe it's about the only chance your friends have." She looked at him earnestly across the Formica tabletop. "It may be that folks up here know the terrain and the conditions and all. But they don't know them birds like I do."

43

Danny Maik wasn't angry with himself that he'd missed such an obvious location. He'd long since given up being upset about his inability to protect Lindy. Now all that was left was to try to undo the damage that had been done. Perhaps then, if he got her safely away from Ray Hayes, he'd find the time to treat himself to the contempt he deserved.

He had advanced as far as he could along the beach, but now it had become necessary to scrabble up the sandy cliff onto the coastal path for his final approach. It was here the first risk would come. As he emerged into the open at the top of the cliff, there would be a moment when he was in direct view before he could reach the shelter of the brush along the far edge of the path. He'd get there as quickly as he could, but if Ray Hayes happened to be looking in this direction as he broke cover, Danny would be visible.

He paused for a few moments just below the top of the rise, his body pressed flat against the rock face, his feet firmly entrenched in the runnels that ran like claw marks down towards the sea. He could hear the waves breaking gently on the rocky shore below him. The faintest of breezes stirred the sprigs of early sea bindweed poking out of the rock all around him. It was a cool day, with a weak sun that suggested more warmth than it delivered. It suited Danny. He was already perspiring, and he knew by the time he'd made it all the way to the place Lindy was being held, he'd be sweating a lot more. It wouldn't be because of the weather, though.

He had no doubt this was the right place. He'd known it as soon as he'd seen it on Quentin Senior's battered map. Off to the east, if he'd have cared to raise his head from the cliff face and look, was the proof. The cranes were a fair way inland. Maik must have driven past the site countless times on the coastal road, but he'd had no idea it was there. It was surprising Jejeune had never pointed it out to him. Perhaps some vestiges of that early secrecy Senior had spoken about still existed among the birding community. Lindy was aware of this population, though. She knew where it was, even if she couldn't have made out what the birds were from this distance. Maik doubted even Domenic Jejeune could have identified the birds as Common Cranes from this far away. But Lindy hadn't said he would be able to identify them. She'd told Maik her boyfriend would have been able to *recognize* them. It was a word you used for something familiar. And that was how Maik knew she was here.

He drew in a breath and risked a peek over the edge. Everything was as he remembered it — the path, the approach, and the sightlines from those windows. It was a risk he had to take. If he made it across the open space, he had cover all the way up to the building.

He hauled himself up over the cliff edge and ducked into a low roll, shuddering a stand of gorse as he crashed through to the far side. He waited, recovering his breath, his ears attuned to any noise from the house. There was no reason to suppose Hayes would have come tearing along the path even if he had spotted Maik. The sergeant had already learned enough to know Ray Hayes was clever, and clever criminals didn't give up their advantages with panicky, ill-advised moves. So, the silence behind the gentle rustling of the vegetation all around him didn't really prove anything. Whether Hayes had seen him or not, Danny knew he had no choice but to continue his approach.

He moved forward in a low crouch, using the gorse as a screen. He elected to go in from the back. He could come up virtually underneath the rear patio without being detected. On it, there was a key to the back door under one of the planters. Hayes would have looked for spare keys, but Lindy wouldn't have told him where this one was. With luck, he would have missed it.

Maik leaned against a bulky steel strut that angled out to allow the patio to project over the cliff edge. He didn't need to peek up to check the layout. He'd been on this patio many times before, taking in those wonderful sea views, raising a glass to this success of his DCI's, or that one of Lindy's. There would be no champagne toast to mark this visit to the cottage, though, only the bitter taste in Danny's mouth at his failure to perform the one duty entrusted to him by Domenic Jejeune.

The kitchen was empty. Maik closed the door gently behind him and listened. He heard a faint hiss he couldn't identify, but there were no sounds of movement. He'd expected some sort of early warning system — pots or pans leaned against the door, even, to clatter a warning of an undetected entry. But there was nothing. A house with four exposed sides should have had some sort of arrangement like that. But Hayes not only was intelligent, he *thought* he was intelligent. He'd be confident that his choice of this location to hold Lindy was clever enough that it wouldn't be considered.

Maik eased slowly along the long hallway, his footsteps on the hardwood floor as light as falling feathers. He pressed himself back against one wall as he approached the living room, trying to stay out of the sightlines. He tried to imagine where Hayes would be. The chair near the window would be his guess, watching for an approach along the driveway. If so, he'd have his back to Maik as the sergeant emerged from the hallway. There would be a split second of advantage for Danny. With luck, it would be all he would need.

Running water. Maik recognized the hissing noise now. It was coming from behind the closed door he had just passed. The bathroom door. But why was the water running? *To wash away blood?* Had Hayes already killed Lindy? Was he now trying to clean up the evidence? Maik spun around and began moving back down the hallway towards the bathroom door, abandoning his stealth in his panic. As he reached for the doorknob, he felt the cold steel point press into his neck from behind. He froze.

"I had hoped you wouldn't be bright enough to think about looking here, Sergeant. See what a price you pay for underestimating somebody's intelligence. What you're going to do now is leave that hand on the doorknob and reach forward and put the other one on top of it. That's right. And now back your feet away. Keep going."

Maik kept backing away until he was at full stretch, his entire weight supported only by his two hands on the doorknob, at arms-length in front of him. In this position, Danny Maik was helpless to launch any kind of assault, but he knew any attempt to reposition himself would result in a knife blade across his carotid artery. Maik had been utterly outmanoeuvred by Hayes, and both men knew it.

"Where's Lindy?" Maik's arms were beginning to tremble with the strain. "What have you done with her?"

Hayes ignored the question. "I really do wish you hadn't come, Sergeant. Things are going to get bad in a hurry now. And it's all going to be your fault."

The pressure of the knife point on Maik's neck had remained constant. There was no shaking in Hayes's hand to suggest any nervousness or uncertainty. He wouldn't be squeamish about spilling Maik's blood. So why hadn't he?

"Where's Lindy?" asked Maik again. His tone was demanding, insistent, despite his position.

"She's just on the other side of that door, as a matter of fact. But I wouldn't advise going in."

"Why not?"

"She's naked."

Maik raised his head despite the knife point, feeling the wave of nausea swell within him. "If you've done anything to her, Hayes, I'll …"

"On your hands and knees. Crawl towards the living room. I know you know the way. Slowly, and don't try to get up. Let's see if we can keep this nice wood floor from getting all covered in blood, shall we?"

Danny was lying face down on the living room floor in a spread-eagle position when Lindy entered the room. She was wearing a white blouse and faded blue jeans. She was barefoot, and her short hair was still wet from the shower.

"Danny," she screamed, dropping down beside him. "Are you okay?"

"He's fine," Hayes told her, hovering over Maik with the knife still firmly in his grip. "He's come to save you." He laughed cruelly. "You really can pick 'em, Lindy. One stretched out here like a bearskin rug and the other one half a world away pretending he doesn't care. And they say heroes are hard to find these days."

"You came alone?" Despite her efforts, Lindy hadn't managed to hide the disappointment in her voice. But it was Hayes who answered for Maik. "And without the bookmark. I doubt this one even contacted your boyfriend. I'm betting he'll have wanted to put this right himself. Silent alarm on the back door, by the way, in case you're wondering," said Hayes, addressing Maik's prone form. "I take it Jejeune didn't bother mentioning to you that he'd had one installed." He shook his head. "There does seem to have been a lot of secrecy going on with the DCI before he left. I imagine the two of you must feel quite betrayed by it all."

Maik could smell the sweet, fruity perfume of Lindy's shampoo as she leaned forward to stroke his face. "Thank you, Danny. You did all you could."

Maik knew Lindy's words had been meant to comfort him, but they twisted into him deeper than any knife blade could have done.

Hayes reached down and hooked a hand roughly under Lindy's arm, dragging her away. "Why don't you go and make us all a nice cup of tea, Lindy, and we'll see if we can't sort out this latest mess that Sergeant Maik has caused." He watched her disappear into the kitchen before turning back to Maik. "You can sit up if you behave yourself. Back flat against the wall, legs stretched out in front of you."

Maik scrambled into the instructed position and locked a flinty, unwavering stare on the other man.

"You don't want to be moving without permission." Hayes let his eyes drift towards Lindy in the kitchen and then back to the knife blade. "Not unless you're sure everything would go exactly as planned. And how's that been working out for you so far, Sergeant Maik? Well enough to take the risk?" He looked back into Maik's stare. "No, I didn't think so."

Lindy returned with three mugs of tea, placing one at Maik's side and another on a coffee table before retreating to a chair on the far side of the room like an obedient pet. No commands, no restraints. What was going on here? It seemed impossible that Hayes had been able to subdue Lindy's spirit so quickly. But there was a compliance in her that went beyond the obedience of fear. The blood ran a little colder in Danny Maik's veins.

"Okay," said Hayes. "Now that we're all settled, we can get on with it. You're going to have to try to keep up here, Sergeant, because I don't have a lot of time to walk you through things. I suggest you do your best, though, because Lindy's life depends on it."

"It's okay, Ray. You can trust Danny. He'll listen to you."

Ray? Maik snapped a look at Lindy. What was he up against here? Whatever Hayes had done to control Lindy, whatever hold he now had over her, his dominance seemed complete.

Hayes walked over to the sofa and sat down. He lifted his tea and took a casual sip, as if weighing the truth of Lindy's words. He set the mug down again and looked at Maik. "I have not been trying to kill Lindy, Sergeant Maik. I've brought her here to protect her from the man who has."

44

A delicate fringe of pale frost trimmed the edge of the water like a lace hem. It was brittle and paper thin, unlikely to survive even a few moments now that the morning light was arriving. But it was a telltale reminder that the temperatures the previous night had plummeted, bringing hours of relentless, unremitting cold that had chilled the men and driven their body temperatures steadily lower. Now, as they lay huddled inside their jackets, the wind blustered around them constantly, the cold air leaching the dampness from the men's clothes and seeping it into their bones.

"I've stopped shivering, Damian." Domenic's speech was thick and slurry. "That's not good, is it?"

"It's okay. It'll pass. Hang in there. Help's on the way. I'm sure Roy is organizing another search."

Both men were lying on their sides, looking out over the water. The island of vegetation beneath them was now so soggy and waterlogged, that even the slightest extra pressure brought liquid oozing up to fill the depressions. Standing was no longer possible; only by laying on their sides to spread their weight out could they keep the water away from the surface of the matted reeds.

Domenic looked at the dead spruce trees on the horizon, hovering like black spectres. There was something magnificent in the way the landscape had shrugged off any evidence of human presence. The Dene had been criss-crossing this land for centuries, but a person could travel for days and never see a single sign of their passing in this park. Humans left no scar on its rocks, no ripple on its waters.

Damian fished something out from between the reeds near his face. He laid it gently on his open palm and stirred it slightly with the tip of his forefinger. It was a small grey-flecked shard, hard and bright. He lifted himself up higher on his elbow and held the fragment of eggshell out for his brother to see.

"I wonder if this one made it," he said. "One more crane towards the five hundred. I would have loved to have seen the day we got there. I'll bet there'll be champagne flowing all along the migration routes the day that bird hatches."

Domenic watched as his brother placed the fragment of shell on the reeds again as gently as if it had been a precious gemstone. Five hundred. The magic number at which the Whooping Cranes would be considered to have sufficient numbers for a viable, sustainable wild population. Five hundred wild birds, from an original population of fifteen. It was going to be an astonishing achievement, one of the great conservation stories of all time. And they were almost there. But Damian had given up hope of ever seeing it. He was telling Domenic the time had come for them to stop lying to each other. They were going to die out here. There would be no search flight coming. No rescuers were miraculously going to happen upon them. This place could hide five-foot-tall white birds by the hundreds. A beaver dam nearly a kilometre long had existed undetected in the park for decades until it was accidentally spotted by a passing satellite. What chance then of the discovery of two humans on a floating raft of rotting vegetation in the centre of a vast floodplain?

Death. Domenic had known it for some time, but to hear it in his brother's words, in the finality, the acceptance of his tone was still a shock. It ran through him like an electric current. The two brothers had been rock climbing once and misjudged the length of the rope. Domenic remembered the sensation as he felt the rope's end pass through his feed hand. The fall had been no more than a few feet then; a short drop and a sharp, sickening jolt at the end. This time, there was no jolt, no end, just a sensation of spiralling downward that felt as if it would go on forever.

The cold was like a membrane now, coating every inch of the men's skin. It seemed to seal their chilled cores within them, shutting out any warmth from their clothes or the low, watery sun that filtered through the cloud cover.

"Is there anything you wish you had done differently, Damian?"

His brother peered out over the dark water for so long, Domenic wondered if he had heard him. Or perhaps just decided not to answer. "It's been a good ride," said Damian eventually. "I wouldn't have changed very much of what I did. I would have liked to see that eighth continent, though."

"Zealandia?"

"Apart from the North and South Islands, it's mostly underwater, but I would have liked to have been able to say I'd been there, that I'd set foot on all eight continents. I had chances to go. I should have done that."

"Do you think there'll ever be agreement about whether it really is another continent?"

"It would have been to me." Damian pounded a weak fist into his chest. "What's in here, Domenic. What you feel, what you believe, that's what's important. That's all that matters."

"I never even got to see the seventh continent," said Domenic quietly.

"Antarctica? Oh, it's magnificent. The space, the silence. It's so, so ..." Damian choked back his emotion. "The world is filled with wonderful places and I've been so blessed to have seen as many of them as I have." He recovered himself slightly and lifted up onto an elbow again. "How about you, Domino? Anything you'd like back?"

"Lindy," said Domenic. "I should have told her what I was doing." His head rocked sideways a little as he shook it weakly, as if he was in danger of losing control of the action. "I shouldn't have lied to her, no matter the reason."

"What I said, the other day, I was wrong. It was a good thing you did. Not just what you gave, but what it cost you."

Perhaps the true measure of how much you loved something was how much of yourself you were willing to sacrifice for it. The thought had come to him once before, but he couldn't remember where. He fought to dredge it up from the depths of his memory, but his thoughts were floating, disconnected. He was having trouble concentrating and the effort wearied him. He drifted off to sleep.

The ice-blue sky of the afternoon brought no warmth, and as the sunset painted its first pink brushstrokes on the horizon, the temperature dropped still further. All around them, nature lay in silence. The reeds were still, undisturbed by even a breath of wind. The water was as smooth as soft grey satin. There were no good places to die, but there could be few more peaceful.

"What will it be like?" Domenic's voice sounded thick, and his speech was slurry again, as if he was having trouble forming his mouth around the words.

Damian looked at his brother. "We'll just go to sleep. We won't know anything about it. It'll be okay."

"I should leave a note. I want Lindy to know why I left. If she doesn't know the truth, she'll never be able to move on. She needs to understand that I did it for her." Domenic paused and breathed deeply, gathering his resources for the effort of producing more words. "Do you think that chip would mark leather? Maybe I could scrape some words into my boot."

It was a futile idea. This place consumed human histories. It obliterated them, swallowing them up into its vast, gaping maw and covering them over forever. No one would ever find any trace of the Jejeune brothers out here. No one would ever read Domenic's etched words to Lindy. But Damian would let his brother hold on to whatever he wanted to now. It made no difference anymore.

"Sure, we can try. But she'll know anyway, Domenic. Danny Maik will set her straight. He's a good man. He'll take care of it."

"Yes." Domenic nodded weakly, slurring the word. "A good man."

Damian withdrew the plastic bag and flipped it across to Domenic. "Here, tomorrow you can write to Lindy, okay?"

Domenic nodded. "Tomorrow. Okay. Lindy." He tried to think of the words to "Hallelujah" once more. Lindy's song; his connection to her now that there was nothing else. But the words wouldn't come; lyrics he'd heard a thousand times floated on the edge of his memory, out of his reach. *The fourth, the fifth.* What next? The major key, something about falling?

"Thanks." Damian's voice dragged Domenic back to the present. "I probably forgot to say it. I usually do."

For coming, he meant, for undertaking this trip into the heart of the Canadian wilderness to find his brother. "I'm sorry for getting you into all this," said Damian sincerely. "Seems like you've spent your whole life getting me out of one sort of trouble or another. My luck was bound to run out one day.

Either you wouldn't show up at all, or you'd get dragged down with me."

Domenic raised his head as much as he could to peer over the clump of reeds between them. He wanted to make eye contact with his brother. He needed him to see the truth his mumbled words might not have been able to convey. "I came because I wanted to, Damian. It was my choice."

"It's all good, Dom." Damian drew a shallow breath. "Lay back down now. Tomorrow we'll write that note, okay?"

"Tomorrow," agreed Domenic sluggishly. "Not now. We'll just rest. Is it okay if we just rest for a while, Damian?"

"Sure it is. We'll just rest for a while."

Domenic closed his eyes. Lindy was waiting for him. Lindy, smiling, with arms open wide to greet him, ready to gather him in. He moved towards her, as happy as he had ever been to see her; untroubled, content, warm.

45

Maik stared at Ray Hayes as if he were a hologram.

"You don't believe me, Sergeant." Hayes leaned forward and casually tilted the knife blade from side to side. He pushed out his bottom lip. "Or at least, you don't want to. It can't be easy for you to accept that I've had to step in and do your job for you, because you were too incompetent to keep Lindy safe."

Maik's expression didn't reveal what he thought of Ray Hayes's comments. He watched the glinting steel of the blade as it turned. No matter how good he thought he was, the outcome of a knife attack was too unpredictable for a man as intelligent as Hayes to be relying on it alone. He had another form of protection. Maik couldn't see it yet, but he knew it was here somewhere.

Hayes took his eyes from the knife blade and looked at Maik. He shook his head. "One-dimensional thinking, that's your problem. Right, wrong, black, white. If I were to ask you why you think I was responsible for the attempts on Lindy's life, you'd say three things. First, the circumstantial evidence: the fact that I've got form for this sort of thing, not to mention a particularly strong motive." Hayes waited, but Maik didn't tell him he was wrong. "Second, you'd point to that bookmark — the physical evidence left at the scene, placing me there. And the third reason you'd offer is that Domenic Jejeune thinks I'm guilty. And we've all learned to trust the DCI's impeccable instincts, haven't we, Sergeant? But tell me honestly, do I seem like the kind of person who's going to leave incriminating evidence at the scene of a crime? And have you asked yourself why, after two attempts to kill this woman from a distance, I'd suddenly decide I had to do it at close quarters like this? Even somebody like you must find these things a bit mystifying."

Lindy was watching Maik intently, as if she was trying to gauge his reaction. She was trying to remain impassive, but Maik could tell she believed Hayes. Whatever story he was weaving now, whatever he had already told her when it was just the two of them here together, Lindy was buying it. And that was Hayes's edge, his protection from Maik's wrath. The person who he'd let down believed that Hayes had saved her. She'd demand Ray Hayes be given a fair hearing. And Maik knew he was in no position to deny her.

"You come in with us, you'll get a chance to tell your side of the story," he said evenly. "If what you say is true, we'll find a way of proving it."

But Hayes was shaking his head. "At the moment, your only concern is to get Lindy away safely. You'd promise me the moon to make that happen. But once we got back to the station, if it turned out your career might be on the line for not informing your superiors about a kidnapping, well, you've got evidence that puts me at the scene of an attempted murder. You've got nothing to support my claims that somebody else was responsible. In the face of all that, things could start to go a bit sideways for old Ray, couldn't they, especially if an arrest might be the only thing standing between you and early retirement with no pension?"

He likes the spotlight, this one, thought Maik. He wasn't sure what he could do with the information just yet, but he stored it away.

"Carcerophobia," announced Hayes. "Ever heard of it, Sergeant Maik? Frankly, I'd be surprised if you had. You don't strike me as much of a crossword man. How about you, Lindy? You're the wordsmith."

She shrugged. "Something to do with incarceration?"

"Very good." Hayes nodded approvingly. "Though you might have done a bit better with the *phobia* part. A fear of incarceration. Not just a dislike of it, you understand, a bit of annoyance at having your basic human freedoms taken away and getting banged up in a concrete cell for most of your day. Anybody would be upset about that, unless you're one of those idiots that can't function in any other setting. No, carcerophobia is a full-blown phobia, with a range of accompanying psychological and physiological symptoms. Sweats, nausea, panic attacks."

"And you have it?" Maik didn't do much to keep the skepticism from his voice. It seemed to him the best way to avoid the condition was to stay out of jail in the first place. If Hayes did have a fear of being imprisoned, it wasn't strong enough to prevent him from getting mixed up in attempted murder and kidnapping.

"I do," confirmed Hayes, "and I tell you all this for one reason." He paused and looked at each of them in turn. "So, you will understand that I will never, under any circumstances, be going back to prison."

Maik inclined his head. If he could have been assured of Lindy's full co-operation, he might have tried to take Hayes now, when he was in his full pomp, distracted by his limelight and his self-importance. But she would need to listen to Danny, do exactly as he said, when he said it. And he wasn't sure she would. There was something in her look, some glimmer of uncertainty that told him she might hesitate, wonder whom to trust, just for a second. And for Hayes, so close to her and armed with a knife, that would be all it would take. Lindy's safety was the priority here. Maik needed to show her he could be trusted to get things right this time. And if that meant indulging Hayes for a few moments longer, then that's what he'd have to do.

"So, if not you, then, who? Give me a name, something we can get out on the wires. As I see it, we pick up this other bloke and you're in the clear."

"Peter Mahler. And don't worry, you won't have very far to look for him. He'll have followed you here."

Maik moved uneasily. "What are you talking about? I didn't see anybody."

But Maik's denial sounded unconvincing, even to him. He'd been focused on ensuring his own approach to the cottage went undetected. He hadn't spent a lot of time looking over his shoulder. Hayes would know this. More importantly, so would Lindy. He looked at her and saw that same look in her eyes: the look of someone trying to have confidence in him, wanting to, but not quite being able to find it all the same.

"A man named Peter Mahler is coming here to kill you, Lindy," said Hayes, his eyes still on Maik. "He's already out there. That's right. On top of all the other mistakes he's made, Sergeant Maik has led him right to your very door. Got a lot to answer for, has the sergeant, I'd say."

Whether this Mahler was real or just some imaginary threat Hayes had dreamed up, Maik knew what he had to do now. "You need to come with me, Lindy. Mr. Hayes here gets the benefit of the doubt for now, but I need to take you away from here."

"On foot? Across all this open land? You've had better ideas, Sergeant. You know as well as I do a target is most vulnerable when being moved. Mahler will be close, Lindy. He wouldn't have let the sergeant here out of his sight." Hayes nodded, looking at Maik again now. "If you want to know where somebody is being hidden, you don't look for them yourself. You let somebody else do it for you, somebody with better resources, more manpower. Somebody like the police, say. And then you follow them." He gave a small smile. "Trade secrets. Before I knew any better, I passed a few on to Mahler."

"Lindy, can you go and check all the doors and windows?" said Maik. He pulled out his phone and switched it on. Lindy was standing hesitantly, looking back and forth between him and Hayes. "Don't worry, we'll be safe here. I'll get a car with a covering team to come and pick us up. We'll hold up here until they arrive."

"Wait." Hayes's tone turned Lindy's gaze towards him and drew Maik's attention from his phone. "If Mahler sees police cars, he'll be gone. And with him goes your chance to get him. We could end this now, Lindy. It could all be over. Mahler disappears now and who knows when the police will get another shot at him. Do you want this hanging over your head until he tries again? It could all be over today. You could go back to your normal life, with the DCI. With Domenic."

Maik was shaking his head. "Mahler's not going to try anything now. Not if he's seen me come in here."

"If he doesn't see any cars, he's going to think I've already dealt with you." Hayes ran his thumb along the edge of the knife blade. "He won't be expecting both of us. He'll think it's just me he has to worry about. I'm telling you, this is our chance."

"And I'm telling you, he won't come." Maik looked across at Lindy. "Don't listen to him, Lindy. We need to get you out of here now."

"The sergeant knows he'll come, Lindy. This is the chance Mahler's been waiting for. You and me together. He wants us both. This is his opportunity, and he knows he won't get a better one. He'll come, Lindy. Listen to what I'm saying. We can end this now. It can all be over. Mahler out of your life forever. How does that sound, Lindy?"

She shook her head uncertainly. "I don't know …"

"It's too risky," Maik told her. "I have to get you to safety." He scrolled up the phone screen with his thumb.

"Why not let Lindy decide?" Hayes's question seemed to still everything in the room. Maik stopped dialing. Lindy stared at Hayes. "You're the reason she's in this mess, Sergeant. You let me grab her. You let Mahler track you here. She must be sick and tired of other people letting her down. Let her make this decision herself. You owe her that much."

Maik looked at Lindy, his guilt burning into him, tearing at his logic, his instincts, everything that told him to get Lindy away.

Hayes saw his opening and pounced. "The threat will never go away, Lindy. Mahler will always be out there, watching, waiting for another chance. Do you want to live with that every day of your life? Listen to me and it could all be over."

Lindy looked from one to the other, eyes wide. "I don't know. I'm not sure. I —"

"We'll get another chance at Mahler, Lindy. And in the meantime, I'll keep you safe … we will, the police," said Maik.

"How are they going to do that? By keeping you cooped up in your house all day?" Hayes spread his hands. "You've had a taste of that already. How does a few weeks of this sound, Lindy? A few months?"

"Lindy, it's too dangerous." Maik could see her faltering, wanting to believe his assurances that he'd be able to protect her. Her look was like a laser entering his heart. He saw now that she couldn't trust him, and he knew the battle was lost.

"Stop. Please. Both of you. Just stop." The hands Lindy held up to each of the men were shaking. She turned to Maik, her eyes brimming with tears. "I can't do this anymore, Danny. It's already cost me too much." She shook her head. "No more. No more. It has to end. I want you to let Peter Mahler come here. I want it over."

Maik lowered his head and looked to the ground. Like Hayes said, it was his fault Lindy was in this situation. And now, one way or another, he was going to be the one to end it.

46

It started with the light, so bright and intense it enveloped him. It came from above, blotting out Domenic's surroundings, pinning him to the ground with its intensity. The light stayed above him, its steady, penetrating glare unwavering. It seemed to be drawing him towards it, promising warmth and comfort. Promising release. He wanted to reach out, to pull himself into this tunnel of light. But his body was an immovable weight.

The last thing he had seen was Lindy's face. He remembered that. The thought pleased him. But the dead shouldn't have thoughts, should they? They shouldn't be able to connect ideas, to be aware of the conscious workings of their mind. Nor should they feel coldness. He was cold. Too cold. He drifted back into the darkness.

Perhaps he was spinning now. Everything seemed to be in motion around him: his clothing, the reed stems on which he was lying, even the dark water beside his face. The air churned with movement, the noise filling his ears, rising to a roar. The light came through his eyelids again, penetrating the cocoon of his sleep. It was dragging him to the surface of his consciousness. He wanted to wake, to open his eyes and claw his way out of the darkness. He wanted to rise towards the beckoning light. But he couldn't. Sleep dragged him back down. It smothered him, blocking out the light and the sounds, bringing him peace. Quiet, dark peace. And then he heard the angel speak. "Two with vitals. One's in bad shape."

The voice was not soft, not possessed of the sweet tone that sang a thousand heavenly hymns. It was sharp, insistent, charged with urgency. *Two. Vitals.* Vital. Important. It was important that he show them he was alive, important that he drag himself out of this sleep. But he couldn't. His weariness weighed him down. He couldn't move or even open his eyes.

There was a blast of noise. But not a noise from heaven; harsh, like a burst of irritation. Another voice. "There should be three. Repeat, three."

"Negative. Two only. No sign of a third."

A pause. And then words he couldn't understand.

"Negative. The temperature is dropping fast. We won't get two chances at this. We'll need to take them both at the same time."

One's in bad shape. Was it Lindy? Was Lindy in bad shape? But the blackness dragged him down again. It was cold up there, cold and wet. Warmth was waiting for him below. All he had to do was let himself slip back into it, drift down into nothingness.

"We have a problem." The tone stirred awakening in Domenic again, though he was still below the surface, still immobile. He heard the sound of splashing, and felt an icy droplet on his face. "The structure of this mound is completely gone. They're already lying in water. Any attempt to set foot on it and it's going to disintegrate completely. A lift is impossible. We're going to have to roll them into the craft."

"It's too dangerous. This water's close to freezing. If it bucks while we're getting them in, we could lose them in the water. They're too fragile to withstand that."

Them. *Two with vitals.* But Damian was here with him, too, he remembered. *Two only. No sign of a third.* Who was missing? Where was Lindy? Domenic's mind clouded with confusion. Panic seized him. The mental exertions exhausted him and he relapsed once more towards unconsciousness. But he could hear his anxious angels again now.

"We have to risk it. There's no way to fit harnesses on them unless we get them into the craft. We can't wait. This one's on the brink. We have to roll them."

Domenic floated up to the edge of consciousness again. *Take Lindy,* he wanted to tell them. *Save her.* But he couldn't move, couldn't speak.

"This one first. Get the blankets ready."

Domenic felt something grabbing at the fabric of his jacket. He was rolled slowly onto his side, and felt the wetness seeping through his clothes. He smelled the musky, stagnant odour of the water close to his nostrils. Coldness pressed against his face, something wet and slippery. It was manmade. Rubber? Moving, rocking, it bounced slightly as it dipped under his weight. The surface gave as he pressed into it, but it offered resistance, pushing him back up. And then he rolled and bounced down with a jolt and was still again. There was a tiny puddle of water beside his face, but soon a blanket blocked it out. A dry blanket. A warm blanket. He lay there for a long time, the sound of shouts and heaves just beyond his range, the water rocking gently beneath him, but no longer wet. He felt the craft buck violently, then urgent, panicked shouts of alarm. Something heavy bounced into the bottom of the craft beside him. It was not moving. *One's in bad shape.* The light came in closer now, and the whirling motion, the fluttering of ten thousand butterfly wings. *Two with vitals.* The craft began to move and Jejeune slipped into sleep once more.

47

Lauren Salter gave a deep sigh and looked around the empty room. Another quiet night in. Max was at football, grandfather Davy assuming the role of touchline-pacer-in-chief. Her dad and Max would be stopping off for pop and chips somewhere afterward to conduct their post-match analysis, with Davy managing to slip in a few sly references, no doubt, about how good he used to be when he was a lad. She smiled to herself. With Max's father largely out of the picture since the divorce, it was as close to dual-parenting as she could offer her son. She knew it was good for Max to have such a positive male role model in his life, but it inevitably meant he was going to gravitate more toward Davy as time went on, revelling in the stories of what it used to be like to be a boy growing up in these parts. She sighed again. It was the right thing for Max, but that didn't mean the right thing couldn't hurt sometimes.

She considered the pile of papers on her desk — printouts, loose sheets of foolscap, notes scribbled on torn-away scraps. It was fact-gathering, details accumulated seemingly at random, regardless of relevance. It was what detectives did when they lacked a clear sense of direction. If all she was going to be left with someday was her career, she thought ruefully, she was in for some pretty unfulfilling nights if her progress in this case was anything to go by.

Putting together the evidence against Albert Ross was like trying to reassemble a mosaic. She was convinced she already had all the necessary pieces somewhere in this disordered mess in front of her. But every time she tried to form some sort of coherent idea of what had happened, the parts didn't seem to fit. All she got was some fragmented image that suggested what the final picture should look like, but never quite did.

In some ways, the certainty of Albert Ross's guilt had made things more difficult. Salter had no questions left to ask. Ross had motive, he had means, and he had opportunity. But in the absence of any evidence, the only proof she could ever get was through a confession. And how, exactly, did you get a confession from a person who couldn't remember what they had done? There was no well of secrets to tap into, no hidden hoard of regret or remorse to unlock. There was just a blank slate named Albert Ross, whose only defence was that killing Wattis Wright should have made him feel better, but it hadn't.

Besides Ross, she'd only found one other person with a motive, and for Jennie Wynn to have killed Wright, she would have had to have been simultaneously at his house and on the road home from Norwich with her dog. As useful as it would have been sometimes for Salter to be in two places at the same time, she'd not yet found a way to make it happen. And neither, she knew, had Jennie Wynn.

Her mind went back to her first interview with the woman, and those intricate movements she had performed in her Tai Chi routine. A criminal investigation should be like that, thought Salter, one set of actions leading into the next, until in the end there was just one long, seamless sequence of manoeuvres that resulted in the truth. *Part the Wild Horse's Mane* — what are the facts? *Grasp the Bird's Tail* — what do they tell you? *The White Crane Spreads Its Wings* — this is who killed Wattis Wright.

She pushed back from the desk and stood up, putting her hands on her hips and stretching her neck from side to side. A walk, that's what she needed, a stroll somewhere to blow away the cobwebs. She went to the front door. The night was quiet, the air still. Across the narrow street lay the river, twisting like a dark serpent through the heart of the town. She followed the towpath along the edge of the river, but turned away from the waterfront this time, choosing instead the other direction. Passing the narrow bridge that led into the old section of Saltmarsh, she continued on until she reached the farmlands on the outskirts of town, where the night traded the harsh glow of streetlamps for the light of a thousand stars. She strolled along the path beside the river, recalling the days she and Max had come here to feed the birds stale bread from a plastic bag. *Ducks*, she had called them all then. Now, thanks to her DCI, her vocabulary was filled with names like Mallard and Wigeon and Shelduck. *Innocence lost*, she thought.

The wind picked up a touch, coming in low over the fields, and she turned her face into it. Farther along the riverbank, Salter could see the lights of the Demesne at Saltmarsh reflected in the dark water. The one from Susan Bonaccord's window would be among them, she knew, destined to burn long into the night. She could hardly imagine Bonaccord throwing up her hands and sneaking out for a walk along the towpath, where the wind could track her down like a fugitive. Susan Bonaccord would stay hard at it, head down, diligently searching for a solution, no matter how long it took. It was what career women did.

What she needed was not another answer, Salter realized, but a question, *the* question. It was what Jejeune was so good at, finding that question, the one he hadn't asked yet. It was always there somewhere, moving in the shadows behind the facts; like one of those backup singers Danny talked about, present but never noticed, important but ignored. Once he had that question, Jejeune's cases fell into place. Not always immediately, and certainly not without complications, but the question shone a light on the path he needed to follow, and it inevitably led him to the truth. So what question did Salter need to pose? What was the one thing she had not yet asked that would be the key to unlocking this case?

One thing was for sure. She wasn't going to find it out here, on a darkened towpath at the edge of town. She'd need to get back to her desk and start sorting through all those papers again. She turned around and headed back along the riverbank towards town. She noticed the small bridge again. A new direction, she thought, instead of retracing her steps. The bridge led to a maze of narrow streets, where large Victorian homes lurked behind high hedges. She enjoyed a walk through this part of town in daylight, with its solid, reassuring structures and its stately, mature trees. She realized now that it had a different character at night, more sinister, more menacing. She quickened her pace slightly and made a turn onto a wider road. And there it was, in front of her: Wattis Wright's house. The yellow police tape was still draped across the doorway, exactly as she'd left it. Above, the darkened windows of the upper storey stared out at her like sunken eyes, asking when she would find justice for the home's owner. *Don't fail him.*

She thought about Albert Ross, standing here, screaming at Wattis Wright, demanding to know why he'd changed his mind now that he had the money. Albert Ross. Standing here. She had changed the sequence, she realized. *Grasp the Bird's Tail* had come afterward in Jennie Wynn's performance, not before. She stared at the darkened, blank facade of Wattis Wright's house. The stirring began to grow with Salter's first pass through the reordered facts, but it wasn't until she ran through them for a second time that she realized she had found her question. And she knew then that she had her solution. It would mean going back to the notes now, those torn-off scraps, those sheets of foolscap. But she knew with a strange, unassailable certainty that everything she found would fall into place. Even if someone somewhere could come up with an alternative explanation, she knew this solution was the correct one. Because all the pieces fit; the big ones like motive and means, and opportunity, and the small ones, too, the nuances, the hesitations she had picked up in her interviews, the choices of words, and pauses, their delivery. Everything.

She realized she was experiencing the assurance that Jejeune must feel, that clarity that made it possible for him to pursue his theories with such conviction. You could listen to all the other interpretations, all the other plausible points of view, the opinions, the rationale. It was just background noise. You had your answer, and nothing anybody said was going to change that. Salter had found her missing piece, her elusive question lurking in the shadows. *Why here?* The White Crane had spread its wings.

48

The room in which Domenic Jejeune awoke seemed familiar, but he couldn't understand why. As the fog of his sleep slowly cleared, a memory of being here earlier began to emerge. Blankets, a hot drink, somebody in a bright orange coat checking his heart rate, taking his pulse. There had been other people in the room, he recalled, people moving around urgently, speaking into phones, grouped in corners chatting. He had recognized none of them. He remembered others gathered around the bed, too, watching as sleep tugged at him. He wanted to stay awake, resist the urge to drift off so he could stay in this room with these people. But he couldn't fight off the weariness, and the watching group seemed content to let him slip towards unconsciousness once again.

The grey metal frame and starched white linen of the bed he was in had an institutional feel. As he turned his head, the bed seemed to be swaying slightly. The mattress felt damp through the sheets beneath him, and his heart started to race as he put his hand down under the blankets. But the mattress was dry, the bed still. It was just the ghostly imprint of the days of lying on a moving bed of reeds with the dampness seeping into his body, he realized.

He looked around the room. The corners were in deep shadow but a pale light illuminated the area immediately around the bed. There was a small nightstand holding a jug of water and a glass, and at the foot of the bed his discarded clothing was piled on a wooden chair. In the shadows, he saw a person moving; a nurse, perhaps, tiptoeing around to avoid waking him. But she was not interested in him. She was searching through his clothes, his pockets.

"What are you looking for?" he asked.

The question startled the woman and she spun to face him. "Oh, you're awake. You had us worried for a while there. How you all doing?"

"Well. Better," said Jejeune. "How long have I been here?"

"Twelve hours, give or take. They got you stable, got your core temperature up, and then they let you sleep some. I'm Verity, by the way. I came up here with Traz."

"Traz is here?"

Verity had stayed in the shadows, but Jejeune could see her nod. "Came up soon as he heard you'd gone missing in the park. That's some friend you have there. You and your brother. They've airlifted Damian to Yellowknife, by the way."

Jejeune rose slightly in alarm.

"No, it's a good thing. With real bad hypothermia, the victim can become so brittle that moving them is risky. The fact that they think he's in good enough shape to withstand being transferred is a good sign. They'll keep him there at the hospital a couple of days for observation, but the prognosis must be okay. You had less severe symptoms, so they thought you were good to complete your recovery here."

"Has Traz gone with Damian?"

She shook her head. "He needed to arrange something. Said to tell you he'd be back soon, though, if you woke." She shrugged and gave a small smile. "I told him I could look in on you until he got back."

"You and Traz met the night he got into Aransas, is that right? And then you decided to travel together?"

"We were heading the same way," said Verity easily. "I got a ride and he got company. Sometimes things just turn out that way, huh?"

"What was it you were looking for in my clothes?"

"I wasn't looking for anything, Domenic. I was just straightening up your things, that's all. Maybe you're still a little groggy or something." She softened her voice slightly. "The RCMP was asking about the woman, Annie Prior. Traz told them she must have died out there. He said you and your brother would never have abandoned her if she were still alive. If she wasn't with you, it could only mean that she was dead."

"She drowned," Jejeune said flatly.

Verity Brown stepped out of the shadows to stand at the foot of the bed. The room was still dim, but Jejeune could see her features in the half-light. Enough to tell she was looking directly at him.

"You're from Scenic, South Dakota, aren't you?"

"With an accent like this? No, I'm from Louisiana. I spend my summers up there, though."

"How far is that from the Black Hills?"

Verity shifted slightly back towards the shadows. "Well, ain't you a curious one. 'Bout an hour, I would guess, give or take."

"There's a lot of American Indian history in that part of the world. Oglala, Wounded Knee. I imagine the university there would have an excellent cultural anthropology pro-gramme. It'd be a good place to meet someone interested in First Nations sites, like the Dene's for example."

Verity stood still, staring at Jejeune through the shad-owy light. "I have no idea what you're talking about," she said evenly. They stared at each other along the length of the bed. Nothing moved. Even the air in the darkened room was still.

Through the half-light, the sadness in her expression came through to Jejeune when she spoke again. "You know, whatever happened to that poor woman out there in the park, I'm sure nobody ever intended for anybody to get hurt."

The sound of the door latch shattered the silence like a gunshot. "Hey, he's awake!" said Traz. "Okay if I flip on the light?"

In the dazzling flash of illumination, Jejeune took in his surroundings. He was in a back room at the Park Offices; a makeshift recovery room. Filing cabinets lined the wall, but otherwise the sparse room bore the signs of disuse.

"So, you've met."

"We were just talking about Damian," said Verity.

Traz looked at each of them in turn. There was a strange, stilted uneasiness between them. Jejeune saw his friend register it, and deflected his puzzlement with a question. "How is Damian? His condition must have deteriorated in a hurry. He seemed to be doing okay, better than me, anyway."

"You don't know?" Traz folded back the door, and hanging on the hook, Jejeune saw his own olive jacket, and next to it, the tawny tiger-stripe one. "When they found you, Damian wasn't wearing a jacket. You had two, the one you were wearing and this one, laid over the top of you."

Jejeune looked down at the blankets on his bed, letting the pulse of emotion settle in him for a moment.

"He'll be okay, JJ. They got to him in time." He turned to Verity. "Did you tell him yet?" He shook his head. "No, you wouldn't have, would you? Not your style."

"Tell me what?"

"Verity's the one you and Damian have to thank for getting you out of there. She worked out where you were by tracking the cranes."

"He don't need to hear about all that," she said, turning away slightly. She hadn't made eye contact with Domenic since the lights were turned on. Perhaps it was just modesty. Traz looked at them both again for a second before continuing.

"The cranes were giving the area a wide berth," he said. "As you know, Whooping Cranes are extremely site faithful. Their preference is always going to be to return to a spot where they've successfully bred in the past. Verry got hold of the telemetry data from Aransas. She went through it all, JJ. Every record." He looked across at her but she was looking at the floor and didn't return his gaze. "All the tracked Whooping Cranes that have arrived in Wood Buffalo so far have headed for their previous nesting sites. Except for two. There's an area that hosted two successful nests last year, but a tracked bird from each pair hasn't returned there this year. The birds have arrived in the park, but they're moving around. There didn't seem to be any reason both would have selected a different breeding site. Verry thought it might be because there was human disturbance in the area. She pinpointed your location for the search team and they found you on the first pass."

Traz scooped an arm around the woman's narrow waist and hugged her into him. The pride shone out of his face like a beam of light. "Isn't she something?"

"I … I really don't know what to say," said Domenic.

"*Thank you* might be a start," said Traz.

"Yes, of course. Thank you, Verity. And thank you for my brother, too. For Damian."

"Welcome, I'm sure," she said without looking at him. She squirmed away from Traz's embrace. "I'm gonna leave you two to do some male bonding. I'll go find us some food."

Traz let his eyes trail after her as she left. "Isn't she unbelievable?"

"Yes." Domenic's pause before his answer was perhaps a heartbeat too long.

"She saved your life," Traz reminded him. "No one else could have done that."

"And I'm grateful, really," said Jejeune. *It's just that....* The words didn't follow, but Jejeune's tone suggested they should have. But whatever misgivings he had about Verity, they were going to have to wait.

"Roy's been monitoring your number, in case it suddenly became live again," said Traz cautiously. "He got your carrier to give him access to your voicemails. There's a lot of them, JJ. From the U.K."

Jejeune was drawn to an upright position as much by Traz's guarded delivery as by the news itself. "A lot?"

"From Danny Maik. He wanted you to get in touch. He didn't say why, but I get the impression he's not the type of guy to use the word *urgent* unless he means it."

"When did he call?"

"A couple of days ago. Twice within an hour and then a few times after that. The calls from the others are more recent. One from somebody called Lauren Sergeant, maybe? She seemed to be having some trouble remembering who she was, but she knew what she wanted to ask. If you'd heard from Danny Maik. He seems to have gone completely off the grid. That one came in yesterday." Traz paused. He looked at his friend as if assessing how far his recovery had come, whether he was ready to handle the next part.

Jejeune gave him his answer. "The others, Traz. Please. All of them."

Traz sighed. "Two from DCS Colleen Shepherd. The first one was asking the same thing. Had Danny Maik been in touch, had he mentioned any new lines of inquiry to you?" Still Traz hesitated. Jejeune began to turn back the bedclothes, reaching weakly for the bed rail to haul himself up. Because he knew. Even before Traz turned his sad stare on his friend, the detective knew what the second call was. "Shepherd asked if Lindy had been in contact, JJ. She hasn't been seen in a couple of days. Nobody knows where she is."

Jejeune sat unsteadily, holding on to the railing for support. "Do you have your phone?"

"We've tried the numbers multiple times — Roy, and me just now. They go to voicemail." He handed Jejeune his phone anyway. He knew Domenic still had to call. Helplessness needs tasks to perform, no matter how futile, no matter how hopeless. Jejeune listened to the pre-recorded greetings from Maik and from Lindy in silence before handing the phone back to his friend. He'd already worked out the easy part. Hayes had taken Lindy and Maik had gone after her. Why Maik had gone alone, why he was out of contact, he'd have to leave those questions until his mind was a little less clouded. But even now, one thing was crystal clear to him: he needed to be there, not in a makeshift hospital room six thousand kilometres away.

"I need to get to an airport," he said, staggering slightly as he pulled on a shirt and jeans, mud-stained and spattered, but at least now blissfully dry.

"Northwest Air can't fly single-engine planes with passengers after dark."

"Then I'll rent that Jetstream they've got out at the airfield. What will it cost? A couple of thousand? I'll pay it."

"These guys aren't cowboys, JJ. They already know the RCMP want to question you about Annie Prior." He paused for a second. "She didn't make it, right?" Jejeune's eyes gave him his answer. "The Mounties said they will give you one more night to get your strength back and they'll come by around noon for a chat. The pilots and the police have to work with each other every day around here. Even if there's no explicit order, I don't think anyone would be too keen on flying you out of town tonight, no matter how much you offered."

"I can't wait another day, Traz. I need to go now."

Traz nodded. "I know you do. Which is why Gaetan Robideau's Durango is outside, fueled up and ready to go. There's a flight out of Edmonton leaving for London tomorrow morning at ten." He looked at his watch. That's fourteen hours from now. If we drive straight through we can make it."

"We?"

"I'll take the first shift while you sleep in the back. You can spell me when you feel up to it."

Domenic shook his head slowly. Verity Brown hadn't said many things he'd believed earlier on, but she'd got one thing right. Traz was some friend.

49

The wide sky slipped towards grey, and the evening light brought a stillness that seemed to settle over everything. The sea breeze had died away to nothing, and the movement of the vegetation around the cottage had ceased. Not a leaf stirred on a tree, not a bird crossed the empty sky. But it was not the kind of stillness that brought peace. This was a sinister presence, ominous and foreboding.

Danny let the curtain at the kitchen window fall from his fingertip and went to the front of the house, peering out to scan the empty driveway. The fading light painted pockets of darkness along the edges of the trees. It was a time when even the shadows seemed to lurk with stealth. But there were no signs of movement.

"No point looking out there all the time. Mahler can approach from any number of directions." Hayes looked around the cottage. "Nice spot this, but not easy to secure. You'd have thought Jejeune might have considered that. He must have known the kind of enemies he was likely to attract."

Lindy watched the two men from her chair with the quiet intensity of a spectator at a chess match. She had offered little more than cursory comments to the men's discussions, as if she was afraid her contributions might be taken as an allegiance to one side or the other. But for Danny Maik, the balance of power between him and Hayes wasn't the important one here. It was the one that lay between the three of them and the man who was coming for Lindy that had him concerned.

He walked to the far window and looked out along the clifftop path that led to the cottage, the one he had used for his approach. His skin was starting to crawl with all the unknowns, the uncontrollables. They should have gone when they still had the light. He and Lindy. *Buy into Hayes's story if you like, pretend you believe all this business about him only grabbing Lindy to protect her. Leave him here at the cottage, let him escape if you have to. But get Lindy out, somewhere safe, while you still have the chance.* This way was madness. What had he been thinking? He pulled away from the window, ready to tell Lindy they were going. But as soon as he saw her, sitting quietly on the chair, her small, nervous smile trying desperately to show her confidence in him, he faltered. He owed her an end to all this, and perhaps he could deliver it. So, he didn't ask her to get up. He didn't move towards the front door. He just stayed there, looking out of the window, vigilant, alert. And troubled.

"So, tell me about this Peter Mahler," he said to Hayes. It wasn't an idle inquiry. Maik hadn't completely given up on the idea that Mahler could be some kind of partner of Hayes's. Perhaps Danny was being set up, sitting here like a fool while Hayes waited for reinforcements to arrive. Many parts of Ray Hayes's story held true; he'd had plenty of opportunities to hurt Lindy if that had been his goal, and he was a long way from being stupid enough to leave incriminating evidence at the scene of a crime. But there were gaps, too: unanswered questions, things in his account that didn't make sense.

"Mahler testified against his latest cellmate so he could get his own sentence commuted," said Hayes. "They just have a talent for making friends, some people."

"Is he one of the DCI's old collars?"

Hayes shook his head. "He's not one of Jejeune's. If this was just something between the two of them, I'd have let them get on with it. If Mahler was trying to kill Lindy to get back at Jejeune, what business of mine is that?" He shrugged. "It's me Mahler wants. He just wants to use her as part of his plan."

He looked across at Lindy, who averted her eyes.

"So why come out of hiding, then?" asked Maik. "Why make it easy for Mahler if he's coming after you?"

"The bookmark. He told me he left a cigarette lighter with my prints on it at the scene of the office explosion, but you lot missed it. Let's face it; you didn't really look too hard at that as a crime scene. You all had it down as an accident. But once you recovered the bookmark with my fingerprint from the car, I was on your radar. So now, the only way to clear my name is to handle it myself. I can hardly rely on you lot to do it for me, can I?"

"I still don't understand what any of this has to do with me, Ray," said Lindy quietly. "You and I have never met before. Why does Mahler think I can help him to get you?"

"A prison cell is like a confessional," said Hayes. "You find yourself telling people things you really should be keeping to yourself. With Mahler, it was women. Nasty, twisted stuff. He's got this act, see, all inoffensive and non-threatening. Gets him in close, and then, when their guard is down, he moves. The police never got him for any of them, but from the way he was talking, there's at least a couple of women out there who he's treated to his own particular kind of attention."

Lindy watched as Maik eyed Hayes carefully. Perhaps he was buying it, perhaps not. With Danny it was always hard to tell.

"So, now Mahler wants to make sure that information goes no further?" he asked.

Hayes looked across at Lindy and shook his head. "See what I mean, Lindy? One-dimensional thinking." He turned to Maik. "No, Sergeant, not quite. I told Mahler I don't want to know. I don't want to hear this stuff, what he's done, how he's done it, how it makes him feel. But he keeps on, so eventually I just shut him out. Completely. Every time Mahler comes into the cell, I pick up my book. *The Consolation of Philosophy*," he announced with a flourish. "Not exactly your kind of reading material, I daresay, Sergeant. Pity, though. Gives you a perspective on things — what we can control, what's outside our influence. I'd go so far as to say it saved my life in there, that little book. See, the thing people don't realize is there's a freedom in prison, too." Hayes tapped his temple. "Up here. You create your own world. As long as you don't let anybody else in, it's yours. Nobody can take it away from you. And when you get down to it, freedom of the mind is all a person really needs."

"You're telling me Mahler wants revenge because you preferred the company of Boethius over his?"

Lindy managed a small smile at Danny's sly comeback. Hayes wasn't going to comment on it, but he hadn't missed it, either.

"One day, I come back into the cell, and the book is all torn up into little squares. *Ran out of toilet paper*, says Mahler. He's actually smiling about it, treating somebody else's property with such disrespect, never mind a treasure like that. So, I tell him I'm going to get one of the magazines from the library, the ones with those heavy waxy pages, and I'm going to fold it into a nice sharp point. And then one night, he's going to wake up and I'll be there, waiting over him, ready to drive it into his eye socket." Hayes paused. "Well, poor old Peter didn't sleep much after that. Every night, after lights out, I'd remind him that might have been the last time he was ever going to see that room. Or anything else, for that matter. Sleep deprivation can cause some very unpleasant side effects. Eventually, it got so bad he had to go to the infirmary. Trouble is, I got used to having the place to myself while he was away, so as soon as he came back, I decided to send him there again. And so it went on."

"And now he's coming for you," said Maik. "So just how does wiring Lindy's car to a battery settle old scores with you? How does setting off an explosive device outside her office cause you any great distress, exactly?" asked Maik, doing nothing to disguise the skepticism in his tone.

Hayes offered him a cynical head shake. "You don't understand revenge at all, do you, Sergeant? You find the most vulnerable spot, the open wound, the exposed nerve, and then you dig your blade in as far as it will go, grinding and twisting all the way. Mahler saw me in the full throes of my carcerophobia a couple of times." Hayes looked at both of them. "He doesn't want me dead. He wants me back in prison. For life."

Maik was quiet for a moment. If you killed a member of a policeman's family, the rest of them would move heaven and earth to find you. If you killed somebody close to a detective as good as Domenic Jejeune, the chances of you being brought to justice went up that much more. But Maik saw the rest of the picture now, too.

"This was never about Lindy, us waiting here. You want Mahler arrested so he's out of *your* life, not hers. If I'd have left here with Lindy and put out a warrant for Mahler, he'd know framing you for her murder was no longer an option. She would have been free from all this. The only one left under threat from Peter Mahler would be you." Maik scrutinized the other man's face carefully. "I should just stand aside and let you and your playmate sort out your differences between you, and then mop up the pieces after. But I'm not going to do that. I'm going to call for that car to pick us up, and then you can give me a description of this Peter Mahler. I'll have an all-points alert put out and get a couple of teams out here with dogs. If he's in the area, we'll find him."

But Hayes was no longer listening. His eyes were staring unblinkingly into the kitchen. "You did make sure all the doors and windows were secure, like you were told?" he asked softly, not taking his eyes off the spot in the kitchen.

Lindy nodded.

Maik followed Hayes's stare to a point where the delicate lace curtains above the sink moved almost imperceptibly, as if wafted by a faint breeze. "Including the one in your bathroom, after you took your shower?"

Lindy's eyes flared wide with horror, and Maik knew any other options he might have been considering had just disappeared. Peter Mahler was already here.

50

Domenic Jejeune had never drawn such comfort from the interior of a moving vehicle. Nestled deep in the passenger seat beside Traz, the darkness and cold temperatures that lurked outside were no threat now. Somewhere out there beyond the black emptiness was the vast, raw wilderness that had almost killed him, but the memories of his ordeal that drifted to him now were quickly dispersed by the reassuring glow of the dashboard lights and the steady flow of warm air from the heater.

"You're pretty quiet, JJ. Still tired?"

"I was thinking about that time we dubbed those Leonard Cohen tracks onto Damian's CDs," said Jejeune quietly. "He brought it up while we were out there."

"And of course you stepped up like the good friend you are to tell him it was all your idea and I had nothing to do with it."

"He'd already worked out it was a two-man job. Technical know-how and an inside man." Jejeune paused, and for a moment the only sound was the chip of loose gravel from the unpaved road against the undercarriage of the car. Up ahead, an occasional irregular shape was trapped in the Durango's high beams, momentarily becoming some grotesque, fantastical creature, until it melted back into the form of a bush or rocky outcrop.

"I was surprised to see Verity up here," said Jejeune quietly. "I thought you said she was only going as far as South Dakota with you."

Traz nodded. "She was all set for a quiet few weeks on her grandmother's porch, but as soon as she knew you and Damian were in trouble, she said she'd come up with me."

"So she changed her plans, just like that?"

"In a heartbeat. She wanted to do anything she could to help. It's what she's like." He took his eyes off the road and looked across at his friend, his face tinted by a faint tinge of blue from the dashboard light. "Right about now, I'll bet you're thinking she made the right decision."

"And to think you two just bumped into each other like that. How did it happen, exactly?"

Traz smiled at the memory. He affected a Humphrey Bogart side-mouth drawl. "It was late, see, and I was sitting at the bar going over my finances with my accounting team, Bourbon and Despair. She walked into the room like a vision from a sailor's dream. Her perfume filled the air like the smoke that hangs in a jazz club, the kind of place where Coltrane's licks made you feel the sound of pain. Her legs were as long as a night in jail and her eyes were as blue as a broken heart. I could tell by the way she wrapped her mink stole around her shoulders that she was a classy broad."

"You realize a comment like that is considered highly inappropriate these days."

Traz dropped the accent. "You're right. Let's make it a silk scarf that told me she was a classy broad."

Domenic smiled. "Either way, to paraphrase something somebody said to me recently, you still ain't no Raymond Chandler."

A set of headlights flashed by heading east, the presence of another vehicle on the highway unusual enough that both men watched in the mirrors until its red lights had faded into the distance. In the renewed darkness of the car's interior, Traz waited for to Jejeune continue, but he just kept his eyes fixed on the road ahead.

"The woman who died, Annie Prior," said Traz quietly, "was she Damian's girlfriend?"

Traz saw his friend shake his head. "Not at first. She hired Damian to help her with her research. Later …" He shrugged.

Traz moved his head slightly. "When I first went to see Gaetan Robideau, he said she'd been to see him. He said you'd been there, too, asking about her. When I went back this time, to ask him where I could rent a car, he offered me this one. He said it was time to start the healing. Did he have something to do with her death?"

Jejeune shook his head again. "No, but he feels responsible for it."

"Because he made a deal with her? Promising her access to the Dene sites in return for those photographs?"

"He told you that?"

Traz nodded. "But he knew the council would never sanction it. I guess that's where his guilt comes in. Because he sent her out there on a fool's errand. He deceived her into thinking there was a chance that they would, just to get those photos."

Jejeune was quiet for a moment. His grasp of the Dene culture was shaky at best, but even he could understand the sacrifice Robideau had been prepared to make to protect the thing he loved. *Integrity, truthfulness, honour:* all cornerstones of his upbringing as a Dene, all abandoned to save the precious waters of the park. How much birch sap would it take to cleanse Robideau of his sins? he wondered. Was there enough in this park? In all of the Dene lands?

"Was Damian in on this?" asked Traz. "Was he part of this plan to help Prior get access to those sites?"

Jejeune shook his head. "Damian knows less about anthropology than he knows about saying *no* to pretty women. He was just there to capture the cranes and retrieve the photo chips."

"So, it was just the two of them involved, then? Just Prior and Robideau?"

Jejeune stared at the unbroken darkness as it drifted past the car, as if looking for something in it. Perhaps there was some guardedness in Traz's voice, a hint of uncertainty? Or did he just want it to be there, to make his task easier when the time came? He couldn't find the will to go there yet. But he couldn't manage casual conversation with Traz in its stead, either, not now they had tested the edges of the topic. "Okay with you if I grab a couple of hours more sleep?" he asked. "I'll just stretch out in the back for a while."

Dawn broke with a pink sunrise. On both sides of the car, the spiky silhouettes of conifers lined the road like tiny mountain ranges, dark against the soft, rose-coloured glow of the sky. Domenic stirred in the back seat and sat up to look through the windscreen.

Traz saw his friend in the mirror. "Welcome back," he said, pulling over. "About time for a stretch, anyway."

He looked up and down the highway as they got out, a long lonely ribbon of tarmac stretching arrow-straight through the wilderness, as relentless and uncompromising as truth. "You know what's strange about this road?" Traz said. "Not a single billboard. You drive through the U.S., and it seems like there's one about every ten metres. But up here, take away the road markings and you could travel for hours without any evidence of human existence whatsoever." He looked around again. "Once, that kind of seclusion would have really appealed to me. Now, though," he shook his head, "I'm realizing it's kind of nice to have somebody to share things with."

Jejeune looked out at the unblemished green carpet of conifers rolling out to the horizon in all directions. From here, you could almost believe this forest stretched to the ends of the earth. The prospect of finding two people lost in this landscape seemed impossible, and his gratitude grappled with what he had to do. But in the end, he knew his duty would win out. It always did.

"I'm guessing you don't mean share them with me," said Jejeune quietly.

Traz smiled. "We just connected. We see things the same way, we like the same stuff — well, mostly. It's just, I don't know, there, in the air between us. You know, don't you, JJ? You know when it's the right one. It must have been the same for you when you first met Lindy."

The comment was like a dagger into Jejeune's heart. He could tell from his friend's voice that it *was* like when he met Lindy. Real. Certain. Unshakeable. How would he feel if Traz had been the one trying to destroy that? A wave of regret overwhelmed him. But he knew he had no choice. It was who he was. He did what was necessary. He did what was right, however wrong it seemed. "Did you ever think about what a coincidence that was, the two of you meeting like that, and her needing a ride in exactly the same direction you were heading?"

Traz turned sharply to look at his friend. "What, you think Verity was just in that bar looking for a lift?" He shook his head. "That's not how it was, JJ. It was my idea. As a matter of fact, she even refused at first."

Traz looked into his friend's eyes, but he seemed not to care for the expression he found there. "You think she was just playing me? No, you're wrong."

But it was there in his voice now, the sound of a man fighting against a rising tide of logic, fighting to deny what his own senses were telling him. Traz was scrabbling around frantically for a grip that would allow him to hold on to his fantasy world where happy coincidences occurred in cowboy bars and soulmates dropped out of the sky into your life.

Traz shook his head again. "Come on, JJ, let me have this one, okay? Give that suspicious policeman's mind of yours a rest for once, and just accept this for what it is. Fate, baby. Karma. I'm telling you, this is the real thing."

But Traz knew it wasn't. Jejeune could see it in his eyes. And that was why, instead of standing out there on the gravel shoulder of this empty road in the crisp morning air, waiting for his friend to continue, Traz slid into the passenger seat of the Durango. "You want to catch that flight, we should be moving. Just remember to keep to the speed limit. We don't want your name coming up on the RCMP's radar if you get stopped for speeding."

51

Maik put a finger to his lips and flattened himself against the wall beside the open doorway, rolling the finger now, as a sign to them to keep the conversation going.

"Your boyfriend should be here by now," ad libbed Hayes. "What am I supposed to do with you if he doesn't show up?" He set the laptop beside him silently, but he did not rise from the sofa. "Still, we'll give him a bit more time, eh? After all, he's got a long way to come."

Maik edged along the wall, fingers feeling for the doorway's moulded surround. He turned into a crouch as they touched it, bringing his hands in front of him at waist height, shoulders pitched slightly forward. It was the best position for rapidly disarming an assailant at close quarters. But the stance offered no protection against a blow to the head. As Maik spun low through the doorway, the barrels of the shotgun smashed into his temple with venomous accuracy. He reeled back into the room and collapsed, clutching his cheek.

"Hello, Linds," said a familiar voice. "Sorry, no coffee today. Just me."

Peter Mahler motioned with the shotgun and Maik scooted along the floor farther into the room, the blood flowing freely from his wound. Levelling the gun towards Lindy, the person she had only known as poor, sad Jeremy kept his eyes on the two men. "Anybody looks like they're even thinking about coming in this direction, I'll drop her where she stands."

Danny stayed put, his eyes not leaving Mahler's face.

"I seem to remember you were a knife man, Ray," said Mahler. "On the table. Far side."

Hayes reached behind him and withdrew the knife from his belt. He placed it carefully on the low coffee table between them.

"I needed to be close, Lindy," said Mahler, moving cautiously into the room. "Old Ray here was playing hide and seek. No point trying to pin a murder on somebody who's not around, is there? But as soon as he surfaced, I needed to be there, ready to act fast, to make sure he was still around to be put in the frame.... Steady."

Maik held up both hands to show his movement had been to check on his wound only. The blood was running down onto his shirt collar, soaking into the material. But the sergeant was still seated on the polished wood floor, still watching, still obeying.

"Cuffs," said Mahler. "Ray's left hand, to the metal frame."

"Just the one hand?"

Mahler had the gun pointed directly at Lindy's chest. Danny wasn't going to risk getting the instructions wrong.

But it was Hayes who answered. "One hand, Sergeant." He turned his eyes on Mahler. "I shot the cop. And the girl. All while cuffed? That's your plan, right? Two dead bodies and gunshot residue on my hands, my prints on a shotgun that has somehow fallen just out of my reach, where I can't wipe them off? It's make-believe, Mahler. You're insulting their intelligence."

"Always about intelligence with you, Ray, wasn't it? But who is it the cops have been looking for in connection with two previous attempts on her life? You grabbed her; your

DNA will be all over her car. You think they'll be interested in some story about somebody else being here? There's only three people in this little menage à trois of yours, Ray — you, and the two people you killed. The cop, and the girlfriend of the man who put you away. The man who was always that bit more intelligent than you. One cuff," he said to Maik. "And then back on the floor."

Lindy could see Maik's bloodstained hand shaking. She stepped forward reflexively. "Jeremy … Mr. Mahler. Danny's lost a lot of blood. He's badly hurt. Let me help him."

"I wouldn't worry about it," said Mahler, turning to look at her. "It's not going to matter to him for much longer."

Perhaps it was a stumble, dizziness, brought on by the loss of blood. Perhaps it was something more. It didn't matter to Mahler. He backed away from Danny's lurch in his direction and brought the gun stock down on Maik's skull with sickening force. The sergeant crumpled to the floor heavily. He was lying on his back, his eyes staring up into the barrels of Mahler's gun.

"Big mistake, Sergeant."

Lindy screamed and raced across the room. Mahler turned to raise the gun towards her, not even seeing Ray Hayes's approach until the blow from the side hit him. He reeled away off-balance, fighting to level the gun barrels in Hayes's direction. Hayes clawed to push them away, grappling frantically with Mahler for control of the weapon. The two men hauled each other back and forth, Mahler wrenching the gun away, Hayes latching on again desperately. He lost his footing and slipped back, dragging Mahler down on top of him. They bounced onto the cushions of the couch, locked in a death roll over the weapon, twisting and tearing at the gun.

The thunder of the gunshot reverberated through the room, its echo rolling like smoke into every corner. Lindy jammed her hands against her mouth in horror as Mahler rolled off onto the floor. Hayes slumped back against the couch, his shoulder a mess of wet purple pulp. Holding the weapon in one hand, Mahler awkwardly snapped the cuff around Hayes's still-juddering wrist and fastened the other end around the metal frame. He stood up and backed away, wiping his mouth with the back of his hand, breathing heavily.

"So, what are you going to do now, genius?" said Hayes, panting between the words. He winced with pain as he tried to move his arm. "One shell left and two of them. Or did I somehow miraculously reload, too, while I was handcuffed? Give it up, Mahler. They'll be coming. Quiet place like this. They don't hear many gunshots. They'll be on their way already."

Mahler was drawing deep breaths of air into his lungs and blinking sweat from his eyes. He looked from Maik to Lindy and back again. "One left," he said. He swivelled the gun towards Lindy and backed her away towards the wooden chair. He fished in his jacket pocket for a length of rope and tied her tightly to the frame. She offered no resistance. She was sobbing quietly, not at her own plight, but for Danny Maik as she caught sight of him on the far side of the room. He'd passed out, blood still flowing from the wounds on his head and temple. He was so pale. She wasn't even sure he was breathing.

Mahler leaned forward and picked up the knife from the table, holding it delicately by the blade between his gloved fingers to avoid removing Hayes's prints. "You did her first, Ray. With this. The copper came in, and saw what you'd done. He managed to get the one cuff on you, but then it all kicked off. You caught one in the shoulder, but you managed to get the gun off him and split his head open with it. Then, with him lying there, all dazed and helpless, you did him, too." Mahler nodded to himself. "Yeah, that's what happened here."

"They'll never buy it, Mahler. They'll see through it in a minute." But there was no conviction in Hayes's laboured, gasping words. Only desperation.

"A defenceless cop, shot where he lay? Oh, they'll buy it, Ray. They'll want to, see. They'll want their pound of flesh for this one." Mahler nodded. "And you'll be it. They're gonna lock you up in the deepest, darkest place they've got for this. You're never going to see the light of day again."

He leaned the shotgun against the edge of the coffee table and approached Lindy. She looked him in the eyes, but there was nothing of Jeremy in there, nothing to connect with. "Please," she said. But she knew it would do no good. He came around behind her and laid a gloved hand on her shoulder. It felt cold through her thin blouse. He brought the knife around and pressed the blade against her neck, still holding it by the top edge.

"Goodbye, Lindy."

It was the last thing she would ever do, so Lindy was determined to make it count. She reared up off the seat and lunged backward at Mahler, driving her heels into the ground for extra leverage. The chair back drove deep into Mahler's chest, sending him backpedalling across the room. The knife rattled away across the floor as he fell. Lindy followed him, tripping over him and falling to the floor, the chair splintering on impact. She twisted her body to thrash the spindly wooden frame into Mahler as he lay beneath her, her arms still strapped to the wood like a crucifix. Mahler pushed her off and rolled to the side, lunging for the gun as he went. But his efforts only dislodged it and it slid off the table edge, bouncing as it clattered onto the floor. Lindy crashed the chair into him again, driving him sideways as she wrenched her left arm free from the tangle of wood and rope. From the couch, Hayes strained forward as far as possible and tried to hook the gun towards him with an outstretched heel, grunting in pain at the effort. Mahler lunged forward from his knees, grasping for the shotgun. Lindy scrabbled for the weapon herself. Hayes. Lindy. Mahler. Only one of them could reach the gun. Only one of them did.

52

Lauren Salter rose to her feet and ushered the woman to a seat on the far side of the table. If DCS Colleen Shepherd wondered perhaps whether it might have been the role of the senior officer in the room to take charge of proceedings, she said nothing. She was content to sit and observe for the moment.

"Thank you for coming in, Ms. Bonaccord. There are just a few details we need to clear up. You've brought in your copy of the signed agreement, as requested?"

So it was Ms. Bonaccord, not Susan? The woman's expression suggested the point wasn't lost on her. Now she was trying hard to pretend it didn't matter. She withdrew a slim black folder from her bag and slid it across the desk. Salter opened the folder and looked at the crisp loose sheets inside. She nodded and set them to one side, between herself and the DCS.

"Additional information, you said?" Bonaccord flickered an uncertain smile toward the watching DCS, like someone who suspected a threat, even if she was not sure from where it might come.

"About your statement." Salter made a show of riffling through a set of papers in front of her. It was theatrics, meant to raise the tension for Bonaccord as she waited for Salter's questions. But it was all a bit transparent and choreographed for Shepherd's liking. Salter would get away with it for now, with Bonaccord looking unsettled and agitated, but if the woman had a seasoned legal counsel sharing that side of the table, the sergeant's clumsy act would have been a tip-off about her inexperience. And a good lawyer would pounce on that. It was an item for the mental agenda Shepherd was compiling for the post-interview meeting with her new sergeant.

Salter drew a statement sheet to the top of the pile. She consulted the document carefully, and spoke without looking up. "You stated that you never let that receiver out of your hand once you answered the call from Wattis Wright."

"Not as far as I know." Bonaccord seemed to realize she might need a more unequivocal answer. "Yes. That is correct. Not until the police officer arrived. I seem to remember I was holding on to it quite tightly when he tried to get it out of my hand."

"And you were there in the room, Room 111 at the Demesne at Saltmarsh when you answered the call."

"Yes." Bonaccord tried another small smile in DCS Shepherd's direction. Perhaps it was just going to be a clarification of earlier details after all. "I have actually covered all this in my statement to you, Lauren."

Shepherd looked across at her newly minted sergeant, in case she wanted to defer to her senior officer, to put a little distance between herself and the interviewee, now that Bonaccord had reminded everyone that the two of them had so recently been on first name terms. But Shepherd knew Salter wouldn't let this one go. She was prepared, she was poised, and she was confident. A little overconfident perhaps, but Shepherd was prepared to see where Salter was going to take the interview before she made any move to intervene.

"The SmartSuite log for Room 111 shows that the system was requested to answer the room phone at 8:30. You made that request?"

Bonaccord nodded. "The system is voice-activated," she explained to Shepherd, who was looking as if she wished her sergeant might have given her a bit more background on this line of inquiry. "You simply address the system with any one of a number of pre-set commands, and it will perform the task."

"Even answering the phone?"

It wasn't clear who Shepherd was asking, but Bonaccord got in with her answer first. "You ask for it to be put on speakerphone. You don't need to lift the receiver. Though you can afterward, obviously."

Salter nodded in a way that suggested all this was leading in the direction she intended. Shepherd had no idea where that was. Salter had clearly picked up a few things from working alongside DCI Jejeune. Not all of them were good. The DCS would be reminding the new sergeant later that it wouldn't hurt to keep her superiors in the loop in future. But she was doing okay. A little bit full of herself, perhaps, with the excitement of closing in on her first arrest, but that was forgivable. The juices would be flowing; the heart rate would be up. It would be hard not to get a little carried away.

Salter raised her head and looked directly at Bonaccord. "You said in your statement you heard Wattis Wright being killed somewhere between eight thirty-five and eight forty. I take it you don't want to change that."

Bonaccord's confident smile from a few moments earlier had disappeared now. She sat forward again. "No. I used my phone to dial the front desk, as you know. I already suspected it might be important not to terminate the landline call. According to my phone, the time I made that call was eight forty-six. Wattis Wright would've been killed shortly before

346

that. I told you, I stayed on the phone for a few moments, trying to speak to him. I don't know how long."

Salter nodded. "Your GPS confirms Room 111 as the location of your phone from about six thirty p.m. onward that night."

Too much, thought Shepherd. The woman had made a call on the phone from her room. Had it really been necessary to verify her phone was in that location? Again, such zealousness was understandable in a new sergeant, but it was one more item for Shepherd's post-case review. The list was growing.

Bonaccord, too, looked shocked that Salter had taken the trouble to confirm such a minor detail. "Of course my phone was in my hotel room. Where else would it be?"

Shepherd had not encountered Susan Bonaccord before, but even she realized the broker's assertive tone as an attempt to regain control of a situation she felt slipping away from her. Somehow, somewhere, Salter had struck a nerve. All she had to do now was be patient. *Softly, softly. Let it sink in, whatever it was. Let Bonaccord think about it, worry about it, get uncomfortable. And stop fiddling with those bloody papers.*

"It's important, you see, because if your phone was there, you wouldn't have had to be in the room to answer that call from Wattis Wright."

There was a beat of silence as both Bonaccord and Shepherd digested the comment. *This is where you stop, Sergeant,* thought Shepherd. Not another word now. Let her come to you. Let her tell you what happened. But Salter didn't heed her DCS's silent warning.

"See, the way this could have happened is quite simple. You could have called your mobile with a burner phone, leaving the line open. Then you could have left your phone in your hotel room and gone to Wright's house, taking the burner with you."

"Sergeant …" There was urgency in Shepherd's tone, but not enough to stop Salter's building momentum. She steamrollered over her DCS's interruption and trundled on. "At Wright's house, you could have waited outside, unseen, in those bushes until exactly eight thirty. You knew he'd be calling you precisely at the time he'd arranged. Punctuality was another one of those old world values of Wright's that you found so quaint. As soon as you heard him ask the hotel switchboard for your room number, you could have spoken into the burner phone and had your mobile issue the command to the system in your room. 'Benson, answer the telephone.'"

"Sergeant Salter, a word please, immediately …"

But Salter was gathering speed, her eyes on the finish line. She had Bonaccord in her sights and she was closing in. She held up a hand to still Shepherd's warning and barrelled right through. "As far as the front desk associate knew, that was you in the room picking up the call. Then, with your alibi in place, you rang Wattis Wright's front doorbell, and when he answered, you stabbed him to death. With him still on the call to your room."

Silence.

Shepherd lowered her gaze to the desk, so Bonaccord wouldn't see the look of despair on her face. *You had her*, she thought, *you bloody had her*. You'd done all the hard work, put it all together, and you couldn't keep your mouth shut long enough to reel her in. Now Salter had told this woman, this suspect who hadn't even been read her rights yet, all her reasoning, all her logic. Bonaccord was clever enough to stop talking now and let a lawyer pick through Salter's claims and come up with plausible explanations for all of them. It was a total bloody catastrophe.

Bonaccord recognized it, too. Shepherd could tell from the faintly disguised smugness in her smile as she spoke. "And why on earth would I want to kill Mr. Wright?"

"Sergeant Salter, I think it may be wise to suspend the interview at this time while we review our position." The case still had a pulse, barely, but if Shepherd was going to salvage anything from it, she needed to stop the carnage now. She'd get Danny Maik on it, whenever she could find him. She'd get him to have another go at Bonaccord, a more measured approach this time, more patient. There may still be enough good police work here to close this out, but not with the runaway train that was first-case Sergeant Lauren Salter at the controls.

"You killed him because he refused to sign the agreement."

Shepherd was too shocked by Salter's answer to offer any protest. Bonaccord was actually laughing now. "Sergeant, you have a document in front of you that manifestly proves the opposite. This is ridiculous."

Bonaccord looked at Shepherd and raised her eyebrows in an expression that mingled astonishment with exasperation. Shepherd couldn't disagree with either the sentiment or the woman's comment. But as inexperienced and reckless as Salter was, the sergeant wasn't stupid. Shepherd waited in silence to see what Salter had to say.

"That signature is a forgery. It's very good, and I'm aware that it would be hard to prove now that Wright is dead, but Mr. Wright didn't sign that document. I think he told you he was backing out of the deal. Once he saw his dishonesty in black and white, he realized he couldn't go through with it. He knew Jennie Wynn was entitled to a share of those rights. Their decency never really leaves them, you see, those men with those old-fashioned values. Even if they might wobble a bit in the face of temptation, their sense of morality is always there at their core. Wattis Wright was going to back out of that deal until you could renegotiate for the rights with both of them. And Wynn, I'm fairly sure, would have driven a far harder bargain than the one Wright had agreed to."

"You're wrong, Lauren. Wright signed that deal. That agreement is legal, it is valid, and it is binding. No court in the land is going to find otherwise." Bonaccord looked at Salter directly, locking onto her with a frank, challenging stare. Whatever friendship had existed, whatever connection they may have once shared, there was nothing between them now. This was a battleground, and Bonaccord was in her comfort zone. Now it was she, not Salter, moving in for the kill. "I had no motive whatsoever to kill Wattis Wright. And no opportunity, either. The system at the Demesne logs all entries and exits. They will prove I was in the room all night."

"The system monitors doors only, though, Ms. Bonaccord, isn't that right? It doesn't record the opening and closing of windows, not even for the ground floor rooms — a bit of an oversight, that, from a security perspective. I might have to have a word with them about it."

Salter looked up to show Bonaccord this was her battleground, too. And she wasn't backing down. "Your reputation was on the line, wasn't it? The show's producers had told you they needed those rights, and you'd promised to deliver them. There were plans that had already been drawn up, there were people counting on you, for their jobs, for their roles in the new production. Contracts have been signed. Six-figure losses were in the cards if you failed to deliver. Your reputation would never recover from something like that. You, who had poured everything you had into your career, who never compromised a single moment of your personal time for it. For somebody who'd sacrificed everything she had to be Susan Bonaccord, professional fixer, that was a lot to see destroyed by one cantankerous old man who was having an attack of the guilts. One *decent* cantankerous old man."

Salter picked up Bonaccord's copy of the agreement. "There was a copy of this agreement on Wattis Wright's desk, next to the uncashed cheque," she said. "We were meant to believe this is a photocopy Wright made of that agreement, one he signed and mailed off to you earlier that day. Have I got that right?"

Bonaccord said nothing, her eyes locked on Salter. Shepherd, too, was looking at her sergeant intently. The DCS had discreetly trailed her arm out along the desk, in the direction of the recorder. She was poised to snap it off and declare an immediate end to the interview. No more requests, no more subtle interventions. If Salter started going off the rails again, she would end things. But it didn't look like that was going to happen now. Salter was composed. She was in control. And she was ready.

"Those big photocopiers, like the one Wattis Wright had in his office, the one used to make this copy, they were very popular at one time, but then they disappeared virtually overnight. Hospitals got rid of them, and the military." Salter looked across at Shepherd. "Even the police departments. Security concerns, somebody told me recently. At first, I thought he meant concerns about somebody leaving sensitive documents on the glass after copying them. But that didn't seem to pose a large enough threat to warrant abandoning these things wholesale. So you know what I did? I *googled* it. Turns out the real security concern was data storage. People found out the hard drives on these old photocopiers were storing tons of ultra-sensitive data; medical records, police files, military secrets. Anybody who knew how to access the memory of these copiers would have access to everything the machine had ever copied, all time and date stamped. Eight thirty-six," said Salter. "That's when this document was copied on Wattis Wright's photocopier. Being in possession of it puts you at the scene of Wattis Wright's murder at the exact time your own testimony says it was being committed."

Salter learned fast. This time she said nothing. She simply sat there watching. There was no smugness on Susan Bonaccord's side of the table now, no self-assurance. There was only a woman who had ceased to exist.

Perhaps it was because the silence still hung so heavy in the interview room that the constable's entry seemed so startling. Certainly, both police officers had started to rise from their chairs before the breathless young man even began his report. He flashed a glance at Bonaccord, but decided he didn't want to wait to get the officers out into the hallway. "Report of firearms discharged, ma'am, two shotgun blasts. They came from DCI Jejeune's cottage."

Salter and Shepherd snapped a shared glance at each other. Neither needed to ask where Danny was now. They knew. And where Lindy was, too.

"First responders are on the scene. No IDs yet, but there are multiple victims."

"Injuries?"

The constable's eyes said it first. "Worse."

By the time Shepherd had issued her terse command for the constable to stay with Bonaccord, Salter was already halfway down the corridor. Shepherd had caught up to her before they reached the station doors.

53

The sky was a palette of frosted pastels; pinks and lilacs and blues. Beneath it, dark mounds of drumlins rolled away in the distance. On both sides, stands of birches flickered past, their white trunks like a giant picket fence. Beside him in the passenger seat, Traz's silence reminded Jejeune of all his friend had done for him, all he was still doing for him. But he knew he had to see things through to the end, as bad as it was going to be.

Jejeune saw an abandoned building in a field, tethered to the highway by a narrow road that was slowly being reclaimed by the wilderness. He pulled off the highway and guided the Durango over the rutted surface, stopping beside the building. As the two men got out, Jejeune realized it had once been a chapel. The paint was peeling from the exterior in great scales, as if the building was sloughing off dead skin. Tattered shutters dangled from rusted hinges, flapping listlessly as the wind blew through the open windows. Through a hole in the roof, a shaft of light pierced the interior and flooded the space with a pale glow. Jejeune stared at the building now as he spoke.

"Annie Prior would have needed someone on the inside, Traz, to fit those cranes with the cameras. Aransas would have been the best place. It would have been easy enough to attract the birds to baited traps."

"Come on, JJ, those devices could have been fitted any-where along the birds' migration route. Damian trapped cranes in Wood Buffalo without patterning them to bait. Is that all you've got?"

"The cranes at Wood Buffalo were fitted with VHF col-lars, which made it easy for Damian to locate them. He sent you coordinates for all the stopover points. You already know whether there was any possibility somebody could get close enough to transient birds elsewhere, at Cheyenne Bottoms or Salt Plains, for example, to fit those devices. And there wasn't, was there?"

Traz was silent.

"Prior knew she would only have a short time after the cranes arrived to remove the collars and cameras before the park staff started their nesting survey. But to anticipate when those cranes would be arriving in the park, you'd need to know exactly when they had departed from Aransas."

"Anyone at Wood Buffalo could have called in to request that information."

"I don't see anybody from the Canadian Wildlife Service asking on behalf of a cultural anthropologist, do you? Not without wanting to know what her interest was."

Traz was shaking his head. "Verity would never be involved in anything like this. She loves those birds. The extra weight of all that monitoring equipment could have put their entire migration in jeopardy. She would never do that."

The protest was almost frivolous, but Jejeune wouldn't treat it that way. Traz saw it as his duty to protect Verity now, so Jejeune would field every question, answer every objection, until his friend was ready to accept the truth. "Ultra-lightweight housings, Traz," he said reasonably. "They would have had negligible impact on large-bodied birds like the cranes. At worst, the extra drag might have forced the birds into an additional stopover or two, if the weather was particularly bad."

Traz said nothing.

On the hillside behind the chapel, the tarmac road ran like a scar through the dense blanket of fir trees. It had been an incredible feat of engineering to drive an access road through this wilderness. But did humans really have any place here, wondered Jejeune, where surviving was the only rule, and things like friendship and loyalty and betrayal played no part?

"Verity was going through my things when I woke up." Jejeune fished in his pocket and withdrew the blue photo chip. "She was looking for this."

"No." Traz was shaking his head now. "You must have this wrong. It was dark in that room. You were probably still a little messed up. Hallucinating, maybe."

"She wanted these photographs, Traz. Perhaps she still intended to give them to Robideau, maybe she was just going to destroy them to cover her tracks." Jejeune shrugged, "I don't know. But she thought I had them, and she was going to take them."

Traz had fallen silent again. Jejeune looked at the ruins of the chapel, this place where faith had been abandoned, and belief in something greater than yourself had been carried away by the harsh northern winds. Traz hadn't asked him the question. He had once told Domenic not to check into somebody unless you were prepared to live with what you found. Traz had looked into Verity Brown, Jejeune knew now, and whatever he had found, he was prepared to live with it. He would make whatever compromises he needed to, sacrifice whatever he had to, in order to have his companion in this world. Traz hadn't asked Domenic the question, and that meant he already knew the answer. For Domenic, that answer was the one piece of the puzzle left, the one unknown. He knew Verity was guilty. He knew what she had done, and how she had done it, and when, and where. In the end, what did it matter if you didn't have the whole picture? So, he would let Traz keep it to himself — the answer Domenic didn't have, the answer to the question Traz had failed to ask him: *Why?*

The oncoming car rocked the Durango with its slipstream as it hurtled past. So many of the vehicles heading north had single travellers, as if the drivers were not so much on a trip, thought Traz, but a quest, to test themselves against the north, to find their own limits, their own tolerances. Perhaps he and Domenic had done that, too. The silence in the car had existed between the men long before Jejeune had drifted off into a deep sleep. Traz looked across at his friend now, his disquiet masked by slumber. Traz's own feelings had spun through a spectrum of emotions since the two men had got back in the car. Resentment had been there. Anger, too. But now, there was mostly just sadness — for a friendship that caused Domenic to care so much that he had to tell him.

Them, too. Till they got rare. Gatean Robideau's words still rang in Traz's ears. Whooping Cranes. Part of the feast at these Dene gatherings, their bones part of the detritus buried at these sites. Bones that would have been recovered by Annie Prior during her excavations. Bones holding the DNA of long-dead birds whose migratory instincts were intact, uncompromised, pure. Bones that would have given Verity Brown the back markers for her genetic modelling.

It would have been a vital source of new data, one that would have garnered any researcher the respect of her peers. Data drawn from sources no one else had, or could ever have. Data that would earn you the right to be considered worthy

356

to hold an opinion — more, to voice it without facing ridicule or contempt. And who wouldn't want that? Who didn't deserve it? And how far would we go, any of us, for a chance to secure it?

Domenic stirred and blinked himself awake. Traz looked across at his friend again. Through the window beyond him he could see farmland. The human landscape was gradually replacing the wild one they had left behind, encroaching ever nearer as they hurtled south on this highway. Soon there would be a town, then another, and another. And then, finally, the airport. And choices.

"Welcome back," said Traz. "We made good time on that last stretch. We're only a couple of hours out, at most."

Jejeune realized Traz wasn't just giving him their ETA. He was telling him how long he had to inform his friend of his decision.

"A crime was committed, Traz, and a woman died because of it. That's not something any police officer can ignore."

"Sometimes people die because of their own choices. There doesn't always have to be a reckoning, JJ. She saved your life."

It was the statement of a man bargaining for the freedom of somebody he loved. It was an unspoken appeal, too, to a friendship and all that meant, all that lay beneath it. But Verity Brown had broken the law. She'd played a part in an illegal scheme that had cost a woman her life. Domenic had a duty to make sure Annie Prior's death wasn't just chalked up as one more reckless, irresponsible soul lost to the wilderness. What else that duty demanded, though, he didn't know.

They talked about other matters, anything and nothing, until Traz swept the Durango around to the departure terminal at Edmonton Airport and pulled up to the curb. Jejeune made no move to get out. He stared out through the windscreen. Traz did the same.

Like someone stirring from sleep, Jejeune slowly reached into his pocket and withdrew the small plastic bag with the blue disc inside. "It seems as if people have been reminding me, since the day I landed, that I have no jurisdiction in this part of the world," he said. "This is evidence in Annie Prior's death, and as such, I have no right to take it out of the country with me." He pressed the bag into Traz's palm. "I'm grateful to Verry, Traz. Truly, I am. But Annie Prior is owed something here, too. Somebody needs to do the right thing for her." Did his loyalty lie with the the living or the dead? Traz was looking at him now, and Jejeune knew his friend could tell the question remained unanswered. He opened the door and reached over to offer a hand. "Thanks for the ride, Traz. It's been ..."

Traz nodded sadly. "Yeah," he said. "Me, too."

54

Domenic Jejeune stared solemnly through the window in DCS Colleen Shepherd's office. The flat landscape seemed drained of colour, the stands of grass moving uneasily in a constant wind. A solitary Kestrel hung suspended in the white sky, banking its wings constantly to hold its position in the blustery conditions. How many times he'd sat here in this office, thought Jejeune, in how many different situations. But never one like this.

Shepherd was standing the other side of the desk, a telephone cradled to her ear. She was half-turned away from Jejeune, not to shield the words, he decided, but perhaps to avoid having to look at him.

"That is correct, sir. One female fatality, two males recovered from the site, both in serious condition." She listened to the voice on the other end of the line for a moment. "No, those were the only ones involved, as far as I know." Her half twist in Domenic's direction suggested she might be about to verify something with him, but in the end she reconsidered and turned away again. Shepherd listened to additional comments from the other party and nodded briefly. "Of course, I'll keep you apprised of any changes in the situation. Thank you, sir."

She replaced the receiver and sat down opposite Jejeune, offering him an apologetic look. "I'm sorry. I imagine that was the last thing you wanted to hear me discussing. The Chief Constable offers his condolences. I'm not sure he quite understands the nature of the relationship between the two of you." Shepherd paused for a moment. "Still, there will be plenty of time to set him straight."

"Yes," said Jejeune quietly, "There will." He looked out the window again. The Kestrel had moved farther off to hover over another patch of pale meadow. The landscape looked the same as he remembered it — the faint swell of the field as it approached the horizon, the line of dark pines marking the far boundary. It seemed incredible to him that after all that had happened in his own life recently, a place like this could remain the same. But despite all he had been through, the world had not changed. Only his world.

Jejeune had come straight to the station from the airport, refusing offers of food and rest until he had interrogated Shepherd about what had happened at the cottage. He'd read the report, now resting on the edge of her desk, and then asked more questions. As always, he wanted every detail, no matter how small, how insignificant. He had lingered over a couple of passages in the report, riffling back or forward between the pages. A contradiction? Some troubling inconsistency? No doubt there was. It was a hastily prepared draft only. But there was no doubt about the report's major findings. Of the terrible events that had occurred at the cottage, there was no question at all.

"You should get some sleep. There's nothing you can do here at the moment." Shepherd paused. "I'm afraid the Chief Constable is adamant that his decision will stand, Domenic. You'll have to remain on leave until this business of removing evidence from a crime scene is reviewed." She looked at him over the top of her steel-rimmed glasses. "It's entirely likely you'll be looking at suspension, you understand. There was no harm done in the end, of course, and that will undoubtedly work in your favour, but I wouldn't expect the Conduct Review Panel to be willing to brush this under the carpet completely. Evidence-handling protocols are there for a reason, Domenic, and if they are breached, there must inevitably be consequences."

Jejeune nodded silently. A suspension wasn't the foremost thing on his mind at the moment, but the DCS's delivery, her tone, her carefully chosen words of admonishment, all had a familiarity to them that he found strangely comforting. It was almost as if, after the constant sense of dislocation he'd felt in the weeks of his self-imposed exile, the two of them had suddenly slipped back into their previous roles. And even if Shepherd's message itself wasn't particularly welcome, it was hardly unexpected, either.

He nodded mutely and stood up to leave.

"Domenic, after all that's happened, it would be quite understandable if you wanted to consider your future. Please know, there will be no pressure on you to make a decision. You should take all the time you need." She paused. "That is unless you've already decided." But the small smile she gave him suggested she didn't really expect an answer, and she didn't wait for one. "Go and get some rest now. There are a number of matters that will require your attention, I'm sure, but you need a clear head for some of the things you will have to deal with."

"I'd like to stop in and see Sergeant Maik, if you think he'd be up for a visit."

"Maik?" Shepherd's eyebrows rose in surprise. "Sorry, it's just that I'd have thought Lindy would have been your first visit, that's all." She looked at him cautiously. "Danny Maik was unconscious at the time of the shooting. I'm not sure he will be able to provide any more details than you already have."

Jejeune shook his head. "It's not that. Ray Hayes is a master of transferring guilt. He will have tried to convince the sergeant that it was all his fault, that it was his mistakes, his failings, that caused all this. It's important that someone tells him he wasn't to blame."

A momentary look of irritation flashed across Shepherd's face. Jejeune nodded in understanding. "You'll have already done that, I know. But I think it will be important for him to hear it from me. I'd like to express my gratitude to him, too."

Shepherd nodded. "It was an extraordinary piece of work, tracking down Hayes and Lindy. The sergeant and I will be having a serious heart to heart when he returns, about his decision to handle the situation on his own, but truly, Domenic, I'm not sure anyone else could have managed to achieve what Danny Maik did."

"He's a good officer," said Jejeune, nodding. "A good man." The comment resonated with him for a moment, though he couldn't have said why. "I'm going to stop by the cottage, too. I take it SOCO have finished processing the scene?"

"They have. But do you think that's wise?" Surely the man didn't need to pile on any more despair, revisiting the place of so many previous happy memories?

"I just need to grab a few things."

"Domenic, will you allow me to give you a little piece of advice? Don't leave it too long before you go and see Lindy. I understand your reluctance, obviously, but it's something you need to do, and putting it off won't make it any easier. You need to face up to things as soon as you can. It's necessary. For both of you."

The emotional investment she made in her officers must have cost her dearly at times, but it was part of what made Colleen Shepherd the kind of DCS she was, and despite their differences in the past, it was the kind he would still have wanted to serve under. He wasn't sure whether that would be possible now, but he acknowledged her advice with a grateful smile. "I know. I'll go tomorrow. I just don't want her to see me looking like this." He paused. "I want to get cleaned up. I'd like to look my best for her. After this long, she deserves nothing less."

Shepherd lifted a sheet of paper from her desk. "I understand your brother is recovering well. I know it must have been playing on your mind, having to leave to come here while he was still in hospital."

Jejeune nodded. They'd kept Damian in for an extra night's observation in the hospital at Yellowknife. But it hadn't prevented two officers from the territorial RCMP from visiting him at his bedside. Jejeune was sure his brother would have told them everything he knew. That wasn't to say his account would be complete, but for the time being it would be the official record of what had happened out in the park, both before Domenic arrived and after.

"He was able to tell the authorities exactly where to find the woman's body," Shepherd continued. "I wish I'd known her name when I was speaking to the Chief Constable: *female fatality* has such a coldness to it."

"Annie Prior. I doubt Damian will know how to contact her next of kin, but the park staff should have something on record. It's required information on the Extended Stay forms." *Extended stay*, he thought ironically. He stood up. "I should be going."

Shepherd nodded. "Do wish Lindy well from me when you see her. She was understandably reluctant to dwell on the details, but she did at least manage to corroborate Hayes's version of events." Shepherd looked at Jejeune. "Mahler's death has been officially recorded as being the result of a weapon being discharged during a struggle with Hayes. Mahler's arms were raised slightly when he was shot, consistent with him being in the act of falling back, having lost his grip on the shotgun. It must have been horrific for Lindy, watching someone shot like that at such close quarters. It's the sort of thing that stays with you." Shepherd looked out the window, though she didn't seem to be seeing anything out there. "She's been through a difficult time, Domenic. I suspect she'll need some counselling if she's to come to terms with everything that's happened."

Jejeune managed to raise a smile from somewhere. "She'll love that."

She returned her gaze to Jejeune. "I've seen it achieve some remarkable results, but it will take time … a long time. You'll need to be patient." Shepherd paused. "I suppose what I'm saying is, you might want to prepare yourself for the fact that she may not be ready to pick up where you two left off, at least not yet."

Jejeune looked at his DCS to see if there was anything behind her words, to see if, perhaps, Lindy had already said as much to her. But there was nothing in Shepherd's look beyond the concern for the well-being of one of her officers, concern for a person she thought of as a friend.

Shepherd softened her tone. "There is one other thing." She looked reluctant to continue, but Jejeune could antici-pate what was coming. He tried to give her an expression that would make it easier for her. "The RCMP wanted a word, and I got the impression that sooner would suit them better than later. I did explain that you'd just got back, and there were a number of personal matters you'd need to attend to, but I suggested we might set up a video call here for tomorrow afternoon. I'll be available."

They would have asked for a senior officer to be present at the interview, thought Jejeune, and the *here* meant they wanted it conducted in a controlled setting. It explained how

Shepherd had such up-to-the-minute information about Damian's condition, too, when he had only just received the news himself. But he nodded at Shepherd's suggestion anyway. If the meeting had been scheduled for the morning, he would have asked for a postponement, but by the afternoon Domenic would be able to tell the Canadian police everything he knew, as his duty required. Whether it was his duty, too, to share the things he merely suspected was a question he was still struggling with. By tomorrow, he would need an answer.

He looked out of Shepherd's window one last time. The Kestrel had gone, moved on to more fertile hunting grounds. The sky held no birds now; it was a wide, white emptiness, with not even a single fold in the cloud cover. A blank slate to start over? Or a shroud to lay over what had once been his life here? He didn't know the answer to that yet, either. But he soon would.

55

"You just missed the DCI." Maik peered past Salter as if checking whether Jejeune's car might still be in sight. He remembered his manners and stood aside to let her enter his house. She was carrying a hold-all, which she set down in the hallway without explanation. Maik helped her out of her jacket and hung it on the coat rack, ushering her into the living room. Standing behind her as she entered, the room suddenly seemed dull and uninviting to him. It was as if Salter's entrance brought light and vitality, and it had only served to highlight the drabness of the room's decor. Time to redecorate, he decided; a project he could look into during his forced recuperation.

"Wine?" he asked. He held up a hand. "I know, your fitness regimen and all that, but surely a small glass is in order, to celebrate closing your first case?"

"Go on then. A small one."

He returned from the kitchen and handed her a glass. He hadn't poured one for himself. "Still got a tea going," he explained.

She was sitting facing him, and leaned forward slightly. "I see Norwich had a good result today."

"It was yesterday, and a goalless draw against that mob is hardly a good result. They're bottom of the league by five points. Any other test questions?"

She smiled sheepishly. "Concussion is serious, Danny. Pretending otherwise could be a big mistake. Somebody is supposed to keep an eye on you overnight, just in case. I doubted there'd be a long lineup of volunteers, so I thought I might as well put my hand up. I brought a bag. I can use the couch if the spare room's not made up."

"It is," said Danny simply. "So, tell me, Detective Sergeant Salter, how did you crack it, in the end?"

With later cases, he wouldn't ask, and Salter wouldn't say. Her deductive reasoning would become apparent as one read through her report. Seasoned officers were content to let it stay there. But this was her first case, the first time she'd trusted her cleverness to lead her to her conclusions, and Maik knew she'd want to share it. He knew, too, that she'd be shy about it, and get that lovely rosy glow on her neck and cheeks before she told him.

"I asked myself how they knew — Albert Ross and Jennie Wynn. Wattis Wright wasn't going to broadcast the fact to Wynn that he had successfully stolen her rights, and if he did intend on backing out on his investment plans, he wouldn't have asked Ross round to see him. He'd have gone to Ross's to deliver the news. It's the proper way to do it, the way you … that type of man … would handle something like that. So, if there were to be any fireworks, they'd have been at Ross's house, not Wright's."

Danny nodded. "So, it must have been Susan Bonaccord who told them both the deal had been concluded."

"Two people with a history of IED, each receiving news that would make them angry, at the very least. Their motives provided Bonaccord with all the cover she needed. I never even looked in her direction."

"That business with the remote phone command," Maik shook his head in admiration, "that would have had any of us old dinosaurs spinning around in circles. And then, at the other end of the technological timeline, that old photocopier Wright had. All things considered, you had your work cut out for you. It can't have been easy coming to terms with the cutting-edge stuff at the hotel and the wonders of prehistoric equipment like that." Danny held up his mug. "Anyway, to closing the case ..." he paused and looked at her significantly, "and leaving doors open."

Salter's colour turned slightly deeper. "Oh, you heard about that."

At some point Susan Bonaccord had offered her confession. Perhaps she had done so while Salter and the DCS were at the hospital. Perhaps the two officers had needed to work on her some more once they got back to the station. But if Maik's grasp of the timing might be slightly off, the details of what Salter had done afterward had made it through the station's grapevine clearly enough. She had gone to see Albert Ross at the nursery. She told him Wattis Wright had foregone a larger potential payout through future royalties in favour of a smaller lump sum up front. It was the kind of thing you might do, Salter had suggested, if you needed ready cash, like if you planned to make an investment in something. It wasn't that his will had failed him, it was simply that he had decided Jennie Wynn should have the chance to invest in Ross's nursery, too. In the end, unless Ross made peace with his other demons, Salter's visit wouldn't change much. But somewhere down the road, in the quiet hours, it might be enough to convince Ross that someone once had enough faith in him to want to back his enterprise And if it did, then it might make a difference. A small one perhaps, but sometimes that was all you could hope for. The gesture told Danny that Lauren Salter had what she needed to become a successful detective sergeant: a concern for the dead, but also for the living they left behind.

"It's not that I don't appreciate you coming," said Danny, "but I'd have thought you'd have better things to do with your weekend."

She shook her head. "Max is sleeping over at a friend's house." Perhaps it was the thought of the upcoming stream of such lonely moments that encouraged her to take such a long drink of her wine. She looked into the empty glass, then set it down self-consciously.

"Another?" asked Maik.

Salter smiled her refusal. "So, what did the DCI want?"

"He wanted to know what I could remember."

"And you told him you were concussed, unconscious in fact, so you couldn't really remember anything of what went on.... Just like you told us in the official questioning, right?" Salter looked at Danny frankly, watching for his reaction.

"I told him I wouldn't be able to add anything to the official record."

Salter continued looking at him for a long time, trying to decide if that was the same thing, but she found the blankness of Danny's expression disconcerting, and eventually turned away. "Perhaps I will have another one after all," she said. "Want another tea?"

He shook his head and watched her leave. It was good she was staying, he thought. A night on his own would have had him mulling over his reaction to the DCI's visit. Try as he might, a quiet, empty house was no place to avoid troubling thoughts. The hesitancy at the doorway had been strangely at odds with the DCI's usual confident knock. A brief greeting, and then into the living room to get down to business. Except this was no normal business. This was DCI Domenic Jejeune asking questions to which his eyes suggested he might not want answers. And although Danny recognized this, he had no intention of withholding anything, or misleading his

DCI. It would have been pointless, anyway. By this stage in their relationship, Jejeune could read him better than any man he had ever known, and Danny knew that he would not have been able to conceal the truth from him.

It's the blood, Danny, Jejeune had told him, *the blood that's not on the gunstock.* Even without the DCI's body language, the uneasy pacing, the constant looking around the room, the rare use of Maik's first name would have signalled to him how important the issue was to the DCI.

His response to Jejeune had been what he told Salter. He was dazed, completely out if it for the most part. He couldn't confirm anything that had happened. But he couldn't deny Jejeune's unspoken premise either. He couldn't offer him explanations about the absence of blood, or how a gun that must have landed in one place could have ended up where it did instead.

He couldn't explain any of that, and he knew that meant Jejeune would leave his house carrying all the same doubts he had arrived with, perhaps more firmly entrenched given that Danny had failed to offer any alternatives to them. He had no idea what his DCI would do now, with his unprovable theories and his unanswered questions. The man who had left these shores had been so certain of things, but this one who had returned seemed different somehow. It was as if his time away had taught him something about the imperfections of this human world of ours, about where a person had to make a stand, and when he should stand aside. About priorities and compromises, and what parts of yourself you needed to hold on to, and what parts you had to be willing to let go of in order to let life in. Danny knew all this because he, too, had struggled with these questions recently. He had looked into his coming death, staring at the cold, dark openings of the twin barrels in Peter Mahler's hands, and he had realized that he had no more chances left. This was his time to die. Something had changed within him when he came back from that moment, something profound. Now Jejeune had his suspicions and Danny knew what they were. But as soon as the DCI had left this house, the startling realization came over Danny that it no longer mattered to him. Even if he shared Jejeune's suspicions, as he believed somewhere in the back of his mind he might, he was willing to make his peace with them. He wasn't sure if Domenic Jejeune could live with his uncertainties, but Danny knew he could. His priority now was to make the most of the reprieve he'd been granted. There was nothing he could do that would change what had happened at the cottage. All he could do was to get on with what happened after.

Salter returned from the kitchen carrying her glass of wine. She set it down and rummaged through her bag. "I thought you might like to see this," she said, producing a DVD. "The original dance routines of the Shammalars. I had tech burn a copy for me. You probably don't have a DVD player, though. Or do you?"

"It's over there by the phonograph," said Maik. Once more, the blandness of the room struck him as he looked around. But he knew it would take more than a few licks of paint or some bolts of wallpaper to transform this room. There was more to be overcome. This room, this house, held the past. He stood up to take the disc, but Salter squeezed in front of him. "I'll do it."

She slid the disc into the slot as Maik clicked on the TV, and the grainy black-and-white footage came to life. The music swelled, pouring into the silence of the room, and Salter began swaying slightly, holding her wine glass loosely off to one side as she danced. "I suppose you're going to tell me they took these moves from old Motown routines," she said over her shoulder, her gaze still fixed on the screen.

"If they did, they've changed them a bit," said Maik. Salter realized he was standing behind her, but she didn't turn. "The hips, for one thing, and that shoulder turn." She sensed his body close behind her and felt his hand on her shoulder. "More like this." He eased her shoulder forward slightly, and rested a hand on her opposite hip. "And this." From behind, he brought his cheek alongside hers and she felt his soft breath on her neck. He wrapped an arm around her waist and together they swayed gently to the music, Danny leaning comfortably against her, and Salter still resolutely facing the screen as the tears flowed down her cheeks.

56

Domenic Jejeune walked along the coastal path, buffeted by the familiar greeting of the onshore winds. The soft whisper of the waves breaking against the rocky shore rose up from somewhere at the base of the cliff. He stopped when he saw the figure ahead of him. Lindy was sitting on the edge of the path, feet dangling over the side of the rock face, looking out to sea. She looked as sad as he had ever seen her. For so long, his dreams had revolved around this moment. But in them, Lindy greeted his return by running up to him, long hair flying behind her, a delighted smile on her face, to fling her arms around him in a hug. Even from this distance, he could tell there would be no delighted smile, no hug. Not even Lindy's newly cropped hair would be flying in the breeze. His heart flinched at the thought of approaching her, but he knew he had to.

She remained still, staring out over the sea, as he approached. The flat morning light had coated the rippling surface of the water with glitter. On the horizon, a low bank of cloud was tinged with pale orange. The sight was as enthralling as it had ever been, but Jejeune had eyes only for the person looking at it.

"I've always thought that, in heaven, it'd be easy to tell the people who were from this part of the world," said Lindy, still staring out. "They'd be the ones looking homesick." She scrambled to her feet and looked at him.

He was right. There was no hug. No smile. "You look great," said Domenic. "Your hair —"

"I'm growing it out. I made a couple of changes to my life I'm not sure I should have."

"Was the diesel version another of them?" He looked over his shoulder, back towards the cottage at the far end of the path. "The Jetta's parked in the driveway," he said simply. Farther along the path, a small bird dropped into a gorse bush. Domenic thought he caught a flash of blue on the head. The light out here, it was always playing tricks.

Lindy looked past him, towards the cottage, and he saw the pain shimmer behind her eyes. "I can't go in there, Dom. I told you that on the phone. Here's okay, but not inside ..." She shook her head. It was always windy up here on the path, *their path*, and sometimes it made Lindy's eyes water. "I've decided to sell up," she said. "In fact, there's a note from my solicitor winging its way to Canada as we speak."

The shock left Domenic without words. The sound of the wind baffled against his ears. Out on the water, the rising sun had shifted the sea through shades of colour and settled on a soft dove grey. Tiny flecks of white foam crested the waves as they gently rolled towards the beach.

He nodded. "I can understand —"

"No, Dom," Lindy shook her head firmly, "you can't. Something terrible took place in there, something horrible and evil. I don't want to set foot in that place ever again, not even to clean it out. I'll get a service in to do it, or something."

"I can do it, Lindy. If you want to sell, we'll sell. We can start again somewhere else."

The fugitive shape popped out briefly from the cover of the bush, and Domenic was all but certain now. The size was right, the shape. And the colours. The chest was red. Surely, it was no trick of the light?

"We can't just hit the reset button, Dom," Lindy looked at him. "We just can't go back to the way things were. Too much has changed for that. Things have happened. Things that can't be undone."

"I'm so sorry, Lindy," he said. "I had to handle it like this. It was the only way."

"No, it wasn't. Not the only way. You wanted to deal with it *for* me, not *with* me. We should have discussed it, but of course you're too bloody arrogant to even consider that somebody else might have a point of view that deserves hearing. So, you left me here, to go through … *that* …" She choked back her emotion and flapped a hand at him.

She had not raised her voice, but the words had landed like blows. He turned away from her, seeking escape. The dark shape of a Sparrow Hawk was approaching low over the fields. Along the path, his bird sat backlit on top of the gorse bush, readying itself to flee from the approaching predator. Was there blue? Red? He couldn't tell, but he knew in his heart there was. And he knew that when the Painted Bunting flew off, it would not return. Once it had slipped away, it would be gone forever.

He turned back to Lindy. "Perhaps we could go away somewhere. I'll be getting some time off. I took evidence with me. To Canada."

She nodded. "The bookmark. Did you bring it back?"

He nodded. "I wanted to give it to you today, but they need to keep it for the inquiry."

"You were going to give it to me? I gave it to you, Dom. That bookmark was *my* gift to *you*." She managed a little choking laugh. "You never really did get the hang of that re-gifting thing, did you?"

"I'm looking at a suspension," he said. "Thirty days at least, I would guess. Longer, most likely. We could go away somewhere, anywhere you like, just the two of us."

Lindy shook her head. "It'll just be window dressing. They'll reinstate you as soon as a big case comes along. Despite everything, they'll find they can't get by without you." The inference in Lindy's flat tone was clear: perhaps some people could.

"Lindy, what happened in the cottage ... I think I know. There was none of Danny Maik's blood on the gunstock." *It's okay, Lindy,* he was telling her. *You can let me see your pain. You can let me into your darkness.* He was fighting for his life, their life. Along the path, the gorse branch was empty. His prized lifer had disappeared forever. He couldn't allow Lindy to escape, too. Not without trying everything he could.

"Sergeant Maik's blood was on the barrel, but the report says Mahler also struck him on the scalp with the stock. There should have been blood on there, too. Some trace, at least."

He paused, but Lindy was unable to raise her eyes to look at him. She was shaking her head, silently pleading with him not to continue. But it was important now that he carried on. He had to show her he knew. He knew the truth and he could accept it. He had the evidence; he had the facts. And Lindy, with every word, with every feathery breath and half-choked sob as she looked back past him to the cottage, confirmed it all.

Lindy looked up and flapped her arms at her sides in frustration, her cheeks wet with tears that were not from the wind. "Oh, Dom. Why did you have to be you?"

"The rug in the living room has been moved. There's a deep scar in the wood beneath it. That scar wasn't there when we had those floors refinished. It's from the shotgun's locking mechanism, isn't it? It happened when the gun hit the floor. When it fell away from the table and landed in that direction."

He waited. Lindy had to tell him the rest. It had to be her decision. If she didn't tell him, where would that leave them? He didn't know. But it would be Lindy's choice now. Everything would be up to her, just as it should have been all along.

"He said we were in it together now," she said softly, staring out at the sea as she disappeared back through the tunnel of her memories. "Oh, Dom. It was so awful." She began sobbing and her grief poured out of her in great waves, like the rolling grey-green swells beside them. He pulled her in close and held her, letting her cry into his chest, while the sounds of the sea washed over them and the bare branches of the gorse bush danced in the breeze.

When the worst had passed, Domenic guided her to the edge of the path where she had been when he first arrived. They sat together and he put his arm around her shoulder.

"I couldn't think," she said. "I was holding the gun. Jeremy ... Mahler ... was on one side and Hayes was on the other. They were both screaming at me at the same time. Hayes was telling me to pass him the gun. Mahler was telling me not to do it." Her voice sounded detached, disconnected, as if she needed to distance herself from it; needed to be somebody else, reporting on the events, not Lindy, living them again. "My hand was shaking. The shotgun was so heavy. I couldn't get my other arm free to hold it steady. Hayes kept saying the same thing. The same words. Over and over again. His voice never changed. *Pass me the gun, Lindy. Pass me the gun, Lindy. Pass me the gun, Lindy.* And all the time, Mahler kept telling me not to. *Don't give it to him, Lindy. Don't do it.* I remember wondering what would happen if Mahler came towards me, whether I would shoot him. I wasn't sure. I didn't know if I could." She paused and looked down. She had her knees gathered to her chest and she was trembling slightly despite Jejeune's embrace. "It was so loud. And the smell, the blood.

377

Afterward, Hayes wiped the gunstock so my prints wouldn't be anywhere on it. He'd picked the gun up off the floor, he said. Mahler had come at him and he'd shot him in self-defence. I was never near the gun. Our secret. I was a part of it now, but he'd keep me out of it. Self-defence. Remember Lindy, self-defence. You never had the gun."

Jejeune looked out over the waves rolling into the shore. When the tides drew them back out again, they would leave no evidence they had ever been there. Blood, fingerprints, sins; they could all be made to disappear, too. They could all be washed away. Except from someone's memory. It had not been self-defence. Jejeune had mapped it out in the cottage. Mahler must have been close to three metres away from Hayes when he was shot. His hands weren't up as he fell; he was surrendering. An unarmed man, hands raised, at that distance. There was no imminent threat to life. Ray Hayes had murdered Peter Mahler. And he'd made sure Lindy was complicit in his crime.

"You didn't know, Lindy, when you passed the gun to Hayes. You didn't know he would kill Mahler. You had no way of knowing."

But Lindy was shaking her head, and tears began to well in her eyes again. "Mahler kept telling me, 'Don't do it, Linds. Don't give him that gun. He's going to kill me if you do.'"

"But still, you didn't know. Mahler was dangerous, a genuine threat. You were right not to listen to him. You couldn't know what Hayes was planning to do."

Lindy was silent for a moment. "I did, Dom," she said quietly. "And that's what makes it so awful. I told myself exactly that at first, that I didn't know Hayes was going to shoot him when I passed him the gun. But I did." She clenched a fist and pounded it into her chest. "In here I did. I knew if I gave him the gun, he'd kill Mahler. And I think part of me wanted him to do it, Dom. I really do."

Jejeune was silent for a long time. He'd unfolded his arm from Lindy's shoulders, though he couldn't remember doing it. They sat side by side, watching the heaving of the sea, the light glinting off the surface in everchanging hues.

"You have to tell them, Domenic."

He said nothing.

"Hayes said it makes me an accessory. He couldn't have reached that gun without me. I gave him the weapon he used to kill Mahler. I made it possible. He said I'd go to prison if anybody ever found out. But he murdered Peter Mahler. You can't let him get away with that. You know what happened now. And you have to report it, whatever the cost."

Jejeune shook his head. "You didn't know, Lindy, not for certain."

"It has to end. I want you to let Peter Mahler come here. I want it over. I said that. Hayes remembers every word. He said if it ever came out in an inquest, a coroner would take it as an indicator of premeditation on my part. If I denied saying it, Hayes would tell them Danny had heard it, too. Don't you see, Dom? He'd make Danny Maik lie to protect me. He'd drag him into it as well." She shook her head. "Where would it end? Hayes murdered a man. That is the truth, and in the end, the truth is all that matters."

Was it? Once, perhaps, when it meant holding strangers to account, or seeking justice for the innocent. But people made choices all the time about what they were prepared to believe, what they were willing to overlook, to forgive. He gazed along the path, at the bare gorse branch, the empty sky. Choices. Domenic could have the life he had been longing for, the one with Lindy by his side. But only if her secret stayed between them. Hayes was right. There was no way to absolve Lindy of her guilt in Peter Mahler's death. You could only hide it, let the world continue turning and keep the secret buried deep within you. Was happiness worth that? Or were the values that had guided you your entire life worth holding onto, even if they promised to rob you of everything you ever wanted?

Lindy sat silently, knowing every question Domenic was asking himself. Her life, her future rested with him now. But then, she realized, it always had. Perhaps she could forgive herself, in time, convince herself as the years passed and the memories faded that she had only been protecting herself from a man who had already tried to kill her twice. She'd taken the necessary steps to end the threat, the only ones available to her. Yes, she thought, she might be able to believe that, in time. But could Domenic? Or would he decide his loyalty belonged to the dead instead of the living? A man had been murdered. Justice was owed to the victim, and it was in Domenic Jejeune's power to deliver it. Not to do so would mean turning his back on everything he had ever stood for, sacrificing every principle he had ever held. Could he do that for her, give up all that he was, all that he had ever been? Would he?

He turned from the sea to look at her. She met his gaze, and she could see the answer in his eyes.

THE WHOOPING CRANE

The survival of the Whooping Crane (*Grus americana*) is possibly the most celebrated success story in the history of the North American conservation movement. At 1.5 metres (five feet), the Whooping Crane is North America's tallest bird, and its white plumage and black mask make it one of the most recognizable. By the beginning of the twentieth century, habitat loss and hunting had put unsustainable pressure on the Whooping Cranes. By 1941, the world's wild population numbered just fifteen birds. A comprehensive recovery plan was put in place to try to ensure the survival of one of the continent's most charismatic bird species.

Migrating cranes need to complete a gruelling eight-thousand-kilometre (five-thousand-mile) annual return journey from Aransas, Texas, to Wood Buffalo National Park in Canada. Natural remedies such as habitat preservation and restoration greatly assisted in conservation efforts, as did hunting bans. But the Whooping Crane recovery plan has also featured a number of innovative human-led interventions. Whooping Crane chicks have been fed by human hands disguised in crane-head puppets, they have had courtship "dances" demonstrated to them by humans, and they have been led on migration flights by ultra-light aircraft. In 2015, a fifteen-year project to establish a second migratory population of Whooping Cranes between wintering grounds in Florida and breeding territories in Wisconsin was terminated. Though the birds were able to complete the annual migration, they were unable to breed successfully in numbers that could have made the population viable. This left the Aransas/Wood Buffalo birds once again as the only wild migratory Whooping Cranes in the world.

In 2018, the number of overwintering Whooping Cranes in Aransas was estimated at 505. With the number of five hundred wild individuals generally accepted as the benchmark for a viable self-sustaining population, the goal of the conservationists now seems to have been met. The success of the Whooping Crane recovery plan is a testament to the continuing efforts of a large number of people across North America, and beyond. It is thanks to their hard work and dedication that one of the most iconic bird species in the world may continue to grace the skies and wetlands of North America for future generations.

ACKNOWLEDGEMENTS

My thanks to Kirk Howard and the team at Dundurn, especially my editors, Allison Hirst and Jenny McWha, who always indulge my requests for extended deadlines with such grace and good humour. Bruce Westwood, Michael Levine, and Meg Wheeler at Westwood Creative Artists continue to provide advice and insight for which I am extremely grateful. The handling of last year's launch of the Birder Murder mysteries in the U.S. by Oneworld Publications reminded me how fortunate I am that the books are in their hands. My thanks to Juliet Mabey, Jenny Parrott, Margot Weale, Harriet Wade, and Becky Kraemer for all their hard work. I am also indebted to Mike Burrows for his careful scrutiny of the text and a number of valuable observations and insights.

I was fortunate to receive the wisdom and guidance of many people during the research for this book. Wade Harrell, Whooping Crane coordinator at Aransas National Wildlife Refuge, and Curtis Wolf, director of the Kansas Wetlands Education Center, both found time in their busy schedules to take me on personal tours. I thank them for their insights and expertise. Rob Alschwede at the Rowe Sanctuary in Nebraska provided some wonderful anecdotal tales about crane behaviour. In the Northwest Territories, I was treated to the combined input of Wood Buffalo National Park Site Superintendent Cam Zimmer, Resource Management Officer Sharon Irwin, and Visitor Experience Manager Janna Jaque. The information they provided was invaluable in putting this story together and I am profoundly grateful to each of them. Brian Harrold of Northwestern Air in Fort Smith was kind enough to talk me through a hypothetical rescue attempt in the park, and also share the details of his experiences in a number of real-life situations.

I am particularly indebted to Chief Roy Fabian of the Kat'lodeh Ché First Nation and Georgina Fabian for providing some insights into Dene culture. A work of fiction necessitates taking liberties with the facts, but I hope I have managed to properly represent the practices and beliefs as they were explained to me. I also trust that, in doing so, I have been able to reflect the great respect I have for the Dene people and culture. Any errors or inaccuracies, of course, remain the responsibility of the author.

As always, my travelling companion on my research trips, my wife, Resa, was both my inspiration and guiding light. I am happy to report she has also maintained her track record with regard to her forecast about the books. Simply put: Resa's predictions state the opposite of inaccuracy with unerring precision.

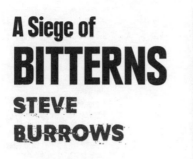

Birder Murder Mystery 2

A Pitying of
DOVES
STEVE
BURROWS

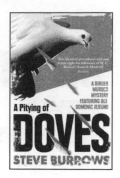

When murder strikes a north Norfolk bird sanctuary, why would a killer ignore expensive jewellery and take a pair of turtledoves as the only bounty? And why is a senior attaché from the Mexican Embassy lying dead beside the body of the sanctuary's director? Chief Inspector Domenic Jejeune is all too aware the case is sorely testing as the clues weave from embittered aviary owners to suspicious bird sculptors. For the truth of it is that with murder, everyone pays a price...

'One of the most delightful, old-fashioned
mysteries of recent years'
Daily Mail

'A tremendous whodunnit'
London Free Press

Birder Murder Mystery 3

A Cast of
FALCONS
STEVE
BURROWS

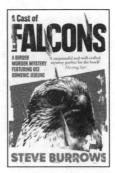

As a white falcon circles, a man plummets to his death from a cliff face in western Scotland. At a distance, another watches; later he tucks a book into the dead man's pocket. When the police show DCI Jejeune the book, he knows it's a call for help, and that it could destroy the life he and girlfriend Lindy have built for themselves in Saltmarsh, a north Norfolk village.

Meanwhile, back in Saltmarsh, the brutal murder of a researcher involved in a climate change project highlights his controversial studies. Might there be a deadly connection between the deaths?

'Most entertaining'
The Times

'An excellent mystery whose conflicted protagonist faces hard decisions'
Kirkus

**POINT
BLANK**

Birder Murder Mystery 4

A Shimmer of HUMMING-BIRDS

STEVE BURROWS

A brutal murder in Saltmarsh opens up some old wounds, as long-time nemesis Laraby is drafted in to investigate in Chief Inspector Domenic Jejeune's absence. Meanwhile, Jejeune is hoping an overseas birding trip will aid his fugitive brother's manslaughter case, but nothing is as it seems as danger lurks around every corner in his quest for justice. Soon, Jejeune learns that something is afoot in Laraby's case – should he speak up and lose his beloved job on the North Norfolk coast? Or stay silent, and let a killer escape justice?

'If you are interested in birding, this series is a must. If you don't know an owl from a canary nor care to... I would still recommend this series. It is just that good'
Reviewing the Evidence

'Burrows intertwines avians with the classic whodunnit in a completely original way'
Audobon

POINT BLANK

Birder Murder Mystery 5

A Tiding of
MAGPIES
STEVE
BURROWS

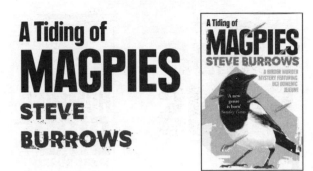

When his most celebrated case is suddenly reopened, Detective Chief Inspector Jejeune's long-buried secrets threaten to come to light. Meanwhile, his girlfriend, Lindy, faces an unseen threat of her own, one which Jejeune may not be able to protect her from. More than ever Jejeune will have to rely on the help of the stalwart Sergeant Danny Maik, but Maik is learning things on his own that have caused him to question his DCI's actions, both past and present. In the current case, and in the former one, the facts seem clear enough. But often the most insidious lies hide behind the most honest-seeming truths.

'A rattling good read'
Birdwatching

'An excellent police procedural'
Mystery People